Confessions of a Naughty Librarian

BACHELOR BAY
BOOK TWO

DEBORAH SCHNEIDER

MOON VALLEY PUBLISHING

For all the librarians who protect everyone's right to free and open access to materials at their local public library.

Banning books is censorship and attempts to suppress ideas and information. This author supports intellectual freedom and the right to read whatever the hell you want to read.

Chapter One

BRIENNE

"HE'S BAAAAACK." Shelby nodded toward the man sitting in the chair across from the library reference books.

"You know, Cute Scruffy Dude," she said in a husky whisper.

Brie glanced up at the same time the man raised his gaze from his phone. Their eyes met and held for a moment too long.

She felt a blush of heat warm her face and looked down quickly, pretending the children's picture book she'd just checked in was the most fascinating thing she'd ever seen.

"He never checks out a book, but he certainly checks you out, Brie." Shelby didn't even try to hide the comment with a whisper. When Brie glanced over at him again, the man

1

grinned as if he'd heard what her co-worker said, and it amused him.

"Shush!" Brie demanded, a little too loudly, then wanted to slap her own forehead for reacting like a stereotypical librarian.

Brienne Henderson worked hard to dispel anyone's version of a staid, uptight librarian who demanded absolute quiet in the Horseshoe Island Public Library. Currently, she sported light blue hair and wore a navy-blue A-line skirt, matching sweater set, and pearls.

It suddenly struck her that other than the hair, she wore an outfit that could be featured on a Pinterest board labeled "Librarian Chic", and she grimaced.

She'd dressed in one of her most conservative outfits for the library board meeting earlier. Brie constantly tried to impress the members and assure them she was a mature, responsible adult who could handle the duties as manager of the library.

And not just temporarily. She wanted to be appointed as the permanent library manager.

The hair color resulted from making a bet with her teen advisory group they wouldn't read over a thousand minutes each over the three months of the summer reading program. Much to her surprise, all twelve members of the group had read more than that. She'd lost the bet and dyed her hair pastel blue, one of her favorite colors, so she really didn't mind losing.

It delighted her to create a banner for the library that boasted about the challenge. She glanced at the stars and fireworks on the proclamation: *Teen Council Members Read 14,000 Minutes!* stretched across the tiny corner of the library she referred to as the teen center.

A momentary flash of pride for the kids' accomplishment whipped through her. A sigh of despair followed.

She certainly couldn't be proud of the designated teen area, a pitiful space. It consisted of a few well-worn beanbag chairs spread across a small area, and some posters of celebrities holding their favorite books to encourage teens to read on the wall. A low shelf with a display featuring young adult books, graphic novels, and the few teen magazines the library could afford to subscribe to divided the teen space from the children's area.

She hoped when the final plans to renovate the library were revealed, her dream teen area would be included.

Brie shifted her gaze to take a quick peek at the man she and Shelby referred to as "Cute Scruffy Dude." He still seemed intensely interested in his phone, so she took advantage of the opportunity to study him.

He had long legs that stretched comfortably across the well-worn carpet. His broad shoulders filled out the flannel shirt he wore, and she and Shelby had admired him from behind more than once as he left the library.

Blond highlights streaked through his thick, chestnut brown hair, as if he spent a lot of time outdoors. He wore it long, but guys on Horseshoe Island seemed to prefer that style. Maybe as a tribute to the island's flower-child past.

You'd discover hippie culture alive and well on the island. Brie's own parents were living proof of that, even though they'd been born at the end of the Haight-Ashbury era of the countercultural revolution and had only been preschoolers when Woodstock happened.

Cute Scruffy Dude shifted in his seat and looked up, as though aware of her scrutiny. She dropped her gaze again to the computer monitor in front of her. She'd already checked in all the books in her pile, so she clicked a button to clear the screen.

"Has he ever come to the desk to ask a question?"

Apparently, Shelby had no intention of giving up on the conversation about the quiet stranger.

"Nope. He's never applied for a library card, asked a reference question, or sat at a computer." Brie shook her head. "He doesn't appear to be interested in any of the services we offer except access to the internet."

It made him mysterious. For the past month, he'd show up a few times each week, sit in one of the more comfortable chairs, always in a place he could view the main desk, and then look at his phone the entire time he visited.

Even though Shelby reported he'd surreptitiously observe Brie during his visits, he didn't seem to be a creepy stalker. At least he never waited for her in the parking lot or followed her through the stacks, and since that had happened a couple of times, she appreciated his discretion.

Some men harbored a familiar fantasy of the sexy librarian, who only had to remove her glasses and let her hair down to become a sexy nymph.

As if, she thought. She didn't spend five years studying for her degrees and ten years on the job to be treated like a bimbo.

A sideways glance toward the mystery man revealed his attention focused again on his phone.

Sometimes, when their gazes locked, his full lips curved into a grin, and one sweet dimple appeared on the left side of his face.

A handsome face that hid beneath a scruff of a beard. He usually wore a gamer T-shirt under a long-sleeved flannel shirt. Worn dark jeans gave him the rugged hipster-logger look so popular in the Pacific Northwest. A lot of men adopted that look on Horseshoe Island. With fewer than six thousand permanent residents scattered around this remote location accessible only by a state ferry, private boat, or private plane, the island kept things casual.

She and Shelby had concocted a variety of stories about

the man. Brie's favorite suggested he could be a forlorn musician who lived in a camper at the state park, wrote songs about the woman who broke his heart, and waited for his big break. Her story explained the reason he used his phone constantly. He hoped for a text message call to fame.

Shelby pointed out that story could describe Brie's ex-boyfriend, Caleb.

Brie had to admit to the truth of Shelby's observation. She and Caleb had dated for over three months, mostly exclusively —or at least she'd only been with him. Until she discovered they had different definitions of what monogamous meant. He'd informed her members of his band wanted to explore polyamory.

He broke up with her because she refused his invitation to join them. Caleb told her being in a monogamous relationship with one guy at a time made her old-fashioned. He called her boring and sexually repressed.

And worst of all, he'd insisted she was frigid. She wondered if he'd put a little more effort into having sex with her, maybe attempted more foreplay, if she might have responded differently.

Caleb made her feel unfulfilled, insecure, and frustrated. There wasn't anything sexy about that.

Cute Scruffy Dude stood, and a stab of disappointment struck her. Any hope he might come to the desk today to request a library card application, and she'd finally discover his name and address, evaporated.

It would not be snooping because their mission was to encourage those who paid the taxes to access all available services. She always encouraged residents to use the library.

The man didn't head out the door and instead moved toward the non-fiction shelves. She seized the opportunity to discover more about him. Even if it only involved his interests and hobbies.

She grabbed the cart with books needing to be shelved and followed him.

Brie tried to be discreet, moving along the shelves while glancing through the spaces above the books to locate him. He stood in the 641-section, indicating he could be interested in cookbooks.

As she advanced down the row, glancing at the books organized on the shelves, she tried to figure out what she could say to him. Library policy didn't insist that patrons identify themselves to be in the building. That didn't stop her from wanting to discover more about him.

She had to admit, she really was snooping. Tall, gorgeous men didn't just fall out of the sky onto this island. It took some work to get out there.

"Would you recommend this book, Brienne?"

She jumped. His voice, as smooth and deep as aged whiskey, startled her, and her heart beat a little faster. *He knew her name*.

Then she remembered she wore a name tag. And he'd been visiting the library for weeks. Of course, he knew her name. They didn't exactly have a vast staff.

Clearly, her attempt at subterfuge had failed. She left the book cart at the end of the row and proceeded to the shelves where he stood waiting for her. She moved closer to see the title he held in his large, thick-fingered hand. Close enough to inhale his scent of cedar with a soft undertone of rich coffee and, possibly, a touch of pepper? Up close, his beard appeared more groomed than she expected.

She wondered if his scruffy look could be more of an intentional effort than neglectful grooming.

She glanced at the cookbook and gave him her friendliest librarian smile. "That's from one of the Northwest's best-known chefs, but the recipes can be complicated. What kind of food do you like?"

Brie transformed from a nosy local busybody into a librarian answering a reference question without missing a beat.

"Meals someone else prepares. But there aren't as many restaurant choices on the island this time of year, so I'm realizing I should learn to cook more."

Brie stepped closer. Close enough to see the deep forest green of his eyes. She licked her lips as she processed the information he shared. No reference to cooking for his family, just for himself. Clue #1 about Cute Scruffy Dude. He might be single.

Not that it mattered to her, as she intended to remain a staid, respectful professional as she helped him.

"I think this might be a good place to start." She handed him *The Domestic Goddess Cooks at Home* from the shelf of books in front of him.

"She's a local celebrity, you know," Brie informed him. "In fact, she just finished filming the first season of her new television show here on the island."

He nodded as he took the book from her. When their fingers touched, a small spark of something flashed between them.

Cute Scruffy Dude glanced at a few pages and paused to study one recipe. "Spanish omelet, one of my favorites."

"You just need to complete a library card application and you can take it home with you." She pointed through the window toward the local market across the street. "A quick stop at the co-op on your way home to get some ingredients and you'll be all set for dinner tonight. I've made that recipe, and it's so easy. You shouldn't have any problem fixing it.

"Your family will be impressed!" she assured him.

Brie realized her voice sounded overly cheerful, as if she were talking to a preschooler at story time.

He set the book back on the shelf. "I'll just order an e-book copy."

"The library provides e-books in addition to print books," she chirped. Now she sounded like a salesperson. Which she sometimes had to be when it came to library services. Many patrons didn't know about all the things they could access with a library card.

He grinned down at her. "Is that so?"

She felt silly. He probably already knew about all the things he could do with a library card, and he didn't need or want any of them. Which annoyed her.

"Is there some reason you don't want a library card?" As soon as the words left her mouth, she recognized she'd overstepped. She had no right to interrogate the man. If he didn't want a library card, she shouldn't care. As an intellectual freedom warrior, she'd just trampled on this guy's First Amendment rights.

She backed away from him. "I'm sorry, that's none of my business." She could feel her face heat with embarrassment. She turned to retrieve the book cart and finish shelving.

"Wait, Brienne." His voice stopped her. "I need to ask you something else."

She blinked, waiting more eagerly than she should for a patron to ask her a question. He pulled out his phone and held it out toward her. Did he have a technical question? Patrons often brought their devices to library staff members with questions about how to download e-books or use the free databases.

Maybe he didn't know how to download the digital copy of the book she'd just promoted.

"Could you read that message?" he asked.

It shocked her to see Violet Lancaster as the contact. The message read:

Brienne is your best bet at the library. Ask her to meet with you OFFSITE!

"Violet is in Iceland. Why is she emailing *you*? Are you related or something?"

He grinned again, and the dimple on one cheek appeared. She stood staring at him, spellbound for a few seconds. Dimples on men were a major weakness for her.

"They actually have the internet in Iceland," he responded. "Technology is moving around the world quickly."

She frowned up at him. She didn't appreciate the sarcasm.

"I think you know what I mean."

He took the phone back and slipped it into the front pocket of his flannel shirt. "I don't want to talk about it here. Can we meet outside of the library for coffee or lunch?"

First the invitation, then the proposition. The message from Violet sparked Brie's curiosity. But she knew to be careful with strange men. Her father had a list of dangerous things a modern young woman shouldn't do stuck to his refrigerator.

This guy could have faked the email, although it seemed like a lot of work if he only wanted a date with her. And she suspected someone who looked like him probably never had a problem getting dates.

Even so, her spidey-sense went on high alert. She needed to check her sources.

"Why can't we talk in the meeting room or my office?"

He shrugged. "That's Violet's rule. She never wanted to talk here and always met me outside of the library."

That sparked Brie's curiosity. What had Violet been up to and how did it involve Cute Scruffy Dude? Could there be a library mystery they were trying to solve together?

Perhaps the library board was embezzling funds? A jolt of happiness flashed through Brie at the idea of Marion Rush-

Talbot, the president of the library board and her main tormentor and nemesis, being dragged out of the library in handcuffs.

He sensed her confusion. "It's nothing bad. It's actually something pretty great; at least Violet thought so. But there's a lot of planning that needs to happen and she wanted to keep things quiet until some of the important decisions are made."

Brie's interest flipped up a notch. At the very least, she wanted to discover what had been hush-hush enough that her former boss and mentor felt she needed to have secret meetings outside of the library with this man. Could there be a scheme to give the library remodeling contract to a board member's friend or family member for kickbacks?

She nearly laughed out loud at those absurd ideas. She'd lived on Horseshoe Island her entire life, and growing up here tended to be both a blessing and a curse. In a tiny, isolated community, you learned the true character of the people around you. When you were a permanent year-round resident, everyone pretty much knew everyone else's business.

It had to be something else, and she loved a good mystery. Could there be a library ghost like in a Nancy Drew story?

She immediately hoped so, however unlikely.

She glanced at Cute Scruffy Dude and frowned. "I'll check with Violet, and if she confirms this is for real, I'll meet you on Thursday around ten at Java the Hut. Do you know where that is?"

He flashed that sexy grin again. "So, if you don't show up, that means I didn't pass the background check?"

Brie swallowed and forced her gaze to remain on his face, as much as she wanted to move from looking into his amazing moss-green eyes to inspect his lean, heavily muscled body.

A flutter in the region below her belly warned her to return to reality. Her mouth felt so dry she wondered if words would come out when she spoke.

She licked her lips again and noticed the pupils of his eyes dilate for a few heartbeats.

"If I had more information about you, like from a library card application, it might make me less suspicious of your motives."

"I'm wondering. Is there some kind of sales commission for the number of cards you register every month? You're kind of pushy."

She felt the heat of her temper warm her cheeks. What an arrogant a-hole. He might be good-looking, but he was also rude.

Brie intended to find out who this guy was, and she'd start with the FBI list of their most wanted fugitives. She sensed he was hiding something.

"Well, this has been a fascinating conversation, but I have things to do, so thanks for the invitation, but I'll pass." She shot him a dismissive look, lifting her chin and glaring at him.

"You should really talk to Violet." He said it with a teasing edge to his voice. Like a kid taunting his friends that they'd be sorry if they didn't join the game.

His comment irritated her even more, and admitting he might be right made her tighten her fists in aggravation.

"Fine, I'll contact Violet. If she vouches for you and your *something pretty great*, then I could call or text you." She gave him an icy smile. "If I had your name and number."

"Cole, and I prefer the anticipation of seeing if you show up for coffee. It makes things interesting."

That voice hit her again. She didn't know much about good scotch, but she imagined drinking it would create a sensation like when he spoke to her. A rich, smooth blend that sent a lightning bolt of heat flashing through her body.

Which was ridiculous, because Cole whatever the hell his last name was, had the good looks that ensured he got what he wanted from women. The last thing she needed right now would be an infatuation with a man out of her league.

"And Brie," he leaned toward her, "I don't have a family."

Before she could summon a response, he headed toward the front door.

Brie steered the cart back to the information desk and parked it. Shelby twitched her head in the direction of the back room and Brie nodded. There weren't many people in the library right now and things wouldn't get busy until after school let out.

When Brie shut the door to her office, Shelby nearly exploded with excitement. "You actually talked to Cute Scruffy Dude?"

"Cole," Brie offered. "His name is Cole. And he's not really that scruffy when you see him up close."

Shelby danced from one foot to another. "What did he say?"

Brie considered sharing the mystery of Violet meeting Cole outside of the library with her co-worker. Then she reconsidered. Violet Lancaster had been her supervisor and mentor. In fact, they were still friends. Violet had introduced her to some of her best book buddies as Brie grew up on the island. The older librarian pushed her to pursue her degree in library and information science. She trusted the woman. If Violet wanted her to keep a secret about the library, Brie would use her research skills to discover more before sharing any information.

"He asked about cookbooks." She tried to be nonchalant. "He said he wanted to learn to cook."

"So, he's single!" Shelby crowed triumphantly.

"Do I need to remind you that you're engaged?" Brie responded, followed by a laugh. "You seem awfully interested in this guy."

Shelby tossed off the observation. "*You* should definitely

be interested. I found my Prince Charming. Now it's time for you to wake up and escape from the fortress of celibacy, Sleeping Beauty."

Since Brie broke up with Caleb, this discussion had a familiar ring. Shelby encouraged Brie to get out and date more. The small pool of permanent residents on the island posed a problem. Most of the men were boys she'd known since childhood, and they were firmly in the friend zone. Probably the reason she'd been attracted to Caleb in the first place—he'd been a newcomer. Different and unknown territory.

"He wouldn't give me his full name or phone number."

Shelby stared at her. "You asked him for his phone number? You go girl! I'm proud of you."

"No." Brie could feel her cheeks warming. "I mean, I told him he had to get a library card to check out the book, and he wasn't interested. I think he's hiding something. Maybe he's in the witness protection program or something."

"Is that where your mind automatically goes when a guy is shy? Men don't share; you should know that by now. If I want information from Ryan, I have to shake him down for it."

Brie imagined Shelby tying her hot firefighter fiancé onto a chair with a bright light over his head. She giggled. "I suspect you have some interesting methods to make him talk."

"I could teach a workshop." Shelby wiggled her eyebrows suggestively.

Brie burst out laughing. "I can imagine the expressions on the faces of the library board members if I suggested something like that."

"Mrs. Rush-Talbot would have a coronary at anything that might suggest s.e.x." Shelby giggled. "Her precious son must have been conceived by immaculate conception. By the way, how did the meeting go this morning?"

Brie sighed. "Pretty much as usual. I still cannot make her

understand how important it would be to have dedicated teen space as part of the remodeling project. She makes a horrible face every time I mention the teens, as if she smells something bad."

Shelby nodded.

"And the only support I get is from Rosalie Ortega. She's not intimidated by the dragon lady, and willing to speak out."

Brie almost told Shelby about Cute Scruffy Dude—Cole—meeting in secret with Violet. The buzzer from the front desk sounded, and Shelby gave her a sympathetic look.

"I know they're going to offer you the manager's job permanently. You just need to have more confidence in yourself."

With that, the tiny blonde who reminded Brie of Tinkerbell scooted out the door.

Brie hadn't mentioned that she learned an additional candidate had applied for the manager's position. Someone the dragon lady knew well. An older man, who had an "impeccable reputation and resume", according to Mrs. Rush Talbot.

Confidence. Brie wished she could get some of that from reading a book. Not that she hadn't tried. It seemed like she had read everything in the self-help section of the library and then some.

In college, Brie had been the quiet one, a bookworm who would rather live in a story than deal with real life. If her friends hadn't pushed her to get out of the dorm occasionally, she would have been consigned to introvert hell.

These days, when observed by outsiders, her world would appear limited. She lived in a cottage on her parents' farm, still hung out with friends she'd gone to middle school with, and loved her job at the library, where she'd attended story times while growing up.

Library patrons would be surprised to learn she dreamed

of traveling the world and living a more adventurous life. But her parents were getting older, and they needed her help on the farm more each year. So, she stayed on Horseshoe Island. She had a steady paycheck and enjoyed her work.

If her life seemed boring, she had no reason to complain. There were people in the world who would exchange places with her in a heartbeat. She had a nice place to live, enough to eat, and an interesting job that paid well enough to cover her expenses, and then some.

Her mind wandered to consider her encounter with Cole. She conjured a story about him. He could be a famous novelist hiding from his fans while writing his new bestseller. That would be interesting. Or struggling to find himself while living in his parents' vacation home? She'd heard about people doing that. They tended to choose the warmer summer months to stay on the island and usually disappeared along with the tourist crowd in the fall.

The tourists abandoned the island during the dark, rainy months the residents referred to as "the gray." People with summer homes and camps might come back for the holidays, but they didn't choose to live on the island year-round.

Cute Scruffy Dude—Cole—certainly intrigued her. Brie never expected him to tell her he wanted to talk to her about a library project that involved her former boss. It might explain the reason he visited the library so often. His visits could be an effort to observe the operations and staff.

Brie hated to bother Violet while she traveled on the retirement trip she'd spent years planning. Still, she itched to contact the older woman, and decided to text her.

BRIENNE HENDERSON

Met Cole today. He told me you were talking to him about the library. He wants to meet with me. Is this for real?

She jumped when her phone chimed a few minutes after she sat at her desk.

VIOLET LANCASTER

MEET WITH HIM!!!

A short and curt message. Violet never wasted words. She could be brutally honest when dealing with her staff. Something Brie admired about her. Violet's mantra had been, *cut the BS and get to the point.* Brie's text messaging app chimed again.

VIOLET LANCASTER

IT WILL BE WORTH YOUR TIME. JUST MEET WITH COLE AND LISTEN TO HIS EXCITING AND INNOVATIVE IDEAS!!!

Brie tapped a pencil against her keyboard and considered her choices. If she met with Cole, she'd get to hear about the "exciting and innovative ideas." She couldn't pretend the man didn't intrigue her. In fact, after the messages from Violet, her curiosity about what they'd discussed exploded.

The way Violet responded to her inquiry added to the mystery. She typed in all caps and used multiple exclamation points in her messages. Things so out of character for Brie's former boss that it added another layer of mystery.

Despite the way he'd teased her, Brie understood his meetings with Violent must have been important.

She didn't need to like the man to listen to him. Now she really wished she could call or text the stranger known as Cole and ask a few more questions. Unfortunately, he hadn't shared any of his contact information.

What had he said? That he preferred the anticipation of discovering if she'd show up for their date.

Professional meeting to discuss library business! she reminded herself.

She leaned back in her chair to consider her discussion with Cole.

Everyone she knew exchanged phone numbers so they could check in before any meeting and make sure people planned to be there. Texting, sending calendar meeting reminders, and double-checking with friends was a familiar routine.

Apparently, not for the man formerly known as Cute Scruffy Dude, aka Cole with no last name. He planned to go to a coffee shop, wait around, and see if she appeared. She couldn't decide if he had too much confidence or too much time on his hands.

Either way, she'd enjoy a break in her regular (boring) routine. Undercover investigation or wild goose chase, it didn't really matter to her. Curiosity propelled her forward.

If it ended up as an opportunity to have coffee with a gorgeous man, that might be a bit of good luck. She hadn't been on a date for months. And if the library benefitted somehow, she'd consider it a delicious cream cheese frosting on a tasty carrot cupcake.

Yum!

TRUE CONFESSION: I can't believe I finally worked up enough courage to talk to Cute Scruffy Dude. I've been watching him sit in the library for weeks, and I'm still wondering what's going on with him. Meeting him for coffee means I'm stepping out of my comfort zone. But I'm tired of sitting on the sidelines and it's time to take more chances in my life. Being careful, cautious, and avoiding danger might mean I'm safe, but it can also be boring as hell.

Chapter Two

COLE

COLE SAT AT THE TABLE, staring out the window at the water as it lapped onto the shore of Shadow Bay. The sunlight made the smooth water glisten, and he made a note to take a photo when he left the café to send to his sister.

She loved all the photos he sent her of his new home on the island. Kate had a residency in child psychiatry at Seattle Children's Hospital. She glowed with excitement when she spoke about working with children and making a real difference in the world.

She also worked long hours and rarely visited him. Her commitment to her dream and her field of study inspired him.

Which brought him back to reality. Would Brienne Henderson show up for their meeting? Violet had assured him Brienne would be excited about their project. In fact, she'd insinuated the young librarian would be more interested in ways to use technology in the library than Violet herself.

Violet had referred to herself as a dinosaur, but she didn't fool Cole. She understood 3D printing, photo imaging software, AI, and soundboards, as well as anyone who didn't work in the tech field.

And she shared his vision of how patrons of the Horseshoe Island Library could benefit if they had access to the latest, most advanced technology. Especially the kids.

Kate had been his motivation. She'd challenged him to do something besides spend his money on man-toys and hang out with Wyatt and Dylan, his business partners. They'd made a lot of money when they sold their gaming business a few years ago, when they were all facing serious burnout and various personal issues.

The move to the San Juan Islands had been Dylan's idea. His family owned a vacation home there, and he'd invited his friends to stay with him for a few months. Those peaceful months convinced them all they'd discovered a perfect place to hide out and de-stress.

When they'd finally got bored, they'd created Three Geeks, a bar that proved to be a great place for them to hang out and remain incognito. Cole had volunteered to be the business manager since that had been his role at their company.

Wyatt built a camp on nearby Spencer Island. He'd always been a loner, and since the death of his wife, he'd become even more so. Cole and Dylan would leave him alone and respect his privacy—for a while. Then they'd head over to the island and hang for a few days. They knew alone time could turn into loneliness and then depression all too easily.

Dylan possessed the best social skills of their group. He'd learned the art of being easygoing during a childhood of surviving blended families. Developing his natural charisma and charm gave him the emotional tools to manage his father's multiple wives and all their kids. He claimed since he never knew who planned to show up at any family event, he'd learned to cope with surprises.

His attachment to the camp on the island involved his mother, who had passed away when he was young. He purchased Windswept because she'd designed it.

Cole and Wyatt teased him, calling him the "Golden Boy." With his blond hair and ocean-blue eyes, Dylan had movie star good looks besides being a talented musician. His practiced charm captured hearts easily.

Not that it solved the major problem of his life, his ex-wife Sami. She'd asked Dylan for a divorce two years ago, but for some reason, he couldn't get over her, and had never signed the final papers. He obsessed over her social media when she posted pictures of exotic vacations with an ever-changing cast of men. It drove Dylan nuts, but nothing his friends could tell him changed anything. And when Sami got in trouble, which happened with an unhealthy frequency, Dylan came to her rescue.

A vintage turquoise Ford Bronco pulled into the parking lot. He grinned as he watched Brienne step out of the vehicle. Even though she arrived ten minutes late, he didn't care.

She'd showed up. After the suspicious way she acted when he'd invited her for coffee, he actually hadn't been sure she would.

He'd noticed the Bronco in the library parking lot and wondered who owned it. It made sense now that he thought about it. She had a fun vintage style, wearing cute sundresses with strappy sandals during the summer and skirts with sweaters in the colder months. The vintage Bronco matched her retro vibe.

She wore a red and black sweater, one of his favorites, with curve-hugging jeans. He'd noticed the first day he visited the library that she had a knockout body. Watching her cross the parking lot, he admired the way her outfit accented her luscious breasts and curvy thighs.

Heat rushed directly to his dick.

Her blue hair hung loose, falling down her back in waves. Red shoes with polka-dot heels made him smile. She had a fashion sense that combined rockabilly with quirky schoolmarm.

His decision to leave his sunglasses on while sitting in the café meant none of the other diners could witness him checking her out.

Maybe he'd spent a little too much time at the library observing her. Initially, he'd gone to see the woman Violet Lancaster praised as being brilliant and incredibly capable. According to Violet, the youth services librarian was smart, systematic, and sensible.

He'd add sexy as hell to that list!

Cole removed his sunglasses and stood as she walked through the door. She turned toward the counter before he could stop her. The barista's face broke into a huge smile.

"Hey, Brie! The usual?"

So, she had a "usual" which meant she visited Java the Hut regularly. Then again, according to Violet, she'd grown up on the island. No doubt she knew nearly everyone who lived here.

"Just the double shot mocha today. Mom made breakfast this morning. The hens are laying so many eggs I'm tired of omelets."

"I hear you. You should ask Keegan if he can take some off your hands. Add it to the regular order from the farm."

Brienne pointed behind the barista. "Is Keegan here?"

The barista shook her head. "He's over on the set of *Domestic Goddess*. They're shooting again this month. Rumor is Bailey's new network liked the Blue Moon Lodge renovation shows so much they asked for some special holiday episodes."

Bienne reached into her purse and pulled out her wallet. Cole held up his hand to get the barista's attention. "That's on me."

Brienne turned and her smile smashed into him like a bolt

of lightning. She could do serious damage with the wattage of that look.

"You tantalized me with your offer," she said. "So here I am, ready to listen. I admit I'm intrigued. Violet used capital letters and exclamation points in her messages to me about you."

So, Violet had acted as the intermediary and convinced Brienne she should take the meeting. He'd be sure to text her later to thank her.

"You must be a regular here," he observed. He didn't sit until Brienne pulled out her chair and sat first.

"Keegan's an old friend. I've known him since elementary school. I never doubted he would end up opening a café. He talked about it since we were in eighth grade together."

Cole wondered how it would feel to still be friends with the kids you grew up with. He counted himself lucky to still be close to Wyatt and Dylan. They'd met at the University of Washington back when they were first-year students. They were the guys who spent long hours in the computer lab practicing their coding skills.

In their sophomore year, they'd rented an apartment together after discovering they were more than gaming enthusiasts. They were fanatics who spent every weekend playing video games through the night.

They were proud to call themselves "geeks" and by graduation, they'd founded an online gaming platform that transformed the industry. Their first fantasy game, *Mystic Moon*, won awards, acclaim, created the cornerstone of their business, and established a massive fanbase.

When her order arrived at the table, Brienne puckered her lips and blew on the hot coffee.

She didn't notice the air suddenly being sucked out of his lungs as he watched her bright pink lips touch the edge of the cup. He imagined his chair tipping backward to spill him onto the floor.

Shaking his head to clear it, he discovered his feet were still flat on the floor as he sat at the table. It just felt like he'd fallen.

Grabbing his own coffee, he took a huge gulp to calm his nerves and get his bearings before glancing up to find her soft gray eyes fixed on him. Waiting.

"So, what's the big mystery?" she asked as she drummed her pink nails on the table. "Do we have a ghost in the library? Should we gather our Scooby-Doo crew to deal with it? If so, I'm Velma."

"Wait, I thought every girl wanted to be Daphne."

"Every girl I knew wanted to be Shaggy—because he had a great dog. But I'd rather be the brains of the operation than the chick who's always getting herself into trouble and waiting to be rescued."

"Interesting observation." He grinned at her.

"Boys always have the best choices, anyway. There are three males. Which one would you be? Fred Jones?"

Cole enjoyed the way she teased him. He hadn't expected their conversation this morning to be fun.

"Actually, I have a friend who's a dead ringer for Fred. He always insists on driving too. I'd be Scooby-Doo, because the show is really about the dog, isn't it? He's the actual star because the show's named after him."

She leaned her cheek on one hand and her full lips turned up into a satisfied smile. "Not to mention the Scooby treats."

He nodded. "Best part of being a dog, if you ask me. That, and sleeping on all the furniture."

She laughed. The sound made him smile at her. He already felt comfortable talking to her, and that didn't happen often with women.

He'd developed an icy façade as protection when dealing

with new female acquaintances. Her warmth melted that glacial reserve quickly.

"You must have a dog!"

Cole grinned. "I do. He thinks his name is 'Stop That.' Climbs on my furniture, barks at every squirrel he sees, hogs my bed all night, and I adore him as much as he worships me."

"What's his real name?"

"Oscar the Slouch, and believe me, the name fits him. He's a mixed breed I got as a rescue. Fun personality, sloppy personal habits."

"Sounds like my ex." She hurried to take another sip of her coffee.

The boyfriend must be permanently out of the picture. Good. He had never liked that long-haired, unkempt grub who carried his guitar around town to signal to everyone he considered himself a serious musician.

He'd convinced the guys to go with him to a show in town one night that featured the now ex-boyfriend's band. The drummer's performance surprised them. He had some talent. Dylan called their lead singer dynamite. He'd talked to her after the show about connecting her to some people he knew in the business. He predicted she could forge an actual career in music. But the other woman, who played keyboards, and Brienne's ex, the grubby guy with no talent, spent more time exchanging sly looks with each other than playing.

"Bad breakup?"

"Bad relationship altogether."

He wanted to ask her if she currently dated anyone new, but that seemed nosy. Especially since he'd promised her this would be a professional meeting. While he definitely felt a powerful attraction to her, he needed to focus on his mission.

Brienne frowned at him across the table. "Did Velma ever get to drive the Mystery Machine?"

He blinked at her for a moment. Then he gave her his

known-to-make-women-sigh-and-offer-their-phone-number-to-him sexy grin.

"Jeepers. We couldn't let a girl do that. But we gave her a taser once in the episode about the witch of Skull Island."

She nodded with a smile. "So, you've met the library board president, Mrs. Rush-Talbot?" Then she glanced around her as if to make sure no one overheard. "Did I actually say that out loud?"

He nodded, but she didn't really seem worried.

"I've heard a great deal about her. Violet described her as impossible to deal with and committed to getting her own way."

He shifted in his seat. "Did Violet tell you anything about our meetings?"

"She never mentioned you until a few days ago, which adds to my curiosity." She took a sip of her coffee. "And my suspicions."

Brienne leaned closer. After a glance at her breasts, displayed to perfection by the low-cut sweater, he worked to snap his attention back to her face.

She didn't notice his gaze had wandered. Or she could be too polite to say anything.

"She controls the board like a general commanding the army. She doesn't allow discussion after announcing her decision and expects the other members of the board to approve whatever she wants."

"Violet mentioned she's demanding and has some very specific ideas about the library renovation."

Brie sighed deeply, and he could tell by the silence before she spoke, she tried to be careful about what she said. "That woman is stuck in the dark ages. I'd be shocked if she didn't call her employees serfs. She hates technology, and she calls computers and the internet tools of the devil. Every tech upgrade we request, she complains as if the money is being siphoned out of her personal bank account."

He frowned. Violet had told him the president of the board had outdated ideas of what a library should offer to the community. This sounded much worse.

"I want a teen space included with the design for the remodel, and she fights me every step of the way. She says teens are obnoxious and make messes. I swear she lures children to her gingerbread house in the woods!"

Brie sat back in her chair and brushed a wave of blue hair from her cheek. "I'm sorry. That's so unprofessional of me. I hope you'll keep anything I say today confidential."

He nodded. "Of course."

"We had a very tough board meeting the other day. I asked them to consider including a larger teen area in the library expansion. You would have thought I'd asked if I could offer a bomb-making class as an after-school activity for kids."

She grabbed her coffee cup and a bit of the liquid sloshed over the side, then wiped up the spill with her paper napkin. Her cheeks had bright spots of color that matched her lipstick. "I can't seem to convince the board members we need to make the spaces inviting, so teens and kids will want to hang out at the library."

Her rosy cheeks and clenched fists transmitted her concern for the younger patrons of the library. Brie's enthusiasm for her job impressed him. She reminded him of Kate, and the comparison surprised him.

"That's actually what Violet and I talked about. She told me about your concern that the library board seemed more focused on ways to serve adults and older patrons than children and teens."

Her head snapped back, and she stared at him, her mouth forming into a pout. She wore a delicious expression of annoyance.

"You and Violet discussed *me*?" She didn't sound pleased about that revelation. "What exactly did she say?"

Uh-oh. He shouldn't have mentioned that. No one liked to think others were gossiping about them behind their back.

"Nothing personal." He shook his head to emphasize his words. "She mentioned you had some great ideas for the remodel. Ideas the board ignores."

That seemed to placate her, at least for the moment. He had to admit, though, the way her eyes sparkled, and her cheeks burned crimson when her temper rose, it would be worth riling her up just to enjoy the view.

"There's so much we could do, even if funds are limited. If we purchased a few tablets or laptops, we could use free software to teach coding classes. A larger space with room for tables would be great, so the kids could do crafts and maybe we could even scrape together some money to purchase a couple of screens and a few new game consoles."

"It doesn't matter." Brie pushed her nearly empty cup away and gave an exasperated sigh. "They won't listen to me. All they want to talk about is building a coffee bar in the library's entryway as part of the remodel."

She leaned forward again, and Cole reminded himself to keep his gaze glued to her face.

"We have coffee bars all over town," she said. "Why in hell would we need one in the library?"

He couldn't answer that question, so he decided it might be a good time to make his offer.

"What if you weren't constrained by the budget? What if you had all the money you need to get that teen space you dream about?" He waved one hand in the air. "Not just a few items, but enough funding to create a technology center."

"A technology center?" Her eyes widened. "I can imagine all kinds of things to put into that. Be specific. How much more money are we talking about, and where is this sudden windfall coming from?"

He drummed his fingers on the table a few times while considering how to phrase the offer. Finally, he sat up straight and pinned her with a serious look, then cleared his throat.

"I represent a foundation." That sounded too businesslike. He paused for a few moments. "A group of donors." He hoped that sounded more friendly.

"Donors?" One eyebrow rose as she frowned. "Do they live on Horseshoe Island?"

He nodded. "Two of them live on the island, and one lives…" He paused again, considering how much to disclose. "On a different island."

Now her expression turned suspicious. "And they all want to donate money to the library?"

His head bobbed, and he wished he could crawl out of their conversation. He didn't prepare for her questions because he assumed once he told her about the donation, she wouldn't care about the identity of the donors.

She'd moved her cup and leaned forward again. An expanse of soft, round, creamy skin tempted him. He reluctantly dragged his gaze from the titillating scenery and tried to focus again.

"Where they live isn't important." It became difficult to remain sitting comfortably. "These are wealthy individuals who want to give back to the community."

He paused, waiting for another question. She tilted her head and blinked at him.

"Wealthy donors. That's interesting. What exactly do they want to do?"

"They want to give the library funds to create additional spaces for children and teens as part of the renovation. That includes a makerspace. Violet explained to me those are spaces that offer technology equipment like 3D printers, game consoles, and craft supplies. The funds I'm talking about could provide all the equipment and tools you need."

She frowned and remained silent for a few moments. Then she laughed out loud, and this time it sounded more like a bark than a cheerful noise.

Then she glared at him. "Did Violet actually believe this bullshit you're peddling? I don't know how you convinced her, but I've been working on this library renovation for years. If a group of rich folks who wanted to toss a bunch of money at the library existed, I'd know about it."

She leaned even further across the table, giving him an expansive view of her sizeable assets. He couldn't drag his gaze away from her.

Her response stunned him. Violet had been excited when he'd first approached her with the idea. The more they met and developed concepts for the renovation, the more excited she'd become. He couldn't understand the reason Brienne rejected his offer so quickly.

She stood, forcing him to look up at her. "Thanks for the entertainment. I don't get punked often, but you had me almost believing in miracles. You're good. I'll let Violet know she pulled one over on me." She turned and stalked out of the restaurant.

Cole stared at her back. He'd been ready to offer this woman a lot of money. Well, at least a lot of funding for the library. And she had the audacity to laugh in his face.

What kind of woman laughed at money?

He chased her outside and caught up with her as she opened the door to her Bronco.

"This isn't a practical joke. I represent some people who want to make a sizable donation for the library renovation." How had things gone so wrong so quickly?

She slid into the driver's seat, closed the door, and put her arm on the edge of the open window. She glared at him before tossing her hair.

"Can you prove it?"

"What?" He wasn't sure he'd heard her correctly.

She put one hand on the steering wheel and turned the key with the other. She prepared to leave, and he had an inkling it would be difficult to get her to meet with him again if he didn't respond to her challenge.

"I can!" he yelled, in order to be heard over the noise of the engine.

She leaned back and turned to face him. "Okay, you've got five minutes. I'm listening."

He swallowed. "Can you meet me at Three Geeks bar on Monday?"

"Are you asking me out on a date? I'm flattered but not interested."

Despite his ego taking a bruising today, he needed to convince her to come to his office at Three Geeks.

"I'm the manager there. I'll meet you in the daytime when there's staff around. So, it's not a date, or a creepy come on ..."

He swallowed. "I need to show you something, and it's in my office."

It hadn't been this difficult to convince a woman to meet up with him for a long time. He couldn't compete with Dylan in the looks department, but he stayed fit, tried to be charming, bathed regularly, and was rich. Really, really rich!

Which was the reason he hadn't had a date for nearly a year. He wanted to meet a woman who didn't consider his money his most attractive feature.

Maybe he'd just met her. Of course, she didn't know who he really was. He and his friends had worked hard to protect their identities.

"It's a public place and there's something I need to show you. It'll prove everything I've told you is true."

She tilted her head again to stare at him, skepticism written on her face as clearly as if she'd sketched a question mark on her forehead.

A final plea. "What would Velma Dinkley do? Wouldn't she develop a hypothesis, collect the facts, and then find out if the culprit is lying?" He hoped appealing to her sense of humor might work.

"So, you're using the Scooby-Doo defense?"

He grinned. "Absolutely!"

She took a deep breath. "I'm off on Monday. I'll see you around one at Three Geeks and I expect to be wowed by this proof you're going to show me."

"I'm going to work hard to impress you. I guarantee it." He stepped away from the vehicle.

Cole watched as she donned her sunglasses, then backed out of the parking spot, and waved as she drove away.

He sensed the nice librarian he expected to jump up and down at his proposal presented a problem. She could make his job tougher than expected. Violet had assured him, once Brienne learned what he and his partners planned for the library renovation, she'd be thrilled.

If by "thrilled," Violet meant suspicious and distrustful— he'd hit the mark. Brienne challenged him.

He waved at the barista through the plate-glass window. She blew him a kiss in return. He'd left her a twenty-dollar tip, and she'd slipped him her phone number.

Crumpling the paper with the number on it in his pocket, he slid into his truck. Cole recalled soft gray eyes as they snapped at him with a fierceness he admired. Brienne was funny, smart, and feisty.

He looked forward to tangling with her again.

TRUE CONFESSION: Making a human

connection is always tricky. Whether it's bumping into each other, an online connection, or a friend of a friend, you know first impressions are also opportunities for judgment. Overcoming the fear of failure enough to take a chance on a new guy is a challenge. Still, every hill or mountain you climb makes you eager to climb the next one, if only to see what's beyond the next turn. The fun isn't conquering something; it's the challenge just beyond the horizon.

Chapter Three

BRIENNE

AS BRIE SWERVED BRONCO BILL, her pet name for her truck, down the winding, barely two-lane country road on the way to her cottage, her thoughts were a tangled mess.

Cole, the cute scruffy dude, turned out to be an enigma. The information about a bunch of rich folks willing to fund her dreams for the library scrambled her thoughts. Like in a magical story, a group of fairy godmothers, or godfathers—since she didn't have many clues about the donors—swoop in to grant her wishes.

Then she considered Cole. Handsome—beneath the scruff—green-eyed, sexy-as-hell Cole, whatever his last name, the international man of mystery. He tantalized her in oh-so-many ways.

She twisted the wheel as Bill slipped a bit on a curve. She needed to slow down. "Whoa, Billy!" she muttered as she touched the brakes.

She needed to ignore her attraction to the man who might represent a group of donors to the library. She'd see about that next week. A sexy distraction would be fun, but Brie didn't need anything that would mess with the richly detailed plan she'd designed for her life. She intended to keep working hard and earn the library manager position permanently. All she needed to do was stick to the plan and avoid distractions.

A distraction like a quick fling with a drop-dead gorgeous guy could mess up everything.

She slapped her forehead. Where did the idea of a quick fling even come from? "Focus, focus, focus," she whispered out loud. She'd ignore the magnetic pull of attraction that grew stronger now that she had talked to the man.

Brie turned onto the gravel road and passed the sign that read "Diggin' Dirt Farm." The rough road led to her parents' farmhouse and then up a hill to her own cottage. A cottage hand-built by her mother and father back in the 1980s when they'd settled on Horseshoe Island.

Her older brother, Ryder, had been born in the cottage. In fact, he loved to tell people when he ran for President someday, he had an Abe Lincoln story to tell. She'd pointed out how egotistical it was to compare himself to Honest Abe. He brushed off her observation and insisted origin stories were important, not the specific details.

Ryder worked as a lawyer at a prestigious law firm in Seattle. When he eventually ran for office, Brie had no doubt he'd get elected. Tall, handsome, and charismatic in a way that drew people to him with no effort made him a perfect candidate for office. Brie considered him a player—dating several women simultaneously and never committing to any of them.

And the mess with her friend Taffy, who had dated her brother off and on for years, needed sorting out.

She parked near her parents' farmhouse. After climbing out of her truck, she took a moment to stare at the home she'd grown up in. The original farmhouse dated from the late 1800s. It had been built for a mail-order bride arriving from New York to marry a man she'd never met.

How hard would that be? Brie wondered. Trusting your life to someone who wrote you a few letters. How did you know what kind of man you'd be marrying? Women took the chance he could be the person described but what if he were a drunk, abusive, or a serial killer?

Brie shuddered. She needed to adjust her holds list to change her current choice of psychological thrillers to cozy mysteries. Or contemporary romance.

Not a great idea. Reading happy-ever-after stories would only add to her recent bout of sexual frustration. Although finding a new book boyfriend might help her fantasize when she...

"Brie. What are you staring at?" Her mother straightened from clearing out one of the flower gardens in the front yard.

Working on the farm since the mid-1980s, when she'd climbed into a minivan with her handsome new husband and set out traveling from the Midwest on the adventure of her life, Charlotte Henderson had always insisted on having a flower garden.

As an equal partner in managing the farm, she still indulged in her passions of growing flowers and weaving. When her weaving turned into a profitable business, they started raising goats and sheep for the wool. Her mother used a traditional floor loom to create artistic masterpieces that were shown in galleries around the world and sold for amounts even Brie, who admired her work, couldn't believe.

Brie's father discovered innovative ways to produce income from the farm by selling their fruits, vegetables, and products to local restaurants as an early adopter of the farm-to-table movement.

He loved sharing the story about following their dream to move after tiring of the long winters in Minnesota. They'd always been pragmatists, and they researched the most temperate places in the West before deciding to move. Their priority had been a milder climate with little snow, fulfilled by the Pacific Northwest. Getting the amazing views of mountains and water made them even more serious about building a life here.

They arrived in Seattle in September, the golden month, with extended warm days. Gorgeous orange and gold sunsets and heady, sun-filled days gave little warning that the long, cold, rainy weather lurked just beyond the horizon. "The gray" could ambush you like the villain in a screamer flick. Waiting oh so patiently, breathing heavy enough to hear—if you were careful enough to listen.

And when "the gray" descended upon the Northwest with endless cloudy, overcast days, the light so weak it seemed like the sun had absorbed every color before departing, the couple had reconsidered.

They were ready to pack up and go back home to live with Brie's grandparents when a stroke of luck, or what her mother called "goddess guidance," hit. They noticed an ad in the local alternative newspaper looking for farm help.

Since they both grew up on farms, they knew it would be hard physical labor. The advertisement for workers to join an agricultural commune on an island in the Salish Sea promised five-acre plots could eventually be purchased by the commune members.

Warren and Charlotte took a chance and answered the ad. They met Amber and Mark, the couple who were designing an organic farm cooperative on Horseshoe Island. A few days later, they drove their van onto a Washington State ferry from Anacortes to the island and fulfilled their destiny.

At least, that's how her parents told the story. Brie suspected a great deal might be missing from the narrative. As she grew up on the farm, she discovered a few more details, like the real reason for leaving Minnesota—their dedication to organic—and then bio-dynamic farming, and the way they'd designed their lives to match their dreams.

It made Brie jealous that somehow her parents found a way to organize the various strands of their dream to weave together a lifestyle many people envied.

She'd discovered over the past few years as she helped patrons in the library that people often settled for lives they didn't plan, design, or even want. They let their dreams dissolve into the shadows of their daily life without even putting up much of a fight.

And sometimes she wondered if that was her fate.

Brie joined her mother in pulling dead leaves from the garden. The dark purple dahlias were still blooming, and Charlotte cut a few and gently put them aside with a small pile of flowers and cuttings she'd use to create a simple arrangement. Her artistry took shape in her home as well as in her studio.

"Where's Dad?" Brie asked.

"Planting garlic in the north field and checking on his rutabagas. He wondered if you were planning to come back after your coffee date this morning."

"Not a date, Mom," Brie insisted. "A business meeting."

Her mother didn't respond for a few seconds, but when she finally lifted her head, she gave her daughter a knowing look. "Having coffee with a man you don't know? Sounds like one of those online dating setups."

"I'm not doing online dating anymore, Mom."

Brie wanted to share the information about her meeting with Cole. He never actually told her she shouldn't talk about their discussion, but since he'd refused to share his last name, she suspected he wanted her to keep quiet about the offer they'd discussed.

Which might be a good idea since Brie didn't even believe him. She still needed proof of his offer.

She wondered how much information she could share without giving too much away.

"We discussed a donation to the library. I'm always looking for ways to find more resources. You know that."

"I remember when you were ten and set up a lemonade stand to buy new children's books for the library." Her mother laughed.

Brie smiled at the memory. "I had exactly four customers, you and Dad and the next-door neighbors. You all gave me more money than the twenty-five cents for frozen lemonade and water warranted. I ended up handing Violet Lancaster twenty dollars in cash. It seemed like a fortune then.

"Violet always favored you. She recognized a kindred soul. Your love of reading and books became apparent before you attended kindergarten. I remember you always begged for one more story before bedtime."

"So, I tended to be a greedy little thing even then?"

Her mother shook her head. "Greed for knowledge has never been a crime in our home. And I'm delighted you might have a donor interested in funding the library."

Brie stood and kicked at some red and gold leaves that had fallen recently. She'd need to use the blower to clean up the yard soon.

"Is it weird that I'm so skeptical? I mean, it seems like a wonderful thing, but why would some rich people suddenly care about our little library? Don't they want to build hospital wings and solve world famine or cure infectious diseases? You know, big things like that. Or they build rockets to launch themselves into space."

Charlotte put her hand on her back as she straightened. In the warm afternoon sunshine, Brie noticed how the cinnamon highlights in her mother's hair glimmered in the light. Her petite mother said her constant labor on the farm helped maintain her slim figure. She and Brie's father still made a handsome couple.

"Do they live on the island? Maybe they know how important the library is to this community. And it's a matter of scale. There are billionaires today who give away more money than most of us can even dream of having."

Brie considered her mother's comment. When she thought about an amount of money, it related to what she earned in a year. She struggled to imagine thinking in terms of eight figures, much less the number of zeros in a billion dollars.

"I don't think they're super-rich people, but I really don't know. It's possible they're just multi-millionaires, the poorer rich folk. Cole, the man I met with, said they have something incredibly special they want to fund. Violet seems to think it's all on the level, so I'm forced to consider the offer."

Her mother shook the dirt off her hands and set her trowel in the old, red wagon that Brie played with as a child.

"Are you going to discuss this with the library board? How do you think Marion will react to this plan? From what you've said, she's worried about the cost of the renovation."

Brie wondered if she visibly shuddered when her mother said the name of the library board president. Even the mention of that name made a cold shiver run down her back. Marion excelled at making it seem she was all sweetness and lovely manners—until she wasn't.

She'd use her syrupy, old-lady voice and compliment something—your shoes, the outfit you wore that day, something you talked about doing. Then she'd insert a verbal icepick in your neck with sharp words that stripped you of even a shred of dignity and confidence.

Marion had a special gift she used to embarrass and harass her victims.

That's certainly an interesting choice, and not what I'd do, say, wear, but then again—it's you, dear.

Marion possessed a talent that transformed a compliment into criticism, and she used it as a weapon against Brie regularly now that she'd assumed the duties as temporary manager of the library.

Marion Rush-Talbot turned into an enemy the day Brie succeeded Violet Lancaster as the library manager. Brie knew the two older women disliked each other, but until Violet retired, she didn't realize the depth of their mutual contempt, and never learned what had made them enemies.

Every board meeting had been a battlefield for the two women, and the only thing that saved Violet for many years was the allegiance of two other board members who disliked Marion as much as she did. They formed a voting bloc that steered the board to make some progressive decisions. One member had retired from the board, and only Rosalie remained as an ally to Brie.

Marion clearly voiced her opposition to the renovation of the library. But Violet had leveraged local funding with state and federal grants that finally convinced most of the board members to approve the renovation.

For revenge, the board president blocked many of the suggestions to create inviting spaces for children and teens in the renovation plan. She complained about computers replacing bookshelves in the center of the library space and felt children were noisy, messy, and spoiled. In fact, she'd stated more than once they didn't belong in a quiet place like a library.

If the woman could keep kids out of the library, she certainly would. "Old-fashioned" didn't even begin to describe the woman. A matriarch in her eighties, her family had once been influential in Seattle. Her father sold off most of the land he'd inherited on the island, but kept the camp at Eagle Point.

Marion remedied that by marrying a wealthy businessman who could see the future of the tech industry in the Pacific Northwest. He invested in two companies that vowed to put computer technology in every home, at a time when many people called it unrealistic.

Things worked out well for Marion Rush-Talbot. She expanded the family compound and she and her son spent nearly every summer on Horseshoe Island. When her husband suffered a heart attack in his early sixties and died, Marion moved to the island full-time.

No one really understood the reason for the move. Brie imagined if she were rich, she'd move to a place with more people and culture. She'd live in France for a year, then move to Croatia and Italy. All her winters would be spent in warm places unless she wanted to ski in the Swiss Alps, even though it had been years since she'd been on a slope.

Her mother's voice snapped her out of her daydream. "It might have something to do with her parents. I heard they were strict with her and her brother, and apparently, he died tragically when he was a teenager. That must have been hard on Marion."

Brie leaned forward and yanked at weeds that had turned dry and brown and felt a shadow pass over her. As much as she teased about her older brother, she'd be devastated if anything bad happened to him.

She could feel sorry for Marion Rush-Talbot, but that didn't give her the right to bully Brie.

"Careful, Brie. I'd like to have irises next year. They're my favorite." Her mother grabbed her trowel again and fell to her knees to poke at the roots in the flowerbed.

"What I mean is that even those we think have had every opportunity in life have secret pain they don't share with others," Charlotte continued. "Marion values her position on the library board and in the community. I don't doubt she enjoys using her power, but to me, it looks like protection when she fights against things that are actually good for everyone."

"I don't have enough information to approach the board yet about the donation." Brie took a deep breath, trying to calm her emotions. "Cole wants me to meet with him next week to prove his offer is genuine."

Charlotte lifted her head to study her daughter. "That seems promising. Why do you sound like you'd rather clean the pigpen than meet with him? Is Cole an unpleasant man?"

Brie wrinkled her nose. "Nothing is as bad as the pigpen." She pulled more weeds. "Cole is pretty enigmatic. He spent hours at the library before he approached me, watching the way we interact with patrons, and studying our procedures."

"Don't mention that to your father. He'll assume the guy's a mass murderer stalking you. You know how he is, with all those murder mysteries and police procedurals he watches on TV."

"Not to mention his love of those true crime books. He warned me last week there were men sweeping the internet to find single women who lived alone to attack. He wanted me to move back into the house."

Charlotte laughed. "Ann Rule strikes again! He checks all the doors and windows every night now and puts his shotgun under the bed. I do not know why, since the thing is an antique, and it doesn't fire anymore. All he can do is aim it at someone to intimidate them."

"It seems weird to think of Dad with a gun. Didn't he march to protest against wars?"

"He did. But he lets his imagination run away with him. Just don't mention this strange man you've been seeing."

"I'm not seeing him, Mom. We're meeting to discuss library business."

Her mother nodded. "How old is this man? My age? Your age? Or in between?"

This conversation headed in a familiar direction. Her parents showed no disappointment when she broke up with Caleb. They had pretended to like him for her sake, but they professed they knew he wasn't the right man for her.

"He's thirty-ish," Brie finally answered.

"Since this man has offered to support the library, I don't see that it would hurt to meet with him again." Her mother scratched her nose and left a small smudge of dirt. It made her look younger.

"In a public place, of course," Charlotte added. "A woman has to be careful nowadays. And don't leave your drink unattended."

More wisdom from the nightly news? Or true crime shows?

"He wants me to meet him at Three Geeks on Monday."

"I've heard about that place. It's supposed to be quite a hopping joint on the weekends. At least during the summer." She frowned at Brie. "What exactly is the difference between a geek and a nerd?"

Brie considered pulling out her phone and asking Siri. Her reference librarian inner voice stopped her. She trusted herself enough to explain this in simple terms.

"A geek is more interested in technology and learning about specific subjects, while a nerd is more of an intellectual, interested in different fields of sturdy." She paused. "Or possibly it's the other way around. I forget."

"Just curious," her mother observed. "Isn't 'geek' something you'd be called as an insult in high school? Although there are those guys who will show up to fix your computer, so I could be wrong. I wonder why they named the bar that?"

Brie wondered the same thing when she'd first heard the

name of the business. She thought it could be a way someone turned a negative into something positive. Maybe even a middle-finger salute from someone who'd been bullied growing up.

From what she could see from the few times she'd glimpsed Cole in his T-shirt, his body had the chiseled look of someone who worked out. He didn't exactly look like a guy anyone would pick a fight with in a bar. He looked more like a bouncer.

"Nerd, geek, it doesn't matter. I heard the place is cool, but I won't be there partying. This is strictly a business meeting in the middle of the day. I plan to dress sensibly and be very professional. I need to consider my reputation as the library manager."

"More's the pity," her mother sighed. "You need to lighten up, Brie, and have more fun. You're young and lovely. Take advantage of that now, because age creeps up on you faster than you can imagine."

Brie worried about that every day as she stared into the mirror. The tiny lines forming at the edges of her eyelids scared her. Time marched on and she faced a future that appeared to be predictable, comfortable, and boring. She craved safety and predictability, but a little adventure would be nice.

She should take her mother's advice and visit Ryder for a few days. He had a huge social network. Of course, all future politicians needed that, he explained to her. He had an amazing apartment in a trendy neighborhood filled with restaurants, bars, and nightlife. He'd told her to come to visit anytime.

At least it would break up the monotony of her everyday life.

Then her imagination swung to a pair of moss-green eyes and a dimple deep enough to fall into. Damn Cole, who presented just enough of a mystery to keep her intrigued.

Her mother stood and stretched. "If you finish here, I'll go in and fix us some lunch. Your father should be back soon."

Brie watched her mother walk back to the house and considered her own current situation. How did a woman her age find a partner if she wanted one? Not necessarily for a lifetime, or to get married and settle down.

Just a nice, smart guy who had a great sense of humor. He could be a tiny bit gorgeous, too. She wouldn't object. She wanted to meet someone interesting who gave her the shivers with a look, melted her with a kiss, and took the time to satisfy her with a slow, languid session of sexy time.

Wasn't that every modern single woman's dilemma? Meeting Mr. Right at the right time? It didn't help when she flipped through magazines at the library to read articles with headings like, *No Baby No Time?* and *Aging Eggs? Put Them in the Freezer!*

Brie didn't believe being single and, in her thirties, meant she faced life as a spinster.

Spinster? She shook her head. Good thing she'd taken a break from reading historical romance novels. They messed with her brain, even as they fueled her dreams of a handsome hero twirling her across the dance floor at a ball.

She'd tried online dating, but it didn't work out well for someone who lived on an island. The gene pool tended to be small in her neighborhood. There were lots of men she'd grown up with and few she wanted to be with.

Her brain skipped to Cole again. She'd noticed when a new man appeared in the library recently and now it was hard to ignore a handsome, inscrutable guy who refused to share his full name. Could he be messing with her, insisting they meet outside of the library, suggesting their meeting today over coffee at Java the Hut, then teasing her with the next meeting at Three Geeks, where he promised to show her proof of funding for the library?

He hinted at information about the donation, but refused to divulge the names of the donors. Could he be protecting them or himself?

At least she'd learned he worked at Three Geeks, so at least she had a clue to follow. Everyone in town wanted to know who owned the newest bar on the island. She'd heard it was an amazing place with a spectacular view out at Salmon Point. They hosted popular bands from the mainland on weekends.

The island's soon-to-be-famous builder, Max Cumberland, had constructed the place. Photos online showed huge beams, multiple outdoor fireplaces, and second-floor game rooms, not to mention a concert hall that attracted crowds during the summer.

If she met Cole there on Monday, at least her curiosity about who owned it might be satisfied. Then again, the man seemed to enjoy keeping his secrets. He appeared confident she'd show up. His suggestion the proof he offered would excite her revealed an arrogance she found annoying. She'd suffered a little too much from male egos the past few months.

It astonished Caleb when she refused to become part of his polyamorous group. He insisted she needed to experience sex with multiple partners. To share the love, as he put it. When she declined, he dumped her.

Brie had no interest in joining his poly group with the other band members. She didn't even like several of them. He raged at her and called her a prude who clung to an outdated ideal of a committed monogamous relationship that ended in picket fences and happily ever after.

If she'd cared more for Caleb, she might have agreed. But her interest had been waning, the sex less than satisfying, and he bored her.

It's possible she had old-fashioned ideas about love and marriage, but she could point to her parents as an example of a successful long-term, loving relationship. They'd been together for nearly forty years, and she witnessed their commitment and devotion to each other every day. Even the smallest gesture, from her mother's hand sweeping across her father's hair at the breakfast table, a quick squeeze as they passed each other in the house and the way they sat together reading or listening to music in front of the woodstove on winter nights reinforced her ideal of a successful relationship.

Some of her friends in college swapped out sex partners like seasonal wardrobes, but that didn't interest her. She'd had one long-term boyfriend in college, but she knew it would end at graduation.

She'd never felt loved or cherished when they were together. It was a comfortable arrangement, like boots she'd taken the time to break in and couldn't let go of until they fell apart. She accepted the terms of their relationship. Fairly good sex and companionship seemed like worthy goals.

Actually, it had been mediocre sex. Sean lacked imagination.

Brie considered her choices. She had a non-existent dating life, and she couldn't remember the last time someone had propositioned her. Her weeks were filled with work and helping her parents on the farm.

Of course, she needed to solve the mystery of the rich donors who might want to donate to the library. Brie didn't think Cole planned to divulge their names. He seemed very protective of that information.

She needed to investigate. A search through the public records about expensive new homes on the island served as a starting point. Cole had confessed that the donors lived here.

He'd shared a scrap of valuable information.

A good reference librarian could be as tenacious as a hotshot reporter chasing a story or an FBI agent trailing a perp. Brie needed to gather as much information as she could to use as fuel for her next meeting with Cole.

Cute Scruffy Dude would discover a librarian could be a determined foe on a quest for information. Finding things out was her superpower.

TRUE CONFESSION: Why are we so intrigued by a mystery? With facts as close as asking our phone a question, we still want to dig, search, uncover things, and solve puzzles. Perhaps it's our never-ending quest to discover the secrets of humanity. With our attempt to learn all we can about others, maybe we hope to understand ourselves better. The fact that I can't find information about Cole makes him even more interesting. I guess that says a lot more about me than him.

COLE

"**ARE** we going to raise the fuckin' sails today or just motor around?" Cole glared at his two companions.

"Ain't we in a sweet mood today?" Dylan observed from the wheel, brushing his sun-bleached blond hair from his eyes. "Get busy and remove the cover instead of sitting on your ass telling us what to do."

Cole stood and made his way down to the boom that held the mainsail on *The Sylph*, Dylan's sailboat. There wasn't any point in stomping, because in his bare feet he couldn't make enough noise to telegraph his mood.

A mood that could most easily be described as "royally pissed off." His last encounter with the prissy librarian, who seemed to think he was a con man or crazy, had bothered him for days.

He unsnapped the bag surrounding the main sail and removed it. Despite his mood, he carefully folded the covering and stowed it in a small, hatched compartment.

After unfastening the sail ties, he started attaching the mainsheet to the mainsail before returning to the stern and plopping back down on the plush cushions of the seating area. "Maybe if either of you would take an interest in Three Geeks once in a while, I wouldn't have to act like such an asshole."

Wyatt pushed the button on the electric winch to unfurl the mainsail, then lowered his sunglasses to frown at Cole. "You never let business bother you, so Three Geeks isn't the problem. What's going on?"

The wind filled the sail and heeled the boat in the water as if it had been picked up by a giant hand. Dylan turned the wheel to take advantage of the steady breeze.

"I think his little librarian is bustin' his balls," Dylan offered. "The old lady librarian was easy to manage, but the new younger one doesn't trust him."

"Trust him? What the hell does that mean?" Wyatt shrugged his broad shoulders. "We're giving the library a million bucks. People should hold a parade in our honor and dance in the streets."

Cole leaned back and put his sunglasses on. "She's not *my* little librarian. And I haven't told her about the amount of money yet, just mentioned a donation."

The other two men stared at him. "Why the hell not?" Wyatt finally asked. "I thought the old lady librarian had everything set up. We give them the money and they build the makerspace when they remodel the library. You told us she was thrilled with the idea."

"Her name is Violet. And yes, she supported the project. But she retired and now I'm dealing with the temporary manager. Violet had to practically give me a letter of recommendation just to get Brienne to talk to me."

"So, give her the dollar amount," Dylan suggested, "and that'll get her excited."

Cole didn't answer right away. He didn't want to admit to his buddies he felt an intense attraction to Brienne. He wouldn't mind asking her out on a date, but he sensed she wanted to be taken seriously. Her cool attitude showed her desire to keep things between them professional.

The last thing he needed to do was mess up their plan for the library by trying to hook up with her. Despite her resistance to his proposal, he couldn't seem to have a conversation with her without flirting.

He'd watched her blush when they had coffee at Java the Hut. She had a sense of humor and that made it even more fun to talk with her. Which was part of the problem.

Cole didn't tell her about the money because he wanted to find an excuse to see her again. So, he'd set up the date. The *meeting*, he reminded himself, to see her again.

"You didn't hit on her, did you?" Dylan shot him a mischievous look. "Is she one of those sexy librarians, the kind with a bun and glasses who looks so puritanical but then lets down her hair and turns into an insatiable sex kitten?"

Cole stared at one of his best friends. "You're watching too much porn, Dylan. Maybe it's time for you to give up your sex doll and find a real woman."

"Fuck you, Cole. If you didn't rub one off every day, you'd have no sex life either."

Cole flipped his friend the bird and slipped down the steps and into the galley to grab some beers. Dylan hit a bit too close for comfort. The reality was none of the three geeks, named by others during their college days, were getting any action.

Wyatt had lost his beloved wife, Amy, to ovarian cancer a couple of years ago. He'd met her in college, and they married right after graduation. They'd been planning to start a family and when Amy couldn't conceive, she'd visited a specialist. Instead of a baby, she'd had a hysterectomy at age twenty-five. She'd died of cancer a few months before her thirtieth birthday.

Amy's death contributed to the reasons they ended up in the San Juan Islands. Cole and Dylan recognized Wyatt needed a change of scenery after her death. They'd all purchased sailboats, and on nearly every weekend, they ended up visiting Dylan's family estate on the island. Finally, they all realized they shared a desire to step back from the successful gaming business they'd built and simplify their lives.

The weekend escapes turned into living full-time in the San Juan Islands. Cole threw himself into the building and managing of the bar because he needed to keep busy. Dylan and Wyatt worked together on graphic novels that became best-sellers.

Despite being good-looking, single, and rich, they all struggled to meet women they could trust. They'd slipped into incognito lives that resembled the witness protection program more than early retirement from running a successful business.

"Hey, you brewin' that beer down there?" Dylan yelled from above.

"I'm bringing up some snacks for you guys. You're bottomless pits." Cole grabbed the beer, two gigantic bags of chips, and a container of dip. He balanced the food as he climbed the steps to topside.

When he got on deck, he handed the beers around and put the chips and dip in the middle of a table near the bench seats. Dylan nodded at Wyatt. "You wanna take the wheel for a while?"

Wyatt was always game to steer the boat. He sailed more than any of them, probably because being out on the water served as an escape. They rarely mentioned Amy, maybe to avoid reminding Wyatt of his loss, but sometimes Cole wished men could be better at talking to each other about their feelings.

Dylan sometimes mentioned his ex-wife, a model who latched onto him when they made their first real money from the business. He'd been dazzled by Sami's beauty, her worldliness, and sophistication. They had a whirlwind romance, followed by an opulent wedding. Within a year, they separated.

Sami wanted to be an actor, and she traveled around the world, tracking down auditions and often hooking up with inappropriate guys along the way. It seemed like every few months, Dylan got a call from her. He functioned as her white knight, rescuing her from self-imposed messes.

It had developed into an ugly pattern, but Dylan couldn't seem to extricate himself from Sami's web of chaos. Wyatt described it as a co-dependent relationship. Sami created havoc to bring Dylan back into her orbit, and Dylan kept hoping when they got together, it would be a reconciliation. He'd even refused to sign the final divorce papers.

Dylan represented the true romantic in their group of friends, believing his first love would be the one to last until the end. Cole had long ago given up on that notion. For him, romance was a temporary arrangement in pursuit of company, fun, and sex.

It worked out well for both parties if neither expected any long-term commitment. Cool and casual meant there were no strings attached.

Which brought him back to Brienne.

He took a swig of his beer. He figured she'd be a fairy-tale-finish sort of woman. The kind who'd accept nothing less than a Hallmark movie ending.

"Brienne," he said to Wyatt and Dylan, "is a librarian who grew up on a farm here on the island. I'm guessing getting an out-of-the-blue donation from a bunch of rich guys who want to remain nameless might have set off her corruption detector."

"Shit, why can't rich people just do something good for the world without being accused of a crime anymore? Back in the good old days, altruistic motivation was good enough.

When Bill Gates started giving money away to solve world problems, everyone called him a hero. Now, if you give money away, you're under suspicion."

"Sucks for us," Wyatt offered, "being so rich we can give a million dollars away and then people don't even appreciate it."

"I suspect it might have to do with large donations to politicians and the public thinking we don't pay our own way," Cole said. "She didn't turn us down, but she's definitely suspicious. I figured I'd take it slow, introduce her to the idea in stages."

"Better raise the jib; the wind's picking up," Wyatt said, looking at the sail. The boat slipped into a trough, then tipped to the left before heeling and slicing through the water like a thoroughbred horse released from its stall.

He admired the way the boat handled in the water. A French architect and an English designer created a company that built what he considered some of the best sailboats in their class. Wyatt purchased his first, but it only took one sailing trip for Cole and Dylan to decide they needed matching vessels.

The men made sure they went sailing as often as possible. Sometimes together on the same boat, but once in a while they raced each other around the Salish Sea.

"So, what does your little farm-girl librarian look like?" Wyatt asked. "Since she's not one of Dylan's high school wet dreams."

Dylan saluted Wyatt with a middle finger.

"She has blue hair," Cole said. "Apparently she made a bet with some teens to encourage them to read more over the summer. When she lost, she dyed her hair."

Dylan frowned. "What shade of blue, like flag blue, or ocean blue?"

Cole had to think for a moment. "A kind of light blue, I'd call it...mermaid blue."

"Uh-oh," Wyatt said. "You better be careful. We know how you are about mermaids."

They teased him because when they all purchased sailboats, they chose names based on the elemental creatures in the first successful video game they designed. The quest in the story featured four witches who had to learn to use magic and slay the ancient evil sorcerer who threatened their fantasy kingdom.

Mystic Moon was one of the first subscriber online games, and its success astonished the gaming industry. Their company produced a lot of other games, but the guys all had an emotional connection to that first accomplishment.

Wyatt named his boat *The Sylph*, after the elemental wind spirit. Dylan favored the flame-haired witch in the game with the power to control fire, choosing *The Sea Dragon* for his sailboat, and after some consideration, Cole finally settled on *The Siren of the Sea*.

An interesting coincidence since the first time he'd seen Brienne with her blue hair piled in a tousled bun on her head, he'd thought of the beautiful witch in the game who could control the element of water. Wyatt created the art for the witches, and his drawings of sexy, full-figured fantasy women drove them all crazy when they worked twenty hours every day and barely left the tiny apartment they shared.

The witches inspired devotion from people around the world who played the game. There were merchandising deals, spinoffs, even talk about a television show or movie. That game spawned an entire company, and the three men never took their good luck for granted.

"I blame it on that stupid mermaid movie my sister was obsessed with. She must have watched that damn thing a thousand times. I can probably still sing those fuckin' songs."

The other two men stared at him for a moment, then burst out laughing.

"Go ahead, do it now, Cole. Let's hear the one about how great it is to be underwater. You know, the one with that lobster that could sing and dance," Wyatt said.

"It's a crab, fool," Cole responded.

"I have to admit, that mermaid chick was hot. I liked her better with a tail than with legs," Dylan commented.

"That sounds kinky," Wyatt said. "It might explain your attraction to redheads, though. Especially one troublesome little redhead who needs you to rescue her and bail her out of trouble on a pretty frequent basis."

Dylan stared off into space for a few moments. Frowned, then swallowed a gulp of beer before responding.

"That's over. I signed the papers a few weeks ago." He shrugged and crushed the can. "She wants to get married again, and I want to be free."

"It's time to let go," Cole suggested.

Dylan's jaw tightened. "I hoped—thinking maybe, someday—she'd realize we had something special. When she told me she planned to get married again, I decided I wanted to move on with my life too."

The boat ripped through the water as the group of men stared at each other.

"Listen, Dylan," Wyatt said as he spun the wheel to tack into the wind. "I know what it means to fall in love with someone you think is your forever person. It happened to me, and when Amy died, a part of me died too.

"Eventually, though, you need to admit things have changed. Sami's been over your marriage for a long time. I mean, I don't want to hurt your feelings, but I never thought she cared as much about being married as you did. To be honest, she loved the wedding and all the media attention."

"Fuck you, Wyatt. Just because you've been in therapy doesn't make you an expert on my love life."

Cole held up one hand. "No, but if you had a fuckin' love life, he'd be happy to give you some terrible advice."

Wyatt nodded at Cole. "Get Dylan another beer and let's cut out all the psych shit. We were talking about your librarian, who looks like a mermaid."

"She has mermaid hair; that's all I'm saying," Cole yelled over his shoulder as he ducked back down the steps into the galley. "And she's also a wholesome, sweet girl-next-door type."

The groans from the other two men showed they knew that meant trouble for Cole.

"She's not your usual type, but maybe you're attracted to her for that reason," Dylan yelled after him. "Is it possible she's the hot librarian who fuels a thousand male dreams, but in an innocent, nice-girl package?"

Cole ignored the comment. He'd given them enough information and needed to proceed with his plan to reveal their proposal for the library renovation to Brienne.

If she even showed up at Three Geeks on Monday. She might think he set up the meeting as a trick and ghost him. She'd flat-out refused him when she thought he wanted a date.

Not that he'd mind dating her. In fact, since their meeting at the coffee shop, his imagination had gone into overdrive considering ways he could entice, charm, and seduce her.

No! Not *seduce*. Not his plan. Then he imagined Brienne stretched across his bed, naked and wanton—with her blue hair covering the nipples of those full breasts. He put his head down and tried to capture his breath.

The bulge in his jeans appeared too conspicuous to go topside for a few minutes. He lifted his head and rubbed the cold can of beer across his forehead. He hoped it wouldn't be necessary to move the can of beer lower.

Smart, sweet, wholesome girls were not his jam. He preferred being with hard-edged, experienced women who understood Cole enjoyed great sex, avoided long-term commitments, and sought a "happy ending," and not a "happy-ever-after ending."

This attraction to Brienne didn't make sense. He planned to meet with her to discuss the makerspace project, convince her he and his buddies were on the level, and work with her to present the proposal to the library board.

That would be the extent of his involvement with her. Purely professional, building on sexual tension, playful flirting, teasing at the edge of seduction...until he fucked her all night long.

He snapped open the beer and took a long gulp before admitting his attraction to Brienne Henderson could turn into more than a lusty itch.

It could be an extended yearning that would grow like a banked fire, torch all his plans to act cool and ignite a sensual hunger that left him craving her company, her touch and more.

He took another long gulp of beer. He was really and truly screwed, and not in a good way.

∂✧℃∿✧

BRIENNE

"Is that your new tail?" Pure jealousy edged Shelby's voice. "Is it from Fantasy Tails?"

"It's a brand-new design. Look at the colors! It should float in the water beautifully." Raina blushed. "I'm not bragging, just pointing that out."

Shelby stroked the mermaid tail and exhaled. "It's beautiful and the photos for the calendar will be amazing. I confess, I'm insanely jealous."

"As if." Brie snorted. "You have the most gorgeous

wedding gown I've ever seen. We're buying mermaid tails while you're planning a fairy-tale wedding to a real-life hero. It's not even close!"

"I'd trade this designer tail for a fiancé as studly as Ryan in a heartbeat," Raina offered. She wiggled her eyebrows at Shelby and the group dissolved into laughter.

"So, do we know when we can arrange the last shoot for the calendar?" Luna's edgy, tough-girl voice interrupted the laughter.

Brie shook her head. "They've already closed the pool at the resort. There aren't many other options on the island unless we find someone with a private pool."

The women glanced at each other. Shelby grinned. "I don't have any rich friends. How about you guys?"

The group of friends known as the Mermaid Posse remained silent.

"I have exactly one famous friend, Bailey Holmes, and while I hope she makes a ton of money on her new show, I doubt she'll have time to build a pool so we can do a photo shoot in the next few weeks," Brie said.

"Maybe we could put an ad online: *Needed: lovely, heated swimming pool for a group of mermaids to lounge around. Send photo of pool*," Raina suggested, then grinned.

"Ooh," squealed Shelby. "That won't bring out any weirdos or creeps. With that message, we'll get all kinds of legit invitations."

"Not to mention the photos. Dick pics, anyone?" Brie added. "Not the sort of thing we want connected to a calendar to raise money to purchase children's books for the library."

"I'm actually shocked Old Lady Talbot gave her approval for this project," Shelby said with a sly grin. "We aren't exactly buttoned up and proper in our mermaid costumes."

Brie shook her head. "She didn't like the idea, but we raised so much money for books at the Independence Day celebration, she couldn't argue with success. As long as the calendar represented the library in an, and I quote, 'serious, tasteful manner,'" Brie shifted into a snooty, high-pitched voice, "'with all the problematic body parts properly covered,' then she'd approve."

"Do you think my seashell bra will properly cover my problematic body parts?" Luna asked. She held the piece of fabric she worked on against her substantial breasts. She was a tall woman with long, thick, wavy black hair who fit the description of statuesque perfectly.

The women in the group surrounding her laughed.

"I think you're gonna need more fabric than that to cover your substantial bit of real estate," Raina said. "I also think any of us would be happy to be blessed with your bounty."

Luna laughed as she shook her head, and ripples of dark hair curled around her face. She possessed an astonishing figure packed into a substantial package and Luna never apologized for a body that often drew suggestive glances, wolf whistles, and improper propositions.

She demanded respect and knew how to put men in their place when necessary.

"My grandmother tells me the women from my family have always been proud of their curves." She winked. "Besides, Brie could give me some serious competition when it comes to being a full-figured gal."

The other women turned to study her. Brie's cheeks heated into a blush. "If only I was as confident as you are. I'm never going to achieve that tiny waist and flat-hipped look magazine models have, no matter how much I diet and exercise."

Luna studied her for a moment. Her dark eyes shimmered with intensity.

"Why would you even want to look like that, Brie? You need to model yourself like 1950s movie stars. Elizabeth

Taylor, Susan Hayward, Sophia Loren. If you think you're fat because you're not a size zero, that's a problem with society, not you."

"Brie, you need to celebrate who you are, not what someone else wants you to be," Raina added.

The tall, athletic redhead with long legs and a muscular build made Brie a little jealous. How she maintained her figure while owning a busy restaurant and catering business was a secret her friends begged her to share.

Shelby gave Brie a sideways look. "I know at least one guy who seems to like exactly what he sees!"

Brie wanted to shush Shelby. She didn't want to talk to the posse about Cole yet. They'd had one coffee date. No. *Not a date*. A meeting. A serious business meeting to discuss serious business.

Too late. Raina and Luna erupted into a cascade of questions.

"We've been calling this guy, who's been hanging around the library, Cute Scruffy Dude," Brie explained. "You know the type—tall, muscles in all the right places, sun-streaked hair, sexy as hell single guy, with long legs, and a tight ass."

Her friends stared at her.

Luna finally broke the silence. "I *want* to know the type. But not even one man who has recently walked into my place comes close to that description. I'm definitely planning to visit the library a lot more often."

She smiled, then briefly closed her eyes, and exhaled, as if she could imagine the man Shelby had described.

"Now tell us every single detail about Cute Scruffy Dude," Raina insisted.

"There's nothing much to tell." Brie shook her head. "He's been coming into the library for the past few weeks, sits, uses the wi-fi to check his phone, and never checks out a book or any library materials. He doesn't even want a library card."

"But he spends a lot of time checking Brie out," Shelby interrupted. "He watches her and then pretends he's not looking if one of us catches him."

"That's kinda creepy," Luna pointed out. "Do we need to call Sheriff Clements?"

Brie shook her head emphatically. "Now you sound like my father. Cole isn't a stalker. Violet suggested he talk to me."

That statement silenced the room for another few seconds.

"Violet Lancaster sent you a man. Wow! That lady has skills!" Raina burbled. "Maybe she can find one for me."

"It's not like that." Brie paused and nibbled on her lip. "He wants to talk to me about a donation to the library. For the remodel." She tried to make her shrug as nonchalant as she pretended to be. "Since I'm the temporary manager, Violet told him to contact me." She glanced around the table and frowned. "But you can't tell anyone about this."

"Cute Scruffy Dude could have done a quick scan on social media if he just wanted to make a donation. I think he wants to take something out of the library, and I think it's Brie." Shelby wiggled her eyebrows and grinned.

The group dissolved into a chattering mob. Each woman had a suggestion for how to find out more about Brie's not-so-secret admirer. She hated to spoil their fun, but she needed to stop the gossip before it started.

"His name is Cole, and he works as the manager of Three Geeks," she said when the noise finally settled down. "We had coffee and discussed a grant to the library building fund. End of story."

Raina shot her a suspicious look. "You let him get away? Did he talk about his beautiful wife and three exceptional children?"

Brie glanced at the silver and white bra she worked to bedazzle into a mermaid top. "He's not married," she stated with an emphasis on the not.

"And...?" Luna asked. All the women seemed to hold their breath, waiting for Brie's response.

"And that's the extent of it. You now know what I know." She shrugged again, hoping to shut down the conversation.

Shelby dropped the piece of green netting she held onto the table and gave Brie a pitiful look. "I swear he's not that boring. I see deep secrets and layers of mystery beneath that gorgeous surface. Did you look at his profile or search for his name online?"

Brie wanted to scream. Of course, she'd tried to research Cole that afternoon. Unfortunately, the search didn't go far. She summoned her helpful reference interview expression and plastered it on her face.

"All I have is his phone number and first name. He's being pretty secretive about who he is and the identity of the donors he represents."

"So, he could be a serial killer who's scoping you out to be his next victim." Raina's voice rose in panic. "Are you sure we shouldn't get the sheriff involved? What if he tries to kidnap you the next time he comes to the library?"

Brie stood up and patted Raina on the shoulder. "You and my dad should get together and create a plot for a TV show. Cole's not a stalker or a serial killer. He works for the owner of the Three Geeks Bar. That person, whoever they are, is interested in donating funds for the library remodeling project. That's it."

Shelby paced across the room, her face scrunched into a frown. "How do you know he works there? He could be lying. Creating a backstory so you won't suspect his motives before he kidnaps you."

Putting her hands on her hips, Brie shook her head in dismay. "First, you guys want me to seduce him; now you think he's going to murder me. It's kind of hard to keep up."

Luna's head tipped up from sewing more bangles onto the

bra top in front of her. "I don't think anyone suggested you seduce him. That's totally on you, Brie."

The group erupted into a fit of giggles.

Brie felt the heat of embarrassment ignite on her cheeks. She should ignore the good-natured teasing, but she wanted to throw out a tease of her own to the members of the posse.

"I guess I'll find out for sure on Monday, because he wants to meet with me again, this time at Three Geeks. He says he wants to show me something."

"Tell him to send the dick pic and save you some time," Raina suggested, tossing her auburn braid over one shoulder.

Hoots and groans signaled the group's opinion of that suggestion.

"Hey," Raina added. "I'm just trying to keep it real."

"If you meet him at Three Geeks, there will be other people around. It's not like he can tie you up and kidnap you in front of a bunch of customers," Shelby pointed out. "And you can text us when you get there, and also after the meeting."

"Gee, thanks, Mom. I'll be sure to do that!" Brie said. "Any other instructions? I've never been alone with a man before, in case you didn't know."

The three women stared at Brie. Their stern, no-nonsense expressions clearly signaling they weren't kidding. They all narrowed their eyes, and there was no hint of a smile on any of their faces. They'd stopped working and folded their arms. This was some serious shit.

Brie threw her hands up in the air. "All right. I'll text you when I get there and promise to let you know when the meeting ends. You'll be informed at all times."

The other women in the Mermaid Posse nodded. Brie knew they were just trying to ensure her safety. But with overprotective parents, friends who acted like guardian angels, and an entire island filled with people who seemed to think she couldn't take care of herself, Brie had an aching need to prove she was a capable grownup.

And maybe a wish for the opportunity to do something a tad thrilling and a tiny bit naughty.

Brie pictured Cole's moss-green eyes, the inviting curve of his smile when he flirted with her that revealed the deep dimple on the left side of his cheek.

She was more than a bit interested when she considered the naughty part. She had a feeling Cole, whatever his last name was, would make letting loose and being wild a whole lot of fun!

TRUE CONFESSION: True friends are the people who offer you free advice, even when you don't ask for it, who point out you're heading in the wrong direction, even when you're searching for adventure and excitement, and listen to you complain after you ignore their good advice and wander off the path. A good friend is a rare treasure, and when they'll don a mermaid tail and help you with your crazy idea to help the community, they're priceless.

COLE

"WHAT'S up with you today, Cole?" Matt asked. "Are you pissed off at someone or just angry at the world?"

Cole winced. He'd spent the morning acting like an asshole, and he knew it.

"Sorry. Just trying to keep track of a bunch of things. Distracted, I guess."

Matt grinned at him as he moved a keg of Pirate's Grog beer across the floor. "Well, whoever she is, I congratulate her on the power to confuse and unsettle you."

Cole frowned. "There's no she. Well, not one like you mean."

Matt straightened up and gave his boss a knowing grin. "Sure, no mere mortal woman could ever confuse the calm, cool, collected Cole Moore."

Cole snorted.

"You like women, Cole. I've watched you flirt with dozens of them. You seem to flit from one to another without a thought, but I've never seen you bothered by one."

Cole fumed at the observation from his employee. Matt should just shut the fuck up and mind his own business. Then again, Matthew O'Donnell wasn't a bartender. As a trusted member of his security team, the man sometimes helped with minor tasks at the bar to maintain a low profile.

"I met with the librarian. You know, the young one."

"Sweater Girl? You spoke to her after weeks of skulking around the library? Good for you, man."

Now that he'd met her, he regretted giving Brienne a nickname based on her rockin' hot bod.

"Her actual name is Brienne. And we met for coffee to discuss business." Cole knew his voice had a defensive tone.

"Of course. You're the most obvious person in town to be interested in library business," Matt said. "In fact, I suspect you'll soon be on the library board. With every other old codger on the island."

Cole growled. "Libraries bring information to the masses. The guys want to fund some projects on the island, and they asked me to find out more about the plan to remodel the library."

Matt stared at him for a few moments. "Hey, I'm just bustin' your balls, Cole. I get it. You're the guy Dylan and Wyatt send to get things done. If Team Geek wants something, you make it happen."

Cole nodded. "Since I'm the one who pushed the idea of creating a foundation, thanks to Kate sending me on a major guilt trip, they assigned me to find out more about the library."

"Your sister's a bundle of 'save the world' energy, isn't she?" Matt laughed. "So, Sweater Girl isn't making it easy for you to hit on her? I'm delighted to hear it. A good-lookin' rich bastard like you needs a challenge occasionally."

Cole felt a sharp pang of guilt. He was taking advantage of the donation to the library to meet with Brienne again. She expected a professional business meeting this afternoon, and he kept imagining ways to seduce her.

Not that he expected her to fall into his arms. Honestly, it'd be disappointing if that happened. He'd determined Brienne Henderson would be the sort of woman who required patience to be slowly enticed to his bed.

That would be part of the pleasure for him. Part of the foreplay. He could easily find women eager to enjoy a good fuck even when they didn't know he had a lot of money.

Those women bored him.

There was a spark between him and Brienne. He felt it, and so did she—even if she pulled away from him. Maybe she'd learned to be distrustful after her recent breakup or just tended to be cautious because of her job at the library. A professional woman in a very public position couldn't afford to act impulsively.

He'd observed her in the library. Brienne appeared to be thoughtful, kind, and professional. She could be funny and open when interacting with families and teens. Little kids adored her and even the most jaded curmudgeon seemed to respect her.

His observations of Brienne Henderson surprised him. She appeared to be the sweet, kind-hearted, helpful librarian to those who visited the library. He wondered if her face hurt at night from all the bright, cheerful smiles she bestowed on everyone who entered the building. If it was an act, she deserved the Oscar.

The color of her hair shocked him at first. Once he discovered the reason she'd dyed it, he admired her commitment to getting teens to read. Something that seemed like an impossible challenge. He'd loved playing video games as a kid, but his mother had demanded quiet reading time every night.

He admired her. And he wanted to get to know her better, a major change for Cole when it came to women.

Preferring casual arrangements, Cole's partners

understood in advance he didn't do commitment. He enjoyed sex with them, but he'd never been curious enough to attempt to figure out any of the women he'd been with. Short-term arrangements, with no permanent ties, worked best for him.

He should run away from Brienne as fast as possible. Instead, he created more reasons to see her. He sensed the usual invitation for dinner and drinks to be followed by a predictable round of sex afterward wouldn't appeal to her.

Or maybe *he* didn't want it to work as usual. She could be fun and unpredictable. He wanted to discover if she experienced the same powerful attraction he did. While he knew it would be wise to avoid her, the temptation to see her again overwhelmed his good sense.

He wanted—to be surprised. He craved a conversation that took an unexpected turn, elicited a smart retort, and delivered a sexy double entendre. A conversation with an intelligent vixen possessing the body of a goddess. Yet he understood she didn't owe him entertainment or distraction.

Cole climbed the stairs to the second floor, then continued up to what he called his "Boss Man Aerie" at the peak of the building. When Max Cumberland helped design this structure, Cole insisted his office be high above the other floors, with one wall nearly all glass.

That glass wall gave him a spectacular view. The dark blue and gray of the Salish Sea, the green of the evergreen trees scattered at the edges of the water and the changing shadows across the sky, as the weather moved in and out of the islands, never failed to thrill him.

He glanced around the room and appreciated his masculine lair, decorated in dark woods, leather furniture, and chrome accents. He'd hired the same decorator who designed his house. A tall, leggy blonde who made it clear early in their business relationship that she'd be a willing bed partner. When she finished the job, they ended their affair. It had been over a year, and he hadn't met another woman he wanted to spend time with since then.

Not until the first day he'd wandered into the library to learn more about the new manager. Violet insisted he take his time to approach Brienne. She'd told him to watch her interactions with patrons, observe her working and, most of all, to be patient.

It didn't take long before he looked forward to his visits several times each week. He always pulled out his phone and connected to the Wi-Fi immediately after arriving at the library. Then he pretended to be engrossed in looking at his messages or checking social media.

Not that he ever appeared on any social media platform. He'd paid a lot of money to get as much of the information about him scrubbed from the internet as possible. The land purchases the geeks made on the island were coordinated from a corporate account with multiple layers tied to small companies to help conceal their identities. If you had enough money, you could buy anonymity.

His phone buzzed with a text message.

BRIENNE HENDERSON

I'm here. The sign says closed on Monday. I hope this isn't a trick. Where do I go?

His fingers worked the keyboard. She'd shown up. Again. That's two points for him.

COLE

CUTE SCRUFFY DUDE: Two employees here. No worries.

Her answer came quickly.

BRIENNE HENDERSON

LOL! Very funny name. Updating my contacts list. Open the door.

He grinned as he typed a message that he'd be right down. An unexpected flicker of excitement flashed through him. He couldn't exactly describe what Brienne did to him, but he recognized anticipation when it hit.

When he arrived at the bottom of the stairs, she stood at the bar chatting with Matt, and Cole's excitement turned into an irrational flare of jealousy. Which didn't make sense. Cole had no right to feel possessive.

As irrational as his emotional response might be, he couldn't control it. From the way she stood, leaning toward Matt, tipping her head back to maintain eye contact as her luscious pink mouth opened to laugh with him, she seemed to enjoy flirting with his employee.

"You didn't say please." His voice sounded harsh and annoyed, and he regretted the tone the instant the words left his mouth.

Matt and Brienne paused in their conversation to stare at him. Matt took a step back from her. He had a gift for reading body language. It's what made him an elite bodyguard.

"Fortunately, Matt noticed I waited for you at the door, so he let me in."

He reconsidered his strategy and tried to steady his emotions. Emotions he found confusing. He was the guy with nerves of steel, just as Matt said. Cole worked hard to maintain a cool, calm, indifferent attitude. He had a reputation as the "guy in control" at all times.

Only his best friends, family members, and Sal knew the truth about what it took for him to maintain that image.

Apparently, unless it involved this sweet, sexy-as-hell librarian. He took a deep breath and worked hard to make his expression friendly and his attitude mellow.

"I'm glad you're here." He moved closer. Close enough to

catch a whiff of her perfume. Something spicy and flowery at the same time.

He liked the way she smelled. It was sensual and enticing, yet fresh and sweet.

It fit her.

"To be honest, I wasn't sure if I believed you about this place. But here you are, and Matt assures me you're actually the manager."

Cole glanced at Matt and raised his eyebrows. "I'm surprised you didn't do a background check on me, Velma."

She turned her stormy sky-gray eyes to gaze at him and flashed him a look of victory. She waved a familiar-looking business card in his face.

"Oh, I'll be checking you out," she grinned. "That's an official library term, by the way, now that I know your full name, Mr. Moore."

"Would you like a drink? A glass of wine or beer?" Matt asked her.

Brie shook her head. "This is work. I'm officially on the clock, so just some sparkling water for me."

She turned to Cole when Matt left to get her drink. "I'm surprised you set up our meeting for today. The sign on the door says you're closed on Monday?"

"We are, which means I have time for meetings."

Her pink lips curved into a smile, and he could swear her gray eyes sparkled. "It's kind of you to give up your day off to see me."

"I have a flexible schedule. I'd like to move forward on the foundation grant as soon as possible. You're the only thing standing in my way."

Matt set a bottle of water and a glass on the table. He put a smaller glass filled with an expensive Scottish whiskey in front of Cole.

She thanked Matt with a brilliant smile, and Cole felt an unfamiliar sensation jab him in the gut.

Jealousy.

"I hired a new chef. He's in the back creating the menu for fall. We're trying to source our food locally." Cole had no idea why he said that. Possibly in an effort to distract himself from the enticing woman sitting next to him.

"It makes all the difference for local farms and businesses to sell to restaurants. The transportation costs are lower, it's a stable market, and it keeps the money in our own community. That's always a plus." She chattered on, unaware of the lustful thoughts running through his head.

"It sounds like you know what you're talking about."

She glanced away for a moment, took a deep breath, and her mouth formed a crooked smile. "I grew up on a farm and I'm still there. I live in a cottage on Diggin' Dirt Farm and help my parents with chores in exchange for free rent."

"Diggin' Dirt Farm," he repeated. "How big is it?"

She rolled her eyes. "It's getting to be too big for my dad to manage. He loves the farm, but he's slowing down a bit. My mother owns a weaving business, and she's so busy she can't help as much anymore. We used to hire teens to work after school and on weekends, but most kids don't want to do physical labor anymore."

Cole caught a bit of that intoxicating scent again. She wore a crisp white blouse and a navy-blue skirt with a ruffle along the bottom edge. She looked innocent and sexy as hell at the same time.

He'd noticed her shoes when he came down the stairs. Navy blue and white polka dot heels with a ribbon that wrapped around her ankle. Despite being on her feet for hours at the library, she wore the sexiest shoes and boots. Even when she wore jeans, she often sported a pair of vintage-looking heels as part of the ensemble.

He wished he could lean over and look at the shoes again. They were sexy and cute at the same time. Just like the woman who wore them. Her vibe combined vintage rockabilly with a touch of sex kitten.

Cole liked everything about her, and it worried him.

"My parents came out here from the Midwest in the 80s. They were searching for their dream," she went on, seemingly oblivious to the way Cole gaped at her.

"They became part of a farming commu...cooperative." She took a sip of her water. "Here, on the island. Horseshoe Island."

She'd changed "commune" to "cooperative." Interesting.

"What kinds of crops do you grow on the farm? Do you have any animals?"

"We grow fruits and vegetables, and we have chickens, pigs, sheep, and goats. We're pretty much as self-sustaining as possible."

He leaned back on his stool. "Did you enjoy growing up there?"

Cole grew up on a farm in eastern Washington, and he'd loved it. They had acres to roam, a pond to swim in, dogs, cats, and a variety of other pets. It had been a cross between *Peter Pan* and *Huckleberry Finn*.

She took a deep breath, then let it out slowly. "I loved it when I was young. Now that I understand how much work it takes to be profitable, I'm not sure it's worth it."

When she looked up at him, he could see sadness reflected in her eyes. Did she feel stuck here on the island, on her parents' farm? Maybe he could offer her an occasional escape. He had access to an incredible number of resources.

The apartments in Seattle, New York, London, and Paris. The private jet. A flexible schedule to take time off when he wanted to.

His imagination took off, and he needed to return to reality.

"Do you make your own cheese from the cows you milk?"

"Goats." She frowned at him, as if she knew what he'd been thinking about. "We milk the goats to make our own cheese. And they provide wool for some of my mother's weaving projects."

He'd been joking, but her answer made him grin. "I'd like to try some of that cheese. Maybe our chef can figure out how to use it here."

She poured more water from the bottle into her glass and studied him. "You didn't ask me to meet you to discuss goat cheese. Although I warn you, if you ever meet my father and bring up that topic, be prepared for a long, boring lecture. After ways to kill people and rutabagas, it's his favorite subject."

Cole laughed. "He sounds like a true Renaissance man." Then he considered her words and frowned.

"Should I worry about the killing people part?"

She sipped her water and dabbed at her lips. Lovely, enticing lips painted an intense shade he'd named Tickle Me Pink.

"You probably should worry a bit. He's convinced you're a serial killer hiding out on the island. When he found out you were watching me at the library, he became concerned. He calls you 'that stalker guy.'"

"Given the choice, I prefer 'cute scruffy dude' instead." He took a sip from his own glass.

She blushed, and he felt heat rush to his dick. He couldn't decide if she was a sweet innocent playing with fire or a sexy minx drawing him in? It would certainly be interesting to discover exactly what game Brienne played best.

"You weren't supposed to hear that. I guess our whispers were a bit too loud."

He let his gaze wander from her bright pink lips to the open space at the top of her button-up blouse. He caught a peek of her white lace bra and every word he planned to say died on his lips.

How could any man resist her intoxicating mix of innocence and eroticism?

He looked away from her cleavage and took a deep breath to regain control. "I'm more concerned about your father's threats of homicide. How serious should I take that?"

"On a scale of what he doesn't know won't hurt you? I didn't mention our meeting today."

"That bad?" He put his hand on the back of his neck. "Will I need to hire a security detail?"

Matt brought her another bottle of water. When he heard that remark, he frowned at Cole.

Brienne bestowed one of her best I'm-the-friendliest-girl-in-town smiles upon Matt. It startled him and he bumped his hand against the edge of the bar. A grimace showed it hurt.

Cole felt a moment of vindication and wanted to warn him. *No poaching on my territory!*

And the minute he formed that thought, Cole wanted to punch himself in the face. Except he also wanted to claim this woman, to tell every man on the island to back off because she was his. Even though she wasn't.

What was happening to him? He relied on Matt to protect him, and this jealousy over Brienne confused him. He needed to get it together and concentrate on the purpose of their meeting.

Even though the things he really wanted to do included kissing her enticing lips and slipping one hand down the neck of her blouse to move that provocative bit of lace aside so he could...

This was the worst business meeting he'd ever attended.

He couldn't even remember what they were supposed to be talking about.

The library? A makerspace? Donating money? He worked to gain control of his over-active imagination again.

"You'll warn me if your father decides to come after me? Right?"

"I promise, but he gets these ideas from all the detective shows he watches. He just signed up for a new streaming service, so from now on he'll be watching British detectives solve mysteries. I expect he'll be talking about much classier murders."

"I'll be sure to wear my tuxedo should he decide to come after me."

She leaned forward, moving closer to Cole. There was that glimpse of lace peeking out at him. Cole squirmed as his dick joined the party again.

"He's overprotective. My mother too. It's the downside of living with your parents when you're a grownup. I swear they still think I'm twelve." She twisted in her seat and glanced away from him to look out the glass doors that led to the fireplace deck.

"I thought about applying for a job in Seattle, but I needed to come back to the island after I got my master's degree. They really needed my help on the farm."

She returned to being the sweet, innocent farm girl. How could he not be charmed by a woman who obviously cared so much about her parents and her community? If there was a wistful hint of dreams not fulfilled, she seemed to do a good job of dealing with it.

"Maybe I should meet your father, just to assure him I'm not a stalker or serial killer."

She rested her gaze on him for a few heartbeats and heat rippled through him.

"Maybe you should," she whispered, her incredibly full

lips puckered, and she looked like she'd be interested in witnessing that event.

Not that it was ever likely to happen. He needed to focus on the reason for their meeting today.

They'd set up a meeting, not a date, he reminded himself.

"I told you about the makerspace project the foundation wants to fund as part of the library renovation. I have something upstairs to show you."

Her eyebrows folded into a frown. "My friends had some less than complimentary ideas about what you invited me here to show off."

He straightened as he considered her comment. She'd talked to her friends about him. That was a good sign, wasn't it?

Although it didn't seem her friends were thrilled about their meeting again today.

"I hope they don't think I'm a stalker or serial killer, too."

She picked up her glass and swallowed a drink of water. Her stormy eyes glittered with good humor.

"Should I be offended by the way you're talking about me to your family and friends? They don't seem to think much of me," he finally asked.

She shrugged. "It's all conspiracy theories. You're mysterious. Possibly even dangerous." She blinked at him. "I suggested you might be in the witness protection program."

"I know I should feel better about that, but it doesn't seem like a vast improvement to my character. Everyone thinks I'm some sort of criminal, but at least you believe I'm a reformed one. Good to know."

"I'm sure you're going to enlighten me soon about who you are, and I'll apologize for everyone who has misjudged you. Including me."

He slipped off the stool and waved toward the stairs to the

second floor. "Come upstairs with me and I'll prove I'm a man of honor and integrity."

She stood and walked in the direction he'd motioned. He followed her.

"That's a pretty tall order, Mr. Moore." She glanced over her shoulder at him. "And I plan to investigate you the instant I get back to my office. Or I might not even wait until then. Does your Wi-Fi work in the parking lot?"

"Our internet service is directly from a satellite. And good luck with your search, Velma," he responded as she started up the stairs. Then his mouth went dry, and the blood rushed once again through his body to his dick to produce a significant erection. She'd been sitting when he came down from his office. He didn't have an opportunity to notice how the tight skirt highlighted her ass perfectly. A very perfect ass, he might add.

Every step put a swing in her hips. Every swing made him painfully aware of his official status as an "ass man."

He'd watched her at work as she moved around the library, and he'd noticed she had a nice wiggle in her walk. Today he observed the perfect combination of seeing her up close from behind, and that skirt.

That ass in that skirt mixed with a devastating wiggle would feature in a lot of his fantasies in the coming days.

When they arrived on the second floor, she stopped. The room featured doors marked for different rooms. One had a sign for Gaming, and another designated a movie theater. The largest area of the room had a stage at one end. Chairs were stacked along the edge of the space, but it was otherwise empty.

"I heard you were doing concerts here, but I never managed to attend one. People were talking about it all summer."

He nodded. "We're planning to turn the natural hillside

slope into an amphitheater for outdoor concerts next year. We sold out quickly every weekend, so there's definitely interest in more live music events here on the island.

"Keep going up to the top." He pointed to the next set of stairs.

She pursed her lips and frowned. "There better not be chains up in that tower."

"I keep all the chains in the dungeon in the basement."

"Good to know," she replied, and put one sexy shoe on the first step of the next flight of stairs. "I confess, I'm intrigued."

Oh, he shared in that intrigue. Mix it with confused and horny as hell just from watching her climb the stairs. Cole wasn't in particularly good shape to conduct a business meeting. He could use a cold shower.

"Oh, wow!" he heard her shriek.

Brienne must have arrived at the top room where his office was located. The view always impressed people. He climbed the rest of the stairs to join her.

She stood in front of the wall of glass overlooking Seal Harbor. "It's so beautiful up here," she gushed as she turned to him, her smile stretching from ear to ear. "You have an amazing view. How do you ever get any work done up here?"

She turned back to the view. "I wouldn't be able to keep from watching the clouds, and the boats, and the birds." She turned to smile at him again. "I bet you even occasionally see J-Pod swimming by. I'd never get anything accomplished working in an office like this."

He'd designed this office to impress. There were incredible views from the other floors, but the aerie gave visitors a bird's eye view of the landscape.

"That's the reason my desk and chair face in the opposite direction. It's the only way I can get any business done. This," he said, gesturing to take in the water, clouds, and trees beyond. "This is my daily escape. With a view like this, I don't mind coming to work."

She turned back to face him; they were close enough that he could appreciate her scent again. Close enough to feel the heat rising from her skin, and to see the high color in her cheeks from the climb up to the room at the top of the building.

Close enough to pull her into his arms and enjoy one taste of those tantalizing lips. Something he wanted to do but fought against. He took a step back and pointed at a leather couch across from his desk.

"Please sit."

He forced himself to be perfectly relaxed. At least on the outside. Inside, he simmered with a lusty hunger he could barely control. It shocked and irritated him. Women didn't affect him like this. Ever. Until this delightful, voluptuous librarian slipped into his world and shook things up.

"I think you should come over and sit next to me. If I try to talk to you while I'm looking at that view, I won't be able to pay attention." Her voice held a hint of an apology.

If he sat next to her, felt that heat, smelled that fascinating perfume—he couldn't be sure he'd be able to maintain control. Pulling her into his arms would reinforce the idea he might be a scary stalker.

"How about I stand over here?" he suggested. "It'll be easier to show you what I want to share with you."

She sat and folded her legs carefully to the side. Ladylike. Then she shifted, and the tiny, tempting piece of lace peeked out at him again.

Either she played him with a tease, or she didn't know the effect she had on him.

Why did his mouth feel sandy? He cleared his throat. It didn't help. He dipped down to the small refrigerator built into the bookcases surrounding the room.

He grabbed a bottle of water, then glanced at her.

"Would you like some more water?" he inquired.

"No, thank you." She shifted on the couch and sat up straighter, which made her plump round breasts more tantalizing even without the provocative lace teasing him.

He put the cold bottle of water on his forehead. The room had to be at least a hundred degrees. The air conditioning must be broken.

Cole worked to bring his attention back to his task for the day. The reason he'd invited her to Three Geeks. He took a few steps to move next to an easel stand with several large poster boards sitting on it. A label on the back of the top one read ***Horseshoe Island Library Remodel***.

"When we talked at Java the Hut, I tried to explain what my employers wanted to do with their donation to the library building fund. I realized pictures are better than words."

Cole flipped the first board to reveal an architectural rendering of what the library would look like with the addition of a makerspace and more room for the children's and teen areas.

Brie rose slowly from the couch, never taking her eyes off the illustration. She stopped in front of him, staring in awe.

"It's, it's...amazing. Everything I've ever wished for." She pointed. "Is that a recording studio?"

"Yes!" he said. Her excitement delighted him and distracted him from how close together they stood. He could feel the heat rising from her body, and took a step back while pointing at the drawing.

They'd been too close. He needed to stay out of her personal space.

"And a fiber arts workshop with sewing machines and a serger?" She moved closer to the easel as she pointed out details of the design. Even closer to him, despite his effort to put more space between them. He could lean down and slide his tongue along the tender skin behind her ear, then let it slip down her throat to settle on the full round...

"I see 3D printing stations. Are there two of them?"

When he nodded, she gave a squeal of delight. Some women craved diamonds and pearls. This woman seemed thrilled with technology. He could have sworn there were tears in her eyes.

She crashed into his arms, her head resting against his chest. "It's everything. Really and truly everything I could ever imagine for our patrons. I don't know how I'll ever repay you if we can make this happen."

Holding her in his arms, Cole considered some interesting ways she could do just that. But he kept those to himself as he enjoyed her gratitude.

TRUE CONFESSION: Passion and desire are two of the most confusing things a human can experience. They act on the primitive parts of our brain. On Maslow's Hierarchy of Needs, sex is right there with oxygen, food, and water. It's basic, but attraction is so much more complicated than discovering your favorite foods or the best brand of sparkling water. Sex is about finding a partner who can respect your needs while fulfilling their own. That's complicated shit.

Chapter Six

BRIENNE

BRIENNE DIDN'T DARE LOOK up from the firm, heavily-muscled chest she leaned against. She'd peeked at him when he visited the library. True confession time: she'd stared at him when he seemed distracted and hoped he wouldn't notice.

She'd never imagined under the flannel shirt there could be a body like this, with thick muscles beneath the T-shirt with a giant yeti on it. Cute scruffy dude Cole had ripples and bulges in all the right places.

Her brain skittered off to unruly places when she considered the word bulge. Then she shifted to her current reality.

She had her arms around the waist of hunky Cole Moore, a man she barely knew, who might not even be who he said he was, and she liked it. Oh yeah, she really liked it. She'd acted impulsively—again.

The big question: what to do next?

Acting properly embarrassed and asking for forgiveness usually worked for her in similar situations.

Taking a deep breath, she backed away from him and

straightened her blouse. She noticed several of the top buttons had come undone, but she didn't want to draw Cole's attention to her wardrobe malfunction.

Too late, she noticed his gaze focused on her breasts. He'd discovered the peekaboo view.

Her cheeks warmed, and she crossed her arms. Then she realized her action only pushed her boobs up more and made them nearly pop out of the top of the blouse.

When his gaze quickly moved up from her chest to her eyes, his quirky grin made the dimple stand out. Clearly, her actions amused him.

"I'm sorry. That was...I don't know why I did that. I mean, give you a hug." She wanted to escape down the stairs, but she couldn't. They were still talking about the library renovation.

Despite her inappropriate behavior, she needed to salvage what remained of their meeting. She retreated to the couch, turning to refasten the buttons before she sat down as demurely as she could manage.

Relief flooded through her when Cole took several long strides to his desk and flopped down in the enormous leather office chair. He appeared more comfortable with the safe distance of a few feet between them.

Probably because he thought she might launch herself into his arms again at any moment.

Not that the idea didn't hold a lot of appeal. The few moments of his stunned silence when he'd tightened his arms around her and she'd balanced against his body would probably fuel her daydreams for a long time. Not to mention her fantasies after bedtime.

Her friends were right. She needed to start dating again.

"No need to apologize, Brienne. I'm thrilled you're excited about the possibilities the funding presents." His voice had a funny hitch as he glanced at his computer.

"I wish we could discuss more of the details now, but I have to meet with our beer distributor in about five minutes."

He might be making that up to get rid of her. She'd understand if he did. She'd turned a business meeting into a groping session and crossed the line.

"Let's set up another meeting soon," she suggested, hoping she hadn't blown the opportunity for funding now that it seemed a real possibility. "We should discuss budget and the timeline."

She hoped that sounded business-like and professional. She stood, smoothing her skirt around her hips. His gaze flitted over her, and then he focused on his computer monitor again. She could take a hint.

"Great." She picked up her bag and walked across the room to his desk. Without thinking, she leaned over and held out her hand.

Cole blinked at her for a moment, then reached across the immense desk to shake her hand. His expression seemed a bit strained. The hug must have flustered him. He worked at a place with *geek* in the name. She'd truly embarrassed the man.

"I appreciate your offer of the donation. If we can do this, it will be so amazing for the library, and the kids, and the community," she gushed.

He nodded and clicked his mouse as he looked away from her to the computer again.

"I'll just see myself out," she offered, afraid she'd already taken up too much of his time.

He glanced at her, then quickly directed his gaze back to the computer before nodding.

Brie knew she'd been dismissed, so she headed down the stairs. When she was halfway to the next floor, she heard him blow out a huge breath and swear loudly enough to echo in the stairwell.

Glancing down, she noticed her blouse buttoned wrong.

The attempt to fix the gap while in his office had exposed a view of her white lace bra and an expanse of skin.

Skin covering several of her ample assets.

Clearly, she'd disturbed Cole Moore, and that was the reason he'd been so eager to get her out of his office. Her inappropriate hug, added to a peep show, had sent all the wrong messages. She should go back up and apologize to him again, except it would probably make things worse.

"Awkward," she whispered as she continued down the stairs. That should be her middle name.

꧁ઝ⌇ꞈ꧂

COLE

"Holy fuck!"

Cole leaned back in his chair. His dick was as hard as a rock, and beads of sweat dotted his forehead. It surprised him sweat wasn't dripping down his face.

Brienne, the nice, sweet, girl next door librarian, managed to excite him to a full erection several times this afternoon. It started at the bar when he'd watched her lick those lush, pink lips. Then there was the walk behind her up the stairs to his office, with a view of her exceptionally fine ass.

The clincher, though, was when she slipped close, put her arms around him, and gave him a hug.

Every single sex-connected synapse in his body snapped to attention. Not to mention a significant organ that demanded all the blood from the rest of his body.

He could have sworn for a time he forgot to breathe. Her soft curves, her enticing scent, and those full breasts snuggled up against him made time stop for a few minutes.

Then she'd backed away from him, the color on her cheeks

signaling her embarrassment. And one more button on her blouse somehow magically came undone.

That shouldn't have been the thing that took him over the edge. But it did. It was just a tiny bit more creamy white skin edged with pristine, snowy lace that short-circuited his brain.

When she turned away to settle herself on the couch, he'd rushed to his desk. He needed to put some distance between him and the voluptuous librarian.

After she sat, he noticed she'd tried to adjust the buttons on her blouse. But she'd left him with a peek-a-boo view that fueled his libido even more.

He didn't think she teased him on purpose. She had a sweet, innocent vibe. And that was not his type. At all. Or at least until now, it hadn't been. This little librarian spurred fantasies he needed to ignore. He had to get his mojo back.

Cole concocted the appointment with the beer guy to cut the meeting short because he was afraid he might embarrass himself, and her, with the raging boner in his pants. He had some invoices to review and a staff schedule to update this afternoon, but no more meetings.

He'd sent her away because he couldn't trust himself with her, and that thought scared him.

If Brienne had moved closer, if she'd given him one sultry look, one ounce of encouragement, he'd probably now be on his knees with his head between her legs, and his tongue eagerly tasting her.

Cole slapped himself on the forehead. He had to stop this shit. Brienne was a professional woman, and they had a professional relationship, and that sounded boring as hell.

He could get laid. That hadn't been a problem for a long time.

The problem, at the moment, involved red-hot lust for a woman he should put on the "Do not touch" shelf of his sexual fantasies.

She'd already warned him about her father and his shotgun. That should serve as notice this nice, wholesome woman was off-limits. He preferred to keep his life simple, without a lot of complications.

And a woman like Brienne Henderson came with a ton of complications and expectations.

Except maybe he needed that. One-night stands had lost their appeal a long time ago. He'd traded lust for desire, and it failed to satisfy anymore.

But a slow, passionate seduction, with a clear understanding between them it was all fun and games with no strings attached...that could be incredible.

Would Brienne be open to that kind of arrangement? She seemed a delightful combination of innocence and sexiness. And he couldn't decide if it was contrived or real.

Or could he be fixated on an outdated stereotype? Did she overtly flirt with him, or did his attraction to her fire his imagination?

He stood to gaze at the view. It was one of those gorgeous, clear September days that could convince you that the weather in the Northwest was all mild temperatures with a week or two of occasional gentle rain.

Those who lived here knew the truth. These were the halcyon days that fooled you. Made you think there would be endless weather like this ahead.

The locals knew better. "The gray" headed straight toward them. These were the sweetest days because the weather would change soon, and the rain would come. Misty, cold, stormy days of pouring rain that made you forget sunlight ever existed.

He glanced at his phone as it played the theme from *Superman*. Wyatt.

"What's up, Wy?"

"I was thinking I'd enjoy kicking your ass on the water this afternoon. You interested?"

Cole snorted. "That'll be the day. Did you ask Dylan?"

"Yup. He's in. What about you?"

"I'm at the bar. I can meet you at Dylan's place around two."

"Shit. It's supposed to be your day off. What are you doing over there?"

"I needed to meet with someone. But I'm done, so I'll see you soon."

"Better bring your fuckin' A game, because the wind is picking up and the water's gettin' choppy," Wyatt warned him.

"You just described my favorite conditions for sailing. Get ready for some serious competition," Cole responded before ending the call.

Sitting back in his chair, Cole flexed his muscles. A fast run on the water sounded like a perfect distraction. But it bothered him that he needed something to keep his mind off Brienne.

He recalled the moment she moved against him, his surprise, then the way his arms slid down her back to hold her. She fit so perfectly against him.

"Fuck it!" He jumped up and started down the stairs. He'd get on the water and sail that woman right out of his head.

Although his head might end up being the least of his problems. Ignoring her when it came to other parts of his body might still pose a challenge.

༄ঙ৫ঙৎ

BRIENNE

Confusion scrambled Brie's brain. She tried to avoid confusion. When she faced a problem, her focus shifted to organizing things into neat imaginary piles, like Marie Kondo assisting a client. There were always obvious distinctions, and she used logic to figure things out.

Hold something close to your heart. Did it hold value, or should you let it go?

Then she'd held her ear next to Cole Moore's chest and listened to his heartbeat. Tall, long-legged, voice like aged whiskey—Cute Scruffy Dude. She'd heard a thump, then another, and a beat that grew faster and faster as they stood hugging each other.

It was supposed to be a moment of joy. A response to the excitement of seeing the design he'd revealed for the library renovation and makerspace.

She'd intended for it to be a platonic gesture. A friend thanking a friend.

Except they were *not* friends. She'd only discovered his last name minutes before they sat in his office, and could barely count him as an acquaintance.

She'd met a stranger at the library, and they'd talked a couple of times. Hadn't she warned her preschoolers of stranger danger, yet today she ignored her own advice.

Instead of planning her after-school teen gaming group, she searched online for any hits on his name. She'd shifted her priorities because of him.

Despite her threat to look him up from the parking lot, she'd waited until she got back to the library to begin her research. After entering his name into a search engine, she focused on her computer screen to view the results.

At first, she didn't find anything about the man she'd met with earlier. Nada. She found a Cole Moore who was an accountant and one who wrote a series of science fiction novels. They had great reviews, and she made a note to find out more about him.

She didn't find one image of the good-looking Cole Moore she'd wrapped her arms around earlier that day.

It seemed impossible. No internet pages with news of him. No social media accounts. Nothing except a reference to C. Moore, the Manager, on the Three Geeks website with a company email to contact him for more information.

Other than that, it was as if he didn't exist. At least on the internet. And if you didn't exist online, did you really exist at all?

Brie recalled her friends' suggestions he could be a serial killer hiding out. The vibe didn't feel right. She hoped that if he were a creepy, sinister type scoping out potential murder victims, she'd at least feel uneasy around him.

Maybe her Scooby-sense had a temporary malfunction. After all, Ann Rule considered Ted Bundy a nice guy.

Confidence in her own judgment didn't stand up to scrutiny today. She'd let her emotions run away with her and embarrassed herself and Cole.

She could imagine him telling his friends how the silly little librarian threw herself into his arms, nearly begging him to screw her.

Wait, what?

A shiver slipped down her spine as she shook her head and removed her reading glasses. That was not what happened! Her imagination filled in the blanks and somehow turned a perfectly innocent response to good news about the renovation project for the library into an erotic encounter.

She considered her options. With no real leads on Cole Moore, either the man didn't exist, or he wanted to hide the specifics of his life.

Sometimes people used their middle name instead of their

first name. Maybe she could tease out that information the next time they met.

Or she could just ask him why he appeared to be the "invisible man." She cringed at that idea, then wondered why she'd be reluctant to ask him some personal questions. That was what you did with new friends, right? Got better acquainted.

She sat back in her chair and considered why the idea of slotting Cole into friend territory bothered her. The few times they'd talked, he'd been polite and businesslike.

She was the one who went off the rails with that hug.

Brie stood and checked her reflection with her phone, making sure all her buttons were fastened correctly before going out to set up the teen program.

She hoped to limit herself to one humiliation per day.

The Next Morning

"This is strange. You never come here for breakfast." Raina frowned down at Brie. "Eggs at home getting boring?"

Brienne stared at the menu. "Mom's great at inventing recipes, but if the chickens don't slow down soon, even she's going to run out of ideas.

"I'll take the apple pancake. And a mocha, heavy on the chocolate." She handed the menu back to her friend, the owner of The Mermaid's Lair restaurant.

She loved this place, with its pale-blue painted wood walls, clean white granite counters, and seascape décor. A sculpture of a well-endowed mermaid with strategically placed curls to make the art family friendly hung behind the coffee bar. More sea creatures were featured in a collection of paintings from a local artist scattered around on the walls.

"Morning chocolate coffee sounds like a sleepless night," Raina commented.

Brienne nodded. "There's a lot going on—with the library, you know, the board and the renovation." She took a sip of water.

"Yeah, the library." Raina shot her a suspicious look. "And maybe that guy following you. When you texted us, you said you had a successful meeting and were heading to work."

Brienne fought the blush, but she knew her cheeks had turned a pink that matched her lipstick. Raina was too observant, and she'd notice.

"So, exactly what happened at this meeting? You're blushing, so *something* happened. Right?"

"I don't know what you're talking about. We discussed a library project. End of news flash."

"Uh-huh." Raina slipped her pencil into the pocket of her apron. "You know I'm going to wheedle the information out of you eventually." She laughed as she walked away.

Brienne pulled a folder from her leather backpack and opened it to glance at the printout with budget items organized in neat rows. If Cole were serious about the donation to the building fund, these numbers would skyrocket. It could mean so much for the renovation, because the plans he'd showed her yesterday were amazing.

A shadow fell over her, obscuring the light. She glanced up to discover Cole standing across from her. She nearly jumped out of her chair because it seemed as if she'd conjured him by magic.

"May I sit?" he asked, that seriously sexy grin generating heat in the place between her legs. She swallowed and reminded herself to behave.

Good manners demanded she agree to let him sit with her. It was what business acquaintances would do in a professional relationship. The man was an important *business*

94

acquaintance. One who held the carrot of a large donation to the library on the end of a stick.

A very big stick. Then her mind went sideways at an image she conjured, and she snatched her glass of water, took a huge gulp, and coughed.

He pulled the chair out across from her and sat.

When she finally recovered enough to speak, she studied him for a moment. "I'm concerned you *are* stalking me. Do I need to call my father?" She tried to keep her tone light.

He turned the full wattage of his smile on her. "I noticed your Bronco parked in the lot. I need some coffee, so I thought I'd stop in here so we could chat."

He said, "I need coffee" with a sad, desperate look on his face. Brie nearly giggled.

Giggle. Really? Was she fifteen and talking to the captain of the football team? She straightened her shoulders and tried to slap a serious expression on her face. It proved to be a challenge because she could barely contain her delight at seeing him again.

But she didn't want him to know that. And she had no intention of mentioning how their last meeting had ended. It appeared he planned to ignore her behavior and still wanted to arrange for the donation to the library.

She pointed at the papers in front of her. "I'm reviewing the renovation budget before we have a building committee meeting this afternoon."

"Please don't mention the donation yet. We have a lot more planning to do."

She blinked at him. "I assure you, Mr. Moore, I won't mention anything about the donation or our meetings until I know you're serious."

"Mr. Moore? What happened to Cole? I think we moved to a first-name basis yesterday. Don't you?" He winked at her.

It was a playful wink. A flirty wink. A wink that said, "We

should stop this nonsense and get it on." She imagined her face taking on a scarlet hue once again. Why did this guy bother her so much?

She needed to turn this conversation around to get it back to business.

"I'm not even sure the name you gave me is real." She pointed at him and narrowed her eyes. "You don't exist online except as a contact for Three Geeks. No other websites mention you. You aren't on social media, and the only photos I found belonged to other Cole Moores. How is that even possible in the twenty-first century?"

He stared at her finger, and his grin reappeared. Along with the deep dimple that gave her a tingle in the nether regions.

"Maybe I'm shy and value my privacy. But you should check out the sci-fi author. His books are fantastic."

She cocked her head at him. "Shy?"

"Or maybe your detective skills are slipping, Velma."

Now he'd made her angry. She shifted forward in her seat to stare him down. At least she wore a turtleneck today. No peeking at her boobs for him!

"My reference skills are legendary." She narrowed her eyes. "I think you're hiding something, so I'm perfectly happy to keep this donation a secret until I know more about the people offering the money. Maybe you're laundering cash for a Mexican drug cartel."

His laugh boomed throughout the café. "Wow! You are clearly taking advantage of your Netflix account."

"Of course, you'd say that." She pursed her lips.

"What a brilliant cover."

Raina appeared at the table with Brie's coffee. Predictably, she looked intrigued.

She set the coffee in front of Brie and studied Cole. "Where'd he come from?"

"He's stalking me, as usual."

"Oh." Raina put her hands on her hips. "Is this the cute scruffy serial killer dude?"

Cole sat back in his chair and folded his arms. He tipped his head and gave Brienne a half-smile. "Did you take out an ad in the local paper?"

"No, I put your photo on the bulletin board at the library with a warning."

His smile faded. "What?" He sounded pissed. Which served him right for making fun of her.

She grabbed her cup and took a sip of hot coffee. And burned her tongue. *Damn it.*

Brie needed to be careful. Making the guy who could represent a huge donation to the library angry wasn't her wisest move.

"Just kidding. This is Raina, owner of this place and a member of the Mermaid Posse."

He nodded at Raina. "The Mermaid Posse. I'm visualizing a bunch of mermaids riding seahorses."

"You're close." Raina studied Cole. Her gaze roved over his face and upper body. "We cos-play mermaids and organize photo shoots to raise money for the library. It was Brie's idea. She saw an article about the Seattle Mermaids group and thought some of us here on the island should get together and do it. It's fun and helps the community."

Brie knew her face flamed with a blush. He'd probably think she was silly for dressing up in costumes. Little did he know.

"That's a creative idea. I'm impressed." His dimple reappeared. "Just let me know if you ever need any pirates. I have friends who'd jump at the chance to dress up and capture a bunch of mermaids."

He gave Raina his devastating panty-melting wink, and the woman softened in front of Brie's eyes.

"Can I get you a menu or just coffee?" Raina purred after another moment of staring at Cole.

He glanced at Brie. "I'll have plain black coffee and whatever she ordered."

"You're gonna trust her judgment? So, you're handsome and brave. Good for you."

Before Brie could respond, Raina disappeared around the corner, heading toward the restaurant's coffee bar.

He studied Brie silently for a few minutes. She squirmed under his scrutiny.

"What?" she finally asked. "Do I have a coffee mustache or something?"

"Mermaids? I'm just trying to visualize you with a tail. Intriguing."

He kept staring at her in silence. His green eyes sparkled with delight. She couldn't stand it.

"I know. It sounds stupid, but we've raised several thousand dollars with the meet-and-greet events. We're working on a calendar as part of fundraising for the renovation."

Raina returned with Cole's coffee. "The calendar is nearly finished," she added, apparently having overheard the conversation.

"Have you found a pool yet for the last photo shoot?" Raina asked Brie.

Brie realized she'd spent precious time trying to find information about Cole when she should have been researching photo shoot locations. She looked down at the table.

"Not yet. I'll look later this afternoon. It's too bad the resort won't let us use their pool one more time."

Cole sipped his coffee, then grinned again. "I know someone who has access to an enormous, heated pool," he said. "In fact, it's perfect for photos. It has an all-natural rock setting and a magnificent view of Latham Channel."

Raina and Brie glanced at each other.

"Do you think they'd let us take some photos there? We can finish in a day," Brie asked.

Cole shrugged. "I don't see why not. This time of year, my friend is the only one out there."

"So, will you ask him about it?" Raina leaned forward. "Please, please, pretty please?"

Brie felt a flutter of jealousy. Her friend was tall and willowy, with an athletic figure that displayed her love of swimming and using her paddleboard. Her long chestnut color hair, turquoise eyes, and warm personality had a way of making everyone she met comfortable.

Cole nodded. "I'm fairly sure my friend will agree. He's always up for something fun."

Tilting his head toward Brie, he nodded. "Just text me the information and I'll talk to him."

Raina clapped her hands. "I don't care if you are a stalker. Thanks for your help."

She returned to the kitchen, and Brie smiled at him. "Thanks for the offer. It's really nice of you and if it doesn't work out, I appreciate that you tried to help."

Cole leaned across the table. His dark green eyes captured her with a cold, hard anger reflected in them.

"Now, about this stalker, serial killer, drug runner shit. It's gotta stop. Okay?"

TRUE CONFESSION: How do you get to know someone you've just met? Isn't there a huge amount of trust in meeting someone for coffee, dinner, or having a drink at their place? Not just a safety issue (that's terrifying enough), but how do you let down the emotional shields that protect you? How do you recognize you're vulnerable while also addressing the need to have faith that you won't be hurt? And once you've given your trust, how do you make sure it's not abused?

Chapter Seven

COLE

"**IF WE'RE GOING** to have a respectful business relationship, you need to stop making things up and spreading rumors about me."

He wanted to intimidate her with the force of his words. And the tone, which might have been a bit too harsh now that he watched her reaction.

Her smile disappeared and her lovely pink-hued lips thinned as her eyes snapped with barely contained irritation. In his experience with women, these were not good signs.

"Then maybe you should tell me who you really are."

Cole glanced away from her piercing gaze, pretending to admire the artwork on the wall and the high exposed beams. Then he glanced out at the window at another sunny September day.

He couldn't avoid answering her question for long. Fortunately, Raina rescued them from the uncomfortable silence when she approached the table with two small cast-iron frying pans. She set one in front of Brienne and the other in front of him.

The apple, sugar, and cinnamon smell overwhelmed him.

A golden-brown pancake filled with apple bits still sizzled in the pan. He inhaled the scent before gazing up at Raina.

"I don't know what you call this, but I have a feeling it's going to become my favorite food ever!"

Raina grinned at him. "If you like apple pie, this is my version as a breakfast food. The pan's hot, so be careful." And with that, she hustled back through the door to the kitchen.

Cole glanced down again, took a deep breath, and realized Brienne glared at him. He could almost feel the heat of her gaze on him.

Finally looking up, he figured he'd avoided answering the question long enough. Taking a sip of his coffee, he nodded at her.

"You deserve the truth, and I feel like I can trust you. But swear you'll keep this to yourself. I've made promises to my...employers."

She picked up her coffee cup and took a sip, silent, as if weighing his request. Finally, she nodded.

"Although I'm uncomfortable swearing to something without more information." She paused. "I'll set one condition. No illegal stuff. That voids the agreement."

"Seems reasonable, but we can't talk here." He shrugged as he picked up his knife and fork. "If I'm divulging secrets, we need to be someplace no one can overhear us."

"Three Geeks?"

He cut into the pancake and closed his eyes as the sweet aroma rose when steam escaped the pastry.

"No, we need a place that's isolated. I'm going to have to get permission to disclose some of the information I plan to share with you. My employers protect their identities, as you've discovered."

She sliced into her own pancake and her eyes closed momentarily as she took a deep breath.

A waitress stepped over to refill Cole's coffee cup. Her

mouth full of pancake, Brienne raised her cup, signaling she wanted another mocha.

Cole enjoyed the view of her appreciating the food. He'd spent a lot of time taking women out to eat, only to watch them order a salad and then push the food around on their plates while eating almost nothing.

The reason women thought men didn't want to see them eat bewildered him. Paying for food a date didn't eat made no sense to him.

The waitress returned with Brienne's mocha. All conversation came to a halt as they focused on their food for a few minutes.

"Do you think your friend will share the recipe for this? I'd try to make this myself just to enjoy the aroma."

"It's in the cookbook I recommended to you." Her mouth quirked into a crooked smile. "The one you said you'd buy online instead of borrowing it from the library."

Her voice held a note of sarcasm.

He stopped eating and stared at her. "What are you, the library police? I don't need, nor do I want, a library card."

"I intend to introduce you to all the amazing benefits your local library provides." She lifted her chin and straightened. "By the time I finish with you, I expect you'll be taking advantage of everything I offer. You might even decide to join our Friends of the Library group."

Brienne glanced down at her food to concentrate on slicing into the pancake and didn't notice Cole's expression, as his own fork paused in mid-air and his jaw dropped.

When he linked the words *friends* and *benefits,* heat coursed through his body, even though he suspected her remark was innocent.

She frowned when she noticed he seemed frozen. "Don't worry. I'll figure out some top-secret meeting place for your confession."

"Sure," was all he could force out of his desert-dry lips. He grabbed his water glass and took a long gulp.

"But you better be honest with me, or I'll revive the names and conspiracy theories about your identity and spread it all over the island."

Her words brought him back to cold, hard reality.

"Fine," he muttered.

He didn't know how he'd get Dylan and Wyatt to agree to her terms.

◦◦◦◦◦◦

Later That Day

"Fuck, Wyatt, when are you going to buy some actual furniture?" Cole set the case of beer and a bag of groceries on the kitchen counter.

"Go to hell, Cole. I didn't invite you guys over to party with me. If you don't like the decorating, get out of here."

Cole glanced at Dylan, who carried several bags of groceries with him as he pushed the front door closed with his foot.

"Someone definitely got up on the grumpy side of the bed today, didn't he?"

"Fuck you too, Dylan."

"Work not going well this week?" Cole started taking groceries out of the bag. "Still can't find the woman of your dreams?"

Dylan made a fart noise of derision. "He's looked at a bunch of photos of models and he says they look like they're starving. He wants a real woman. One who doesn't have fake tits and a bottom that's been injected. A natural beauty."

"Isn't that what we all want?" Cole stopped what he was doing to stare at his friends.

Dylan wiggled his eyebrows. "I've seen your little librarian, and I gotta say, she fills out a tight sweater nicely. I'd bet she's a natural beauty."

Cole stared at his friend, aware that if he had laser eyes, Dylan would be a melted puddle at his feet.

"How the hell do you know what Brienne looks like?"

"I had to go into town the other day, so I visited the library. Damn it, Cole, she's hot." Dylan started emptying his own bags of groceries. "The cute blonde who works there is sexy-pixie cute. I got a nice dose of fantasy naughty librarian from those two."

"I should punch you in the face right now and get it over with."

Cole heard Wyatt's laugh from the other room. "Don't get any blood on my floor," he warned them.

Dylan held up his hands. "I didn't make any moves. Just lookin' to see what the fuss is about. I didn't know you were that serious about her."

Cole clenched his fists. Until Dylan mentioned her, he didn't realize he wanted to get more serious. Shit. Brienne was getting to him.

"I need to be careful because she's asking a lot of questions, and I don't know how much I can tell her. That's the reason I wanted us to get together today."

Cole turned to the huge refrigerator—an appliance that seemed unnecessary since Wyatt rarely cooked. He had a collection of sugary breakfast cereal in his cupboards that would make any nine-year-old green with jealousy. In fact, his nearly nonstop gaming on a state-of-the-art system, his beloved collection of graphic novels and comics, and his self-absorbed behavior could have described an average preteen.

Cole stared at the shelves in the refrigerator. There were plastic containers and bowls covered with aluminum foil. Wyatt had actual food in there. He blinked.

Wyatt had been living in his new cabin for over six months, and until now, Cole had never seen any food in the fridge that one of his friends hadn't delivered.

Shaking his head, Cole slid the items he'd brought on one shelf. Then he opened a large container in front of him. It was filled with rigatoni and meatballs.

He stared at the other dishes. It looked like Wyatt had signed up for one of those subscription food plans.

"You taking cooking classes, or did you finally subscribe to one of those delivery services, Wyatt?"

Dylan slid behind Cole and huffed as he surveyed the contents of the fridge. "If I'd known you had this much food, I would have saved myself a trip to the co-op this morning."

Wyatt strolled into the kitchen. He wore gray sweatpants that had clearly seen better days. His broad shoulders and thick upper arms were visible in a faded Yeti Entertainment T-shirt. At least the clothes were clean.

A dragon hair tie held his long hair pulled into a ponytail. He removed his wire-rim glasses and folded them. Cole and Dylan stood staring at him, waiting for an explanation.

"All of that's from Mrs. Scallini."

"The old lady you bought this land from, is she makin' moves on you, buddy?"

Wyatt glared at Dylan. "Why is it your mind goes straight to your dick first thing?"

Before Dylan could answer, Cole poked him, "Because it's been so long since he got laid. His dick is lonely and needs some attention."

"We've all been in a dry spell. I suspect that's why Cole's chasing the sexy librarian." Dylan reached behind him and grabbed a beer. He popped it open and took a large swig. "How long has it been for you, bud?"

"Shut the fuck up, will ya?" Cole glowered at Dylan. He

nodded at the containers in the fridge. "What's the deal with all this food, Wyatt?"

"I hooked her up to my satellite TV and showed her all the stations she can get now. She's grateful, and she's a fantastic cook. Apparently, she discovered the Food Channel and wants to practice the recipes on me." Wyatt grabbed a beer. "There's a pie behind those containers on the bottom shelf. When she found out I didn't cook, she started bringing me food."

He patted his flat stomach below washboard abs. "I've had to work out more, because the stuff she brings me is carb-heavy and delicious." He took a sip of his beer.

Cole stared at his friend. "That was a really nice thing to do." He closed the door on the fridge. "And nice of her to reward you with some food."

Cole and Dylan had been worried since Wyatt moved into the cabin about his diet going to shit. His supply of cereal, sugary snacks, and frozen pizza concerned them. Wyatt could get lost in his games or his art. A day might pass before he even remembered to eat something.

"Mrs. Scallini is grateful, but I got my ass chewed by her granddaughter the other day. Her dog went berserk barking at me, and I told him to shut the fuck up." Wyatt set his beer on the counter. "She and I kinda argued, and she insisted I shouldn't have given her grandmother access for her TV without consulting her first."

Cole stared at his friend. "Pissin' somebody off is a daily occurrence for you, Wy."

"Anyway, I told her Mrs. Scallini wasn't some senile old lady who couldn't make her own decisions and if I wanted to give her something, it was none of her granddaughter's damned business."

Dylan leaned on the counter. "And how did that go?" He grinned at Wyatt.

"About as well as you can imagine. The granddaughter has

a colorful vocabulary, and I know that from all the names she called me. We did not part on amicable terms. Let's put it that way."

"What did she look like?" Dylan asked.

"Here we go again." Cole shook his head.

Wyatt frowned. "I couldn't really tell. She wore a black hoodie and dark jeans. I never got close enough to see her clearly. Let me put it this way. I thought if I got too close, she might smack me. She was furious."

He took another swig of his beer. "What can turn a woman into such a bitch?"

Cole exchanged a look with Dylan. "Men," they both said at the same time.

"It was a bad day; you know what I mean. Anniversary."

"Sorry," Cole offered. "We should have been here for you."

Wyatt shook his head. "I wanted to be alone. You guys understood that."

Cole pulled the container of rigatoni out of the fridge and opened several cabinets in search of a dish he could use to warm it. He found a stack of disposable foil containers in several sizes. A roll of aluminum foil sat next to them.

"Maybe you should visit the Shopping Channel and buy yourself some decent dishes and a set of pots and pans. You live like a college student, for fuck's sake."

Wyatt wandered back to the living room. "Whatever."

Cole and Dylan stared at his back. "Do you think it's a good sign that he engaged with another human being or a bad sign because he had an argument with a strange woman?" Dylan finally asked.

Cole considered the question. "Maybe a bit of both. He's too isolated out here, so at least even if it was an argument, he communicated with the granddaughter. And he's letting the grandmother bring him food. That's a good sign."

"True." Dylan grabbed a bag of chips as he followed behind Wyatt.

After putting the food in the oven, Cole grabbed several more beers. He shambled into the living room. The Seahawks game was on, and as Wyatt sat on one end of the enormous sofa, Cole settled at the other end. Dylan stretched out on one of the beanbag chairs scattered around the room.

They watched the game until a commercial break. Cole knew it was time to talk seriously with his friends.

"Brie is asking me a lot of questions about the donors for the library remodeling project. I didn't expect her to be so suspicious, but I guess all the recent reports of rich people creating fake foundations and using the money for illegal purposes spooked her."

He glanced at his friends. "Anyway, she wants to know more. You guys need to tell me how much I can say."

Wyatt gave a bark of laughter. "Does she have any suspicions about who we are? I think most people around here know I'm rich. Even though I purchased it through our holding company, they can clearly see I built the cabin out here and they know the price of real estate."

He'd purchased twenty acres on the island. There were restrictions on the division and use of land here. Cole knew those restrictions were one of the main reasons Wyatt chose the property. He craved quiet and seclusion. His friends worried about him being too isolated. Too lonely. It had been over two years since Amy's death, and he showed few signs of wanting to join the world again.

Cole and Dylan tried to get him out more. They took him out to eat occasionally. But Wyatt still escaped into the fantasy worlds of gaming and graphic novels. His friends were worried, but Wyatt told them to fuck off when they made suggestions.

Dylan stared at the TV as the game resumed. He finally

turned to look at Cole. "How much can you tell her without telling her anything important?"

"She won't be that easy to fool." Cole set his beer on the floor. "She noticed I wasn't on any social media accounts. I explained it away as being phobic about spreading my name around on the internet, which is true. I think she bought it."

"Considering how much it cost us to get our photos and accounts removed, I hope that worked." Dylan stood up and stretched.

"I think it did for the moment." Cole nodded. "But being invisible on the web creates new questions. Like, who exactly are you if you don't show up on any of the platforms? There are all kinds of rumors spreading around town about me. Like maybe I'm a serial killer hiding out."

"Don't you want her to know you're rich, Cole?" Wyatt stretched again. "Wouldn't that help you since it's pretty clear you want to get together with her?"

Cole had thought about that. He should just confess to Brie he was one of the rich geeks interested in funding the library. Telling the truth would be the simplest solution.

Then why did he resist it so much? Sure, he'd had his share of women chasing him because they knew he had a lot of money. He sensed Brie wasn't the gold-digger type. She seemed honest and open and worked with facts.

Still, he couldn't seem to open his mouth and tell her the truth. He should trust her, but trust didn't come easily for him. Maybe once he got to know her better, he'd be able to be more honest.

Maybe? What if? Honesty and trust? All words he struggled with. His past might catch up to him, and he knew he couldn't tell her everything yet.

"I have an idea. Brie is part of a mermaid cosplay group, and they're looking for a swimming pool to do a photo shoot.

They're putting a calendar together to raise funds for the library. I thought maybe they could use your pool, Dylan."

Dylan stared at Cole. "So, you want us to come out to them at a pool party?"

Wyatt and Cole stared at him.

"Are you trying to tell us something, Dy? Something we should know?" Wyatt put one hand up. "We totally support you in your lifestyle choices."

"Fuck you, Wyatt."

"Is that an offer, Dy? I mean, I'm attracted to you, but I'm not sure if I'm ready to..."

Dylan stared at Wyatt. "I'd do Cole before you. Sorry. I hope I didn't hurt your feelings."

"Thanks." Cole shook his head. "I think. Anyway, apparently, when they're in their mermaid outfits, they can't walk. They need a mertender to carry them around and grab stuff for them. We could volunteer to do that, and you guys would meet Brie. You could decide if we can trust her enough to tell her the truth."

Dylan stretched out his legs. "I never thought giving the library money was going to be this hard."

Cole agreed with him. He imagined they'd just write a check, have Brie present it to the library board, and be done with it. They wanted to remain anonymous because they'd spent a lot of money to disappear into obscurity.

"Do you know who the other mermaids are?" Dylan asked.

Cole reached into his pocket for his phone and pulled up a website. Bubbles swirled around the title "The Horseshoe Island Mermaid Posse." He clicked on an image and handed the phone to Dylan.

Dylan grinned as he studied the screen.

"Raina." He nodded eagerly. "She owns the Mermaid's

Lair, and now that name makes sense to me. I'm in." He handed the phone to Wyatt.

Wyatt glanced at the image on the phone and tossed it back to Cole like it burned his fingers. "Fuck no! That tall, dark-haired one is Mrs. Scallini's granddaughter."

Dylan leaned closer to look at Cole's phone. "Shit, Wy. She's exactly the sort of model you described to me for your project. Big breasts, curves, long dark hair, and that face. She's gorgeous."

"And mean as a junkyard dog," Wyatt added. "Also, she owns a mean junkyard dog who wanted to rip my throat out."

"Does the mean girl scare you, Wy?" Dylan made a sad face.

"You didn't meet her and her wolf dog. If I hadn't been on a huge rock and out of slapping range..." Wyatt finished his beer and smacked the can on the block of wood in front of the couch that served as a table.

"Better be careful. She knows where you live," Cole warned him.

"I'll check on the food." Wyatt stood and headed into the kitchen. "And just leave me out of this stupid plan."

Cole and Dylan stared at each other. Then they started laughing.

"We could have a good time with this," Cole commented.

Dylan nodded, a smirk forming on his face.

"It's about time he came out of his fog. We gotta make sure he shows up for this mermaid pool party. I'll ask Brie about her friend because I suspect she probably had a good reason to confront Wyatt. You know how he is."

"I heard that!" Wyatt yelled from the kitchen.

"Let's go eat and we'll figure this out. At least the two of us can have some fun."

Dylan nodded at the photo on Cole's phone. "I can think

of a lot worse things than spending the day snuggling up with this posse of mermaids."

Cole looked forward to seeing Brie in her mermaid outfit. He'd saved several of the images of her. His favorite was taken underwater. She wore a bra covered with shells and sparkly stuff, with a mermaid tail that matched the color of her hair. A crown made of shells and jewels sat on her head and her hair flowed around her.

She looked majestic, like a sea goddess, and sexy as hell.

He spent a lot of time looking at that image.

Way too much time.

TRUE CONFESSION: I'm convinced when guys sit around watching football, they use a code that translates into dirty talk. I mean, what's the real meaning when you hear an announcer say things like "Just shove it right in the seam" or "It's all about the penetration." And you can't convince me "He sees the hole and gets right up in there" and "He's going deep...and it popped right out" isn't some kind of secret sex language.

Chapter Eight

BRIENNE

"FOR SOMEONE who's just a business acquaintance, you sure seem worried about what this guy is going to think of us."

Her mother continued setting the table, and Brie tried to ignore the remark. She'd invited Cole to come to dinner because he'd expressed an interest in farm-to-table dining. At least, that's how she explained it to her parents.

Inviting a strange man to dinner set off enough questions. If her parents sensed her attraction to Cole, there could be all kinds of shenanigans. Her father loved a good practical joke, and her ex had been a regular victim of his pranks.

Relationships were challenging. When you considered professional roles and setting boundaries at work, things could get complicated. She didn't work for Cole, and he didn't work for her. But he represented a group of donors, and she was the manager of the library. She'd spent the previous evening trying to sort it out.

A big black truck pulled into the driveway, and her heart rate jumped. She pushed her hands, which were damp, down the full skirt of her sundress, and licked her lips.

"Cole's here," she called over her shoulder as she slipped through the screen door.

"Your father is down in the barn if you're looking for him."

Brie winced. She never worried about her mother. The woman had a gift for entertaining and knew how to make visitors feel comfortable.

Her father, on the other hand, could be a jerk when he met one of her boyfriends. Well, he'd been a jerk to Caleb, but he'd turned out to be right, so she couldn't fault him too much. He had a sixth sense about people you could trust.

Despite some powerful fantasies about the man over the past few days, Cole was *not* her boyfriend. They were business associates. Professionals who shared a common goal.

Cole climbed out of the truck as she walked down the driveway to greet him. He gazed at the farmhouse and an appreciative smile lit his face.

Her heart ticked up a beat.

He wore the familiar uniform of a dark T-shirt, jeans, and a flannel shirt, a wardrobe that highlighted his broad shoulders, thick upper arms, and long legs.

Brie held out a hand, intending to greet him with a handshake, but he pulled her into his arms and hugged her briefly before letting go and grinning down at her.

"We're beyond the handshake phase, don't you think?"

"Maybe I'm not the sort of woman who rushes into things."

He studied her for a long moment, then grinned again. "I get that about you. Steady, takes-her-time Brienne."

"Brie. My friends call me Brie."

He leaned back against the shiny truck. "Then we've moved into the friend stage. I like that." He stood straighter and looked around. "At least for the moment."

Brie shivered at the tone of his voice. Friends? That's what she wanted, right? Keep things between them strictly business.

He was good-looking, charming, hot as hell, and totally out of her league.

So why did she spend so much time imagining being in his arms, his mouth slowly moving across her lips, tasting her, and teasing her with long, languorous kisses as his hands explored her body?

"How many acres do you guys have here?" Cole asked, looking around the property surrounding the house.

Brie jerked back to reality.

"Diggin' Dirt Farm is twenty acres. When my parents moved here, they became part of a commune. All the members worked together on five-acre plots. One by one, the other members left and in the agreement, they'd signed, another member had the first chance to buy the plot. That's how my parents ended up with the land."

Cole shot her an amused look. "So were your parents hippies joining the back to the land movement or something?"

People often assumed that when they learned the history of the farm.

"They moved here in the late eighties, after the hippies, and were just kids when all the Haight-Ashbury stuff happened. They tell me they were looking for more temperate weather. The Midwest is muggy and hot in the summer and freezing cold in winter. And apparently the mosquitoes are the size of hummingbirds and as bloodthirsty as vampires."

Was she babbling? That seemed like a lot of information to answer his simple question.

He nodded. She'd need to talk less this evening. As a person who collected facts, she tended to over-share.

"Not exactly a free love, drum circle, smoke pot, and drop out of society kind of group. They worked together on their farms and shared the large building projects, like renovating our house."

Cole turned to look at the house again. "Your father did the work on this house?" She noticed the admiration in his voice. If he kept that up, her father would soon be a fan.

"Dad built the cottage my parents first lived in by himself, but this place," she said with a nod at the farmhouse, "was a huge remodeling project. I guess no one had lived here for a long time, and it was pretty decrepit."

"Howdy there," a voice boomed from behind them.

Brie winced. Her father had joined them.

Warren Henderson was an impressive guy, even though he'd passed sixty a couple of years ago. He was tall and lean, with a full head of thick silver hair that matched his beard and mustache. Her brother Ryder inherited his Nordic body type.

She favored her mother's Irish side of the family when it came to stature, but got his stormy gray eyes with pewter highlights.

He touched Brie's shoulder gently as he stood next to her. She introduced him to Cole, and they shook hands.

"I heard you were interested in bio-dynamic farming, Cole."

Cole slid her a shaky smile and looked confused. "I don't know exactly what that is, sir. I am interested in learning more about working with local farmers to source food for the bar I manage. We're planning to expand the menu later this fall. I'd like to use as much local produce as possible."

"I can tell you all about that, son. Just come with me and we'll walk and talk."

Brie let her father handle the tour. She regretted not spending more time with Cole, but he was her dinner guest. It wasn't fair to leave the final preparations for her mother to deal with just because she wanted to spend a few extra minutes with a gorgeous guy.

Besides, she wanted Cole to know she had excellent cooking skills. She intended to mention several of the recipes came from the cookbook she'd recommended to him.

"So, you left your young man alone with your father?" The skepticism in her mother's voice was clear. "Do you think that's a good idea?"

"He's not *my* young man. He's a business associate. And as far as I know, Dad doesn't keep a shotgun down in the sheep's pen, so for the moment, I believe Cole is safe."

She'd been humiliated when Caleb came to dinner the first time, and her father took down the antique gun hanging above the fireplace in the living room. She understood he issued a warning. It ended up being a wasted effort.

Caleb was so oblivious, not to mention high that night, he'd missed the point. She just hoped there wasn't a repeat performance by her father tonight with Cole.

She had a feeling the information she'd shared about the commune created an image that the Hendersons might be a little odd. He'd think she was a weird woman with a strange family.

Odd?

Strange?

Weird?

Not exactly complimentary descriptions.

Her mother leaned over the stove and sniffed the beef short ribs Brie had made for dinner.

"These smell so delicious; I'm tempted to snatch a taste."

Brie waved a finger at her. "Better not touch anything. This dinner is special."

Oops, now she'd done it. Said too much—again.

Her mother put the lid back on the pan and slid away from the stove. "Then I'll just pour myself another glass of wine and stay out of the prep area."

Brie took a deep breath as her mother emptied the rest of

the bottle of wine she'd used to season the beef ribs into her glass. She tried to remember how much wine had been left.

"I'd better open another bottle of red for dinner," Brie said.

"Don't worry, I already opened two more bottles. We wouldn't want to serve that cheap stuff we buy to cook with to our *distinguished guest.*"

Her mother had started early on the wine. Brie picked up the bottle and tilted it. Yup. Totally empty.

"Don't worry, I'll nurse my dinner wine. I promise to behave." Her mother made a tiny salute.

Charlotte usually imbibed alcohol carefully and rarely overdid it. But on holidays and when they entertained, she sometimes became...giggly.

And she tended to be a flirt after a couple of glasses. Cole presented too much of a temptation for her to resist, and Brie didn't know if she feared the embarrassment or the competition tonight.

Even in her late fifties, Charlotte Henderson still turned heads. Her original dark brown hair had silver highlights. A rigorous skin care regimen ensured she had a smooth, silky, mostly unlined face.

The physical work on the farm kept her in shape and it bruised Brie's ego that her mother wore a size smaller than she did.

"We're all set for when the guys come in from their tour." She raised her wineglass in Brie's direction. "I hope your father isn't being too hard on him."

"Why? What did Dad say? He didn't plan something tonight, did he?"

Her father had once convinced Caleb he should climb into the pigpen to scratch their sow behind the ears. He bet Caleb that he wouldn't do it. That disaster ended up with Caleb being knocked down and covered in pig shit.

Although considering how things ended between them, it seemed justified. Still, she didn't want Cole to become a victim of one of her father's pranks.

"I told him to behave tonight." Her mother glanced at Brie over the rim of her glass. "He promised to be nice to Cole. After all, it's not like he's your boyfriend. You must have told us a hundred times he's just a business friend."

Brie glanced at her mother. Was that a little dig? Her parents had married when they were pretty young, and she had Ryder in her twenties. Occasionally, her mother dropped not-so-subtle hints that Brie might want to consider finally settling down.

A few weeks ago, she'd spent a lot of time showing Brie all the photos of her friends with their grandchildren. Lots and lots of photos. Not exactly subtle.

"I hope Dad isn't planning to walk Cole around the entire twenty acres. Dinner's ready." Brie looked out the huge kitchen window toward the barn.

Her mother straightened. "I'll ring the bell. That'll bring your dad back to the house."

"I don't think it's necessary..." Brie's objection came too late. Her mother flew out the door and a few moments later, the huge brass bell on the front porch rang out with a deep toll.

No doubt now. Cole would think her family was truly odd, strange, and weird. All the above.

Brie wondered about Cole's family. She knew he'd attended college at the U-Dub, as local people called the University of Washington, because he'd mentioned meeting the owners of Three Geeks there.

He'd also mentioned working for them in some sort of tech startup. She found scant evidence of Cole's background online, and that bugged her. Despite his assurances of being a regular, law-abiding citizen, it still bothered Brie that she couldn't discover more information about him on the web.

His remark that her research skills might be slipping still stung.

Brie heard her mother greeting the two men and a few moments later she walked through the door, with Cole and her father following.

"You boys get washed up while Brie and I put dinner on the table."

Brie felt like a character in an episode of *Little House on the Prairie.*

You menfolk git to the pump and clean up while we ladies get the vittles on the table.

Why did that thought come out like she had a Southern country accent? She shook her head to clear it. It was too early to blame the wine because she hadn't even had any yet.

She grabbed two potholders to pull the scalloped potatoes out of the oven. After setting the casserole dish out, she returned to the stove to arrange the beef on a serving plate. It smelled delicious.

When she invited him to dinner, she'd asked Cole if he ate meat. He had an impressive physique, at least what she'd seen of it. What she hadn't actually seen in real life, she'd embellished with her imagination

Then there'd been that brazen, inappropriate hug in his office. While it provided an opportunity for her to get up close and personal with him, the memory still made her blush.

The men returned to the dining room as Brie finished putting the basket of rolls on the table. She smiled at Cole, gesturing toward the food on the table.

"I hope you're hungry."

Her father clapped. "I'm starving, so let's get to it. Charlie," he said, turning to Brie's mother, "you gonna offer grace?"

Her mother giggled at the nickname. Oh no, it was already giggle time. "Let's sing the Johnny Appleseed grace," she responded. "*Oh, the Lord's been good to me.*"

Cole stared at Brie as both her parents sang a blessing. The edges of his mouth lifted into a grin.

Brie shrugged and then joined in. "*For giving me the things, I need.*"

When the musical prayer interlude finished, they pulled out their chairs and sat.

"I never heard grace sung at the table before," Cole commented. "It's nice."

"We have our own way of doing things out here on the farm," her father responded.

Brie fought the temptation to roll her eyes. Her father made it sound as if they were some kind of cult with weird hairstyles and prim-and-proper fashion requirements for women.

Her mother had jeans on, and Brie wore a sundress with V-neckline and an open back. Not exactly a conservative outfit, but she wanted to be a little provocative tonight.

"Did you enjoy your tour of the farm?" Brie's mother inquired as she passed the veggies to Cole.

"Yes, ma'am. Warren explained the bio-dynamic aspects, and it's impressive. I found the cover crop rotation interesting."

She nearly choked on her wine as she took a sip. He thought cover crops were interesting. Her mother was "ma'am," and she could swear Cole now had a Southern accent. Or she imagined he did. Her brain needed a cleanse.

"But tell 'em what really impressed you, son." Her father acted as eager as a kid showing off his Pokémon collection.

Cole glanced at Brie, then leaned closer. She could tell from the way his dark green eyes sparkled and the dimple framing the left side of his luscious mouth that he enjoyed this immensely. Too bad for her. The humiliation kept piling on.

"Let me guess. The size of Becky Sue, our sow? Or maybe the sheep shed where we shear in springtime? Could it be the goats climbing the ladders into the haymow?"

"Your goats can climb ladders? That's awesome." He grinned at her. She resisted the temptation to stab him in the hand. This night must be like a comedy show for him. She'd never be able to overcome the humiliation.

Her father was so excited he waved his fork in the air. "Tell her," he urged Cole.

"The tractor," Cole finally admitted. "I thought he was shi..." He glanced around the table and coughed. "Fooling with me when he told me about it. But there it was, an actual Lamborghini tractor."

Her father leaned back in his chair. "Man's got good taste in farm equipment."

It was the highest of compliments from her father. Brie supposed if Cole had been impressed, it was probably a case of one man admiring another man's equipment.

Brie paused and set her fork on her plate, hoping she hadn't said that out loud. She was relieved as the *menfolk* went on discussing the various outstanding features of the tractor.

She sipped her wine. Then she took a deep gulp of wine—and then she emptied her glass. Cole refilled it for her, and she mumbled her thanks.

The meal felt endless, as if they'd been sitting at the table for several hours. Her father lectured them about all the benefits of a bio-dynamic farm. Cole nodded, agreed, and ate.

At least he seemed to enjoy the meal. He accepted the second helpings her mother forced on him and thanked her for the excellent meal.

When her mother slapped her elbows on the table and leaned closer to Cole, Brie was tempted to remove her wine glass. She couldn't remember how much the older woman had to drink this evening, but they were pouring from the second bottle opened before dinner.

"I didn't make this. Brie did." Her mother's words sounded a little slurred. "The whole thing." Only Cole's lightning-fast reflexes saved the bottle of wine from spilling as her hand grazed it.

Brie coughed, hoping it hid her embarrassment.

"Charlie, you need to slow down. I think you're gettin' a little tipsy."

"Tipsy, slipsy, Warren. I'm just having fun." Her mother pushed her wineglass toward Cole, and he obliged her by refilling it.

Her mother patted him on the arm, then wrinkled her nose up at him. "You're so hard, Cole."

"She's quite the cook, our Brie," her father joined in the effort to totally humiliate her. "She's gonna make some lucky man a fine wife someday."

Now Cole looked like a deer caught in the headlights. Served him right for being all nice and pretending he was interested in the farm.

That said, she needed to rescue him.

"Well, before my parents offer you my dowry and force you to sign a marriage contract, we should go for a walk," Brie said brightly.

"Now honey, you know we're not providing a dowry for you." Her father stared at Cole. "We expect the groom to offer a substantial bride price. It's an old family tradition."

Cole jumped up so quickly his chair teetered, and she had to catch it before it fell backward.

"Sorry. Do we need to help clean up?" he asked. His face seemed to have paled since he'd arrived.

"Don't worry about that, young man. You kids go off and have some fun," her mother said with a wink. Stage two of tipsy. First the giggles, then the winks. Brie was tempted to grab the wine bottle and take it with her.

"Just don't get into any trouble!" her father warned before both of her parents dissolved into laughter.

Brie grabbed Cole by the elbow, leading him out the front door. When they descended from the porch, Brie released him. She had to agree with her mother. His arms were impressive. Even his elbow felt muscular. Wait, how much wine did she have to drink tonight?

"I'm sorry about my parents. They aren't usually like this. I swear, they were out in the fields today and a spaceship kidnapped my actual parents and replaced them with these pod people. I'm hoping the originals will be returned in a few days after the aliens have experimented on them."

Cole laughed. "I wish my family was this funny. Hey, did you know your dad has an antique shotgun from 1892?"

She tipped her head at him. "He's so subtle sometimes, it's hard to understand what he means."

Cole laughed as she guided him down the driveway and pointed him toward a well-worn path through a nearby grove of trees.

"Are you going to make me go home? Because your mother promised me dessert. She said it was apple pie with homemade vanilla-bean ice cream. I refuse to leave until I've had my pie," Cole said.

"Don't worry, I will not deprive you of your pie. I believe that right is guaranteed in the Constitution." She slipped her arm through the crook of his elbow. "Our forefathers and mothers were farmers, after all."

"Where are we going?"

She pointed to lights ahead of them. "To my cottage, where we'll be safe, at least for the time being, and the alien couple won't bother us while we talk."

"Are you sure?"

She shook her head. "As you've probably noticed, they're very unpredictable. I just hope my actual parents aren't undergoing anal probes."

He snorted, and she wanted to slap herself. Apparently, her family suffered from contagious awkwardness tonight.

They walked in silence until the outline of her cottage appeared. The lights had come on automatically. He halted.

"Are you kidding me? When we go in there, I expect to see birdies and bunnies doing your dishes."

"Birdies and bunnies? Really? Are you like five or something?"

He pointed at the cottage. "You're Snow White, living in the woods in this magical little house. I expect birdies and bunnies to be doing your housework. Don't spoil it for me."

"I wish," she said. "I've never figured out how to get Bambi's mother to vacuum for me."

"Do not mention the mother," he warned. "That movie traumatized me as a child. Whoever wrote that story obviously hated children."

"I believe it's the same person who wrote the story about the flying elephant in the circus."

"Stop!" he demanded. "Otherwise, I'll have to call my therapist tomorrow."

"So, you have a therapist?" She might be able to tease out a few more details about his life tonight.

They stood at the bottom of her front steps.

"Doesn't everyone have some kind of trauma they need a therapist for?"

"I don't, but then again, my life has been pretty boring so far. My parents are aliens, my brother is evil, I think I'm a mermaid, and tiny wild creatures do my housework. Just your typical girl-next-door type."

He kept staring at the cottage. "Your father built this masterpiece? I love it, and it fits you perfectly."

She didn't know how she felt about that remark.

"The lines, the gabled roof, even the flower boxes scream Brienne. I can't wait to see the inside."

She cringed as she climbed the steps behind him. What if he made fun of her version of cottagecore? He'd probably think it too prissy and soft and girly? Maybe he hated pink! She'd used a lot of pink in her decorating. She'd accented with white and turquoise, but he might not notice because of all the shades of pink.

What if he thought she was silly and impractical and...?

He opened the front door, stepped into the small entryway, and stopped. She bumped into him because, obviously, she didn't expect him to come to a complete halt. The man needed taillights.

"This is so awesome. I can't even describe it except to say it again. It fits you perfectly."

She hoped his architectural review wouldn't include the words silly, girly, or prissy.

He hadn't moved and still looked around the main room. Finally turning, he shot her a giant grin. A dimple-activating grin that made her womanly parts heat to about a thousand degrees.

She hoped her panties didn't catch on fire.

She tried to imagine how the kitchen with ivory cabinets and an island made from a piece of antique furniture, along with a pink vintage reproduction refrigerator, must look to him. A multitude of pillows covered the sofa, floral-patterned chair and were scattered across the window seat, framed by overloaded bookshelves.

"It's so, so...fluffy," he finally said, taking a step into her kitchen. "And pink." He turned again. "Really, really pink. Like my sister's Barbie dream house."

"There are touches of white and turquoise as accent colors," she pointed out.

"Clearly," he agreed. "But your designer definitely focused on the pink palette as the center of her design."

She wanted to swat him because he clearly enjoyed teasing her. She waved toward the living room. Her turquoise velvet couch sat in front of the wood-burning stove. "Would you like to sit?"

"And settle on just one view of this dazzling boho delight? I think not. I need to see everything."

He crossed the room to look at the bookcases built around a bow window.

"You have a lot of books," he observed.

"Librarian." She pointed at herself.

He nodded as he continued around the room, studying the framed floral prints and several elaborately decorated mirrors on the wall. "So fabulously fluffy," he commented.

She cringed. She should have hidden the pile of embroidered pillows on the sofa in a cupboard. The pastel woven coverlets scattered around the room were gifts from her mother, but the pink-white-turquoise color scheme was repeated in them too.

He finally leaned against the vintage buffet she'd painted white and installed as an island for her kitchen. He looked like he was going to laugh when his butt settled against it.

It was a genuinely nice butt, she reminded herself. Then she warned herself to stop objectifying this man into body parts. Then she admired the muscles that flexed in his arms when he crossed them.

"Where's your bedroom?"

That was bold. Her nipples tingled, and the temperature in the room shot to tropical in a heartbeat.

He glanced around again. "That is, if you have a bedroom." He'd apparently noticed there were no more interior doors. "Or a bathroom?"

"I don't need a bedroom. I sleep in my glass coffin in the woods. The dwarves guard me all night."

He unfolded his arms and stared at her. She licked her lips, and his moss-green eyes went darker. Did he think she was being seductive?

Was she?

"I assure you; I have a boudoir and bathing chamber." She formed her lips into a soft pout. "You have to earn the privilege of entry."

He laughed. "Exactly how does one manage to do that?"

Her gaze slid to the bookshelf that hid a secret door to her bedroom. "Be honest, trustworthy, and kind?"

When she turned back to look at him, his dimple appeared at the edge of his smile. "So, you're looking for a boy scout?"

"No boys need apply. I've had enough of those," she responded with a purr in her voice. It shocked her because she didn't think she'd ever sounded like that before.

His grin disappeared. "Why did you invite me out here tonight, Brie?" He appeared to be relaxed and comfortable, but something hot and dangerous swirled in his eyes.

"You mentioned you were interested in sourcing food for your bar from local farmers. My dad nearly invented the farm-to-table movement on the island." Her voice sounded breathy, like she couldn't make her lungs work correctly.

She licked her lips again. She needed a drink of water, but that would bring her closer to him. Would it be necessary to die of thirst just to maintain an adequate personal space? Was she afraid of him or her reaction to him?

"That's what you said, but I think there's another reason you brought me here." His voice rumbled, deep and sexy as hell.

"I just wanted to help you—because we needed a private place to talk. About the library funding?" Her voice had trailed off in an annoying squeak.

He slid away from the kitchen island and took a few steps to move closer to her. She wasn't imagining it. His eyes were darker, a more shadowed green. The look on his face hypnotized her.

"Brie, Brie, Brie." He kept his gaze focused on her face, the timbre of his voice growing even deeper.

"Yes," she responded, switching her attention from his eyes to his perfectly-shaped mouth.

"What are we going to do?" His tone suggested he had something in mind.

She'd wanted to drag him away from her embarrassing parents, but she hadn't really thought through what would happen once they were alone in her cottage. She didn't know how to respond.

"We should talk, you know, about the library."

He rubbed his chin. "Now that we're finally alone, I'm not really in the mood for talking."

What exactly could be in the mood for? Dessert? More wine? *Foreplay*?

Where had that idea come from? She hoped he couldn't read minds.

"What do you want from me?" His gaze remained focused on her, and she realized he expected her to answer.

"You know, the donation to the library—for the renovation. More information about the donors and..." Her voice trailed off again. She swallowed and realized she could really use that glass of water right now.

He shook his head. "I think you want more than that."

More than a million dollars for the library renovation? She wasn't that greedy. But maybe he wasn't talking about money.

He took another step toward her, and she could smell his earthy cedar scent. It must be expensive to smell that amazing.

They stared at each other for a few long moments. She waited for him to make the first move.

He watched her, silently, patiently waiting for her. Finally, she put her hands on his chest and wondered why puffs of steam were not rolling off him. He felt feverish, and she considered putting her hand on his forehead to check.

Time to be bold and honest. "I want you to kiss me."

There! She'd said it. When the words tumbled from her mouth, she knew that had been her plan all along. She'd swept him out of the main house and walked him to her cottage to demand a kiss and maybe more.

She'd be happy to start with a kiss.

"It would be my pleasure," he responded, leaning down.

And her brain went silent as his mouth captured her lips and moved ever so slowly to slide across them gently. Then he put his hand in her hair, cupping her head, and deepened the kiss. It was still slow and dreamy, making her melt.

She couldn't breathe, no wait, she could. She'd just been too captivated by his lips against hers to remember how.

One hand slipped below to touch the bare skin of her upper back and he pulled her closer against his body. He was all thick, hard muscle, and heat. When he finally lifted his lips from her mouth, he breathed out a ragged groan.

"I predicted it would be my pleasure. And I was right." He didn't release her. And she didn't resist when he leaned down to torture her with another deep, searing kiss.

Her body seemed to short-circuit as her breasts, seemingly of their own volition, pushed against him. Her nipples were hard, and she wanted to tell him to stop because his kisses created a slowly-spreading ache between her legs.

His hand moved lower until it settled on her ass, and he pulled her up and forward until her center settled against his impressive erection. She didn't need to study that move. The message was obvious.

His mouth moved from hers to nibble at her earlobe, and then he trailed his tongue down her neck. Tiny shivers of delight washed through her. His tongue appeared to know several delightful tricks to make her wild and wanton.

And also make her panties wet. *So wet.*

That sweet, talented tongue slid into the space between her breasts. She didn't want him distracted, so she helped by lowering the sleeves of her dress. It was the friendly thing to do, to assist him.

"I've been thinking about you." He paused to stare up at her face. "If you want me to stop, just tell me. Do you want me to stop now?"

"No! Please don't stop." She gave a vigorous shake of her head. The words betrayed her eagerness to have this man touch her.

His mouth discovered her treacherous nipples, and he suckled both thoroughly. Someone moaned. No, wait, she'd made that sound. Had she totally lost control of her body?

His hand holding her ass lifted the edge of her dress and moved to skim the tender length of her inner thigh. He slid the hem higher until his fingers caught the edge of her red lace panties.

Of course, he couldn't see that they were red, but quality lingerie was important to her. Before they were through, he might get the chance to admire them.

If she were lucky.

One thick finger dipped beneath the lace, and she gasped. It slid to part her seam and she would have screamed if he hadn't expected her reaction and captured her mouth again in a deep, sensual kiss that left her ears ringing with a clanging sound.

He lifted his lips from hers. "What the hell?"

No! No! No! For fuck's sake, this couldn't be happening. She was getting the best sex play she'd had in months, possibly ever, and now her parents rang that damn bell!

He slid her down his hard, muscular body until her feet

touched the floor. She wanted to cry when his hand slipped from her hot, aching, slick center.

She closed her eyes for a second. "I'm sorry. They won't stop ringing that freakin' bell until we get back down there. They'll say it's because of dessert, but honestly, they just want to make sure we don't do anything..."

She couldn't figure out how to end that sentence. Silly? Funny? That they'd regret.

He stared at her, then laughed. "You have a really strange family."

So strange, not weird. Which sounded better? How could she attempt to play at being cool when this hunk of a man had just been stroking her clitoris to her extreme pleasure? Some insatiable creature had taken over her body, and it demanded satisfaction.

Too bad Cole had a different idea, and took several steps back. Away from her. "We never talked."

Talk? After what they'd just been busy doing, he wanted to talk? What was wrong with him?

The bell went silent. Brie knew they had a brief reprieve. Her parents were intensely disciplined when it came to dessert. They had pie and ice cream that needed to be eaten and they literally wouldn't rest until it was consumed.

"Talk," she repeated, as if her brain switched to operating with emergency synapses only. Which it probably was. "What do you want to talk about?"

If he said *the tractor*, she'd kill him. The knife block was on the counter right behind him, so the knives were handy for murdering someone.

"What are we doing here?" he finally asked.

How much time did this man have? She could be very descriptive and lay out her demands in specific detail.

The bell started ringing again, so clearly, they didn't have much time. Two sessions of ringing, then her father would start up the hill. Probably with his antique gun to show Cole his actual intent. To make sure he didn't take advantage of his sweet, innocent daughter, and spoil all her fun.

If he knew about the fantasies she'd concocted about this man, her father would treat her like a fairy-tale princess, lock her in the cottage, and throw away the key.

"I'm curious. Is this a hookup, a make-out session, or something that's going to lead to more?"

"More." For a woman who loved words, she couldn't seem to remember many at the moment.

"Okay. More. Coffee dates, dinner, sex?"

"I hope so!" she nearly shouted out her response and worried she might scare him away with her eagerness. "It seemed like we were on the way to that until we were so rudely interrupted."

It was probably good to be clear about expectations right from the beginning, but he was being strangely specific.

He pushed one hand through his hair, messing it up even more than it was before. One look at the two of them and her parents would imagine they'd been rolling around on the floor naked while they cleaned up after dinner and waited to serve dessert.

He frowned. "I have a thing about consent. I want to do things to you." He paused to take a deep breath. "With you. But, for me, it's always casual. And I could be wrong, but I don't think you do casual."

"I'm not that innocent," she quickly protested. "I can do casual." She looked away from his face and nibbled on her lip. "I mean, I haven't had a lot of, you know, experience. With sex. But I can keep it fun."

The way her voice shook on the word *sex* made her sound like more of a prude than a sex kitten. And she had no idea what she meant by using the word *fun*.

He wrapped a piece of her hair around one finger and

grinned. "I don't think you can, and that worries me, but I don't want to resist you, so we'll work it out."

Before she could respond, the door swung open, and her father stood there with his shotgun. He grinned at them. "Just checkin' to make sure you guys are still alive. Didn't you hear the bell?"

TRUE CONFESSION: Sexual pleasure is something adults think about all the time, caught in the confusing web of desire and guilt. Messages about sex are all around us, encouraging us to buy things because they will make us sexy, to listen to sexy music, to watch sexy movies and TV. Then, when we're at the point of saying YES to all these messages, we discover there's an additional condition: Think about what you're doing! Are you ready? Have you considered birth control? And all the questions about the relationship. Tinder date? Hookup? On the path to commitment or just casual? Commit or don't commit? Trying to sort it out is enough to understand celibacy as a lifestyle choice.

Chapter Nine

COLE

"THIS PIE IS AMAZING," Cole said before shoving the last of his second piece into his mouth.

"Brie made it," Charlotte volunteered, beaming. "She loves to cook and bake. She knows Bailey Holmes, who has the TV show, *Domestic Goddess*. Bailey even filmed an episode of her new show out here on the farm."

He suspected Brie's mother had enjoyed more wine since dinner. She'd been very chatty since they'd returned from the cottage to enjoy dessert.

"I've noticed Brie's pretty talented, and I'm looking forward to getting to know her better." He stared at her for a moment and Brie's cheeks turned as pink as her lipstick.

Her father looked across the table to study Cole. "Exactly what are you talking about, son?"

Cole took his time chewing his bite of pie. His attempt at playful banter now seemed out of place. He needed to be more careful.

The erotic teasing in Brie's cottage left him frustrated and eager to move things forward with her. But he sensed her parents were extremely protective.

"I've watched her at the library. She has an amazing gift for working with people of all ages. She seems to try to make every patron she interacts with feel special. I can tell by the way they smile at her. Her customer service skills are top-notch."

Warren's eyes narrowed, his forehead wrinkled, and he didn't look like he believed Cole's explanation.

But her mother nodded. "Brie has always been such a nice girl. She used to sing in the choir at our church, and we're so proud of her being promoted to Violet Lancaster's old position."

"It's only temporary, Mom. The library board hasn't made a final decision about whether I'll be hired to be the permanent manager."

He caught a hint of bitterness in her voice. Cole could see she resented the idea that someone else might be hired to take the position she clearly enjoyed and deserved. She'd hinted that the woman in charge of the board didn't like her.

He wondered if a million dollars might change the woman's mind. Money bought influence.

"I don't understand what that old bitch Marion Talbot expects you to do. You've raised money for the library since you were a child, and didn't you help Violet find some of the funding for the renovation? That old crow needs to retire and let someone with an eye on the future take over. If it weren't for all the money her husband left her, no one here on the island would give her the time of day."

Charlotte had absolutely had at least two more glasses of wine while they were in the cottage up the hill.

Brie shook her head. "No one is going to replace her for the time being, so I need to figure out a way to convince her to let us change the design for the renovation."

She nodded at Cole. "Maybe you can have some influence with other members of the board when we make the presentation about the donation."

Cole sat up straighter. He didn't know what Brie had told her parents about the promise he'd made for the building fund. He'd asked her to keep it quiet, but these were her parents.

"A bunch of rich guys donating to the library seems too good to be true, Cole. Are you sure they're serious?" Warren cut himself another piece of apple pie and sat back in his chair.

Cole wished he'd stopped at his first piece of pie. This conversation seemed to be getting close to the discussion he'd had with Wyatt and Dylan. How much to say without disclosing too much?

"I worked for these men for years at their company. If they say they're going to do something, then it's going to happen."

"It sure sounds mysterious. Billionaires hanging out on Horseshoe Island suddenly decide to be benefactors of the community. I thought their type showed off their money with fancy mansions and giant yachts," Warren observed.

"The two guys I'm working with are more like multi-millionaires," Cole said. "They're not ostentatious; that's why they prefer to remain anonymous."

"Lighten up, Dad. If they want to donate money to the library for renovations, I will not turn them away." She glanced at Cole. "Please let them know how much I appreciate their offer." She turned and tightened her smile at her father.

"I just need to figure out how to approach Marion about this. She doesn't like kids and hates technology. Since Cole's employers want to fund something related to both, I'm going to need to prepare carefully before I talk to the board."

"I hope they can be patient." She glanced at Cole. "This is going to take some finessing."

He had no objection to the time it would take to prepare a presentation for the board. The more excuses he could find to be with Brie, the better.

When Charlotte offered him another piece of pie, he

thanked her, but pushed his plate away. He'd already need to double his workout tomorrow to offset the calories from the meal tonight.

Standing, he nodded at the older couple. "I appreciate the tour of the farm. I'm impressed with the operation, and I can see when we expand our menu at Three Geeks, it won't be difficult to source our food from the island."

Warren took his time standing. He studied Cole with that narrow-eyed look of suspicion he seemed to have perfected.

"Two," Warren said. "If they own a place called Three Geeks, shouldn't there be three rich guys making the offer to donate to the library?"

Cole hoped his face didn't show his momentary jolt of fear. He needed to think quickly.

"Did I say there were only two?" Cole didn't think he'd said that, but he'd been lulled into a complacent mood by the kiss and sex play with Brie in the cottage. Not to mention overdosing on carbs tonight.

When Cole glanced at Brie, a frown creased her forehead.

"I don't think he said specifically two or three donors, Dad." She settled a thousand-watt smile on Cole that made his heart hitch for a second.

She stood and grasped Cole's hand. "So quit the inquisition and let him get going." She pulled Cole toward the doorway.

Her parents followed them. "Isn't it past your bedtime?" She shot them a furious look.

Charlotte wrapped her arms around Cole. "It's so nice to have such a handsome and well-mannered young man dating Brie."

She stepped back and Warren shoved a hand in his direction. The two men shared a hearty handshake. "Just call me if you need to know anything about farming. I'll hook you up with some local producers when you're ready."

Cole smiled at the older couple and wondered if he should say anything to Brie's mother. He didn't know if Brie thought of them as dating, although she agreed there'd be more between them. He liked the sound of *more*. And he wanted to see her again.

As he followed Brie out the door, holding her hand, he didn't know what she wanted, and he certainly had questions about where they were heading.

He hoped she wanted more than a hookup. They had to start somewhere, but when he considered it, he didn't want a one-night stand. He already sensed that with her, it wouldn't be enough.

They'd talked about more and sex, just not specifically what that meant.

"I apologize if my parents embarrassed you. If you can't tell, they're seriously overprotective." Brie paused a step below him and sighed. "And way too involved in my personal life."

She gazed up at him. "It's difficult to live like a grown-up when your parents are still within earshot. I feel smothered sometimes, but I know they mean well." She still held his hand, and he enjoyed the warmth of her palm encased in his.

He tucked a wisp of hair that had fallen across her face behind her ear. "I like the color of your hair. It's different."

She glanced down at the ground. "It's one more thing the dragon lady holds against me. She said it's unprofessional."

They continued walking down the driveway toward his truck. She glanced at his rig.

"I'd say you were compensating for something with this truck, but I had proof earlier it isn't what I'd expect."

So, they were back to sexy talk. He looked forward to continuing their conversation.

"You asked me what I wanted, so I'll be honest. I'm attracted to you, and I think you're attracted to me." She leaned against the fender and put her hands behind her head. The pose lifted her breasts to give him an enticing view.

"I am, very. A lot." He couldn't seem to make his tongue work to form any words. Shit, he could tell she enjoyed teasing him, and he was getting aroused again. His dick seemed to have a mind of its own tonight.

"It's getting late. You need to kiss me good night," she suggested.

He'd wondered if she planned to invite him back up to the cottage to finish what they'd started. Apparently not. He didn't hide his disappointment.

"So no *more*—tonight?"

She laughed. The sultry, flirty sound sent another shot of heat to his already substantial erection. If she intentionally teased him, she had a gift for making it work. Could there be a sexy vixen hiding beneath her innocent surface? He was frustrated as shit while still wanting more of the tantalizing repartee she offered.

"You promised we'd figure it out. So, what's next?"

That question from the lips of the sweet librarian farm girl who he'd just learned once sang in the church choir nearly put him over the top.

Women didn't do this to Cole. He considered himself the master at managing his relationships to keep them on the cool side. Great sex, no promises—always free and easy, with no expectations. He excelled at no-strings-attached dating.

Her question should have given him an opening to set a date and time to see her again. He'd usually be eager if it involved a relationship with no ties or expectations.

But that idea didn't appeal to him when he considered being with Brie. He took a step closer to her and pulled her arms to circle his neck.

He breathed in her flowery scent as he put his mouth against the soft skin below her ear.

"You smell so good. I want a bottle of that so I can put it on my pillow at night and dream about you."

She gazed up at him, her lips parted, her eyes shiny. "Luna created it just for me. You can order it from the Ancient Ways Apothecary."

He slid one finger down the side of her face, tracing her cheek as he leaned into her. Her body fit against his as if she'd been created for him. Heat warmed and enticed him as the finger slid even farther down, to dip into the valley between her full, round breasts.

A sharp intake of breath alerted him the exploration had an effect.

"That makes sense. You'd require a unique, individual scent. Something as rare as you are."

"So, did you just change the subject to avoid answering my question?"

His mouth captured her lips, and she reacted by opening her mouth to him. Her tongue licked across his lips, then she pushed it softly into his mouth.

"Sweet," he murmured as he pulled his head away from her briefly.

"Kiss me again," she responded. He didn't need any more encouragement, as his own tongue plundered her mouth, sweeping deeply, then pulling back. He repeated the rhythm several times before lifting his head.

If he moved his hand between her legs, he'd find her wet and ready for him. Yet, he didn't want a rushed and reckless fuck tonight. He wanted something slow, with enough foreplay to make her willing and eager for him.

Despite a heaviness in his groin that signaled he was destined to spend a long time in a cold shower when he got home, he stepped away from her.

"Did you intend to distract me even more from my question?" She studied him.

"Did it work?"

She put her hands on his chest. "I believe it made me even more eager for your answer."

Her lips were swollen from their kisses, and he smoothed the front of her dress where it had slipped down when he'd fondled her breasts.

Cole rubbed her arms. "You told me you're not that innocent and you have no problem with keeping things informal between us."

"For now." She shrugged. "And so, you know, I'd like it to be something more than a hookup and less than an arranged marriage."

"I don't know." He stared at his shoes before grinning at her. "Your father informed me this farm would be your dowry if I came up with enough bride money to purchase you."

She grabbed his shirt lapels and yanked on them. "Tell me you just made that up or I'll be so humiliated I'll run away from home."

He noticed her frown.

"I confess, I made that up, but he told me your brother has no interest in the farm, so I can extrapolate that all this..." He spread his arms. "Will be yours someday."

She cocked her head at him. "Before your fantasy of marrying me to become a land baron can be fulfilled, you need to demonstrate you can meet my very exacting standards."

She slid one hand across his crotch, and he could swear he saw stars.

"I can at least vouch you have the right equipment, but I think I'll need a test drive." She rubbed her hand against the fabric of his jeans again. "Or several."

"I can put the tailgate down and we can do it right here, right now," he offered. "Technically, it's called a bed."

"That sounds like a plan for another time." She stood on her tiptoes and slid her enticing tongue across his lips, then nibbled at the corner of his mouth before pushing him a step back. The fact he didn't collapse to his knees amazed him. He might not be able to walk steadily enough to get into the driver's seat.

"When?" His throat felt so tight and parched his words came out as a growl.

"I'll let you know." The flirty smile returned.

They stood for a minute, gazing at each other. Finally, she rose on her tiptoes again to put her lips as close to his mouth as she could reach. He bent to give her a tender goodnight kiss.

It didn't put out the fire searing through his veins, but it slowed it down a bit.

"Operators will be standing by," he growled.

She turned and walked toward her cottage.

He opened the cab door, slid inside, and watched her disappear onto the wooded path. He heartily wished he was going with her to see her bedroom, which he imagined was as pink and fluffy as the rest of her place.

Soft and sweet and succulent. That described Brie.

He started the engine, and despite the week ahead of him filled with fantasies of Brie was destined to be frustrating as hell, it also gave him something to look forward to.

Something enticing and fun. A sensual temptation that'd make him eager to get through the week.

That thought made him groan. A man could only stand so much anticipation.

TRUE CONFESSION: When you're a teenager, you always seem to think your parents are the worst. They must tire of hearing about "somebody else's parents" who allow them to do anything they want whenever they want and don't set any rules. Of course, most of us have never met those mythical parents, but until we get older, we still think they exist. Then we grow up and discover our parents weren't as bad as we thought they were, and eventually, most of us realize they cared about us and made rules to protect us. As adults, we fight for our independence and the right to make our own decisions. Even the bad ones. It must be tough for our parents to be forced to let go, and even harder for them to see us stumble and sometimes even fail. The amazing thing is that even if we fail, they're there to pick us up and dust us off again. Just like when we first learned to walk.

COLE

"**DID** you ask your friend about the mermaid shoot at his pool?" Brie smiled at him.

Shit. He'd meant to talk to her about that the other night. His brain cells must have flamed out when they were in the cottage together. So much heat.

Hot, wet, sensual heat. He remembered the tiny sounds she'd made when his fingers stroked her...

He dragged himself back to reality. "Dylan said it's fine. There's no one at the house now except him."

"Are you sure it's okay with the family who owns the place? I wouldn't want to get caught and accused of trespassing."

She lifted her cup to take a sip of coffee. They'd agreed to a coffee date at Java the Hut to talk. Which they were attempting in short fits of conversation, followed by long moments of awkward silence.

He could tell her Dylan owned the place. But something stopped him again. It was an opportunity to be totally honest with her, to admit he was one of the geeks, and rich enough to be part of the foundation offering funding for the library renovation.

So why didn't he say the words?

"It'll be fine. Does Saturday at noon work for you? The weather is supposed to be sunny, and the pool is heated."

She nodded. "I'm off this weekend. I'll check with the posse, but we should all be able to get away."

There was a playful pout on her lips when she said that. Off. Not working. The entire weekend. Was that an invitation?

Cole needed to wake up and take a hint. "I have a boat. A sailboat." The words rushed out of his mouth, and he sounded like a teenager setting up his first date. He needed to play it cool.

"We could go sailing. After, the pool thing." He cleared his throat, then shut his mouth to avoid saying *would you like to*?

He was fucking this up. This adorable, smart, funny woman somehow managed to mess with him and put him off his game. He had to get things back under control.

"You could bring an overnight bag and spend the night on board." He wanted to be clear she understood his intention. Consent was an important issue to him, especially after...

He snapped back from that ugly memory.

"It's up to you. Or we could just go sailing for a few hours."

She nodded. "I'll bring a bag, then we'll see what happens."

Another jolt hit his dick. How the hell was he going to survive until Saturday?

"You'll have a cabin of your own, so no pressure to..."

"I know." She slid him a flirty smile. "Let's just see how things go. We can be spontaneous."

He'd noticed a dock at the water's edge when her father gave him a tour of his property.

"Do you want me to pick you up at the farm? I can bring the boat almost to your doorstep."

She took a minute to consider his offer, then shook her head. "I'll need to bring a lot of gear to the photo shoot, so I'll just meet you there."

He wondered if she'd give her parents an excuse or tell them she planned to be with Cole overnight? He understood her desire to navigate her own life, and he also knew Warren and Charlotte would worry about her if she didn't tell them the truth about where she'd be. And who she'd be with.

She set her cup on the saucer and reached for her bag on the chair next to her. "I need to get going…the Forest School is visiting the library this afternoon and…"

"I have a sexual consent agreement you need to sign."

"What?" She stared at him, a frown digging a deep crevice across her forehead.

"It's a legal document, because the company I used to work for, there were some allegations. Anyway, my lawyer told me this is something I need to cover with potential partners."

"So, if I understand you correctly, before we have sex, I have to sign some papers? Legal papers? What exactly does this agreement say?"

He glanced around the café, grateful they were the only ones sitting in the area with tables. He reached into his jacket pocket, pulled out several folded pieces of paper, and handed them to her.

"Take it home, read over it, and call me later if you have questions." He turned away from her to gaze out the window. He didn't mean for it to sound so perfunctory.

She stared at the papers sitting on the table.

"I know it sounds…"

"Cold, legalistic, suspicious?" she suggested.

She read down the document. "What's an Accidental Violation"?

"It's just a legal way of saying if we do something you didn't agree to in writing, we can have a verbal agreement."

She gave a nervous laugh. "There's a Failure to Perform clause," she glanced at him. "Does that mean me or you?"

"It protects us both. We agree to use contraception, and to only engage with each other during the dates of the contract."

"This is too Christian Grey for me." Brie sighed. "I'm not into that scene."

Cole stood and put both hands on the table to lean forward. "No, it's not like that. It's protection for both of us. Something happened at the business where I used to work, and we were told..."

He grabbed the back of his neck. "I'm sorry. This is so embarrassing. I never should have; I know you're not the kind of woman who would." He closed his eyes.

"I don't want to insult you. Let's forget about this." He opened his eyes and held out a hand to take the agreement back.

"Can I think about it, Cole? Read it, and talk to you about it?"

"Yeah, of course. Maybe have your lawyer review it."

She glared at him. "Yeah, I'll ask my brother to review the terms of my sex contract. That sounds delightful."

"I'm sorry. I didn't know." He sat, trying to think of something to say.

"Stop apologizing." She shoved the papers into her bag. "I need some time to think, and I can't do that right now. Since we're not going to be engaging in any sexual acts this afternoon," she glanced at him and raised her eyebrows.

"No, not today. Or tomorrow," he said. "Later, whenever, after you. If you decide to."

He needed to stop talking.

She stood and started to walk toward the door, then paused and twisted to stare back at him. "If I don't agree to this *agreement*, how does that affect the donation to the library?"

"It doesn't. This is something between us. I want to be with you, and I hope you'll understand why I'm asking you to sign the papers. But it has nothing to do with the donation to the library's building fund."

"Good answer." She lifted her bag to her shoulder.

"Will you tell me what you decide?" he asked.

"Of course. And I will think about this. Seriously. I promise."

Later That Week

"Fuck off, Cole. I told you I'm not going to your little pool party." Wyatt filled a bowl with sugar-laden cereal.

"Mrs. Scallini's granddaughter is a raging bitch. I doubt she'd want to jump into my arms so she can play mermaid." He turned to the refrigerator for milk.

Cole watched his friend eat and tried to figure out a way to convince Wyatt to join him and Dylan at the, well—pool party. Officially a photo shoot for the Mermaid Posse. Brie had told him they needed to finish shots for the calendar so it could go on sale before the holidays.

He had to admit, spending the day carrying Brie around in his arms and watching her pose in her skimpy mermaid costume sounded like a fun way to spend a Saturday.

He'd been surprised when she sent him a message with the still unsigned Sexual Consent Form attached, with all the boxes below oral sex marked with a question mark. She'd put, **We Need to Talk About This**, on the top of the form.

When he asked if she planned to join him on his sailboat after the photo shoot, she'd agreed with several stipulations.

He offered her several choices, including a day sailing trip and returning before nightfall. She'd chosen to spend the night with him, but she wanted her own cabin.

Now he needed to convince one of his best friends to be his wingman. Cole didn't think it was too much to ask, but Wyatt kept insisting that there'd be blood on the ground if he faced the witch he'd met on Spenser Island.

The woman certainly left an impression. Wyatt studied the Mermaid Posse webpage, pointing out he didn't know what she looked like when they'd argued. The sun had already set, and he'd been perched on a rock. Cole watched his friend's face as he studied the photos on his phone, and the few comments Wyatt made convinced Cole something about the woman interested him.

Wyatt ignored women, even though they flirted with him constantly. He had a raggedy, cool guy who couldn't care less attitude that many women found attractive. He only left the isolation of Spenser Island to sail or visit one of his friends. When Cole and Dylan insisted, he should "get out there," their suggestion was met with a hostile silence.

Wyatt had grown withdrawn, angry, and depressed. Cole and Dylan checked up on him often. They were encouraged by their discovery that he'd befriended Mrs. Scallini. They'd decided she must be an exceptional woman if she broke through his reluctance to talk to strangers.

Then again, Cole had enjoyed some of the lady's cooking, and if the woman owned a restaurant, he'd eat there every night.

"It's a couple of hours, Wy. I can't believe two adults can't share the same space for a worthy cause. The women are raising money to buy children's books for the library."

Wyatt dumped the remaining milk from his disposable paper bowl into the sink before tossing it into the trash. He stood with his hands on the kitchen island and considered Cole's comment.

"We're offering to give the library a million dollars. They can buy books with that money and save themselves the trouble of fundraising."

"We require matching funds, you know that. For the library, every cent will count. And there are worse ways to spend a day."

"Her other friends will be there, right?" Wyatt asked.

Cole nodded. "Brie and Shelby, the woman she works with, will be there along with Raina. She's the redhead Dylan's interested in, so you'd be helping him too. You'd serve as a double-wingman."

Cole held his hands up in front of his chest. "I doubt Luna will attack you with all of us there as witnesses, but I promise, if she threatens to beat the shit out of you, I'll be your second."

Wyatt frowned. "So, you'll hold my glasses while she punches my lights out?"

"Absolutely there for you, buddy." Cole folded his fingers into a pledge.

Wyatt still didn't look convinced, even though a small smile lifted a corner of his mouth. "So, if I say yes, you and Dylan will owe me a favor. Is that what you're saying?"

Cole stopped grinning. What exactly did Wyatt want from them? Why did he need to make a bargain? He had more money than Dylan and Cole, so it wouldn't be a financial thing.

Maybe Wyatt harbored a secret, which would be a good thing. It showed signs of life.

"Do you think I can sketch the, um, *mermaids*, since I'll be sitting around pretty much all day?"

"I'll check with Brie, but since they're posing anyway, I can't see they'd object." Cole shrugged. "Just be sure if you plan to use any of their images in your work, you get a release."

"I've done this before." Wyatt shot him a dirty look before heading to the living room. He pointed at the front door.

"I'm going to work for a while, but I'll show up tomorrow. Noon at Dylan's castle, right?"

Cole took the hint.

As Wyatt started up the stairs, he turned back to Cole. "I better not end up a bloody pulp with my eyes scratched out and need to go to the emergency room."

Cole laughed. "I can't wait to meet the woman who has put that kind of fear into you, Wyatt. She's, like, my hero."

"Fuck you, Cole."

∽✺✾✺∽

BRIENNE

"Are you sure you know enough about this Cole guy to be spending the night with him? Alone on a boat. I mean, just a few weeks ago you suspected he could be a serial killer?"

Brie glanced at the landscape from the front seat of her friend's SUV. "I trust Cole. He came out to the farm for dinner last Monday, met my parents, and still asked me to go sailing with him."

Luna choked out a laugh. "Does your dad still pull out that antique shotgun and show it off to your boyfriends?"

Brie didn't find it funny, but her friends enjoyed hearing about her father's antics around any man she dated. Not that there had been that many. Still, Warren loved to pull practical jokes and tease any guy she brought home.

"I discovered they called Caleb 'Shit for Brains' behind my back the entire time we were together."

Luna glanced at her before returning her gaze to the road.

"I will not argue with that assessment. He was a lazy, going nowhere loser. I certainly tried to convince you I thought you could do better."

"Of course, I recognized his shortcomings. What does it say about my taste in men that I'd stay with someone like that? Am I desperate? Willing to settle? Afraid to ask for more in a relationship?"

"All the above?" Luna suggested.

Brie studied her friend. Luna had more confidence than any other woman she knew. With her height, sculpted muscles, and full figure, she carried herself with the grace of a queen. Her tawny skin, thick black hair, and amber eyes were gifts inherited from her Italian and Native American heritage. Men stared at Luna when she walked into a room, then they discovered she didn't take crap from anyone.

On more than one occasion, Brie had hoped some of her friend's self-confidence might rub off on her. So far, while she'd learned to occasionally speak up for what she wanted, she still felt a long way from being assertive enough to set her own direction in life.

"Cole is still pretty secretive, but something happened to him. Most guys I've been with just go with the flow. The other night, Cole wanted me to be clear about my expectations."

She wanted to discuss the contract Cole had given to her with Luna, but embarrassment kept her from asking her best friend's advice. He'd insisted the document protected both of them, and while that might be true, Brie still didn't know what he expected of her.

The lines about using devices on the body and other activities seemed a little too vague. There were lines she didn't feel comfortable crossing.

"Protecting himself from what? Do you think he's going to divulge where the bodies are buried?"

Brie leaned her arm out the window and stared at the sky

and the puffy white clouds dotting it. "I'm sorry I even started those stupid rumors. I think it hurt his feelings. Anyway, he's a gorgeous, sexy, funny guy, and I'm attracted to him. That's all I need for now."

At least until she discovered if the man had some serious kinks.

Luna coughed. "Please tell me you're bringing some bear spray with you on his boat. Also, send all of us a text when you get to wherever you're sailing off to."

"I'll demand the coordinates so I can put them on a note in a bottle and drop it into the Sound. You should get together with my father and write a screenplay—you both watch too many murder mysteries."

"There's a reason there are so many of them on TV. True-life crime." Luna patted Brie's knee. "And I'm just messing with you. I made some inquiries around town. Cole Moore has a great reputation. Matt O'Donnell has been working for him at Three Geeks and says he's a good guy."

"Matt seems nice. Have you ever thought about dating him?"

Luna had been through a series of short-term relationships for almost a year. She told everyone she preferred quick, no-strings-attached flings. Brie thought her history growing up as a military brat affected her relationships. Her father retired after twenty-five years in the Air Force and while Brie envied all the places around the world that Luna had lived, she also understood it had been hard for her friend to move constantly and make new friends over and over.

Antonia Scallini, Luna's maternal grandmother, provided the stability she'd craved as a child. The Scallini family had lived in the Seattle area since before the First World War. They'd become successful importing specialty foods from Italy and there was still a Scallini Italian Foods store in Pike Place Market.

Luna spent the summers visiting her grandmother in Seattle, and when Antonia—also known as Toni—invited her teenage granddaughter to stay with her to attend the local high school, she was eager to settle in one place.

"Your sexy mystery man is bringing some friends with him today, right? What can you tell me about them? Start with cute or not cute."

Brie closed her eyes to enjoy the sun warming her face. It was a perfect day for the photo shoot. Even though September could often be beautiful, it could also be a gamble for weather here on the islands. They'd lucked out, but they had to get the last images for the calendar finished today. They were on a tough deadline to get everything completed in the next month.

"Cole said the guy who has access to the pool, Dylan, is single. I guess he takes care of the property we're going to use. He's a gardener or caretaker or something."

She caught Luna's expression and noticed her hands tightened on the steering wheel.

"Don't worry, I made sure we wouldn't get arrested for trespassing. Cole says the family is cool with the shoot. I guess they don't spend much time at the house anymore."

"Friggin' rich people. They own homes they don't even use while others go homeless."

A sentiment Brie shared. She didn't understand why anyone needed more than one house. Most of the summer folk who owned vacation homes on the island were nice, but occasionally she'd met an entitled asshole who thought everyone needed to submit to their needs.

Last year, a woman visited the library with her children and complained to Brie that there weren't enough copies of the books on her kids' summer reading list from the fancy private school they attended. Brie had pointed out they could only read one book at a time, and she'd put the books on hold for them.

The woman had wrinkled her nose and said they'd order the books from Amazon, since her children were used to always having a variety of choices.

When Brie suggested they donate their books to the library at the end of the summer, the woman had looked at her as if she were a cockroach and stormed out of the building.

Brie had grown up with a healthy understanding that rich people were different. Not better, not even worse—just different.

"Anyway, he didn't say much about the other friend. He isn't even sure he'll show up, which will make things complicated. If we don't have enough mertenders, it's going to make it even more challenging."

"Did you tell Cole about his official title and spell out the responsibilities?" Luna laughed. "Or did you just inform him the guys were supposed to carry us around when we have our tails on?"

"I told him what we call the guys. I didn't mention the find-and-fetch portion." She took a deep breath. "We need these guys, and I didn't want to scare them off."

"Right. Good call." Luna nodded.

"Besides, Cole is eager for our date later tonight. I think he'll do pretty much anything I want to get me out on his boat." Brie could feel the heat rising to her cheeks.

"Use that magic while it lasts, girlfriend. In my experience, it can wear off quickly."

That was one thing Brie worried about. Cole was eager, attentive, and focused on her now. But what if she couldn't live up to his expectations? She'd been with two men, and from their reactions when they had sex, she didn't think they found her skills in bed highly creative or very satisfying.

Caleb had been screwing three other people when he was

with her, so obviously, for him, she left a great deal to be desired in the sack. She probably should have read *Cosmo* more or something. Learned a few tricks.

That's something that worried her about Cole. If he had a check-off sheet for sex acts, he had to be far more experienced than her. She couldn't decide if that scared or excited her.

The instructions on her phone directed them to turn off the road onto a paved driveway. They stopped at an enormous iron gate. Luna pushed a button for the intercom system.

A deep baritone voice responded. "Hello. You must be here for the photo shoot. Take the first right to the pool house. I'll meet you there."

Luna's head swiveled to stare at Brie. "Do you think he's the butler?"

Before Brie could answer, the gate swung open, and they drove through. The driveway curved through a landscape designed to look natural, but too orderly to be wild.

"Impressive," Luna said as they drove on.

Then they passed an immense stone house built on a bluff.

"Shit!" Luna yelled. "That butler must be Alfred, and this must be Batman's house. It's a fuckin' castle, so either that or they've moved Downton Abbey."

The house rose three stories and looked like a manor house you'd find on an English estate. It certainly didn't fit her idea of a summer camp or cottage.

"Who are these people? If I owned this place, I'd never leave," Brie said, awe in her voice.

"Rich mothers, that's for sure." Luna slammed on the brakes, and they both tilted forward. She put the car in reverse. "Sorry, I was so impressed with that house I missed the turn."

They backed up and turned onto a paved parking lot. A smaller but still impressive stone building stood in front of them. Beyond that a pool set in a landscape that might have been conjured by a fairy queen sparkled in the sunlight.

Both women stared in open-mouthed wonder.

Luna turned to Brie. "I want to live here. Do you think it's owned by an old guy who needs a young wife to continue the family dynasty? I volunteer to become Lady What's Her Butt."

"I have no idea." Brie giggled. "But if it is, get in line, woman."

A tall, shirtless man who definitely worked out approached their car. Brie wondered if they'd spiraled into a weird parallel universe because this guy was a dead ringer for Thor. He grinned, and she heard Luna moan.

He stood next to the driver's side and gave them a cocky grin. "Hello, ladies. Welcome to the pool party. Let me show you to the place where you can put your things and transform yourselves into gorgeous creatures of the sea."

The last word was strung out for effect and the drawl made Brie wonder if his next words would be, "All right, all right, all right."

Brie unlatched her seat belt and opened the car door. "I'm Brie and this is Luna. We're mermaids."

Luna's head snapped to glare at Brie.

"Not real mermaids, obviously," Brie added. "We're part of the Mermaid Posse. We're supposed to have a photo shoot here today."

Her words seemed to disappoint the man as his mouth turned down and his eyebrows knitted into a frown. The expression should not have made him even better looking, but it did.

"And I thought real mermaids were coming." His smile reappeared. "I'm Dylan. Cole's already here. And your photographer, um...Taffy? She's here too."

"Hello, Dylan." The sexy purr in Luna's voice telegraphed her attraction to the handsome blond Adonis.

The sparkle in Dreamboat Dylan's sky-blue eyes tempted

Brie to sigh. Then she remembered Cole was a sexy, good-looking guy, too. In fact, she preferred his darker, more masculine look to the beach-boy surfer vibe Dylan possessed.

Besides, Luna seemed interested in him as she leaned toward Dylan and pointed to the back seat where their mermaid tails were folded. "Can you carry these for us, handsome?" she asked, her voice husky. "They're so heavy."

Brie remained quiet, despite knowing that the members of the posse carried those tails around all the time.

Dylan grabbed the tails and flung them over his shoulder as he pointed to the pool house. "You ladies can change in there. It has a bathroom, shower, even a bedroom."

Did she hear Luna giggle after he said "bedroom"? Luna didn't giggle. Or at least Brie had never heard her do it. The blond surfer god had already bewitched her.

Good for her. Go after what you want was Luna's mantra. If obstacles didn't move out of her way, she shoved them out of the way.

The trunk lifted and Brie grabbed one of her suitcases and her makeup kit. She'd come back for the bin that held her crowns and accessories. People had no idea how much paraphernalia it took for a group of mermaid cosplayers to create their magical transformation. For a little while today, they'd become sea sirens.

The path narrowed, and she spied Taffy Zodiac facing two men. Luna noticed her and they both dropped the containers they were carrying and squealed with delight. They ran to envelop her in a hug, giggling and laughing as if they were middle school pre-teens.

They hadn't seen Taffy in several months, so while this exuberant, unrestrained greeting should have been embarrassing, they were thrilled to see their friend. Taffy was the photographer for the shoot today, and they didn't intend to let anything like proper decorum restrain them.

Taffy had a wild, free attitude, and defied ladylike behavior and rules of propriety. For Brie, she served as a fashion influence, mentor, and her brother Ryder's sometime girlfriend. Brie frowned as she tried to recall if they were on or off again.

"Brie."

A deep male voice brought her to a stop, and she glanced up to see Cole striding toward her. Despite touching him several times, his shirtless hot bod stunned her. The ripples of muscle on his arms, chest, abs, and legs made her heart stutter.

The memory of the blond surfer dude who had greeted them dissolved into smoke. This man, with this body, this face, this voice, stopped in front of her and kissed her.

So, they were doing public displays of affection now. Good to know. He surprised her and she forgot to close her eyes when he gave her a warm, soft peck on the lips. Then the kiss ended.

Disappointment flooded through her. It wasn't enough.

"Let me grab those things for you," Cole offered. "The pool house has plenty of room for you to change and get ready for the shoot."

Brie stood dumbfounded by the appearance of a half-naked Cole. Her mouth felt full of cotton and her brain filled with fuzzy static. If a clothed Cole was seriously sexy and a nearly naked Cole mouthwatering delicious, what the hell would a naked Cole be like?

She might find out later and a shiver slipped up her spine. Whether it was fear or delight, she couldn't say. Excitement, elation, or dread—impossible to determine.

She only hoped she'd sort the feelings out before she stretched across his bed naked and willing to do... something. Possibly everything?

TRUE CONFESSION: Cole Moore is a sweet, sexy,

funny, incredibly hot guy and I do not know why he wants to be with me. I should probably thank my lucky stars, not look a gift horse in the mouth, and repeat many more clichés while avoiding thinking about it too much. Then again, I'm a world-class worrier, so I'd hate to miss this opportunity to question his interest and convince myself he has an ulterior motive for asking me to spend the weekend on his boat. Then again, if he wanted to discover what it's like to date a cosplaying mermaid librarian, she could accept that.

Chapter Eleven

COLE

COLE STARED at the woman standing across from him as she issued a series of requests. More like commands, given to them in a stern tone, as if she were a kindergarten teacher directing her five-year-old pupils.

"I'll need you guys to unload all the equipment from my van," Taffy demanded. "And be careful. That shit costs a fortune."

He might have been intimidated, except the pixie standing in front of him had bubble-gum-pink hair, with messy buns on each side of her head. He considered the possibility the hair covered horns. Her T-shirt had an image of vicious-looking teddy bears holding up their middle fingers, and buckles ran down the side of her short black skirt. Her shoes were black high-top Chucks matched with pink and black striped socks.

He noticed a black and white mermaid tattoo on one arm and the other had images of unicorns and bubbles climbing from her wrist to her elbow. A variety of pink and black earrings hung from multiple ear piercings, and a glorious diamond stud decorated her left nostril.

Wyatt stood next to him, a twist of a smile on his face.

"She seems fun. I've been here less than fifteen minutes and I'm already entertained." He smacked Cole on the arm. "I can't wait until all the mermaids get here."

"Taffy!" Two more female voices screamed the name as Brie and a tall, dark-haired woman appeared on the walkway near the pool house.

The women dropped the large plastic containers they carried and scurried to the pixie woman. They gathered into a group hug that involved a significant amount of feminine laughter and squeals.

Cole stared at the small group and grinned. Brie wore a white cut-off blouse with puffy sleeves. A low neckline edged with lace gave him an appealing view of her lovely breasts. Her red shorts exposed curvy thighs and her shapely legs. With her hair in pigtails, she looked every inch the sweet farmer's daughter.

The woman who arrived with her must be the Amazon warrior who terrified Wyatt. Now he understood. Cole stood over six feet, and Wyatt was even taller. This dark-haired beauty could almost look them in the eye. Black hair curled down her back. Her blue and white dress didn't have sleeves, and Cole admired the muscle tone of her arms.

He tried not to notice her other charms and turned to Wyatt, whispering to make sure the women couldn't hear him. "The photos on the website don't do her justice. She's gorgeous."

Wyatt stared at the woman, his mouth open wide enough to catch flies. "She wore jeans and a black hoodie, and it was getting dark, so I didn't see her clearly."

"Too bad you spoiled it." Cole shook his head. "You should apologize and offer a truce."

"Hey Brie." He greeted her and watched as she pulled away from the other women and turned to him. Her bright smile settled on him, and his world lit up. He swore the birds started chirping louder, and the air became perfumed with the sweet scent of flowers.

His heart gave a hitch, and despite the audience, he kissed her lightly on the lips. She seemed surprised, and he wondered if he'd overstepped.

Her plan to join him on the sailboat later might be a quick one-night-only hookup. It could even end up being a three-hour cruise with no sex.

He was fine with whatever decision she made. For Brie, he could be patient.

"Let me grab those things for you," he offered. "The pool house has plenty of room for you to get ready for the photo shoot."

"Hey, you! Manbun!" Taffy confronted Wyatt, her legs planted apart and her hands on her slim hips.

Wyatt pointed at himself. "Me?"

The pixie with the ridiculous name nodded. "Come and help me get the rest of my equipment."

With that, she turned and marched down the path, not even glancing over her shoulder to see if Wyatt followed.

"Get with the program, Wyatt. You're here to work, not goof off," Cole said as he lifted two containers and turned toward the pool house.

Wyatt shrugged, and the tall woman watched him as he followed Taffy with the funny last name.

Then the dark-haired beauty turned to Brie.

"I feel like I know that guy. He must have come into the shop, or I've seen him in town," Luna said.

Cole remained silent. His friend hadn't shown any interest in a woman for a long time. If they could come up with a way to keep Wyatt's encounter with Luna a secret, she'd get to know him and discover he wasn't the surly bastard she'd met on Spenser Island.

Then again, Wyatt behaved like that all the time, so

somehow, they needed to keep him in a good mood for a few hours. A gargantuan task, considering it had been years since the quiet, introverted man cared about joining humanity again. He told everyone his isolated, solitary life in his cabin on the island satisfied him. He called it tranquil.

Cole called it lonely. If this woman could help wake him and bring him back to life, Cole intended to make the most of the opportunity.

The open door to the pool house framed Dylan as he draped several fishtails across the table. They were shiny and colorful.

"Mermaid tails," he announced. "And they weigh a ton." He glanced at Brie and Luna. "I don't know how you gals swim around in them."

Luna approached Dylan with a flirty smile. "Our problem isn't swimming; the water supports us. The issue is getting around on land. That's the reason we need you guys to be our mertenders."

Her gaze scanned Dylan's body, then she slid one hand down his arm. "You certainly look strong enough to carry me around."

"Easy as lifting my little puppy." Dylan moved closer to Luna and flexed his arm.

"We'll see." Luna laughed. "A day of carrying mermaids around isn't for the weak. I promise it will be a workout."

"Less flirting and more unloading." Brie pushed Luna toward the door. "We still have more stuff to bring in, and if Taffy wants to catch the light, we need to get ready."

"I'll help," Cole offered. He looked forward to seeing the women in their mermaid costumes, so the sooner they could get everything unloaded, the sooner they'd be posing.

Wyatt stood outside with Taffy. She sorted various pieces of camera equipment, as he stood next to her. His furrowed forehead and the dark look he shot at Cole signaled he wasn't happy with his assignment, but he'd do what she told him to do.

That satisfied Cole. He'd promised Brie he and his friends would help the mermaids today. Things needed to go nice and smooth, because when they were done, he had a long, pleasurable evening with Brie to look forward to. He couldn't predict what would happen between them later, and that made the anticipation even sweeter.

A familiar throbbing below his waist reminded him to attempt to maintain his dignity. He needed to avoid embarrassing himself. He couldn't walk around with a hard-on, and he certainly couldn't carry Brie around with a raging boner. She'd notice.

He wasn't a teenager getting laid for the first time, so he should be able to manage his lust for a few hours while watching several nubile, nearly naked women lounge around the pool in mermaid costumes.

Cole stumbled to a stop, realizing he and his friends were facing a challenging afternoon. Dylan and Wyatt were going to end up totally pissed off at him by the of the day.

BRIENNE

"Raina! You're finally here. Is that Shelby with you?"

Brie glanced at the last members of the Mermaid Posse to arrive at the photo shoot. "What happened to Ryan?"

Shelby shot her an apologetic look as she caught up with Raina. "He had to go to work. One of his coworkers got the flu, so they were short-handed. I hope it doesn't cause a problem." She tossed her blond hair as she held out a hand to Cole.

"It's nice to officially meet after you've spent so much time at the library." She glanced at Brie and grinned. "But of course, I've heard all about you."

She made it sound as if Brie had shared every detail of her meetings with Cole. He flushed, probably concerned about a few of the salacious things she'd kept to herself.

"I told you he works at Three Geeks, and we've been discussing a donation to the library building fund. We've had a few meetings to discuss that." She glanced at Cole. "That's pretty much all I said."

"Just a few business meetings." His guilty grin nearly made her laugh.

"What is this place? It's amazing." Shelby glanced around her. "I didn't realize there was a castle on the island. Who does it belong to?"

Leave it to Shelby to ask the nosy questions. Brie had been too thrilled with the good luck of finding a pool they could use to inquire about the amazing estate. She glanced at Cole, who just shrugged.

"You'd have to ask Dylan about that. Let's get your things into the pool house. Your photographer arrived early to look at the site and plan some shots."

Raina climbed out of the truck and nodded at Cole. "Nice to see you again."

"Can we help you with your stuff? Mermaids sure don't travel light." Cole looked at the pile of stuff in the back of Raina's truck.

She smiled and her turquoise-hued eyes lit with good humor, then her expression froze when she noticed Dylan rounding the path to join them.

Dylan returned the stare as he suddenly came to an abrupt stop.

"You," Raina growled. Her mouth thinned as she tossed him a look of contempt.

"Does *he* have to be here?" Raina turned to Brie, her voice choked with anger.

Brie glanced at Cole, who turned to Dylan, who looked seriously pissed. He stayed silent, so Cole intervened.

"Dylan arranged for us to use this place today, so unless you want to call off the photo shoot, yeah—he has to be here."

Brie grabbed Raina's hand to pull her away to speak to her privately. She didn't know why her friend was so angry. Her mouth had settled into a line of disapproval and her rigid posture signaled her contempt of the man standing next to Cole.

When Brie thought they were far enough away from the guys, she stopped and stared at her friend.

"What the hell is going on?"

Raina glanced over her shoulder, watching as the men unloaded their mermaid tails and luggage from the back of her truck.

"Remember last month when I told you I'd spent the night with a guy? The first guy I'd been with in a long time."

"The guy who rocked your world and took you places you had no idea existed." Brie leaned closer to her friend to whisper. "Which, I think, is a euphemism for multiple orgasms?"

"Yeah, that guy." Raina nodded. She ticked her head in Dylan's direction and raised an eyebrow.

Realization hit Brie, and she gasped. "No! He's the slam, bam, thank you, ma'am guy?"

"Yeah, the asshole who left in the middle of the night, never called or texted me." Raina pursed her lips. "He's totally ghosted me after a hook-up."

"In my defense, I didn't know he was Cole's friend." Brie turned to watch the men head down the path to the pool house. "What should we do? Cancel the shoot?"

Brie understood her friend's attitude, but she honestly

didn't know what to do. She hated to scrap this one opportunity, especially since the pool area was beautiful. Really perfect for the shoot.

"We need to finish the calendar, and it's getting too late in the year to reschedule. It's not as if we had a choice of sites." She glanced around. "And it's such a magnificent setting."

"It's amazing," Brie agreed. "There are rocks for us to pose on and mature plantings as the background, even a waterfall. Honestly, I think Taffy will get some great shots today."

Brie held her breath. She wanted to support Raina, and she knew how hurt she'd been by the man who'd visited the Mermaid's Lair several times, charmed her friend, and then asked her out on a date.

Raina didn't date much. With her restaurant, catering business, and young son, she didn't have time to invest in a relationship and didn't engage in casual sex. She'd chosen to be celibate for nearly a year.

She'd told her friends about the amazing guy she'd met. How charming, funny, and fantastic looking he'd been. He pursued Raina for weeks, and she'd finally agreed to a date. They'd ended up at the house Raina and Luna shared.

Then, after that one night, he'd ghosted her, leaving Raina angry, disappointed, and discouraged. The members of the Mermaid Posse had taken to referring to him as the "rat-bastard a-hole".

"What's his connection to this place, anyway? Is he the caretaker or gardener, or does he live here?"

Brie shrugged. "I guess he's the pool boy?"

"I bet that's it. He probably hangs around here doing maintenance work all summer and fall, then heads to California or Hawaii in winter to surf." Raina sniffed. "He's definitely a beach bum."

"You don't have to stay. I'll understand if seeing him is a

problem. We can arrange for Taffy to take your photos another time."

"If we want to get this calendar out for Christmas sales, we need to do this today. Taffy's busy, and we can't take advantage of her." She squared her shoulders and gave a resigned sigh. "I can manage one day with the rat bastard if I just ignore him."

"I'm proud of you, girl." Brie hugged her friend. "I'll try to keep the two of you apart if I can. There are three guys and four mermaids, so we can work out the math."

"Please don't tell the others about this. It could make things—uncomfortable," Raina said. "The important thing is to get some good shots. Now show me more of this amazing pool."

"I assure you, the setting will make this worth the pain and effort." Brie paused. "And being able to buy books for the library will make it rewarding. Keep that in mind. We're doing a good deed here."

They walked down the path and stopped when they arrived at the pool's edge. Shelby looked around, as much in awe as the other women had been.

"You didn't lie, Brie. This is amazing," Raina said.

The pool looked like a natural grotto, with rocks forming a wall on one side and a waterfall tumbling down a hill on the other side. More rock surrounded the edge of the pool and blended with the natural plantings of grass, shrubs, and trees. It looked like a natural pond in the wilderness.

"It's perfect," Shelby said. "I feel like I'm in a magical place."

"Hey, bitches!" Taffy appeared close to the pool house. "Get your shit together so we can make this happen." She headed toward the men, who were setting up her strobe lights on a frame above the pool.

Her command got the group moving as they picked up their baggage and hustled into the small building. Luna removed her silicone tail from the wheeled suitcase and stretched it on the couch. "Did anyone remember to bring a waterproof sheet? I forgot mine."

Shelby shouted from the next room that she had one, and they began arranging their costume pieces, makeup mirrors, and luggage around the room. The pool house seemed large until you tried to fit four mermaids and all their stuff into it. Then it was a tight fit.

"Brie, did you and Taffy create a schedule for today?" Raina asked. Of course, everyone knew she had, because she was the organized, list-making, perpetually prepared member of their group.

"Shelby will be the first photographed for the land shots, since her tail is lighter and easier to get on. Then we'll take turns, depending on who's ready. All of us will do land shots before we get into the water. Individual shots first, then several of us together."

"Thank you, oh queen of organization." Luna bowed. "Now, how are we going to divide up those hot guys outside? I'm calling dibs on the Thor look-alike."

Raina caught Brie's gaze and wrinkled her nose. "You're welcome to him."

Luna shot her a confused frown, then shrugged. "Of course, Brie will get her cute scruffy dude, since she's already claimed him."

"I wouldn't say he's claimed, and we can share the mertenders. Taffy's going to need help when we get into the pool, so we can ask whoever is available to help us." Brie swallowed, and then licked her lips.

"Cute Scruffy Dude is probably dying to get his hands on you, so let's get real. He's yours." Luna tilted her head at Brie. "Dylan will be mine and that quiet one with the glasses and manbun—what's his name?"

"Wyatt," Shelby said. "He can help me and Raina unless he's busy. Then we'll grab the closest available guy."

"Sounds like fun," Luna said, wiggling her eyebrows. "And tell Cole we appreciate him bringing along his good-looking friends. Male eye candy is always appreciated."

Raina slapped her tail on the table. "Too much candy can make you puke, so beware if you're tempted to take a bite."

The other women stared at her. "Just a warning. We're here to get the shots for the calendar today, not hookup with these guys."

Shelby started giggling. "Then you better warn Brie, because I believe she's gonna get some action tonight, and the guy is out there."

There were hoots of laughter from the other women. Brie glared at Shelby. She'd only mentioned Cole planned to take her out for a sail on his boat tonight. She'd never even hinted at a hook-up.

"If we don't get ready, Taffy is going to be in here kicking our collective asses." That warning got the members of the group moving, as they efficiently organized their makeup and accessories. Luna and Shelby headed to the bathroom with their stuff, while Brie set up her mirror on the space at the end of the table. Raina sat down across from her.

"Are you sure about this, Raina? If Dylan being here makes you too uncomfortable, you can still leave."

"Fuck that," Raina snapped. She must have realized how loud her voice sounded and looked down at the table for a moment. She sighed and lifted her gaze to meet Brie's. "No asshole is going to ruin a day with my posse. I'll sort this out and it'll be fine."

"You know what they say? 'The only F word coming out of a woman's mouth that should scare you is *fine*,'" Brie said, giving her friend a wicked smile.

There was a knock at the door. "How's everything going in there?" Cole asked.

"Fine!" Brie and Raina answered, then stared at each other and started laughing.

TRUE CONFESSION: When they tell you to beware of a woman scorned, that should serve as all the warning you need. It doesn't mean women only act from emotion and don't think things through. It means you'd be wise to be careful when you insult or deceive one, because if you've ever watched a lioness hunt, you know females can be stealthy, patient—and lethal.

Chapter Twelve

COLE

"COLE!" The call came from the pool house, and he instinctively wanted to run to answer Brie. He nearly dropped the PVC pipe they held over the pool. "Just a minute," he yelled back.

"She can wait," Taffy growled. She pointed to the stand she'd placed to hold her strobe lights and ordered Dylan to latch one lamp to it. Her frame covered the deep end of the pool, and the structure impressed Cole.

The woman might be a tiny tyrant, but she clearly had skills.

When he dropped a plastic pipe on the ground, Wyatt discovered she also had a colorful vocabulary. She'd bitched him out, swearing a blue streak. She used several descriptive expressions Cole wanted to remember for the next time he got into a bar fight.

Which had never happened, but it paid to be prepared.

The pixie swearing a blue streak nodded at Cole. "Better go see what she wants. I hope one of them is finally ready to get started. Those damned mermaids can take longer getting ready for a shoot than I do organizing an entire show."

Cole fought the temptation to ask her what shows she organized, but the petite woman with the fiery temper intimidated him. All three of the men obeyed her. She was only about five feet tall, and her head came to the middle of his chest. Her wide eyes, glitter makeup, and pink hair made her look like a tiny sprite.

Not that any of them would dare tell her so. She had a tattoo of a doll with blood dripping from its teeth on her lower thigh. Cole interpreted that as a warning.

He knocked on the door of the pool house. "Brie, it's Cole. What do you need?"

Brie opened the door, and he nearly took a step back in surprise. She wore a curly blond wig and a fancy white top decorated with ribbons, lace, beads, and crystals. The top highlighted her breasts nicely, and he refused to shift his gaze from the view.

"When you're finished staring at my tits, could you carry Shelby out to the pool area?" Brie said.

He pushed past her, still not raising his gaze from the delicious sight. "I don't think I'll ever be finished with staring at your tits, but I can try to ignore them," he whispered as he brushed against her.

She grabbed his hand and pulled him closer. "I expect you to pay a lot of attention to me today, Cole." He leaned forward to kiss her. This time he made it a hot, deep kiss that sent blood simmering through his body.

When he lifted his head, she had a dreamy look on her face. "Exactly!" she said before pushing him away.

He turned to stare around the room. Items were strung everywhere. He saw mermaid tails, tackle boxes holding makeup, bra tops decorated with a remarkable variety of lace and trimmings, and a jewelry box filled with shiny fake pearls, necklaces, and earrings.

"I must have missed the tornado." He turned to grin at Brie. "Or was it a tropical hurricane?"

"Hilarious," she responded. "Shelby's on the bed in the next room."

Cole followed her. Shelby leaned back against a pile of pillows like a queen, wearing a long curly turquoise wig. Her legs were encased in a green and gold shimmery mermaid tail. Two large seashells with jewels attached covered her breasts, which he quickly tried to ignore. A crown of seashells decorated with jewels and glitter perched on her head.

She looked like a...mermaid. He couldn't control his astonishment as he stared at her.

Shelby's mouth quirked into a flirty smile. "Can you give a mermaid a lift to the pool, mister?"

Cole snapped out of it and nodded. "I'd be happy to oblige you, ma'am." He bent down and lifted her.

"Giddy up, cowboy." She giggled as she wrapped her arms around his neck.

"Just get out there before Taffy turns psycho. You know how she gets if the schedule is messed up," Brie warned them.

The thought of the prickly little photographer getting angry spurred Cole to walk faster. He had no intention of pissing off the scrappy little woman.

When they approached the pool, Taffy pointed to a huge flat-topped boulder near the waterfall. "I'm going to do individual shots there first, then group shots over there, and when we finish those, the mermaids will get into the pool for the underwater photos.

"Sit her down over there," Taffy commanded as she picked up one of several cameras she'd brought with her.

As Cole stretched to put Shelby in the spot in front of the waterfall, she held up a hand. "Be careful. These tails are more fragile than you think. The silicone tails that the others wear cost a fortune."

"So, you don't have a silicone tail?" Cole glanced down at the fabric tail Shelby wore.

She settled on the rock and shook her head. "I'm paying for a wedding in a few months, so the new tail has to wait. But this one photographs well, so it'll have to do for now."

It occurred to Cole that he and his friends could easily afford to buy the Mermaid Posse new expensive tails and not even think about the cost. Then again, Brie and the others might wonder why a bunch of strangers would do that. It had been hard enough to convince her the library donation was legit.

"Let me fix her hair and arrange the tail." He heard Brie's voice behind him. She nudged him out of the way, and he joined the other two guys to watch the women set up the shoot.

"She's magical," Wyatt declared. "Do you think they'd mind if I sketched them?"

Cole shrugged. "You'll need to ask Brie."

Wyatt grinned, and Cole marveled that today his friend seemed more relaxed, had said more, and showed more interest in what was going on than he had for a long time. It was a positive sign his friend might be ready to come out of his self-imposed exile.

"Hey Brie," Cole yelled. "Can Wyatt do some sketches?"

Brie turned to Shelby, said something, and then they both nodded. "Nothing goes on the internet without our permission," Brie warned.

"Gotcha," Wyatt responded as he grabbed his tablet and sat down on one of the comfortable, padded lounge chairs. He was quickly absorbed in his drawing.

Cole and Dylan watched Taffy issue quick orders for different poses, and Shelby followed the directions. Brie stood nearby, ready to hand props to Shelby or rearrange her hair and tail.

A shout from the pool house let them know Luna had finished getting dressed, and Dylan offered to be her mertender.

As the mermaids posed alone or with each other, the time flew by. The guys offered drinks to the women to make sure they stayed hydrated. Taffy made good use of the setting, placing the mermaids at the bottom of the waterfall, along the boulders and even at the edge of the pool.

The women impressed Cole as they worked to get the best shots. He'd expected the photo shoot to be an amateur effort, with simple Halloween-type costumes.

Obviously not the case, as the Mermaid Posse took this seriously, and their makeup, tails, and accessories transformed them.

Taffy finally called for a break, and the men helped the women into lounge chairs scattered around the pool. Cole grinned as he moved Brie to a comfortable spot. Her gold and white tail matched her bejeweled top perfectly.

"Can I get you anything?" He bent to gaze into her eyes, enjoying the soft blush that tinted her cheeks.

"I'd like to fix my makeup before we do the underwater shots. Can you carry me into the pool house?"

Cole stood and bowed. "Today I'm your faithful mertender, and only aim to please you, milady."

"I'll remember that later." Her blush turned from rose to scarlet, as she nibbled on her bottom lip.

He answered her with a slow, sexy grin. Shit. Was this day ever going to end? He'd forced himself to think about puppies, kittens, and rainbows when Brie's soft arms wrapped around his neck and aroused him.

Her full breasts, shown to their advantage in the shell-covered top she wore, and her body snuggling against him when he carried her, caused a reaction that forced him to walk away several times to control the thick stiffness between his legs.

Dylan disappeared to the big house on the hill more than once, and he'd even noticed Wyatt shift uncomfortably after he carried Luna to the pool house. He and his buddies weren't immune to the mermaids' allure.

It made the escape with Brie on the sailboat tonight even more enticing. If his fantasies lived up to reality, it'd be a long, passionate night of steamy sex.

Or not, because he'd set the stage, but whatever happened later between them would be Brie's decision.

His dick twitched, reminding him he needed to control himself. His growing desire as he watched her pose this afternoon signaled a consuming need to be with her. He wanted to fuck her, but he had no idea what she wanted.

She took a deep breath as he settled her on the chair in front of a makeup mirror. He watched as she adjusted her gold and white crown decorated with shells, sequins, and pearls.

"Where do you guys buy all this stuff?" Cole asked, pointing at the crown. "It's pretty elaborate."

Brie finished adjusting her crown and pulled off the white gloves that covered her arms to the elbow.

"We make a lot," she said. "We hunt thrift stores, and we buy craft supplies online. The Mermaid Posse members are DIY experts with glue guns.

"The tails are from a company called Fantasy Tails. They do beautiful work," she added.

Cole nodded. "Shelby told me they're expensive and mentioned she doesn't have one like yours because she's getting married soon."

"That woman has turned into a regular Bridezilla! She insisted on a December wedding, which means fog, rain, or possibly snow for her wedding day, but it's her choice and the posse is just along for the painful, irritating, endless complaining," Brie added, a huge smile on her face. "We're her minions, just doing everything she tells us to do."

She brushed her cheeks with a pink color, then pulled out a matching lipstick. He dropped to his knees.

"Before you put any more of that on, let me test it." He put his hands on each side of her head and gently pulled her down toward his mouth. She slowly closed her eyes and wore a soft, beatific expression on her face. He made the kiss as gentle as possible.

It didn't last. He heard her give a gasp, and he interpreted that sound as a signal. He stood, lifted her into his arms, and carried her to the couch on the other side of the room.

She stared at him, and a playful smile spread across her face. "We don't have much time." She whispered; her voice held a sexy purr.

"This won't take much time," he suggested as he sat and settled her on his lap. His mouth found hers again, and this time, the kiss was rougher, demanding. His tongue slid between her lips, and he heard that faint, breathless sound she'd made again.

A sound that made him groan with pent-up desire. She twisted her body, and his dick went so hard, he knew she could feel it.

As he trailed his tongue down her throat, she leaned back, giving him access to her full, round breasts. He'd always imagined himself an ass man, but her breasts were a feast. He pulled down the edges of the top she wore and enjoyed the view before lifting one heavy breast and positioning it so he could suck the enticing tip.

His tongue laved her nipple before he moved to the other side. She squirmed again, and he thought if this went on any longer, he'd likely embarrass himself.

"Just a teaser." He adjusted the top of her costume to cover her breasts again.

"I need to be honest with you." She wet her lips. "Despite what I told you, I'm not really that experienced." She lowered her gaze away from looking into his eyes. "And if we—decide to, you know..."

She remained silent for a moment, and he touched her chin gently to encourage her to raise her eyes and meet his gaze.

"I want you, Brie. But I won't pressure you to do anything you don't want to do. We're going sailing later, and hopefully," he grinned, "we can have some fun together."

She smiled at him. "Some fun. Hopefully."

"The moment you say we're done, we're done. You make all the decisions tonight. You're in charge. That's the purpose of the agreement."

"So, what if I'm overcome with lust, throw you down, and have my way with you?"

His head fell back, and he put an arm across his eyes. "Is there even a tiny possibility that's gonna happen?"

She traced his lips with one finger. "I'm beginning to think with you, anything's possible."

Cole had no idea how he was going to keep himself together until they finished the photo shoot. He had a raging hard-on, and her enticing suggestion made it even worse.

He needed to put distance between them, so he slid her off his lap to deposit her on the end of the couch. Then he plopped down again on the other side.

"If I don't take a break, I'll have to call Dylan or Wyatt to carry you back out, so I don't embarrass myself."

She burst out laughing. "I'd love to hear your excuse for resigning as my mertender."

"I'm not resigning." He wiped his forehead and straightened. "This is the best gig I've ever had. I just need a breather. Time to clear my head."

"Your head," she repeated.

Someone pounded on the door. "You two better not be naked in there. Breaks over. Get out here!" Taffy yelled at them.

"Is she always this much of a pain in the ass?"

"She can be demanding, but her work is amazing." Brie adjusted the beaded top to make sure her breasts were covered. "She makes us look like beauty queens."

Cole stood, then bent down to lift Brie into his arms.

"News flash mermaid, you and your posse are gorgeous. I'm going to buy a bunch of those calendars and give them away to my customers when they come out."

"Really?" She wrapped her arms around his neck. "That would raise so much money for the library. I'm going to call you the Fairy Godfather."

He carried her through the doorway and toward the pool.

"I refuse to wear a tutu and carry a wand."

She leaned forward and licked the inside of his ear. The progress he'd made with his erection disappeared.

He stopped for a moment and shifted her. "Fine. Just not a pink tutu. Now behave, so I can put you down. Otherwise, I'll have to carry you around like a pet chihuahua for the rest of the day."

When they returned to the arrangement of lounge chairs, Taffy pointed at them.

"I hope you guys got whatever you were doing in there out of your systems for a while. We're losing the light."

A shot of guilt slammed through Cole. He'd probably held things up with his fondling of Brie, but he couldn't resist kissing her, touching her, and his imagination went crazy again.

"Have any of you men been trained as a lifeguard?" Taffy's hard gaze took in the men.

"I have." Dylan stepped forward.

Taffy stared at him for a moment, then nodded. "That

figures. Okay, surfer dude, I'll need you on safety." She handed him a snorkel. "I'm assuming you know how to use this?"

Dylan gave her his best brazenly flirty grin. She ignored his expression and pointed toward the deep end of the pool.

Cole laughed. "She's immune to your charms, Dy."

Taffy looked around to address the group. "I'm not swayed by a bunch of pretty boys showing off their amazing, awesome muscles all day."

"So, you think we're amazing and awesome?" Dylan replied.

"Shut the fuck up." Her voice held a snarl at the end. "When the mermaids are in the water, you're responsible for keeping them safe. Put on the mask and snorkel and hold the pool noodle. If anything looks off, pull them to the surface immediately."

Cole and Dylan traded glances. Clearly, this was serious shit.

"Mermaids, I'm gonna shoot Shelby first, then Raina, Luna, and the final shots will be of Brie. You all know the drill, but I'll remind you. This isn't a game, and you could get hurt if you aren't careful."

Wyatt put his tablet down and joined the group. He nodded at Shelby. "Do you need help to get into the water?"

Shelby nodded, and Wyatt carried her to the shallow end of the pool and climbed in the water to his waist. He reached for Shelby, who was perched on the edge of the pool, and she eased into his arms. He held her for a moment, balancing, before gently pushing her toward the other end of the pool.

Everyone watched as she elegantly slipped through the water, her tail flapping and her arms delicately making waves. She arrived at the deep end and grabbed the end of the pool noodle Dylan held.

Taffy slipped her skirt off, exposing a pair of swim shorts.

She barked more instructions before donning a weight belt and putting on a scuba mask and tank.

She held a camera secured in a plastic box. They watched her walk into deeper water, where she sank to sit on the bottom.

When Taffy waved a hand, Shelby took a deep breath, let go of the noodle, and pushed herself beneath the surface. Her hair floated around her. She posed her arms for several shots, then lifted her head above the water to take a breath.

The posse members all seemed to have held their breath along with her. Cole turned to Brie.

"She made that look easy, but I suspect there's a lot more to it than I can see. You guys must practice a lot."

"We swim at the resort when we can arrange time there and we all take yoga to work on our breathing. We do this for fun, but safety is important. I've never been to the ocean with my tail, but Luna and Raina swam in the water with theirs when they went on vacation to Hawaii. They're the best swimmers, so they can do things the rest of us aren't ready for yet."

One by one, the mermaids posed for the underwater shots. As they finished, Taffy excused them to change out of their costumes. Finally, only Brie remained for the final underwater images in her white and gold outfit.

Cole carried her to the edge of the pool, then climbed in. He marveled at how beautiful she looked. She had a natural beauty, with her soft gray eyes, pert nose, and delicate cheekbones. Her lips were luscious and enticing.

He wanted to kiss those lips until she moaned with passionate hunger. He wanted her to fall into his arms.

Soon, they'd be alone on the sailboat, and he'd have her all to himself tonight. He'd cook dinner for her, they'd share some excellent wine, and whatever happened between them, happened.

He wanted to kiss her, stroke her amazing body, and make her come so hard she'd scream his name.

If she gave him the chance, he was determined to satisfy her. Multiple times. All he needed to do was hold his unbridled lust in check for a little while longer.

And she needed to give him permission. He'd been honest with her. She could see the evidence of his obvious desire for her, but Cole had been clear. If she said no, to anything, that would be it.

Brie needed to feel safe and trust him completely. He'd learned the hard way that destroying trust could leave you broken for a long time.

As she floated in the water, strobe lights went off and outlined her body. Her movements were slow and relaxed. Dylan handed her a length of sheer netting that floated around her. She looked ethereal and otherworldly. Cole got caught up in the illusion.

He snapped out of his daze when Brie rose to the surface. Taffy floated to the top of the water and nodded at Cole. "We're done. You can help her out of the water."

Brie brushed up against him. Her mouth lifted into an enchanting smile. "Is that a flounder in your pocket, Cole, or are you just happy to see me?"

"King salmon," he replied.

She raised her eyebrows as she smiled. "Not humble at all, dude."

He pulled her into his arms and walked through the water toward the edge of the pool. "It's not bragging if it's true."

He set her on the edge of the pool and climbed out. As he reached down to pick her up, she whispered in his ear.

"I'm not sure if I should be frightened or aroused." Her voice held a sensuous edge.

He squeezed her bottom as he pulled her up into his arms. "How about eager and aroused?"

"I like that combination." She slipped her arms around his neck and kissed the corner of his mouth.

Taffy yelled orders at Dylan and Wyatt as he carried Brie to the pool house. Cole guessed they'd be busy dismantling the scaffolding above the pool for at least half an hour.

Raina, Luna, and Shelby were busy packing the bags and plastic containers scattered around the pool house. The space appeared a lot less chaotic than before the shoot.

"Hurry and take your tail off. I'll take it home with me," Shelby demanded as she flicked her hand in Brie's direction.

"I'll get out of the way," Cole said as he carried Brie into the bedroom and settled her on the waterproof cover protecting the bed.

"I'm going to grab a quick shower, but I won't take long to get ready. Could you grab my blue canvas bag from Luna's back seat?"

He nodded and left the women with their suggestive remarks trailing behind him. They all knew Brie planned to join him on the boat tonight. It encouraged him that she'd shared that information with her friends.

He turned the corner of the building to discover Taffy loading her Jeep. She glared at him, and he took a step back, a chill slithering up his spine.

Her pink hair swirled damp and loose around her shoulders. She wore a jumpsuit covered with huge fluorescent flowers and sandals decorated with unicorns. He couldn't figure out her deal. Killer fairy? Pixie maniac?

"I heard you're planning to fuck my girl tonight."

Her wide eyes and tiny frame were deceiving. This woman could be a warrior princess.

"That's up to Brie, and probably none of your business," he answered, his heartbeat picking up the pace.

She twisted her mouth as she stared up at him. "You're right, it's her business. But in case she didn't tell you, her brother is a hotshot lawyer in Seattle. You do anything to hurt her, and he'll dig up something from your past and make your life a living hell."

With that warning, she stormed off to the pool area.

Cole couldn't move. Somehow, whether she knew it or not, Taffy had made a threat that turned his blood to ice.

She couldn't know he'd spent a lot of money to hide his past, and the one thing that terrified him was someone exposing the skeletons in his closet.

Cole took a deep breath, deciding he wouldn't let Taffy's threat ruin the evening he'd planned with Brie. When he got on the boat, he'd text his security team. He needed to keep the door to his past shut tight, locked, and inaccessible.

Especially about some ugly stuff he wouldn't want Brie to learn about him. He cared about her, and even though they played their arrangement as flirty and fun, he knew he wanted more than a casual hookup.

If someone opened Pandora's box of his past, it could destroy any chance of that happening.

TRUE CONFESSION: Everyone loves a secret. Whispered from one person to another, the secret's suspense builds and the story changes until sometimes when it's exposed, it's totally different from the way it started out. It's like the telephone game; we laugh at the way it ends up. What we don't seem to think about is the damage done to the person who has the secret that's been shared.

Chapter Thirteen

BRIENNE

"I'LL JUST BE a few minutes, and Luna's going to take my makeup and jewelry back to her place." Cole watched Brie as she gathered the rest of her stuff.

He shifted a little, glanced at the table, and swallowed. "Can I ask you something?"

She slipped several bracelets into her jewelry box and lifted her gaze to meet his. "Sure."

He put his hand on the back of his neck and shifted to his other leg. "You won't be offended?"

"I don't think so, but unless you spit it out, I can't really say."

"Why do you guys have so much lube?"

His neck turned a shade of red and she almost laughed out loud at his obvious discomfort. "We spread it on our legs when we put our tails on. It works just like on..." She paused.

"Condoms," she finally said.

He swallowed and shifted his gaze to glance around the room. "Sure, that makes sense."

She grabbed the large bottle of lube and held it out to him. "Maybe I should bring this with me?"

"I, um... What?" She'd made him even more uncomfortable. She couldn't resist and laughed at him.

"Relax, I have some in my bag, along with condoms, if we decide to use them." Her smile turned flirty. "A woman needs to be prepared, but the large economy size might be a challenge for one night."

"Then again, we haven't signed the agreement yet." She met his eyes.

"Like I said before, you're in charge tonight." He released his sexy grin. "But, since we already exchanged our health history, using condoms shouldn't be necessary," he froze. "Unless you don't use..."

A flash of heat whipped through her and settled with a tingle in the parts below her stomach. She'd been thinking of being with Cole for days, and now that they were headed to his sailboat, her anticipation was fueled by multiple fantasies of what might happen during their time together.

"I'm on the pill, so it's taken care of." She snapped her jewelry box shut and put it in the large plastic container that held her other accessories. "I'll take this out to Luna, and we can leave. Why don't I meet you down on the dock?"

"Follow the path around the house. It leads to the water," he instructed, sliding her another sexy grin.

As he left the pool house, she touched her forehead. It felt like the temperature in the room had gone up at least twenty degrees in the past few minutes.

She grabbed the container and headed out the door. Dylan waved from the edge of the pool as he skimmed the surface with a net. He probably needed to get things cleaned up before the owners of the property returned.

"Thanks, Dylan, for letting us use the pool today."

After tonight, she didn't know if she'd see Cole again, except in business meetings. As far as she knew, they might just be getting together for the weekend. They shared an incredible physical chemistry, but he'd warned her he wasn't interested in a serious commitment.

They were adults acting on a mutual attraction. If they ended up having sex tonight, she refused to feel even a smidgen of guilt about it. Cole agreed they'd discuss the consent form, and that made her feel powerful and in control.

Or was that just her fantasy world catching up to her?

"Hey girl, snap out of it!" Luna's voice dragged her back to reality. "Are you planning your night with the cute, scruffy dude?"

Brie set her container in Luna's car and frowned. "You think he's scruffy?"

Luna closed the hatch and leaned against it. "I think he's hot as hell and if you don't jump on his boat and bonk his brains out, get out of my way so I can do him."

"Back off, bitch." Brie crossed her arms. "There are two other guys back there."

"Yeah, we had some nice scenery today." Luna smiled. "I thought I'd put some moves on Dylan, but he kept staring at Raina all day. Wyatt is shy, but he could be worth the effort."

She cocked her head and frowned. "He seems familiar, though. I swear I've met him someplace."

"There's some ugly history between Raina and Dylan. My sense is they are never, ever getting back together."

"May your love-life never turn into a Taylor Swift song." They slapped palms. "Ugly history? I'm going to have to hear that gossip when you get back. Quit wasting time and get down to the dock with that hunka-hunka and have some fun." Luna pointed toward the water.

Brie followed her friend's instructions. The path from the pool house wound through a carefully landscaped yard, past the side of the huge stone house, and down to the dock.

Cole waited for her there. He pointed to a sleek sailboat anchored out in the water. A bigger, newer boat than she expected.

"Let me help you," he offered, taking her hand. He steadied the small boat that would carry them out to the sailboat with his foot as she climbed into it. After unhooking the lines, he jumped in after her.

"Pretty nice boat," she commented, pointing to the sailboat anchored in the small harbor.

"It's the right size for comfort, but I can still sail it by myself." He started the engine of the tender, and they slowly moved away from the dock.

The outboard motor drowned out their conversation, so they remained silent until they edged up to the stern of the sailboat. The swim platform was down, and Cole helped her climb on board.

He pointed to a set of steps leading down from the cockpit. "I'll carry your bag down for you. I'm going to take us out for a short sail to one of my favorite places."

Brie headed down the steps, suddenly aware she and Cole were totally alone. Even though she'd agreed to this a few days ago, she felt a shiver of concern. All the warnings about strangers she'd heard throughout her life flashed back to her. There were so many things she didn't know about Cole. They probably should have met at her place again, instead of heading out alone together onto the Salish Sea.

Did she trust Cole? Of course, she did, and that calmed her nerves and strengthened her resolve.

At the bottom of the steps, she stepped into the salon. She admired the boat's clean, modern décor.

What had he called her decorating style? Sweet? Fluffy?

There was nothing fluffy or sweet about the interior of his sailboat. The beautiful wood and shiny brass served as a tribute to Cole's masculine taste.

She wondered if he lived on the boat. If he did, he had to be a neat freak. Which was not a character flaw, just an observation.

"Your boat is very—organized," she observed when he came down the steps.

He nodded and tossed her bag into a cabin. "You can have this bed." He pointed to a door. "The head, er bathroom, is just beyond the galley, and my cabin is over there."

She was grateful he offered her a cabin. It took even more pressure off her decisions when she knew she could retreat to a place of her own.

"You can settle in and then come topside. There's wine in the cabinet over there, so choose a bottle, open it, and bring a couple of glasses up with you."

When he turned and climbed the steps, she relaxed a bit, and took a deep breath. She understood this could be a sailing jaunt or something more. It was up to her.

Brie pulled the hand-painted silk robe, dark green lace bra, and matching thong from her overnight bag and stared at the lingerie. She'd come prepared, just in case.

She stepped into the galley and opened the cabinet Cole had pointed out, and discovered bottles of red, white, and rosé wine. She considered the choices and pulled out a bottle of red.

It was a seven-year-old Cabernet Sauvignon from a small Washington winery. Since she wasn't a connoisseur, she'd trust Cole's judgment.

After opening the wine, she found two plastic glasses and climbed the steps to join Cole in the cockpit. The sails were up, and he tended the wheel. His gaze lingered on her as she poured the wine and handed him a glass.

He took a sip and nodded. "Good choice.

"Why don't you sit over there?" He pointed at an upholstered bench.

She grabbed his glass and set it into a cup holder on the console next to her glass. "I have a better idea," she said, then dipped below his arm to stand in front of him.

"Let me play pirate queen and steer the boat."

She leaned back, and she heard him take a sharp breath before he let out a low groan.

"You've been teasing me all day, so right now, I'll do whatever you tell me to do."

She stared at him. "I like the idea of *that* game."

Her voice sounded velvety soft, and she wondered where that came from. She'd never felt so turned on, or so eager to find out what would happen next.

"Heave ho, matey, and be on the lookout for scallywags," she warned him as he turned the wheel over to her. "Watch your booty and don't let any bilge rats plunder your treasure. Arr!"

"I'm more interested in this bootie." His hand slid down her back to squeeze her ass.

"Don't be thinking I'm some bawd you can toss upon your bed and take your pleasure with quickly," she warned.

"Oh, if I were to toss you down on a bed, I'd take my time and pleasure you very, very slowly." He leaned into her, and she had to work to remain focused on steering the boat.

"I like what you're wearing," he said, his mouth moving tantalizingly closer, studying her for a moment. She wasn't wearing a bra, and her nipples were hard and visible through the thin cotton fabric of her T-shirt.

"I wanted to be comfortable."

His other hand slid beneath her left breast and squeezed gently. She'd encouraged him to have his hands free, and now she questioned that decision. Things were moving fast.

"Beware, you might have to walk the plank if you offend the captain," she warned.

"I'm the captain," he growled, as his hand lifted the edge of the T-shirt to expose both breasts, then he kneaded them tenderly.

"My intentions are obvious. I want to touch you, put my mouth on you, and fuck you. I could ravage you all night long. If you let me."

She didn't answer as his words echoed in her now-befuddled brain. His lips heated a path from below her ear to the top of her shoulder.

"We haven't discussed the terms of the contract," she reminded him.

"Turn around," he demanded. She lacked the willpower to resist and turned to face him.

He lifted her chin. Their gazes locked. His mouth captured hers, taking his time at first, caressing her lips slowly. Then his tongue thrust into her mouth, licking, and exploring, as if she was a delicious dessert and he savored the taste of her.

Heat exploded through her veins, firing her blood as a sensual hunger built, then settled with a languid ache between her legs. His obvious carnal lust for her fueled her own desire.

His kiss deepened. The hand holding her face moved to her lower back, pulling her tighter against him. She discovered the hard ridge of his arousal and gasped.

"Are you okay?" he asked.

"Yes. I just, I didn't realize...you're very..."

"Yes, I am." His mouth slid from licking the edge of her ear to dipping into the space of her clavicle. She shivered.

"I believe we've consented by mutual verbal agreement to several things. If you tell me to stop, I will, because while I want to be with you, I don't intend to spoil it by moving too fast. I promise to work hard to maintain some self-control."

He lifted his head and stared into her eyes. "I want to fuck

195

you. I'm sure you understand that. My fantasies are filled with hearing you scream my name when I make you come. Over and over again. It doesn't matter if it's tonight, or another time. It *will* happen, mermaid."

He turned her away from him and held the wheel with one hand, while he moved the other from exploring her breasts to dipping below the waistband of her shorts.

"Will you unbutton your shorts and let me touch you?" His deep, gruff voice excited her, and she quickly complied with his request.

He yanked on the fabric to pull the shorts to her ankles, and she stepped out of them. He slipped one finger into the slit between her legs. She responded to his actions by becoming wet and eager for his touch. He lifted the finger to his mouth and sucked.

"Mmmm, you're delicious, just as I suspected."

She thought her knees might buckle, but he held her tight against his body. "I believe we've moved beyond previous verbal consent," she reminded him. "Maybe we should have a safe word?"

"How about stop?" he suggested.

"Stop seems sufficient."

He returned his hand to squeeze her mound, then inserted his finger again. This time, he rubbed it against her clitoris. She gave a heavy sigh and closed her eyes.

"Feel good?"

"Oh, yeah." Her breathy Marilyn voice had returned.

When he inserted two fingers into her, pushed, then pulled back to stroke her again and again, she was grateful he still held onto her.

Her heart thumped a staccato beat, and she leaned back against him, aware of his stiff erection as it pushed against the fabric of his cargo shorts.

"Drop anchor here," she demanded as the strokes grew

longer and harder, pulsating against her sensitive clit. "I want you to..."

"Not yet," he said as he pulled his hand away, yanking her abruptly back from the edge of an orgasm. "I promise it'll be worth the wait. And we still need to talk."

He pointed at the upholstered seat. "Sit, relax, and let's enjoy our wine. We'll be at Saka'am Cove soon."

Too aroused to sit calmly, she grabbed her wine and downed it in one gulp.

He grinned at her, revealing his enticing dimple. She wanted to reach for his chin, pull his head down, and slide her tongue across that indentation.

"You said there were some things in the contract you want to negotiate?" He stared at her, the sexy grin edging his mouth suggested he enjoyed her innocence about how things like this were done.

"I have no objection to items one to seven. With specifics."

Cole's grin flashed wider. "Specifics?"

"I don't know about nine and ten, I've never..." And now she could feel the blush warming her cheeks.

"You can refuse, and we can discuss it some other time."

Brie took a deep breath. "The one about restraints. It's just, I haven't ever done...that." Her final word came out as a whisper.

His grin spread wider, and his green eyes sparked with a hot smolder. "Unless you brought some toys with you, we can skip that one too. For now."

Her heartbeat appeared to be edging into catastrophic territory and she thought her lungs had stopped working.

Finally, she managed to take a deep breath. "Fine. Now number twelve: *other activities.*" Her voice ended in a squeak. Which made her feel like an awkward woman who didn't understand all the etiquette of modern sex.

And honestly, she didn't. She needed to catch up on her *Cosmo* articles.

"Come here." She couldn't resist Cole's request and moved closer to him.

He reached for her hand and kissed it. "How about if we agree to keep checking in with each other tonight? The mutual verbal consent clause gives us a lot of flexibility."

He'd explained that the Three Geeks parent company required this agreement whenever one of their employees in management began a relationship. Brie remembered #MeToo had exposed a lot of sexual abuse and harassment in the gaming industry, so it made sense.

"By the way, I gave Luna the name of where we're going and the coordinates. She said you promised to contact her when we arrived," he said.

"My friends are worriers." Another item to check off her *Brie isn't a grown-up who can take care of herself list*. She loved that they cared, and hated they thought she needed to be protected.

"I'm going down below to call her now. Is there anything else you want while I'm down there?"

"Are you hungry? There's a charcuterie board in the fridge and crackers in the cabinet next to the sink."

She frowned at him. "Who are you, Martha Stewart? You're so neat and organized and you plan for entertaining on your boat like it's a fancy dinner party."

He laughed. "I intend to offer you good food, superb wine, and what I hope will be some unforgettable experiences."

His expression turned serious. "I meant what I told you earlier. Every step in the dance tonight is lady's choice."

"I trust you, and that makes me feel safe." She gazed up at him and he smiled at her.

As she prepared to climb down to the galley, she bent

forward to give him an enticing view of her ass and gave a wiggle.

"That's not fair," he yelled as she disappeared below.

She found the cheese tray, unwrapped it, discovered he had a supply of cloth napkins—so Martha Stewart—and opened another bottle of wine.

Before going topside, she noticed they were approaching a small island. She pushed several buttons on her phone. After a few rings, she heard Luna's voice.

"So, did you guys do it yet? How was it?"

"Luna, we're still sailing to one of Cole's favorite places. He told me you have the coordinates for where we are."

"Cole said it's Saka'am Cove, and lots of people go there. There's no public access to the island and you need a boat to get there. It's private, but not totally isolated. I appreciate the call, but girl, get busy."

"Do I need to remind you—you're the one who demanded I stay in touch?"

"Yes, because you're my best friend and I worry about you. Now, my advice is to take advantage of this opportunity. You're alone with a gorgeous hunk of a man. Go enjoy yourself."

Then she hung up.

Brie smiled. She had every intention of following her friend's suggestion.

When she arrived back at the cockpit, Cole pushed a button and a table rose from the floor. She set the food and wine on it before refilling his glass.

"This is a pretty fancy boat. It looks expensive."

"If you buy a new one, it is. Fortunately for me, a guy used it for one season and then he and his wife split up. I had the chance to buy it at a huge discount."

She glanced around before settling on the seat. "That's

actually kind of sad. A marriage breaks up and you get a nice boat. Not exactly a happy ending."

Cole shrugged. "He didn't seem too broken up about it. He had a young woman with him when we closed the deal. I suspect he got what he wanted."

"Rich men are always trading up, aren't they?"

"Sometimes." He turned to study her. "I can't judge every man by the ones who don't take their marriage vows seriously. I don't believe you should get married if you don't plan to stay together."

"Rich guys seem to want busty young women with tight bodies. I think it's showing off how potent they are, and they're probably reacting to some basic instinct to reproduce. Although I can't imagine a sixty-something rich guy is looking for a new family."

"I'm surprised how many older men become fathers." Cole laughed. "You could ask Dylan about that; he has a five-year-old sister from his father's latest wife."

"How many stepmothers has he had?"

"Four, I think."

"See, there's the proof no one wants a committed relationship anymore."

"Long-term committed relationships exist. You might have to look harder to see them." Cole turned the wheel. "When people stay married for thirty or forty years, it isn't exactly fodder for the gossip rags. They're always looking for the clicks, focus on the worst rumors, and don't care who they destroy to get dirt on them."

Brie stared at him. Why did he sound so bitter and angry? Had someone spread gossip about him? Could that be the reason his online presence appeared to be scrubbed? Once again, she realized she didn't really know that much about Cole.

Except he'd just put his fingers in her pussy and nearly

stroked her to an orgasm. Not a background check, but certainly a resounding testimonial.

She put some cheese on a cracker and leaned back on the seat to admire Cole's muscles moving beneath his shirt as he maneuvered the wheel and tacked into the wind. The late afternoon sun outlined his body, and she studied him.

Sexy? Check. Add gorgeous, funny, smart, and charming? Even more check marks.

She had no complaints, so she just needed to settle back and enjoy the prospect of an entertaining evening. She needed to bank the heat he'd inspired and wait for Cole to drop the sails. Then he could drop his pants.

Cole caught her studying him as she slowly licked her lips while gazing at him with a hunger she had no intention of hiding.

His jaw dropped, and she celebrated his reaction with a sip of wine. Then she slid her tongue around the edge of the glass, never moving her gaze from his.

She was rewarded when he gave a deep moan, probably thinking about items five and six, giving and receiving oral sex.

Brie hadn't even started to entice this man. He wanted to hear her scream his name when she came? She intended to get him so hot, he'd beg for release.

And he'd offered to negotiate some terms of their contract later. Brie sensed she wasn't the only one who wanted more than a no-strings-attached hookup.

TRUE CONFESSION: Female pleasure and passion are two of the most misunderstood feelings on the planet. Men desire women who display signs of wanting sex, including blushing, erect nipples, the moistening of lips, touching, and the use of suggestive language. Male desire often wants her to present herself as a wanton temptress while social norms judge her for that behavior. Somewhere between the virgin maiden and the whore, there's a healthy attitude supporting normal desire and sexuality for women. People should mind their own business and let nature take its course.

Chapter Fourteen

COLE

COLE STARED at the bright colors of the orange, yellow, and red sunset. He'd fought the temptation to follow Brie's breathless demand and drop the anchor right where they were. When she'd unbuttoned her shorts, he'd nearly swallowed his tongue.

Her compliance with his requests gave his dick what felt like an electrical jolt.

When she leaned back and rubbed her ass against him, every serious thought evaporated from his brain. He needed to touch her and finding her wet and willing sent his body into sensual overdrive.

It took every drop of his self-control to stop, take a deep breath, and focus on sailing the boat.

Brie was an enticing temptation he wouldn't, truthfully, *couldn't* resist. He knew he had to go slowly, if possible and he could maintain control. Her amendments to the consent form told him her confession of being less sexually experienced were true.

He wanted Brie, and the things she hadn't experienced

presented an opportunity. He looked forward to introducing her to some sensual play.

It made him even more eager to lower the sails, drop the anchor, and moor the boat. He sensed Brie was a willing and creative partner who seemed to be unaware of her raw sensuality.

A partner who had fueled his fantasies for the past few weeks. The first day he'd visited the library, he'd been expecting a mousy, middle-aged, bespectacled librarian who wore sensible shoes and dowdy clothes.

Cole had expected a cliché. Instead, he discovered a blue-haired, curves-in-all-the-right-places woman with a sense of fun and a knack for making him laugh.

He growled when he noticed some of the old men ogling her substantial cleavage as she bent over to answer a question. Cole wanted to punch several of the teenage boys who stared at her ass when she crossed the room. He'd even felt a flash of jealousy when a preschooler snuggled onto her lap, imagining what it would be like to pull her onto his own lap and nuzzle her against him.

Before they'd exchanged a single word, he had fantasized about her. That shocked him because he'd never developed a possessive, lustful craving for a woman before.

The more times they met, the more it grew into a gnawing, almost painful need.

After she hugged him in his office, he'd fought every urge to ply her with kisses, gently remove her clothing, and explore the supple curves of her body. He wanted to quench his erotic hunger by plunging into her again and again until she was too satiated to move.

Cole swallowed and worked to keep his mind focused on sailing into Saka'am Cove. There'd be a full moon tonight, and he intended to take advantage of it to create the most romantic mood possible.

His favorite fantasy, to fuck Brie on the deck with the stars above them, had an excellent chance of coming true. He could easily imagine her voluptuous body glowing in the silver moonlight.

He shook his head to clear it, then pushed a button to furl the jib and waited to drop the mainsail. After lowering it, he set the anchor. The ease of mooring this boat was the reason he loved it so much. It didn't require a crew to sail it and once you reached a destination, it was easy to moor.

Cole stared at the opening to the lower deck. He adjusted himself, aware his erection would still be visible. Even the evening breeze couldn't cool him down. Brie had lit a fire that wouldn't be quenched until he finally pushed deep inside of her.

He hopped down the steps and crossed to the galley, expecting to see her seated at the table in the salon. He glanced into the nearest cabin and saw her bag still sitting on the bed. A few of her things were tossed across the duvet.

Cole turned to look in the opposite direction and noticed the closed door to his cabin. He caught the flap of a piece of paper from the corner of his eye.

A stapled copy of the Sexual Consent Form sat on the table, held down by a nearly empty wine bottle. It was signed and dated. Several items were crossed out, and there were a couple of question marks next to the things they'd discussed.

Cole didn't even realize he'd exhaled a long sigh of relief. Even after their discussion, he wasn't sure she'd sign the agreement.

And as much as he hated to ask her to agree to it, he honestly believed it offered protection for her, too. He took a few steps to knock on the door to his cabin.

"You're the captain. You don't need my permission to come into your own room."

He slid the door into its notch and enjoyed the sight of

Brie lounging across his bed. She'd discarded most of her clothing, and the display of creamy skin against her dark green bra and thong shoved his dick into a full, hard erection again.

Night after night, he'd planned how he'd seduce her. He imagined ways to use his mouth to kiss her, trace down her skin, suckle her tenderest parts, and then slip his tongue between the lips of her pussy to tease her until she came for the first time.

"You gonna stand there gawking at me all day, sailor?"

He threw himself next to her on the bed, turning to gaze into her eyes. "I don't get into port often, so I need to take advantage of every opportunity." He wiggled his eyebrows.

She snorted. "I'm inclined to believe you're welcomed aboard wherever you go."

He leaned his head on his hand as he locked his elbow and stared into her eyes. "I don't screw around, Brie. I haven't been with anyone for a while. To be honest, I'm not even tempted much. At least I wasn't until…"

She rubbed her palm against his chin, tracing the scruff that lined the lower part of his face.

"Until?" she repeated.

He reached out to pull her closer. She slipped a leg over his and he held her ass to nudge her until her pussy was tight against his crotch.

"Until I visited the library and discovered a magical mermaid librarian worked there."

As he explored the soft skin of her lower back and inhaled the delicate floral scent that clung to her, he noticed a teasing light dancing in her gray eyes as she looked at him.

"So, did you visit the library, hoping to capture this rare creature?"

Cole twisted her back against the bed, while covering her body with his. "She seemed elusive at first, but I waited her out."

He slid his hand over the lacy fabric of her bra. "I should have known a mermaid would wear something enticing. I hope you brought a bag full of this stuff with you."

She shifted beneath him. "Mermaids appreciate beauty, art, and a sensual aesthetic. It's because we're intimately connected with water. Anyway, I enjoy feeling silk, lace, and satin against my skin."

Her nipples poked against the fabric of her bra as he continued to toy with them. She shifted her hips and his dick rubbed tight against her. His vision darkened for a moment as he enjoyed the surge of heat that rocketed through him.

"And it's lovely skin, indeed."

"So, what happened to your mermaid?" she asked, while moving her hands to slide against the muscles of his upper arms.

"I discovered that magical mermaid librarians have one weakness."

"Only one?"

He moved his hand across her belly, and her breath gave a hitch.

"I suspect there are many, but this is the one they can't seem to resist."

"Don't keep me waiting. Confess. What is it?"

He grinned at her. "A question."

"You are a tease, aren't you?" Her voice was sultry. "I could ask you to stop, but my willpower to resist you has vanished."

He shifted his weight off her and stretched on the bed. His expression was a hopeful smirk.

"Are you sure about this?"

She seemed to consider the question before answering. "I've been fairly sure all week that sexy time with you was what I wanted tonight. Any doubts I might have held evaporated within the past hour."

"And you signed the form."

"I did," she whispered.

He slid one finger beneath the string of her thong and pulled until she was naked below the waist. His mouth settled on the fabric covering one nipple, and he sucked as his fingers explored the opening between her legs.

She twisted on the bed.

"Tell me what you want," he demanded.

"I want you to fuck me. Fast. And hard." Her answer was a husky demand. "Now."

She took a ragged breath and licked her lips. He understood the invitation, and his mouth captured hers with a kiss. She opened to him, and he pushed his tongue into her mouth, licking, plunging, demanding a response.

She swallowed and took a deep breath when he lifted his mouth from hers. Her lips were swollen, and her cheeks burned a bright, hot pink. Her dilated pupils signaled how aroused she'd become.

Brie was a siren, a vixen, an enchantress.

His dick was hard and heavy and ready to fulfill her request. He stood to yank his shorts and boxers off. When he joined her again on the bed, he noticed her frown as she stared at his erection.

"Brie? Is there something wrong? Do you want to stop?"

He'd fucking throw himself off the side of the boat if she said yes.

She jerked her head up to meet his gaze. He was sure of it now. Her eyes were wide, she nibbled on her lip, and she appeared concerned.

He glanced down. Her gaze followed his to stare at his dick. A frown shadowed her face again.

"I've never been with anyone who is so, well...you know."

He stared at her. "What?" He knew what she was talking about, but his ego wanted to hear her say the words.

She pointed. "So..."

He fought a grin. "So—what?"

"Prodigious?" she suggested, holding back a smile.

He glanced down again. "Are you saying my dick is amazing? Impressive? Or unusual? I'll be concerned if the answer is unusual."

"Too big," she explained, sliding back away from him. "Enormous."

He grabbed her leg to pull her beneath him again. "Nonsense. I'll make you so wet it won't be a problem."

She squirmed beneath him. "Wait. Stop!"

That fucking word again.

He stopped, releasing her as she twisted to the top of the mattress. She folded her legs to sit cross-legged, and Cole gained a perfect view of the lips surrounding her pussy.

She was lightly furred. It fired his blood again.

"I brought some lube, so I'll go get it and we can fix the problem."

His lust-clouded brain cleared for a moment. What the hell? She had to be messing with him.

"What problem?" Before he could assure her again it wouldn't be a problem, she shimmied off the mattress and scurried out the door. While he enjoyed the view of her round ass cheeks as she hurried away, his frustration mounted.

He knew he could make her wet and ready with a few swipes of his tongue. They didn't need lube. Could she be intentionally trying to embarrass him? He didn't think she had that much guile.

Cole glanced down again. He'd never thought of himself in terms of the word "prodigious." Of course, he'd seen enough porn to know he was well-endowed.

"Enormous" seemed like an exaggeration.

Although, she'd admitted she didn't have a lot of experience, so possibly compared to her other lovers, he might be...much larger? It thrilled him to think so.

He heard her in the galley, and she returned with a glass of wine in one hand and clutching a small plastic bottle with the other.

She handed the wine glass to him. He took a gulp, not sure what to expect as she joined him again on the bed.

After she opened the bottle and poured some into her hand, she set the bottle on the shelf next to them. She rubbed her hands together and reached for him. She stroked his dick with smooth, delicate movements. He turned hard and throbbing again in seconds.

Before she slid beneath him again, she removed her lace bra. Her nipples were hard pebbles, and he couldn't resist putting his mouth on her to suck, taste, and tease her.

She moaned, and he knew that if he didn't fuck her soon, he'd probably end up losing it and spurting all over her belly.

When he spread her legs and slipped two fingers into her, he found her dripping wet. He rubbed her clit, and she moaned. Then he removed the fingers, lifted her ass to make an adjustment and then adjusted his hips to slowly slide into her.

She gasped, but didn't tell him to stop, so he pushed deeper. She responded with a sudden puckering of her lips, followed by a faint sound of surprise. Her eyes went wide.

He pulled back. "Should I stop?"

"No," she responded. "Just—go a little slower."

He nodded, unable to tell her he perched on the edge, fighting a climax. Stopping took every drop of self-control he possessed.

His heart raced. Finally, years or maybe only a few seconds later, she put her hands on his arms.

"Now, fast and hard!" she demanded, her voice relaying her need.

To be honest, he couldn't take her any other way. His hips

pushed against her, pressing down, twisting, parting her in his eagerness to be inside of her.

Tight, slippery heat held his full length. Her soft moans as he increased the tempo fed his lust. He positioned one of her legs on each of his shoulders as he kept thrusting, pushing, wild with the feel of her clamping down on his cock plunging deep inside of her.

He'd test her limit, and he waited for her to ask him to slow down again. She bucked beneath him as her eyes closed and she matched each of the powerful strokes into her with a lift of her hips.

Cole stood on a precipice, then his body throbbed, shattered, and he lost control as one last thrust brought him to several long, pulsating, throbbing moments of release. He kept pumping into her, as wave after wave of pleasure rolled through him.

He maintained the rhythm until she gasped his name as she climaxed.

"*Cole.*" Not exactly a scream. He'd need to work on that later.

If he recovered sufficiently.

He shifted to her side when she finally seemed to catch her breath, then he pulled her closer. She snuggled against him, and they breathed in the earthy scent of primal sex.

As he gently kissed her eyelids, he wanted to tell her something, but his throat felt as rough as sandpaper. He coughed to clear it and stared at her.

She opened her eyes as her mouth curved into the smile of a satisfied feline who had been given a large bowl of cream. She gave a deep sigh of contentment.

"That was—so good, Cole. Unbelievably wonderful and so, so satisfying." She lifted one arm to tuck it behind her head. "Every bone in my body feels as though it's been liquefied."

"You are amazing." He considered her for a moment. "Shit, did I hurt you? I reached a point where I couldn't stop. Did you ask me to?"

He'd promised to respect her wishes, to listen to her if she told him to stop. Shit. He might already have proven to her that he couldn't be trusted to keep his word.

"I'm fine." She stroked his chest, igniting tiny flames of heat to warm his blood. He'd just had the best sex of his life and was already getting aroused again.

Brie was like an aphrodisiac. Now that he'd fucked her, he wondered if there would ever be a time when he wouldn't crave her touch, want her, *need* her.

Cole had a sense the more they had sex, the more he'd desire her. The idea of a serious relationship with Brie terrified him and thrilled him at the same time.

This had to be more than a one-night stand. Every word he'd said about keeping things casual now proved to be a lie.

"Did you offer to feed me as part of your trinity of seduction earlier?" she finally said.

He toyed with her still-erect nipple and enjoyed the softness of her breasts. "I believe I made that offer. How about I rinse off quick, then you can get cleaned up?"

She closed her eyes. "An excellent plan."

"You're going to take a nap, aren't you?" He couldn't hide the jealousy in his voice.

"I am, and you'll wake me up when dinner is nearly ready. I'll shower and we'll partake of the amazing feast you've prepared for me." Her voice held a soft whisper, signaling her languor.

"What if it's bologna sandwiches?"

"Don't care..."

He kissed her and climbed off the bed, tossing a soft blanket over her.

She snuggled beneath it. He wanted her to rest. A brief

nap would help her stay awake later. He was eager for their next session. In his imagination he'd already titled it *Slow and easy*.

After a quick shower, he grabbed a beer from the galley and went topside. Popping the top, he took a deep drink. He'd been parched, and the beer tasted so good.

Leaning back on the upholstered bench in the cockpit, he watched the shades of a colorful sunset slip across the western horizon. The outline of the pine and cedar trees on the island looked like sentinels guarding the wilderness. He thought of Brie and his heart filled with an emotion he'd never expected.

Cole took a deep breath of the sea-scented air. A soothing sense of contentment suffused his body.

He'd do everything he could to take care of her. To cherish her for as long as he could.

He felt absolutely, completely happy. The thought jolted him. He stared at the darkening sky as Virgo appeared low on the horizon.

This cove was one of his favorite places. He'd expected they'd be the only ones anchored out here. The island was protected and required a special permit to land on the beach. Although he didn't moor there tonight to explore the landscape.

He'd much rather explore the expanse of Brie's passion and desire. They'd dispensed with foreplay earlier, but he'd make up for it later tonight. He had a vast repertoire of things he wanted to do to her.

After he finished his beer, he headed down the steps. Since he wasn't much of a cook, he'd asked Raina to help him prepare one of Brie's favorite meals. Frying scallops in butter, and reheating rice pilaf in the microwave didn't seem too challenging. Raina had created two salad masterpieces and a fresh fruit plate. He'd grabbed Nanaimo bars for dessert from the Teddy Bear Bakery since Raina informed him they were Brie's favorite.

It had been fun to think of details designed to please and impress Brie. He opened a bottle of Pinot Grigio chilling in the cooler and grabbed a small floral arrangement of dark pink roses for the table.

Her fondness for lacy underthings excited him. He intended to research the most luxurious brands of women's underwear in the world and let her order whatever she wanted.

The door to his cabin slid open and she appeared in the small space. The ends of her blue hair were damp, and a towel wrapped completely around her body. She nodded at him, and her cheeks colored to the rosy blush he loved seeing.

"I need to get dressed." She started toward the cabin he'd assigned her, but he grabbed her midway and yanked at the towel, letting it unwrap.

"You're so beautiful, honey. Don't hide it."

He grinned at her, and her lips turned up into a teasing smile.

"So, you weren't disappointed? I'm a bit too curvy to meet the current standards of beauty."

His laugh echoed in the small space. He let his gaze slowly wander down her body, then he pulled her closer to him. He put her hand on the fabric covering his dick.

"This is what you do to me, mermaid."

She stared at him, her gray eyes darkening to a stormy hue and her eyebrows knitting into a frown of confusion. "Cole, I don't understand what this is, but I plan to enjoy whatever we're doing for as long as it lasts."

"We can talk about it later." He kissed her. "I need to feed you, and I have a nefarious plan to ply you with alcohol so I can have my way with you again later."

"I don't think that will be necessary." She picked up the towel and crossed to the cabin where she'd left her bag. She pulled some items out and he watched her dress from the corner of his eye as he fried scallops.

When she pulled on a navy-blue top and a matching pair of tiny lace panties, his mouth turned to dust. He was as parched as if he'd spent hours walking across a desert. She added the pair of denim shorts she'd worn earlier.

Temptation and lust made blood rush through his body like a tidal wave roaring across the land. He had another hard, full erection, and they hadn't even eaten dinner yet.

"I think you're supposed to turn those over before they smoke," she suggested, and he jerked back to reality. He carefully flipped the scallops.

"Is there anything I can help with, like cooking those to save them from being burned to a crisp?"

He stepped aside and handed her the spatula. "I believe you'd be better at this. My cooking skills are still pretty basic."

"You own a great cookbook, and if you need to discover more recipes, the library has an entire section of 6.4.0.s."

"You're talking librarian to me, and it's sexy as hell."

She leaned back against him as they shared the tiny space. "I understand you're happy to see me, but I'm starving. You'll have to wait."

"Not a problem," he replied, even though being close enough to enjoy her enticing, primal scent drove him mad. "I do have *some* self-control."

"Really?" She turned to quirk a smile at him.

He pushed a button to raise the microwave from the cabinet that stored it.

Brie's mouth opened in surprise. "I didn't even know that was there. No wonder you live on this boat. You have everything you need in a beautiful, compact space. And if you get bored, you put up the sails and just sail away."

"It's nice to be on the water." He grinned at her. "Nicer to be here with you."

He already sensed when she wasn't here with him, he'd miss her.

A nudge of remorse smashed into him. He'd never told her he lived on the boat. She just assumed he did, and he didn't tell her otherwise.

It was another lie of omission. And he sensed she'd be mad as hell when he finally confessed who he was, where he lived, and his involvement with the library grant. He already understood how much she valued honesty. From their conversations, she didn't have a high opinion of some of the wealthy people who visited the island.

Cole knew how entitled some rich people could be, as if others existed only to serve them. He'd once been an arrogant asshole, but he'd tried to escape from that world when it felt empty and left him with nothing but painful memories.

He'd worked hard to deal with his past, and the times he'd shared with Brie had healed some old wounds. She'd taught him how to trust again.

She arranged the scallops on individual plates and the buzzer on the microwave told him the rice was ready. "Spoon some of this on our plates and I'll grab our salads and fruit," he told her.

Brie followed his directions and settled at the table. She bounced on the divan. "Does this turn into a bed?"

He nodded as he set the other dishes on the table and returned to the galley area for the wine.

"I've never used it, though. Most of the time, I don't have overnight guests on the boat. Sailing is my escape and I treasure private time alone."

She spooned slices of cantaloupe and blueberries onto her plate and settled a napkin on her lap. "That sounds lonely. If I had a boat like this, I'd throw a party every weekend."

"It's more like a fortress of solitude for me." He poured

wine into their glasses. "I search for uninhabited places and drop anchor. It's a great way to find some peace."

She cut a scallop in half and forked part of it into her mouth. She closed her eyes, swallowed, and then exhaled. "Every time I eat one of these, I can taste the ocean in my mouth. They're one of my favorites."

Her eyes slanted as she stared at him. "Did you research my favorite foods? Who tattled on me, my mother?"

"Actually, it was Raina. She even told me Nanaimo bars are your favorite dessert."

"Are you telling me there's some of that ambrosia of the gods on this boat?" Her eyes glinted with delight.

"Maybe." He grinned. "You'll have to wait until later to see. It could be a sweet surprise."

She shifted to present him with a view of her cleavage. "I have some sweet surprises in store for you too, Mr. Moore."

Her voice held a seductive purr, and he wanted to push the dishes off the table and take her again. Except she was blissfully enjoying her meal and there was no way he'd interrupt the obvious pleasure she took in eating some of her favorite foods.

Watching her eat in the glow of the boat's lights was almost as much fun as seducing her.

Almost.

In a while, they'd go topside to lie on the mattress he'd spread on the sundeck. They could gaze up at the night sky. He looked forward to stroking her skin, watching her cheeks turn pink with that arousing blush, her nipples grow hard and pebbled, and the delightful cleft between her legs become wet and eager to take him again.

There'd be no rush, and he'd take his time. He planned to watch her arousal intensify as he used his mouth to make her eager for him again. When they returned to Horseshoe Island, they might be exhausted, but the effort to please her in every way was worth the trouble. And it would guarantee she wouldn't forget their night together, or him.

Cole planned to create some delightful memories, hoping after a few days, it would be easy to convince her to keep seeing him.

Now that he'd discovered how sensual Brie could be, he wanted to be the one showing her how to explore her own sexuality.

He was turning into a damn greedy bastard who knew what he wanted, and he'd make damn sure that he got it.

TRUE CONFESSION: The hardest thing to do when everything seems perfect and wonderful is to avoid the "BIG BUT" echoing in your head. Telling yourself it's only temporary sows the seeds of doubt that are planted until they grow to become a self-fulfilling prophecy. You can transform that negative story into a positive one. You might never find a happy ever after, but you can be happy for now and see what happens.

Chapter Fifteen

BRIENNE

IT DELIGHTED her that Cole attempted to include her favorite foods in their dinner. His attention to detail impressed her.

"I'll clean up in here," she offered.

"No way," Cole said, grabbing her plate. "You're my guest. You won't be pulling galley duty."

She started to protest, but he gave her that dimpled smile and she relaxed and decided to enjoy herself. If a man wanted to wait on her, she should let him do it.

"You can go up top to watch the last of the sunset. I'm going to enjoy a whiskey when I'm done here. What can I bring up to you?"

She considered the question for a moment. "I'd like a whiskey too. I don't drink much, so I'll try it."

"Take the pillows and extra blanket from your cabin. It can get chilly on the water this time of day."

He filled the tiny sink with soapy water.

Brie did as he instructed and grabbed the blanket. She added her silk robe to the pile in her arms and climbed the steps.

A breeze had stirred up, and the warmth drained from the day as twilight edged toward night. She discovered a large mattress pad stretched across a portion of the deck. She tossed the pillows and blanket on it, then donned her robe.

The woods on the island echoed with birdsong, and the slow lapping of the waves created a calming sound. If Cole planned more sexy time with her, she wouldn't resist.

In fact, if their last round of sex served as a sign of what might happen later, she planned to be an eager participant.

She flopped onto the thick pad and stretched. This would be a wonderful place to sit with a book and enjoy some sun. She hoped to have time to test that theory tomorrow.

For now, she leaned back to relax and enjoy the comforts offered by a man who wanted to take care of her. The guys she'd dated had always expected her to listen to them talk, mostly about themselves, support them in whatever they wanted to do, and meet their needs, even if it meant ignoring her own.

She could get used to being with a man considerate enough to think of her first. At least for a weekend. She didn't want anyone controlling her, but someone willing to put his own needs aside to consider what she'd like was a pleasant change.

Cole arrived at the top of the steps, holding two glasses.

"I like my whiskey straight, so I made yours that way. Would you prefer it on the rocks or mixed with something?"

"I haven't had enough whiskey to know how I take it, so let me try it your way."

He handed her the glass and slid down to stretch out next to her.

She sniffed the liquid. "It smells like smoke."

"That's the peat. This is a sixteen-year-old scotch from Islay in Scotland, and it's known for its earthy taste. They dry the barley with peat fire. Wet your lips with the whiskey, then take a small sip."

"It's burning a little going down."

He took a sip from his own glass and grinned. "If you'd rather have wine, or beer, or a mixed drink, I'll get it for you."

She took another sip and enjoyed the taste that offered a touch of oak flavor.

He plumped the pillow behind him and pulled the blanket over their legs. They watched the sunset, and she didn't feel a need to make conversation as they enjoyed the peace. She understood the reason he'd chosen this place as an escape.

Finally, she turned to him. "Thank you."

He gazed down at her. "For?"

"Everything. Helping to arrange the photo shoot today, inviting me out here on your boat, that amazing dinner, this sunset." She waved a hand. "It's all been wonderful."

"You left out something important." The edges of his mouth lifted into a proud grin, exposing the dimple at the edge of his mouth.

She licked her lips, and his green eyes shadowed into a darker hue.

"Thank you for that, um, *unforgettable experience*, too."

"I've never heard sex described that way, but for me, it's a fair description."

"I agree." She lifted her glass. "To unforgettable experiences." They clinked their glasses together.

He glanced at the opening at the top of her robe. "What do you call that silky thing? It's not a bra. Is it a corset?"

"It's called a camisole. There's no padding like a bra or lacing like a corset. This is one of the more comfortable fancy things to wear."

"So, you're like a magician, pulling sexy underwear out of your bag instead of a rabbit out of a hat?"

"I warned you, mermaids can be sensual creatures that crave soft, silky, beautiful things."

"And fluffy," he added.

She turned to see the laugh lines crinkle at the edge of his eyes.

"Definitely fluffy," she responded. She took another sip of her whiskey, and she didn't feel a burn this time. In fact, she felt cozy, relaxed, and imagined she grew a bit fluffy herself.

He shifted closer to her, and she leaned against him, enjoying the firm muscles of his chest and arms. For a guy who worked inside at a desk, he was wonderfully chiseled.

"You must spend a lot of time at the gym," she said. "You're really firm all over."

She caught the gurgle of his laugh and looked up.

"Very firm, nearly stiff, I'd say." His grin expanded.

"You know what I mean." She pretended to punch him.

He pulled her closer, and she put one leg over his. His thigh muscles seemed like they could be carved from stone. He lowered his arm to put his palm on her ass, then squeezed gently.

"And you know what *I* mean."

"For all the intimacies of today, you lifting, and carrying me around at the photo shoot, coming out here alone together and having sex, we really don't know much about each other."

"You're the manager at the library and live on a farm." He downed the rest of his whiskey. "Your best friends are mermaids, and your father owns a Lamborghini tractor."

"That's it? According to your research, those are the most important things about me?"

"Also, your father has a scary-looking shotgun that everyone pretends doesn't work, but I have serious doubts about that rumor."

She repeated the punch, this time hitting his arm.

"You also own some very nice undies, and after my

unforgettable experiences with you this afternoon, all I can think about is how much I look forward to the next experience."

She narrowed her eyes and stared at him for a moment.

"With you," he assured her. "We should have so many amazing, unforgettable adventures together. Lots of them."

"Better," she said. "Now, let's see what I know about you. You work for three rich guys who want to give the library a million dollars. Which is an amazing, almost unbelievable thing. You have a lovely boat, and I assume you live on it."

She lifted her chin to glance at him.

"Good, so far," he finally said, nodding.

Why did he look uncomfortable? Like there was more to the story. Which, of course, there must be.

"You also have a big, impressive...black, macho-man truck."

"Agreed. My truck is so big and so macho."

She narrowed her eyes at him. "And a prodigious, impressive..."

"Exactly. What else do you want to know?"

"Where did you grow up?"

He sighed, then gazed off into the darkening shadows of the trees on the island. "On a potato farm in Eastern Washington. My father and grandfather worked the land that's been in my family for generations. They raise beef cattle too."

"So, that's why you're so interested in my father's tractor?"

"You've discovered my secret quest." He gestured with his hand to his forehead. "I'm courting you, my lady, hoping he'll include that tractor in your dowry. Tell me honestly, is there any hope?"

"No." She pouted her lips and slid him a sly glance.

"There's absolutely no chance. My father will never part with that tractor."

His face shifted into an expression of woe. "I hope you realize you've shattered all my hopes and dreams."

"So, you left the farm to go to…?"

"The University of Washington, to major in business management. That's where I met…" He paused. "The guys who started the company that provides me with the luxuries of a macho-man truck and a pretty damn nice boat."

"The three geeks?"

"Yup." He nodded. "After the company sold, I started working at the bar. That pretty much sums up my life."

He yanked the blanket off his legs. "I'm going to get another whiskey. Would you like something?"

"Do you have any sparkling water?" She wrinkled her nose. "I think the booze is catching up with me. When the gals party, I'm regarded as the lightweight."

She shifted on the mattress to avoid seeing his response to her confession. She continued to sound inexperienced, boring, and unsophisticated.

"Now you've foiled my plans to get you drunk and have my way with you."

"You don't need to ply me with alcohol for that to happen, Cole. Just hurry back." She tried to make her voice sultry and inviting. At least she hoped it sounded a little bit sexy.

He quickly disappeared down the steps to the salon, and she heard him swear as he reached the bottom.

"You okay down there?"

"I stubbed my toe, but I'll probably survive."

She fluffed her pillow again and leaned back. The sun stood at the edge of the horizon, nearly ready to slip out of sight. A few stars appeared in the darkening sky, and she sniffed the air. The scent of sea salt and cedar filled her nostrils. If you added a touch of pepper, you'd have the earthy essence of Cole.

She inhaled deeply, realizing she'd remember today, and tonight, for a long time. Closing her eyes, she felt relaxed, and dreamy and...

Cole reappeared with a bottle of water for her and another tumbler of whiskey for himself.

She nodded her thanks, twisted the cap off the bottle, and took a deep drink before offering Cole a sympathetic pout.

"How's your toe?" she asked.

"I'm sure I'll need surgery when we get back to port, but for now, I'll ignore the pain." He gave her long-suffering puppy dog eyes.

"Surgery sounds serious for a stubbed toe. Are you quite sure about that diagnosis?"

"I don't play a doctor on TV, but it seems accurate. I suspect I'll need to distract myself from the pain tonight." Cole sipped his drink, then wiggled his eyebrows.

"Got any suggestions?"

She returned the cap to her bottle and set it aside. "How about I snuggle up against you like this?"

Brie moved back to settle against his side, putting her leg over his again. She rubbed against him like a cat seeking a pet.

Which pretty much described what she wanted.

He took her face in his hand, his fingers gently lifting her chin to position her perfectly, so he could cover her lips with his. The kiss was soft and beguiling, issuing an invitation.

She responded by lifting herself to put one leg on each side of him to settle across his hips. Then she leaned forward to position her silk-covered breasts against the cotton T-shirt covering his hard-muscled chest. She rubbed against him.

His beleaguered groan served as an ample reward for her actions. She nibbled at his lip before plunging her tongue into his mouth, thrusting, and pulling in an imitation of what she wanted him to do to her.

He matched her movements with his own tongue as he

plunged and swiped to open her mouth, dip further and explore.

"You taste like expensive scotch," he growled.

One palm started squeezing her ass before he slipped the other hand beneath the robe and caught the waistband of her shorts. He slowly unbuttoned them, and she wiggled to help him get them off.

Cole rubbed the fabric of her panties covering her mound. She'd considered going commando, but she enjoyed the idea of him undressing her. She wanted to make it part of the fun of foreplay. And he'd promised her they'd take it slow and easy this time.

He slid her up his body, moving his mouth to the deep crevice between her breasts. He fumbled with the tie on her robe. She enjoyed his growl of frustration when it didn't loosen immediately.

Finally, he spread the robe open and leaned back to stare at her. "You're luscious, Brie."

She wiggled to sit across his hips, and the breath he released held a moan. "Shit. If you keep that up, I won't last long."

"You promised me, Cole, and I'm going to hold you to that." She leaned forward to give him a tantalizing view. "We're gonna take this so, so slow. And easy."

With one swift movement, he lifted her off him and turned her onto her back. "Then we have to change positions."

Cole paused to remove his shorts and boxers before returning to his position, covering her with the heat of his body.

Night had darkened the sky, and the temperature continued to drop. Not that she felt chilled. With Cole's body covering hers as he swept his hand over the silky fabric covering her nipples, she felt like a heater blew hot air on her.

His mouth followed his hand, wetting the fabric of her camisole as he traced a pattern from licking one hardened nipple to the other.

Soft, mewling noises encouraged him as she arched her back, pushing against him. His thick, hard erection thrust against her, and she realized he was already hugely aroused. Emphasis on the huge.

A shiver slid up her spine.

"Are you cold?" His voice showed his concern, and it thrilled her. Even now, he thought of her comfort before his own.

"Not at all," she responded.

"We can go below," he suggested.

She traced a finger down his face, enjoying the rough texture of the scruff. "I want you to take me here, beneath the moon and stars, Cole."

A look of concern transformed into one of lusty hunger as the edges of his moss-green eyes darkened with desire. His tongue touched the edges of his perfect lips.

"I'd be delighted to do that, mermaid."

Brie pulled the bottom edges of the camisole up, and he took the hint. He tugged it over her head and tossed it aside. She only wore the lace panties now. He feasted his gaze on her nearly-naked form stretched out beneath him.

"I've fantasized about this—you on my boat, lying here— wanting me, waiting for me to fuck you."

He sounded breathless, and it filled her with pride to be the one capable of making this man want her so much.

Cole kneaded her breasts, his mouth swiping across her stiffened nipples. Flashes of heat whipped through her, and a slow, enticing throb built between her legs.

His mouth moved lower, licking down below her ribs, across her belly to even farther below, settling against the tiny piece of fabric between her legs. He licked at the wet spot covering her sensitive slit before dragging the panties down her legs.

He grabbed the pillow he'd been leaning on and positioned it beneath her, then yanked his shirt off.

When he returned to his task, he parted her with several fingers. She gasped when his tongue found her tender, sensitive clit.

Brie lifted her hips to push herself against his probing, lapping, sucking mouth. She moaned louder as he spread her legs wide, holding her as a prisoner of fervent desire and desperate need.

He gorged on her as if she were a fine delicacy, and she climbed closer, inching toward an orgasm every second his mouth tortured her with delight.

Cole sensed it too, because he paused, and slid to one side. She could see he was heavily aroused, and she took his erection in one hand to slide her fist up and down the slick surface.

"I want to taste you, too." She moved to change her position, but he put his hand on hers. "Don't," he said, his voice a husky whisper. "Not this time. I'm too close. Just tasting you, that…"

Understanding, because of how near she'd been to her own satisfaction, she moved the pillow, but he stopped her. "Leave that there."

His intentions weren't clear, but everything so far with this man had been incredible. She didn't plan to interfere with his technique now.

He pointed at the bottle of water at the bottom of the mattress. "Can you hand me that?"

She watched as he took several sips.

When he gave it back to her and nodded his thanks, she took a drink, then tossed the bottle aside again.

Cole pulled her to him and slanted his mouth over hers in a demanding, aroused kiss from a male who clearly hungered for her body. It filled her with sensual power and roaring heat.

Settling back with the pillow positioned to raise her ass, she watched him.

"Do you want a lubricant?"

"I believe you've made me more than wet enough." She smiled at him. "I should have listened to you the last time, but I felt—intimidated."

A slow grin spread across his face when he caught her meaning. He adjusted the pillow beneath her a bit more. Then he spread her legs as he leaned forward to position himself between them.

The tip of his erection slid into her opening, rubbed against her clit, then pulled back. He repeated the movement, pushing in a bit, then pulling out. It became a pattern, and the friction generating a slick, pulsing beat that fired her blood.

He paused, and she protested with a soft moan. When he lifted her legs to hook them over his shoulders, the sound faded into a breathless, "Oh."

A trickle of fear spiraled through her. He hadn't thrust into her entirely yet, and she could still recall how he filled her when they had sex earlier. She'd refused the lube this time, and she feared that might be a mistake.

"Don't worry, I'll go slow." He seemed to sense her concern. "But trust me, this is going to be so good for you. And we can stop anytime if it isn't."

She did trust him, so she relaxed. He penetrated her slowly, with patience and care, and as he filled her, he lifted her ass a bit more.

She let out a puff of air tinged with a hiss of pleasure. When he withdrew, then moved back into her with a hard thrust, she let her head fall back on the pillow behind her.

He started pumping harder, and she encouraged him with soft sighs and moans. He thrust deeper and faster while he twisted his hips and the tip of his cock hit a secret, hidden spot deep within her. She gasped as she stared up into his eyes.

"Cole. Ohmygodthisissofuckinggood."

Her voice ended with a deep moan, then the small sounds of pleasure she made blended with his deep breathing and words of encouragement.

"Take it all, baby. Let me ride you hard. I'm in so deep; you're so tight."

They were lost in the movements of him thrusting, pushing, lifting her ass to go deeper, and her response, begging him to keep going, to shove his cock further into her, assuring him she wanted him, she wanted it all, that she wanted more.

"Harder, faster," she whispered, and he complied with her demands.

She never wanted this to end, even as she could feel her body edging closer and closer to the gratification that lurked at the edge of her consciousness.

Finally, she reached her climax, her body shuddering as wave after wave of delight washed through her and she experienced the most incredible orgasm of her life. The intensity shocked her, and she couldn't control the noises she made, signaling her satisfaction. The night sky above shattered as ripples of pleasure smashed through her body. She stared up at Cole's face framed by the Milky Way as she clamped tightly around him.

Seconds later, he groaned out his own satisfaction. Spasm after spasm emptied into her as Cole's face contorted into an expression that reflected the pleasure when he found his release. He kept thrusting, and pouring into her. Time seemed suspended in this magical place.

Finally, he collapsed next to her, his chest heaving as one arm covered his face.

A few minutes later, he pulled the blanket to cover them, then he patted a spot closer to him.

She removed the pillow beneath her and tossed it to the side. He'd taught her an important lesson about angles, positioning, and pressure on the right spot.

"That was..." The deep rasp of his voice betrayed his emotion. "Amazing? Earth shattering? Cataclysmic?"

"All the above and more," she whispered.

"Oh yeah," he replied.

The waves washed against the shore, and the boat gently rocked. A soft breeze stirred the night air.

"Are we going to sleep out here?" she finally recovered enough to ask.

"Nope. We're going to just lie here together and stare up at the night sky for a while. Then we'll go below, share a nice warm shower, and enjoy your favorite dessert before going to bed."

It all sounded wonderful, especially the part about the chocolate dessert. But would she be sleeping in her cabin tonight, or sharing his bed?

All she could do was ask. "Do you want me to sleep with you? I mean, it's fine if you don't want me to, if it's more comfortable for you alone in your own..."

Opening his eyes, he stared at her. "I'd prefer to share my bed with you, Brie. That's what *I* want. It's up to you, though."

She snuggled closer to him. "I want to sleep with you. You put off an incredible amount of heat so I can set my cold feet on you to warm them up."

"That'll probably wake me up. I'm a pretty light sleeper." His hand moved down her side, stroking her skin.

"And once I'm awake, it's really hard for me to relax and get back to sleep." His mouth curved into a mischievous smile.

She slid her hand over his chest. "Then I guess we'll just have to figure out some kind of sleep aid for you."

His grip on her tightened. "You are a very naughty librarian!"

She put her hand on his heart and felt the beat as she closed her eyes.

"You have no idea, sir."

TRUE CONFESSION: When someone takes the time to learn more about you and tries to do things for you to make you happy, you should be grateful. Demonstrating that gratitude is important to furthering a relationship, because no one wants to feel their work is unappreciated. The greater the effort, the more appreciative one should be.

Chapter Sixteen

COLE

COLE WOKE WITH A RAGING HARD-ON. A soft, round ass snuggled up against his dick, so it didn't surprise him. He inhaled deeply, enjoying a floral perfume mixed with Brie's individual scent that immediately added to his arousal.

His conscience debated with his lust-addled brain about waking her up or letting her sleep. He could ignore the overwhelming urge to take her again or slowly wake her with his touch.

When he slid one hand between her legs, a finger gliding against her opening while rubbing the outside of the slit, she exhaled. She might be dreaming. Hopefully, an erotic fantasy that he could add to with his touch.

He continued rubbing her pussy, and she rewarded him by shifting to give him more access to the sweet cleft between her legs. He took advantage of her adjustment, placing a finger to rub against her clit.

She moaned softly, so he kept fondling her.

"Cole," she murmured in a husky whisper. "What are you doing?"

He pushed his rigid arousal against the curve of her ass. "I'll stop if you want me to," he offered.

"No!" she responded. "Don't stop. I want to—I mean—I like it." Her voice sounded languid and breathy.

He grinned, then turned her so he could caress a breast while still stroking her between the legs. She leaned even further back into him, clearly enjoying his touch.

When he inserted several more fingers into her, pumping with each stroke, she rubbed her ass against his erection, twisting her hips against him, clearly issuing an invitation.

As she grew wetter, he adjusted her body to position her right leg across his thigh. He slipped into her slowly, taking his time, enjoying the tight pressure surrounding his dick. As he paused, he appreciated the pulse of her body as her tight inner muscles stretched to accommodate him.

He pushed again, still moving slowly, taking his time to fill her. When she lifted her ass up against him, he pulled her against his hips, gently thrusting deeper.

He kept up the rhythm, moving in and out of her while shifting his hand from teasing her hardened nipples to toying with her clit. She encouraged his movements, as her hips arched back in a tempo that matched his measured thrusts into her.

Cole quickened the pace, fighting the urge to flip her onto her stomach and plunge even deeper into her. He wanted to bury his dick to the hilt, feel his balls tight against her pussy, but he recognized the need to move deliberately.

He stopped to take a deep breath, and she moaned her objection. "Please," she whispered, "don't stop."

He resumed the slow, excruciating pleasure of fucking her with gentle restrained movements. Then she pushed back hard against him.

"Faster!" she demanded.

He increased the pace until she panted each breath. His

control barely held as he moved in and out of her. Her inner muscles tensed, and she cried out his name. Her body shivered with her release as her orgasm clenched tight around him. Finally, she stopped bucking back against him.

It only took another thrust for him to climax and spill into her with an explosive orgasm that made him groan with the pleasure of his release.

He pulled her closer, enjoying the way her body nestled against him. He kissed her neck, slipping the kiss down to her collarbone.

"Thank you," he said, his voice raspy from the sensual pleasure they'd enjoyed together. "I'm sorry I woke you so early."

Stretching back into the length of his body, she grabbed one of his hands and placed it on her breast.

"Do we have to get up now?"

"Absolutely not." He squeezed her full round breast gently. "You can sleep as long as you want."

"Good," she replied. "I'm going to stay here and enjoy the afterglow."

She pulled the coverlet over her shoulder and exhaled.

He put one arm across her and planted another kiss against her throat and closed his eyes. The sky had just started to brighten, so he decided to go back to sleep. He wasn't ready to abandon the private love nest they'd constructed out here on his boat. He wanted to keep her alone with him for as long as possible.

Later

A few hours later, he opened his eyes to sunlight glaring through the hatch above them. Brie's gentle breathing signaled she still slept. He stretched and glanced at her, aware it wouldn't take much to arouse him again.

Cole couldn't seem to contain his desire for her. This woman was a walking, talking aphrodisiac. He didn't want to resist her, and like a drug, the more she gave him, the more he wanted. He should be satiated, but the organ between his legs signaled otherwise. Aware he acted like an insatiable satyr, using her body for his base gratification, he fought the urge to wake her.

Of course, she clearly enjoyed their sex play too. He stared at her, the pastel blue hair spilling down her back, reminding him of her posing in the pool wearing her mermaid regalia.

He'd watched her pose as she swept her arms wide, thrusting her breasts forward and twisting her hips to move the tail in slow circles in the pool. The water slowed her movements until she tantalized him to the point of madness, yet he couldn't stop watching her. She was a fantasy come to life.

Now she slept next to him, and he knew he'd better get away from her quickly to avoid further temptation.

But as he climbed from the bed, she turned, and opened her eyes.

"Is it morning?"

"Yeah. I'm going to clean up, then make us some coffee."

Her gaze raked over his naked body as he slid the door open. Then she shifted her attention to his erection, and he wanted to apologize. "I can't seem to be near you without—"

"I'm delighted I arouse you so easily, Cole." Brie's mouth formed a beguiling smile. "It makes me feel incredibly sexy and powerful. And if I don't want to do something, I'll let you know."

She snuggled down into the blankets, moving to the warm place he'd just vacated. "Now hurry. I need my morning coffee."

Cole opened the door to the head and grabbed the hand shower. As he turned on the faucet, he kept the water on the cool side.

His efforts didn't make him less inclined to wish his little mermaid were in there with him to slather soap on and get slick, wet, and aroused. His overactive imagination refused to take a break despite his best efforts.

Brie tantalized him, and he realized he had no resistance whatsoever to her charms.

Even more startling—he didn't want to resist her.

After washing and pulling on clean clothes, Cole knocked on his cabin door. "You can use the head now."

She answered with a soft groan. "I guess that means I need to get up."

It seemed Brie was not a morning person. Or he'd exhausted her with his carnal demands. He'd have to be more careful today, try to stop wanting to fuck her so much.

Which presented a challenge. At this point, he could barely look at her without getting an erection. The bulge in his jeans would be a clear sign to her that he struggled to maintain control.

And if he imagined the dainty lace-trimmed underthings she wore, he'd be lost. When she moved close enough to snuggle against him, lavish kisses on his mouth or rub against him, he'd lose it so fast he wasn't sure he'd be able to respond if she wanted him to take things slow again.

He needed to keep his distance from her despite his desire to pull her into his arms and stroke her soft skin, squeeze the full twin moons of her breasts, run his tongue down her belly, and finally lick her sweet pearl of a clit until she moaned out his name again and again.

His resolve collapsed when she opened the door to his cabin and stood staring at him as if she were reading his mind.

She stretched, her naked body a feast of soft curves and enticing sensuality. Her mouth formed a smile.

"Good morning, sailor." She shot him a playful look.

He answered with a deep, frustrated growl. Her seductive beauty turned him into a beast of carnality.

She laughed before stepping into the head. Clearly, she enjoyed tempting him, and he'd have to figure out a way to deal with the greedy lust that set every nerve in his body on fire. He needed to control his sensual hunger for her.

Or maybe not. She'd admitted she enjoyed having sex with him, and insisted she'd tell him when she didn't want to take part in something he suggested. He didn't need to treat her like a fragile doll, especially when she'd been such an eager participant so far.

And what should they do this morning before he pulled up the anchor? He planned to take her to his favorite restaurant for lunch, but he could change the reservation time.

Then he shook his head to clear it as the microwave dinged.

Working to distract himself, he poured hot water into the French press and inserted the plunger. While he waited for the coffee to brew, he opened the small fridge to take out a bowl of fruit, two containers of yogurt, and several muffins he'd purchased at the bakery.

The water turned off in the head, and he waited for Brie to reappear. When the door opened, she came out, once again wrapped in a huge towel.

A shot of disappointment smacked him. Despite all his inner promises to control his libido, he'd anticipated seeing her naked again.

"The coffee smells delicious," she commented as she made her way to her cabin. She opened her bag and pulled out various items of clothing.

He turned back to finish making coffee. "It's almost ready. Do you want to have breakfast up on deck?"

"Sure," she responded. "I'll get dressed and help you."

He nodded and arranged several mugs, a couple of bowls, and the muffins on a wooden tray. He added napkins and silverware.

When she joined him, he noticed the yoga pants she wore outlined every shapely curve of her body. A sweater bared one shoulder and her breasts thrust out, teasing him.

He indicated the coffee press, trying to keep his mind from wandering into fantasyland. "Would you bring that up? I've got everything else."

Brie nodded and followed him to the top deck. The cool morning air enveloped them in a light mist. He pushed the button for the table and waited to settle the tray on it.

She poured coffee in the mugs and joined him on the banquette. Sniffing the dark brew, she nodded.

"Perfect."

She glanced at their surroundings and closed her eyes. "I don't know how I'm going to stand leaving paradise to go home today. This has been so..." She opened her eyes and her gaze raked over him.

"Amazing."

His eyes focused on her luscious mouth. "Truly exceptional," he suggested, raising his eyebrows to punctuate his observation.

"Do you get to sail often?" She reached for the fruit and dished some into a bowl before adding a scoop of yogurt. "I mean, you're always on the water when you live on a boat, but you know what I mean."

Cole watched her pop a spoonful into her mouth, and when she licked her lips, he felt another jolt to his dick.

"Not as often as I'd like, but let me know when you want to come out sailing again, and I'll make the time." He glanced at the heavily wooded island in front of them. "We could go exploring."

"That's kind of you, but things are going to get pretty busy at the library. We're short a staff person and with the kids returning to school, there'll be the homework crowd and students needing tutoring."

He sipped his coffee. "Speaking of the library, we should make a plan to present the donation to the building committee when they review the plans submitted for the renovation. When do they meet again?"

"In two weeks. We could make a slide presentation, show the board members the plans your architect drew up." She paused. "I mean your employer's architect." She set her bowl back on the table. "Is there any chance the, um, geek guys could be there?"

Cole fixed his eyes on the horizon, hoping he hid his unease. "They prefer to remain anonymous. I'll be their representative."

"Okay," she said. "Then if you can send me the images of the design plan, I'll create the slides. We can work on it together."

He leaned back and sipped his coffee before answering.

"We can get together this week and work on it." He tried to make the tone of his voice sound less suggestive and more professional.

Brie poured more coffee into her cup, then swept her hand to move some hair that had fallen over her eyes. "I'm actually going to Seattle on Tuesday morning. There's training for librarians on ways to incorporate STEM activities into programming. I'll be gone all week."

Cole stared at her, his blood chilling. He refused to believe she'd be gone an entire week. A time frame that had never seemed so vast before now.

"How about if we go together?" he suggested. "I always

have something to do in Seattle, and my employer has an amazing apartment there."

She glanced away from him and frowned. "Your employer seems really generous with perks, but I'm actually staying with my brother. He's been busy, and I haven't seen him for a while."

Cole forgot to breathe. It felt as if someone had tackled him and pushed the air out of his lungs. He'd planned to see her at least once in the next few days, probably more. How could he survive being away from her for an entire week?

Even though until a month ago he didn't know Brie existed, the thought of her gone for a week made him miserable. How had she become so important to him in such a short time?

He didn't want her to see how her information affected him, so he gathered up the breakfast stuff and stood. "I'll take this down to the galley. We're going to stay out here for a while, then I'd like to take you to lunch before we go back to Dylan's place."

"That's nice of you, Cole, but you don't have to do that. I mean, if you need to get back, I understand."

She didn't understand how eager he was to be with her. She probably thought he only cared about sex, and that he'd planned the sailing trip as a hookup.

Maybe that's all she wanted. How the hell could he figure that out? He mulled that over before he settled the tray on the counter of the galley.

He looked up when she leaned down the open hatch. "Do you want me to clean up? You've been a thoughtful host, but I can help."

"There's not much to clean up. Enjoy the sun. We'll be in the gray soon enough."

Pouring out the remaining coffee, he rinsed the carafe

before setting the dirty dishes in the sink. He'd have plenty of time to wash them when they got to Dylan's place.

He'd parked his truck there, and when they got back, he'd drive Brie home. Since Sunday was slow at the bar now that tourist season had ended, he didn't even need to go to work today.

As Cole considered what she'd told him, he thought maybe a little distance this week might be a good thing. He would give her some space since they had the excuse of the library project to get together again. He'd stay busy while she went out of town. It'd work out fine.

She came down the steps, and he stared at her. His jaw fell. The yoga pants and sweater hugged every sweet, voluptuous curve of her body.

"It's still a little cool up there, so I'm going to grab a throw and my book. Yesterday, I imagined the place where we, um, we…"

She nibbled at her lip.

"Where we looked at the stars?" he suggested.

"Yes," she said with that sexy, breathy voice he wanted to hear over and over again.

"It looks like a perfect spot for sunbathing while I read."

Her cheeks turned a bright pink at the reference to the place they'd had sex the previous evening. He didn't know if he'd be able to control himself if he joined her on the sundeck. She was a delightful temptation.

"Sounds great," he offered. "I have a few chores to do, then I'll come up and join you."

She grabbed some items from her cabin and started up the steps again. He cursed himself for turning around to watch her climb to the top deck. Once again, he experienced a jolt of arousal so strong it nearly made him groan out loud.

Cole was tempted to bang his head against the counter. Bringing her out on the boat had seemed like a perfect opportunity to get to know each other better. And that seemed to have worked out well.

He'd been confident once they had sex, that annoying itch would be scratched, and he'd go back to his normal, slightly monk-like existence. They'd be able to plan the library donation without the lingering distraction of sexual tension acting like an electrical circuit jumping between them whenever they were together.

Instead, she'd turned him into an insatiable libertine who couldn't stop thinking about her, and sex, and having sex with her. His plan to get her out of his system resulted in a deeper attraction.

Brie fascinated him, enticed him, and snared him in a web of mutual pleasure. But she was more than a willing bed partner. She was funny, and interesting, and beautiful.

She dazzled him.

The urge to smash his head on the counter returned. He took a deep breath. This wasn't a problem that needed an immediate solution. He had a week to figure out how to manage things with her.

A week when he wouldn't be distracted by seeing her, or smelling her perfume, or touching her.

"Shit," he snarled. Everything about this week was going to suck.

TRUE CONFESSION: Every human who has ever made a brilliant plan will admit if it works out, they're as much a victim of fate as the person who makes no plan and lets the universe decide for them. Sometimes you must go with—shit happens.

Chapter Seventeen

BRIENNE

BRIE SAT on the upholstered settee watching Cole guide the sailboat closer to the dock leading up to the house where they'd held the mermaid photo shoot.

As much as she wished this weekend could last for a few more days, she knew they had to return to reality. She needed to focus on the library renovation, and she knew they'd already exceeded the limits of a professional business relationship. This thing between them had to remain private until they settled the details of the proposed donation.

Despite the amazing sex they'd shared, she didn't intend to endanger her position at the library. Any relationship between them needed to stay on business terms, at least for now, and somehow, she needed to make that clear to Cole.

Making an argument against something she wanted so much presented a challenge. One she didn't look forward to, but found necessary.

If she kept having sex with Cole and someone on the library board discovered they were involved, she could be accused of a conflict of interest. Or they might even suggest he coerced her into a sexual arrangement with the promise of a donation to the library.

She couldn't conceive of Cole doing something so disgusting, but it wouldn't matter to Marion Rush-Talbot. It was exactly the sort of thing she'd use to bully and threaten Brie.

Either way, it wouldn't look good for them to continue being together or to attract public attention. They needed to act with discretion and not let their lust-clouded brains take over.

She resisted the urge to nudge him aside and take over the wheel. She knew where that kind of enticement would end. He'd drop the anchor and before long they'd be back in the cabin below, naked and enjoying more sexy time.

Her nipples pushed against her white lace bra, and she shifted on the bench, aware of the familiar heat building between her legs.

It had occurred to her after lunch that a change of clothes might be a good idea. The strapless pastel dress left her shoulders bare and the V-neckline gave him a peek at her breasts, which were well exposed.

His eyes had glowed with longing when they'd walked to the restaurant. Oceana had a wonderful choice of seafood. She'd admired the Northwest lodge décor, with a blazing fire in a rough-hewn stone fireplace, burgundy painted walls, and an antique bar that stretched across one side of the building. White linen-covered tables suggested understated elegance, and she admired Cole's taste once again.

Today, he looked more polished in a linen jacket and khaki pants. He left the top few buttons of a brown and tan button-down shirt open, which gave her a perfect view of his throat and a tantalizing glimpse of his chest hair.

Their dinner was delicious, and she'd closed her eyes when

she tasted the first bite of the rich cheese sauce and perfectly cooked fish she'd ordered. Their conversation flowed easily, and he listened as she described her ideas for the library remodel.

Caleb never cared about her work, even though he'd often borrowed money from her with a vague promise to pay her back. Of course, that never happened. He'd lied about the loans, his band, his sexual fidelity, and pretty much everything else.

She'd been a silly, romantic fool, which meant she needed to slow things down with Cole. She already knew it would be easy to fall for him. He was funny, smart, and so good looking that she didn't blame the women in the restaurant who flitted their gazes over his face, physique, and beautiful smile.

Hell, if she hadn't been with the man, she'd have checked him out too. She was a big fan of male beauty.

She stirred from her musing as he turned the wheel and winked at her. His smile lit up his face.

And spread the warmth from the burn at her core to an ache in her breasts, to a need to feel his lips on hers again. She ignored the urge and took a sip of her sparkling water. She'd enjoyed the wine at the restaurant, but needed to trust herself to drive home after Cole dropped her off at the Ancient Ways Apothecary, in town.

The stiff breeze tousled his hair, and while she suspected her hair looked like a rat's nest, he looked even more inviting. She wanted to jump up and slide in front of him, like the first night on the boat. She'd lean into him, run her fingers through his hair, then outline his chiseled chest with her hands before unfastening his belt, unbuttoning his pants, and dipping her hand below to...

"I hope I'm not getting you back home too late."

His words interrupted her daydream. She sighed, realizing

if he even suggested they go down below to frolic one more time, she'd be receptive. He'd complained he couldn't stop thinking about her, and she'd been too embarrassed to admit her libido also switched into high gear around him.

She needed to learn to control that immediately! She'd clear her fantasies of being with Cole and keep their relationship professional.

He pointed at a small harbor where a sailboat that looked like his stood moored. She noticed the name on the back, *The Sea Dragon*.

"It looks like Dylan has company, so we'll motor in on the dinghy and pick up my truck without bothering him."

She nodded, afraid the panic of not seeing Cole again might be evident in her voice. Her throat felt scratchy and sore, and she swallowed the pleading words ready to spill out. She hated the necessity of informing him they had to avoid meeting each other in public, but she had no choice. She had to be honest with him.

He'd furled the sails and dropped the anchor with the aplomb of a seasoned sailor. She headed down below to grab her canvas bag, and he climbed down after her. She turned to see his gaze studying her carefully.

"So." He leaned back against the table in the middle of the salon. "We're back."

She had to be clear with him now. "I'll start organizing the presentation for the building committee." She avoided meeting his gaze. "Then you can add anything you need to explain your vision, um, your employer's vision, of the remodel and makerspace design."

"Sure. Sounds great. And we can meet again when you get back from Seattle."

It wasn't clear what he meant by "meet again," but her imagination took a wild turn and rewarded her with a vision of the two of them naked and rolling around on a bed. She forced her gaze from his cabin to meet his dark green eyes.

"We can talk this week, to get things organized, sort it out." Which was not at all what she'd planned to say to him.

"Sounds like a plan," he responded, before taking several steps toward her. He moved close, then closer.

The warmth of his body, the woodsy mixed with the sea scent that followed him, and the way he gently lifted her chin, enticed her. She wanted to resist him. *Or did she?* Her heart thumped and when his mouth sweetly touched her lips, Brie realized it would be nearly impossible to resist the powerful attraction that still crackled between them.

Now that they'd been intimate, it was even worse. She knew the pleasure his mouth, hands, and body could provide. She craved the sensual gratification they'd shared.

Using one arm to circle her waist, he pulled her so close, she was forced to put one leg across his muscular thigh. She didn't resist when his lips settled on hers.

This kiss wasn't a crushing demand for release; it was a lingering promise of more to come.

Cole slid a finger down her cheek. "I wanted to do that here, in private, because I'm sensing you're going to insist we don't meet like this again for a while."

He stopped tracing down her face to wait for her response.

"It's not professional," she huffed. It was a weak argument.

"I know, but I don't give a shit. What we have is so good. It's worth taking a chance, isn't it?"

There were so many things to consider, and she took a deep breath. "It's easy for you to say, but it's my job, my career, and my family's reputation at risk. I can't do anything embarrassing right now. I'm counting on getting the manager's job."

"And being with me would embarrass you?" His forehead crinkled into a frown and his mouth set with a grimace.

She had to touch him, even though she imagined the heat of his body might scald her fingers. He needed to understand what was at stake for her. She wrapped her hands around his thickly muscled lower arms.

"I've wanted to be the manager of the library for most of my life. I watched Violet, and dreamed of helping spread the gospel of books, stories, reading, and literature. This is my opportunity, and I can't jeopardize it because of an overactive sex drive and uncontrollable attraction."

"I have one question," he said. "Do you *want* to be with me?"

Brie stared into his eyes, realizing she could lie, but what good would it do? She'd insisted they needed to be honest with each other.

"I do." She took a step back, forcing him to release her as she dropped her gaze to the floor. "But the timing is all wrong. We're grownups, and we have to learn to put our responsibilities before physical gratification."

"Bullshit!"

Her head jerked up and her gaze caught his.

"Being a grownup means you find a way to do what you want, and be together. You overcome obstacles. I don't want to hide my attraction to you, but I will if it's the only way we can be together. I'll accept any terms except not being with you."

She swallowed at the intensity of his statement. He stood too close, making him too tempting, and it overwhelmed her senses as he towered above her. His physical presence clouded her judgment.

"We can talk about it, but please understand my problem. This isn't easy for me."

He nodded. "Good, because I want it to be a tough

choice. I need you to want me as much as I want you. Every day, every hour, every minute."

She didn't doubt that was already true, but it wouldn't help them resolve this issue for her to admit it. She fought the tears that flooded her eyes.

"I need time to think. Please, Cole."

He turned away from her as he nodded. "Just a warning. We're circling back to this conversation when you return."

"Agreed," she said, hoping for a magical solution to appear before that happened.

As if magical thinking ever actually solved any problems. Just because she pretended to be a mermaid didn't mean she could call up a sea witch to deal with her dilemma.

BRIENNE

A few days later

Brie stared at her computer screen as she waited for Cole to answer her call. They'd used video chats the past few nights to talk about the library project, and she'd promised to talk to him again tonight.

"Hey there, beautiful," he said as his face filled the screen. She recognized the backdrop. He was in his cabin on the sailboat. A familiar rush of desire rippled through her as she remembered the hours of pleasure she'd found there.

She coughed to clear her head.

"Are you sick?" The warmth of his concern for her smacked her in the chest, making her heart jump a beat. How the hell could she even imagine being able to resist this man?

"No, I'm fine." She leaned against the pile of pillows supporting her on the bed in her brother's guest room.

"Maybe a little dehydrated. The room we're training in is stifling. They can't seem to get the air conditioning to work right."

"I believe that's called 'conference hell' when you're stuck in a room you can't escape from and suffering from stagnant air and boring ideas."

She shook her head. "The ideas and resources we're discussing are amazing. I can't wait to implement some of the STEM programs I've learned about."

He looked disappointed. "I hoped it was so dull you'd be coming home early."

"No such luck. My brother planned a party for tomorrow night. I'm supposed to meet all his political friends." She slipped one arm behind her as she balanced the computer on her lap.

Cole sat forward, a concerned look on his face. "Politicians aren't trustworthy. You need to avoid that crowd."

"Don't tell me you're jealous." She pursed her lips.

"I want to rip anyone apart who touches you. It's a primitive urge that I'm not proud of, but I'm trying to be honest."

She laughed. "Most of the people who'll be here are married, so I don't think you need to worry about me meeting anyone."

He shrugged off her comment. "I'll try not to worry—but be sure to warn any bachelors wandering into the party that your boyfriend is a vicious beast."

She stared at him and blinked. Had he just called himself her boyfriend? Was he serious or just joking around?

This was a topic of conversation too important for a video call. She needed to lighten things up.

"I thought since we got so much done on the library proposal, we'd do something fun tonight."

"You're too far away to indulge in my idea of having fun

with you," he responded with a slow, enticing grin that exposed his dimple. The man was lust in a box.

"I thought we'd have story time."

He winced. "I know my alphabet, Miss Brie."

"Of course, you do, Colie."

"Not even going to respond to that name."

She giggled. "How about a grown-up story time?"

"Will there be pictures?"

"No pictures, Colie."

"I'm warning you, Miss Brie."

She couldn't stop a smile from spreading across her face. "Just get comfortable, lean back, and relax. You don't have to do crisscross applesauce if you promise to behave."

"That's not something I can easily agree to, Miss Brie. Especially when it involves you."

She waved her hand at the screen. "Fine. Just listen."

She pulled a paperback from the nightstand at the side of the bed. "The title of this book is *Whistle Down the Wind*. It's about a family of witches during the time of King Charles II, in England."

"I enjoy stories about witches, especially the wicked ones." His grin widened.

She cleared her throat and held the book in front of her, with the cover visible to Cole.

"Hey, that guy lost his shirt. He must be freezing," Cole said.

"Pay attention and listen," Brie admonished, as if he were a preschooler.

Griffin removed the baldric holding his sword. He pulled the tall, heavy leather boots from his feet, and tossed them aside with no regard for anything except the voluptuous, delightful Catlin Glyndwr that was inviting him to seduce her.

Cole sat up straighter. She clearly had his full attention now.

"Voluptuous is my favorite kind of woman. But what the hell is a baldric?"

Brie pulled the book down to stare back at Cole. "It holds his sword."

"Is that a euphemism for his dick?"

She lifted the book to study the page of print and frowned. "I don't think so."

Her eyes scanned farther down the page. "Clearly not, because the author used a different word here."

"What word would that be?" He was clearly curious.

"You're rushing ahead of the story," she complained.

His fingers tangled in the ribbons of Catlin's bodice, and he had a brief impulse to use his dagger to quickly vanquish the pesky fastenings.

"Is dagger a euphemism for his dick?"

Brie lowered the book again. "No."

"So, he wants to cut her clothes off? Sounds a little aggressive."

Brie was inclined to agree. "I guess he's really horny."

Cole shook his head. "What kind of story are you reading to me, Miss Brie?"

She waved her hand. "I'll just jump to the naughty bits."

When she was finally garbed only in her stockings and garters, she gave a pretty shiver, but the expression in her soft blue eyes didn't reflect fear. Griffin breathed a sigh of relief. He needed to calm himself, take his time, and pleasure her with skill. His impatience to take her was making him awkward.

"I like the stockings and garters bit. By any chance, do you have some of those things with you? It would give me a great visual."

"I left those at home," she replied in a whisper. "And stop interrupting."

Sweeping one palm down from her shoulder to slide across a pink-tipped breast, he paused to imprint her image upon his memory. If he only had this night with her, he wanted it to last as long as possible. Likely on the morrow, she would brand him a scheming rogue and demand he return her to her family. His finger circled the tender tip of the orb before he kneeled and took it into his mouth and suckled.

She set the book down, waiting for Cole to make a comment.

He stared at her with a dazed expression on his face. "Why are you stopping now?"

She smiled and lifted the book to read more.

As his lips moved to the other breast, she thrashed against the coverlet. Heat pulsed through him at every touch. Her skin was soft and supple, and he couldn't resist tracing an outline of her curves with each hand.

She glanced at the computer screen to discover Cole's face appeared to blanch. His mouth was open, and his breathing ragged.

"You okay there, big guy?"

"I think it's getting too warm. I need to open a hatch." He disappeared from the screen.

"Keep reading," he demanded off-camera.

His cock throbbed as it pressed against his wool breeches. He thought he might burst before he could push himself into the soft, yielding heat of Catlin's body. Yet, he wanted to take this lovemaking slowly, to appreciate each precious moment with her.

Cole's face reappeared on the screen. "You just made some of that up. No way does it mention his cock."

She held the page of the book close to the camera. She heard him give a whistle. "I've been reading the wrong books my entire adult life."

"Shut up and listen. It's getting better."

Griffin stood to remove his breeches, and Catlin blinked as his cock sprang free. She tilted her head as she examined his body, and a smile stretched across her face. "You are far better endowed than the drawings of Greek statues I've seen. I doubt a fig leaf could cover that very well".

"So, do you think Catlin would describe Griffin as *prodigious*?" Cole asked.

"Do you want to listen to this, or are we going to have a book discussion?"

He rubbed his hands together. "Please continue. I'm excited to discover what happens next with the beauteous Catlin and her lover with the big cock."

"She doesn't even imply that, and besides—she's a virgin so it's not as if she has any basis for comparison—except the statues that were given, um, tiny tally-whackers."

"What did you just say?" His eyes narrowed, and he leaned forward to stare at her through the screen.

"Their weenies were teeny?" She couldn't hide her smile as she wiggled her eyebrows to punctuate the words. "I believe you might say their shlongs weren't very long."

Now she had to swallow a roar of laughter at his expression. He was clearly offended, but she couldn't decide if it was personal or if it was on behalf of all men. Or Greek statues?

He folded his arms. "Obviously, the author of this book doesn't understand how sensitive this issue is for men."

Brie stared at him. "You certainly aren't concerned about it, are you?"

He shook his head. "Of course not."

She could see her unflattering descriptions of men's genitalia bothered him. "Let's jump forward a bit and see what's happening."

He grunted in response.

"Here's a good part," she suggested.

Catlin's eyes widened as Griffin leaned across her body, his mouth trailing hot, eager kisses down her flat stomach, to her thighs, and then even lower.

"What the fuck? Is he going down on her?"

Brie ignored the interruption and continued to read. "This is the really good part."

She moaned when his tongue replaced his finger at that most tender of pleasure spots. She leaned back upon the pillows, twisting beneath him as he savored the sweet woman's honey pouring from her. She desired him, for it was in the liquid heat he tasted with each stroke of his tongue against the satiny delights.

"FUUUUCCCKK!" Cole gasped, his face contorting into a mask of pain. "Stop. Close that book and put it away."

Brie was concerned. "Are you okay? Did you hurt yourself?"

"You're killing me, woman, and I don't want to hear another word of that book until you get back. Then we're going to arrange a—what did you call it? Book discussion?"

"I'm sorry, Cole, but you need to read the book if you want to join my book group." She pointed at him. "No shirkers allowed!"

He leaned back on the pillows spread behind him and wiped beads of perspiration from his forehead. "Oh, we're going to read it. Together. We'll take turns, but not until you're back here on the island."

"So, are you suggesting a private book club made up of just you and me?"

"Absolutely," he responded. "I doubt you'd want to take a chance on having others join us, because I'm not willing to promise I'll behave."

Brie slipped a bookmark into the book and set it aside. "We'll need to discuss this further, Cole, because to join my book club, you need a library card."

He stared at her. "Is this some kind of librarian blackmail?"

Brie wiggled so she could give him a glimpse of her breasts. "Only if it works. Good night, Cole."

She heard a clipped good night, and the home screen appeared before she closed the laptop and took a deep breath. Brie had never indulged in this kind of face-to-face video sex play before, and she was aroused. Her breasts tingled, her body felt electrified, and she knew if she put her hand between her legs, she'd discover some of the "sweet woman's honey" the author described in the book she'd read aloud.

Even through a computer screen, Cole had been aroused by her playful reading. Pushing her computer aside, she slipped down on the mattress, settling against the soft pillows.

Brie closed her eyes. Should she take care of her arousal tonight, or wait a couple of days until she returned to the island to be with Cole?

A few days away from him and she'd discarded any thoughts of ignoring the strong pull of attraction between them. She'd folded to his idea of being together discreetly. It made her feel deliciously wild to sneak around with Cole.

And heightened the attraction too. A crazy dilemma.

An idea hit her with the force of a gale wind, and she smiled. She'd defer gratification until she got back to the island, and she'd plan a sexy surprise for Cole.

If he thought cosplaying mermaids were fun, wait until he saw her steampunk outfit.

TRUE CONFESSION: The people who want to ban books are hoping to convince you an idea is dangerous. They spout off about freedom and the First Amendment, then scream at librarians to yank books with things they don't like off the shelves. There's a reason the men who wrote the Constitution made freedom of speech one of the

FIRST rights. As librarian Jo Godwin once said, "A truly great library contains something in it to offend everyone." So, feel free to be offended and then read something else. Not every book is written for you.

Chapter Eighteen

COLE

COLE TWISTED in his chair and stared out the window at the water, trees, and sky. He'd come in today, even though Three Geeks closed on Monday, and he often worked from home.

He'd hoped to distract himself from thoughts of Brie, and their upcoming discussion about their relationship. Instead, he became even less focused, and it was because of a certain sexy little librarian with blue hair, a kissable mouth, and a body that unleashed a sexual hunger he struggled to control.

His hand moved to rub against his cock. He shouldn't want her as much as he did. But he couldn't stop thinking about her.

She'd promised to let him know when she got back, and he kept checking his phone, waiting for the text that would alert him she'd arrived back on the island.

Even though he didn't know what would happen when he got the message. She'd established some basic rules about working with Cole on the library project. The rules fused into guidelines, and later into suggestions, until Brie seemed to dispense with them altogether before returning to the island.

Not that he objected to her changing her mind about being with him. If that was the plan.

She sent a signal with her reading the other night, but it confused him. They'd kept their video calls professional until her adult story time.

When he finally ended the call, he'd been so worked up he'd stepped into the shower, expecting to take care of business. Then he'd decided to wait. He knew Brie would be back on Monday, and every day he waited made him want her more. He hoped she'd come back as eager to be with him as he was to be with her.

Her grown-up story time had been erotic fun, a way to use their brains for a tease. Hearing dirty talk from her heightened the sexual tension they shared.

There were footsteps on the stairs to his office and he turned his chair back to the desk, waiting for Matt to appear. He probably wanted to ask Cole when they'd be leaving.

Cole should give up and go home. Maybe he'd take the boat out for a while, even though dark clouds piled up in the sky. Fighting a stiff breeze might cool his blood and provide a distraction. If he waited until Brie called, he could invite her to come along.

A shadow fell across the desk. He looked up to discover Brie silently staring at him.

For a moment, he thought he might be imagining she stood there. Then she dropped the dark black coat that covered her down to her ankles, tossed it on the nearby chair and waited for his reaction.

"What... the... fuck?" He started to stand, but she took several steps closer and used a black riding crop with a heart on the tip to show she wanted him to sit.

So he sat.

"I wanted you to see what a corset actually looks like, up close." She posed in a power stance, legs apart, one hand on her hip and the other waving the crop. "I consider it part of your education about ladies' lingerie."

He leaned back, enjoying the sight of her in a red and black thing she called a corset. He'd have bet nothing could possibly make Brie's breasts more tantalizing. And he'd have lost that bet. The way the corset pushed up the generous orbs amazed him. It was a miracle of engineering.

A row of snap-like fastenings kept the corset closed, and he wondered how long it would take to unfasten them to get her naked. It'd be a pleasant task to unwrap her, but would he have the patience?

Once he forced himself to pull his gaze from her breasts spilling over the fabric encasing her, he noticed the way her small waist flared into the curves of her hips. A dark black fabric skirt hung short in the front and long in the back. She wore black fishnet stockings held up by garters that highlighted the soft curve of her thighs.

"Why are you wearing goggles on your hat? Planning to fly out of here in your biplane?"

"Steampunk!" she responded, as if he knew what that meant. "And I prefer to travel by airship."

She winked before turning in a circle to give him a full-body view, and he whistled in approval. He jumped from the chair, but she used the crop to maintain a space between them.

"There's no touching until I give you my permission, mister," she warned him.

He was already hard, his erection signaling he approved of her wardrobe. She pointed to his chair. "I told you to sit!"

He swallowed, wondering if she had trained dogs in the past. He decided playing along was going to be to his benefit. She'd arrived in an outfit that sent a clear signal as to her intentions. It wasn't as if letting her play sex games was a bad thing.

And her dominatrix persona was certainly a turn-on. He sat back in the chair, eager to see what she'd do next.

"I'm not sure this is part of our agreement. Not that I mind. Just saying."

She moved closer, slapping the crop against her hand. "Do you verbally agree..."

"Yes. I agree!" he interrupted her.

"Have you been a good boy or a bad boy while I was away, Cole?" The tone of her voice was commanding.

The closer she came to him, the more blood rushed from his brain to his dick. When she paused close enough for him to reach out to pull her toward him, she slapped his shoulder with the crop.

"Shit," he said, wincing. "That hurt."

"Do you want to use your safe word?" she said, putting her knees on either side of his legs and settling on his lap, facing him. He touched her arm, but when she lifted the crop in warning, he put his hands down.

"Keep going," he demanded.

She lifted her ass, then rubbed her breasts against the cotton fabric of the shirt covering his chest. She dragged the crop down, tracing the muscles.

"What do you want, Mr. Moore?"

They locked gazes. "The usual stuff—world peace, an end to poverty, a solution to climate change."

Her mouth hovered over his, tantalizing him with her dark pink lips. He inhaled her scent. "What else?" she asked in a breathy voice that sent shock waves to his erection.

He moaned as he grew impossibly harder. She was driving him crazy with lust.

"You," he answered. "I want you."

She slid off his lap, and he noticed the black laced leather boots. She was tightly wrapped, making the prospect of undressing her even more enticing. But she hadn't given him permission to touch her yet, so he gripped the armrests of his chair and fought the urge.

His control was slipping by the moment.

She put the crop on the desk and leaned toward him to unfasten his belt. He watched her, appreciating an even better view of her breasts. His palms itched to squeeze and play with them. His self-control stretched taut. A very thin thread liable to snap at any moment.

Tossing the belt aside, she slowly unzipped the fly of his jeans. She paused once to rake her fingers over his cock through his boxers, which nearly made him jump out of the chair.

Finally, she found the opening and wrapped her hand around his erection. He tilted his head back and gave into the pleasure of her touch. She gripped him loosely, sliding her hand up and down the engorged shaft.

She stared down, then lifted her gaze to meet his with an approving smile. "I'm going to taste you now, Mr. Moore, but you still can't touch me."

Before he could muster a response, she fell to her knees and took him into her mouth. Her tongue swirled up the sensitive sides, then she sucked on the tip.

He groaned at the exquisite torture of her mouth and tongue. She moved slowly, tasting, then licking.

When she glanced up to meet his gaze, he nodded. "So incredibly good." His throat felt parched, and his voice sounded harsh.

He finally held up his hands in surrender. "I can't hold back much longer. I need to touch you."

She nodded and stood up. He put his hands around her tight waist and lifted her to the surface of the desk. He stopped, a moan escaping from his lips when he discovered she wasn't wearing anything under the skirt. It made him even more impatient to take her.

He licked the tops of her breasts, dipping his tongue into the deep valley between them. His hands kneaded each one, then he pulled the fabric of the corset lower to uncover her nipples. His mouth worked each one, sliding his tongue around the tips, then nibbling. She bounced up, but didn't ask him to stop. He applied more pressure and her breath caught.

"Tell me if I do anything you don't like, Brie."

She nodded. "And you can tell me what you want or don't want, Cole."

"I can't imagine anything you'd do to me I wouldn't enjoy." He pushed back from the desk and stared at her.

Brie shrugged. "Just in case." Her lips curved into a sexy smile. When the tip of her tongue licked along the edge of her lips, he nearly lost control.

Cole's hands held her thighs apart as he fell to his knees. He slid one finger below the top of a stocking and stroked the soft skin. He kept moving higher until his mouth settled on the outer lips at her center.

His tongue circled around the edge of the folds guarding the velvet inner lining of her opening. He focused on the sides, savoring the honey of her arousal as he licked and suckled her. She was already wet, but he intended to make her drip with desire for him. He'd open her, stroke her with his mouth, and tease her until she invited him to take her.

He slid his hands beneath her ass and lifted her, bringing her closer to his mouth as he gently savaged her with his lips. She made little mewling noises, her eyes closed, and he knew she was intensely aroused.

"What do *you* want, Brie?"

Her eyes opened for a moment, and she blinked up at him before putting her hands on his shoulders. "Help me down."

He did as she directed, then she turned around to lean forward and set her elbows on the desk.

Cole understood what she wanted, and it fired his blood.

He swiped a finger across her pussy and used her own dew to wet his erection before stepping closer behind her.

He paused, waiting, not sure if she wanted him to be gentle or rough.

She lifted her ass, and he understood. He entered her with one hard thrust. She gave a sharp squeak of surprise.

Brie didn't tell him to stop, and he was seized with a craving to angle her body and plunge deeper. To feel her tighten around him even more. He lifted one of her legs to position the knee on the desk, then put one arm beneath her, settling her back on his dick.

As she rode up and down his thick, hard erection, he wrapped one arm around her waist. While she was the one controlling the pace, he enjoyed the sensation of pumping even deeper inside of her. This was the position that allowed him to penetrate her deeply while being able to enjoy access to her gorgeous breasts.

Her small noises grew louder with every stroke, and his voice joined hers to create a melody of hunger, need, and exquisite pleasure. He increased the tempo, fucking her hard, and he felt her inner muscles spasm as she screamed his name when her orgasm made her shudder with completion.

He tried to hold on as long as possible. Finally, it was too much, and he came with an explosive force that shot into her with pulse after pulse of hot liquid.

Cole took several deep breaths, then pulled her back to settle on his lap. He stared down at his pants that sat wrinkled at his ankles, realizing he'd never managed to undress.

Somehow, that made this interlude even more erotic. He'd wanted her so much he couldn't stop long enough to remove his clothing.

She turned sideways and put her arms around his neck, then rested against him. He rubbed a hand across the lacing down her back.

"I like this corset thing. Very nice," he said, still rubbing her back.

"It forces you to sit and walk with good posture, but if I lace it too tight, I can't breathe. A hundred years ago, women wanted a waist so tiny, they'd faint from lack of oxygen."

He nuzzled against her throat. "I think I understand what that feels like. I struggled to fill my lungs with air a few minutes ago."

She laughed, then closed her eyes. "You know this was a mistake. We shouldn't be seeing each other like this."

He rubbed her bare arm. "You came to me, Brie. You want me as much as I want you."

She remained silent for a moment. "I know. It scares me. I'm jeopardizing so much to be with you." She pushed her fingers through his hair as he studied her.

"I'll agree to whatever you ask so I can be with you. If we need to see each other in private, I'm willing to do that."

"If we can keep this thing between us quiet, at least until we make the presentation to the library board, I'd prefer that."

His arms tightened around her. "As long as we're still going to see each other. We can meet on my boat, or at Dylan's pool house, or wherever you want."

"Thank you," she whispered. "It feels sneaky, but my job is important to me."

"Are you planning to wear that to drive home?" He pointed at the corset, boots, and stockings. "It doesn't look very comfortable."

She glanced down at her outfit. "It's not designed for comfort. It's designed to titillate."

"Mission accomplished." He laughed. "Did you bring something to change into?"

Cole unhooked her arms that were circling his neck to release him.

"There's a bag in my car. Would you mind getting it for me?"

His gaze measured her again, from head to toe. "I'm enjoying this outfit, but I'll help you out. I'd hate for something to happen, and the local firemen get an eyeful of what you're wearing."

"At least I'd be a legend. They probably wouldn't stop talking about me for years." Her laughter bubbled through the room as she slid off his lap.

He stood and pulled up his boxers and jeans. She watched him as he zipped up.

"I don't want to be with anyone else, Brie," he blurted out, unsure of why he suddenly needed to be clear about their relationship.

"So, we're not casual anymore?"

"I'm not sure it was ever going to be casual between us. You do something to me, Brie." He grinned. "I think of you too much, want you more than I can handle. The past few days were torture, and I had to force myself to wait for you. I even planned to go to Seattle and wait in the library until you were finished with your training. I'd surprise you with a bouquet, kiss you in front of all your colleagues, and spend the night making love to you."

"You can't do that kind of thing, Cole." She looked appalled. "This is...something between us. I'm not ready to go public. There'd be consequences."

"I understand that, and I just want you to know I'm not ashamed of being with you. I'll wait until you're ready before I shout out to the world that we're together." He kissed her, the warmth of her lips against his signaling their agreement.

"When can I see you again?" He stood in the doorway, enjoying the sight of her settled in his office chair, slapping the crop against her palm.

"I'm off tomorrow. Can you play hooky?" Her voice held the lilt of a tease.

"For you, mermaid? Anything."

She swiveled in the chair and laughed. "I'm going to hold you to that promise, Cole."

He raised an eyebrow at her. "Please do, because I look forward to meeting *all* your demands. They are," he took a deep breath as he stared at her, "very stimulating."

He started down the stairs, her laugh following behind him.

His only wish was for enough stamina to follow through on his promise.

TRUE CONFESSION: Even when you're not teasing your partner into an afternoon of sexy time, there's an aspect of dressing up that's sensual. You can change your personality with a wig, makeup, a costume, and accessories. It's grown-up pretend play and you can try out a unique personality, whether it's a comic book or manga character, a superhero, or a popular character from video games. It expands the imagination, and there's little chance adults are in danger of overdoing imaginary play. Why should we stop playing and having fun just because we're older?

Chapter Nineteen

BRIENNE

"I HOPE you're not rushing into something with this guy, Brie. You don't really know that much about him."

"I know enough, Luna. He makes me feel like..." Brie glanced at her friend. "Like I've never felt before."

Luna lifted her mug to take a sip of coffee. She leaned back on Brie's couch and gazed out the bow window. The sun had just risen, scattering morning shadows across the trees.

"Okay, 'good in bed' is a recommendation, but I'm not convinced you should agree to being exclusive when you just escaped from break-up purgatory. You only just put yourself out there."

Brie fumbled with the espresso machine. "I don't want to go out with a bunch of strangers, looking for something I've already found." She gazed at her best friend.

"I trust my feelings for Cole. He's tender, and funny, and shit, you've seen the man." Brie laughed. "Do you have eyes in your head, girlfriend?"

"I've been in lust before, girl. I'm suggesting you slow down, take it easy. If he's that into you—he'll be patient."

Brie pushed the button and watched the espresso stream

into the cup. She'd expected Luna to be pessimistic when she'd told her what happened at Cole's office. At least her friend had been impressed with the steampunk seduction.

Luna just wasn't impressed with the plan they'd developed to continue to see each other. She questioned the need to hide their relationship, since they were both consenting adults. Brie found it difficult to explain how precarious her position at the library was right now.

Brie's best friend radiated strength and power. She'd tell people to fuck off when they didn't like what she did. Luna had a lot of freedom as the owner of her own business. Plus, she had the security of a grandmother who supported her decisions. Antonia Scallini sold a tract of land her family had owned for nearly a hundred years to help Luna set up her business.

Brie didn't enjoy the same freedom, especially with Marion Rush-Talbot on the library board. If that woman could find a reason to dismiss Brie, she'd do it. The breach of an outdated morals clause in her contract might provide enough ammunition to fire her.

"It's not like we can't go public after the board accepts the donation. Once that happens, there's no potential conflict of interest. We can wait a few weeks to hang out together."

Her cheeks heated. "Our private meetings are a lot of fun. I'm reluctant to give them up."

Luna waved a hand at Brie. "Sure, tease me with stories of your talented lover, incredible sex, and multiple orgasms. It's not as if I'm jealous or anything."

"There were two other hot guys at the photo shoot. I provided an opportunity. I can't help it if you didn't take advantage." Brie finished steaming milk for her latte and grinned at her friend.

Luna made a sour face. "I could have pounced on either of

them, but Raina has something weird going on with Dylan. As for Wyatt..."

She shook her head. "He seems closed down, emotionally frozen or something. The man carried me around all day and didn't seem to notice what I'm proud to point out is an amazing rack and awe-inspiring ass."

"Cole told me he's had a difficult time adjusting to his wife's death. Give him a break, will you?"

When she turned to look at Luna, her friend wore an expression filled with so much sadness it almost brought tears to Brie's eyes.

"I'm sorry, I didn't know about that." Luna's voice was choked with emotion. "You should have told us. I would have been nicer to him. I understand now..."

She stopped talking and shook her head.

"Anyway," Luna set her mug down on the antique trunk that served as a coffee table in Brie's living room. "Maybe your thing with Cole will provide a few more opportunities to talk to the guys. I keep feeling like I've met Wyatt before, but first, you'll need to come out of hiding."

"We're not hiding, we're—keeping things private," Brie objected. "We want to make sure things work out between us before hanging out together in public. You know how the people on this island love to gossip."

It was difficult to explain the circumstances to Luna, especially since Brie had been the one to suggest that she and Cole avoid being seen together in public until after the public meeting about the library remodel.

She glanced at the clock on her microwave. "Cole's going to be here soon, and I need to get ready."

"What do you two have planned today, more secret sexy time on the sailboat?" Luna grinned at her.

"Actually, it's a surprise. I'm not sure where we're going," Brie said.

"But you are assured there'll be *a happy ending*, right?"

Brie stuck her tongue out at her friend. "I can't help it if you're frustrated, girl. Maybe you need to swipe right."

"That's not my scene." Luna wrinkled her nose. "I found out the guys there were only looking for a onetime screw. I've wasted enough time being a booty call."

Brie knew Luna had enjoyed a more adventurous sex life as a single professional in Seattle, and enjoyed a variety of partners and experiences. Things she'd been happy to share with her more reserved friend.

It could be one reason Brie enjoyed Cole's inventive sex play. Much of it new to her, but her excellent research skills came in handy. She found a lot of information online, and in books, about exploring the boundaries of sensual pleasure.

"You're getting that *my boyfriend is oh so dreamy* look again, so I'll let you get ready. I'd tell you not to do anything I wouldn't do, but that doesn't set many limits." Luna stood and grabbed her purse. "So just enjoy yourself."

Brie rinsed the coffee mugs and put them in her dishwasher before crossing the living room to open the bookcase that hid the entrance to her bedroom. When her father remodeled the cottage for her, it had been his idea to hide the doorway.

She wondered now if he'd been indulging her drama queen tendencies or just trying to make it more challenging for men to discover her bedroom.

The room took the pink, white, and turquoise décor to the lacy limits. Her bed with the pink headboard was covered in a floral quilt. A half-dozen pillows, including two white shaggy fake fur ones, were tossed across the top of the bed. A dresser she'd painted turquoise and pink and covered with floral decals stood opposite the bed.

Two shelves surrounded the alcove that held a small dressing table she'd constructed from an antique desk.

Wrapped in tulle, it reminded her of something from the Barbie house she loved as a child. The shelves held a variety of hatboxes, wig stands, jewelry boxes, and containers for odd bits.

The white walls were decorated with a variety of romantic prints from the Pre-Raphaelite Brotherhood.

When she had finally opened the door to let Cole see the room, he'd laughed. He called it over-the-top foo-foo. She'd told him she didn't care what he called it; she liked what she liked.

Opening her closet, she studied her clothing choices. Since she didn't know what they'd be doing today, the appropriate wardrobe presented a problem.

Except Luna predicted one thing correctly. Brie knew something she'd be doing with Cole since they couldn't keep their hands off each other when they were together. She opened the top drawer of her antique dresser and sorted through the lingerie there. Finally, she settled on a vintage-style red bra and matching panties. If you were doing a vintage look, go all the way.

Brie found her favorite red and black button-up cardigan and decided jeans would be a perfect choice to match. She grabbed the ones with a cuff to continue the pin-up look and added bright red heels to the ensemble. She'd bring a pair of Chucks in case they were going hiking, but she loved her red shoes. And she'd discovered Cole appreciated titillation.

She slipped the underthings on and went into the bathroom to finish her makeup. After dusting her lids with a color that matched her hair, she drew black eyeliner to create a cat's-eye look. She finished with bright red lipstick, then studied her reflection.

Her hair color had faded, and she'd need to decide soon if she wanted to keep the blue or go back to her natural chestnut-brown shade. After living with the pastel color for weeks, she might even consider a different shade.

She grabbed her robe before answering a knock at the door. Cole leaned against the entrance, dressed casually in black jeans, a T-shirt of the same color, and a gray hoodie with a Yeti logo on it. She'd noticed he often wore clothing with that logo and decided it must be left-over swag from his job at the gaming company he'd mentioned.

It seemed unfair that a cute guy could get away with wearing about the same thing day after day. Then again, she'd be bored with a basic wardrobe. She loved fashion.

As soon as he shut the door behind him, he grabbed her around the waist to pull her into his arms. His kiss seared her lips, and his hands slipped behind her to squeeze her ass. He pulled her closer against him. It delighted her to discover he already showed he was happy to see her. She slipped a hand down to caress his erection. His deep groan provided a satisfying response.

"Brie, unless you plan to share your bed with me today, you should stop. Not that I wouldn't be thrilled to be invited into your sanctuary of sweet delights."

She pulled away from him. "No such luck, sailor. We're not guaranteed privacy here. I told you, my parents have a key to this cottage."

"You're killing me, Brie, inch by frustrating inch."

She grinned at him, then turned to enter her bedroom. He stood in the doorway watching her finish dressing. As she buttoned the sweater that let just a tiny pinch of red lace peek out, he groaned again.

"I love that sweater. When you wore it with that tight black skirt with the slit up the back, and those black and red heels, it made me…"

She turned to stare at him, her lips twitching. "I'm not sure I'm comfortable hearing about your sexual fantasies when you were watching me in the library. It's a bit disturbing."

Cole shrugged. "I suspect I'm not the only one you affected. When you walked around with a cart of books, the way your sweet ass wiggled, it was worth waiting for. I'd sit for hours hoping you were going to shelve books."

"Sexy librarian is an unfortunate stereotype." She slipped one leg into her jeans.

"In your case, Brie, it's an honest description." He shook his head. "Watching you was supposed to be an assignment that took a couple of hours. But it turned into a major research project. I couldn't stay away."

She put her other leg in the jeans and pulled them up. She gave him an enticing view as she bent forward, and she heard him react with a deep rumbling in his throat.

"Be careful. I don't need to be in your bed to take you." He touched the wall. "This looks sturdy."

Heat shot through Brie like a guided missile. She looked forward to a day of banter and foreplay before they had sex.

She finished her outfit by adding a pair of vintage earrings, then carried her extra shoes to the door and winked at him. "You have a lot to live up to in order to meet my expectations, so take it easy."

"It's a good thing I'm a patient man." His gaze raked over her.

"I guarantee you'll appreciate your reward. Now, where are we going?"

He crossed the room to help her into a black leather jacket.

"I'm liking this look, but you're making my job difficult. I can't decide what persona I enjoy most. Sexy librarian, sexy mermaid, sexy bossy steampunk lass, sexy lingerie lady, or...?"

"I call this sexy rockabilly bitch." She tossed her hair back.

"Is the 'bitch' part a warning or a promise?"

She laughed. "You'll find out. You know what the meme

says—*I may not be everyone's cup of tea, but I'm someone's double shot of whiskey*. So, we'll see how much you like your whiskey."

Brie walked out ahead of him and waited as he shut the door. He took her hand as they walked down the path to the farmhouse and approached his truck parked in the driveway.

He glanced around. "Are your parents here?"

"Nope. They loaded up their pickup and went to town. They had a delivery for several of the restaurants. I guess you're not eager to meet up with my dad again?"

Cole tried to look cool, but the beads of perspiration on his forehead gave him away. He attempted to wipe them, but she couldn't control her glee.

"At least I know one person who intimidates you."

"Your dad is tough. I feel like he'd be patient up to a point. Then he'd have no problem knocking me on my ass if he thought I needed it. He reminds me of my father."

She stopped at the door to his truck as he opened it for her. "My father is an avowed pacifist. That old shotgun he totes around doesn't even work. He just uses it as a warning."

"And I am duly warned," he said as he circled in front of the truck to climb into the driver's side.

She buckled her seatbelt as she glanced at Cole. "Just don't hurt me. That's the only thing that could turn my dad violent. He's protected me and my brother with a vengeance since we were kids. He confronted parents of kids who tried to bully me or Ryder. The crazy thing is that those adults became his friends. It's his gift, to convince people to do something they probably don't want to do."

"That's a rare gift, Brie. My dad has an Irish temper, quick to anger, then dismissing it just as easily. He makes a lot of noise, but never laid a finger on my mother or us kids. He enjoyed a brawl at his favorite bar occasionally, but he stopped drinking when he developed a heart condition, and my mother issued an ultimatum."

"Your mother must be a formidable woman."

Cole backed out of the driveway, then turned to her with a grin. "You don't know the half of it. She's not even as tall as you, and everyone in the family is terrified of her."

She laughed. "Judging from the tone of your voice, she's probably less a terrorist and more of an influencer."

"An influencer who never missed an opportunity to discipline us into good behavior. Just ask my sister."

Brie avoided looking at him. He'd been so private about his family; he'd only mentioned his younger sister before, and she wondered if he had any other siblings.

Luna had been right earlier—she didn't really know Cole. The few things he'd shared with her had only been tiny glimpses into his life. He'd met her parents, her friends, and even several of her co-workers. But so far, he'd only introduced her to Wyatt, Dylan, and Matt, the bartender at Three Geeks.

Could there be something lurking in his past he didn't want her to know about? Added to his being an internet phantom, she had to admit, it was a bit disturbing, considering how much she trusted him.

They were on the road that led to Three Geeks, so she assumed they were going to the bar. It was Friday, so she suspected there'd be a band tonight. A fun night of dancing with Cole and partying appealed to her.

Then it hit her. If they were out together in public, there'd be gossip along with a lot of innuendo and teasing from people she knew.

Before she could voice her concerns, he turned down a paved side road she'd never noticed before. She didn't come up to this part of the island often, so that didn't surprise her.

They drove through an enormous gate, and the road

277

ended at a house. A massive lodge-style home made of timber and stone stood before them.

"Is this a B&B? It looks new, but I didn't see a sign."

Cole slid out of the driver's seat. "You could say it's a private bed-and-breakfast."

He opened the truck door, and she still couldn't take her eyes off the building in front of them. The craftsmanship was amazing, and the design fit perfectly into the landscape of tall cedar and fir trees.

She turned to Cole. "Does this belong to one of your bosses? If we're sneaking in to have some sexy time, I can already predict what's going to happen."

"I think the phrase 'sexy time' gives it away."

She followed him to the huge front door and watched him key a code into the lock pad. She followed him into a hallway with a high arched ceiling and a craftsman-style chandelier swinging high above them. The hallway led into a main room, where a fieldstone fireplace soared up several floors. She spun around to take in the rustic luxury.

It was Pacific Northwest style, combined with a European influence. When her gaze found the windows on one side, she couldn't resist going closer to enjoy the amazing view of the water.

The view took her breath away. When she turned to discover the kitchen, she stood stock-still in awe. The island in the middle of the room had to be the size of her kitchen. There were two European-style stoves, dual wooden doors that must be designed to hide the refrigerator, and broad wooden beams stretched above them.

"You've just spoiled me with serious house porn. I'll never be satisfied with my tiny cottage again because I'm experiencing *Hearth and Home* envy."

"You should see the bedroom. It has a fireplace and an immense bed."

She turned to him. "So, is that the plan? We're gonna mess up your boss' bed, and he's going to catch us, then we'll have to grab our clothes and run out of here naked?"

"Something like that." He grinned at her. "I admit, I'd enjoy the running around naked part."

"I've seen this in a bunch of rom-com novels and movies. It's supposed to be funny, but it just looks horribly embarrassing to me." She walked past him, back toward the main door.

Just as she reached for the doorknob, his voice stopped her. "This house belongs to me."

Her brain stopped functioning. She had to be having a stroke because his words didn't make any sense. This house must have cost millions of dollars. And even though he had a nice truck and an amazing sailboat, Cole couldn't be rich enough to afford this kind of luxury.

Or could he be? She reminded herself she didn't really know that much about him.

Her mouth still wide open with shock, Brie turned to stare at him. She blinked at him for several moments while collecting her thoughts.

"What? How?" she said, obviously having lost the ability to speak using full sentences.

He crossed the polished wood floor and stood in front of her. "I own this house. I had it custom-built to my specifications. It took over two years."

She finally managed to close her mouth. She looked around at the magnificent space again.

"Your house? Where you live?"

It didn't make any sense. If he was rich enough to own a home like this, why would he work at Three Geeks?

"I know it's a shock."

"Oh, it's a shock," she admitted. "Are you... I don't know,

heir to a family fortune, descended from royalty, or a secret billionaire hiding out from the paparazzi?"

Cole's face blanched at the last question, then he shrugged. "Compared to most people, I'm pretty rich."

"Pretty rich? Maybe we need a different modifier. *Extremely, incredibly, unbelievably*. Which would it be?"

"Can we sit down? Maybe have a glass of wine while I explain?" He pointed to the set of leather couches in the middle of the living room.

She stumbled on the edge of an oriental carpet before sitting. It probably cost more than all the furniture in her cottage combined.

"I need to let my dog out of the kennel. Why don't you go pick out some wine and I'll open it when I get back? The wine cellar is behind that door."

He escaped out the sliding glass doors as she still processed the information he'd just shared. He had a wine cellar. She stood to follow his directions. When she opened the door he'd indicated, she found a stone staircase that led down to a room with stone walls. Wooden racks held a lot of bottles of wine.

Still in a daze, she wandered into the cellar. She twirled in the space. There were probably a hundred bottles. She didn't even know anyone with a wine cooler, much less an actual room filled with bottles of wine. How was it possible Cole Moore could be this rich, and she'd had no clue?

And why had he hidden this from her? Clearly, she didn't know enough about him.

The clicking of nails on the stairs and then the stone floor warned her a dog headed her way. A bundle of dark fur slammed into Brie and almost knocked off her feet. A heavily muscled arm caught her.

"Down, Oscar!" Cole commanded. The dog ignored the order and sniffed at her crotch.

"Sorry," Cole said. "He doesn't actually listen to me."

The dog danced around them, clearly delighted to see his master, but equally happy to discover another human in the vicinity. Oscar seemed to be very friendly.

Brie frowned. "Since I've seen you do exactly what he just did, I'm more inclined to believe the dog is modeling behavior he's observed."

She grabbed a bottle of wine from the shelf. It was a rosé with a fancy script in French on the label. Since she didn't know much about wine, she shoved the bottle at Cole.

"Open this, because I believe I'm going to need a lot of wine in order to listen to the explanation you owe me, and I might as well admire the color as I get drunk."

Oscar followed her back up the stairs and to the couch. He jumped up next to her and stared at her intently, drooling.

"Hey Cole, this dog has some of your same expressions, too. Look at him."

"You're hilarious," Cole called from the kitchen.

Cole carried two glasses and the bottle into the living and set them on the coffee table. He sat in one of the enormous armchairs between the couches and poured the wine.

He took a drink and made a face that displayed his displeasure at her choice. Clearly not one of his favorite vintages.

She waited for him to say something, and she let the silence grow. Cole stared at her, looking contrite. She had no intention of rescuing him from this awkward situation.

"I know it seems strange, but there's a reason I didn't tell you about my, the..."

"Huge fortune? So, are you building-rockets-to-the-stars rich?"

"Fuck no." He swept a hand through his hair. "Even if I had that much money, I sure as hell wouldn't use it for that."

She believed him. If he could keep his wealth a secret from her for over a month, he wasn't an egomaniac who craved attention. She still didn't say anything else and waited for more explanation.

He took a gulp of wine, and this time his face wrinkled into a wince.

She studied him. "Rosé, not your favorite wine?"

"This is a Moscato, and it tastes like soda pop."

"It's now my favorite," she responded, tipping her glass at him before taking another drink.

"You have a right to be angry with me." He took a deep breath.

"I appreciate your permission to own my feelings, Cole. How kind of you to offer your approval."

He shifted in the chair. "That's not what I meant."

Brie drained her glass and refilled it. "Would you agree we've shared quite a few *intimate* moments these past few weeks?"

She gulped her wine.

"And yet in all our moments of being naked together, you licking my pussy, and me sucking your dick, of exchanging some serious bodily fluids, it never occurred to you to tell me the truth about who you are?"

"You make it sound dirty and sordid. I never thought of us that way, Brie." He stared at her.

"We fucked, Cole." Her gaze didn't shift from connecting with his. "I fucked a guy who pretended to be someone else. Was that the game you played? Fool the little librarian?"

He jumped to his feet. "It was never a game. I have my reasons for doing what I did, of being—secretive."

Cole turned away to lean against the fireplace, his head down. "This is embarrassing to talk about."

Brie emptied the remaining wine into her glass. "You know what's more embarrassing, Cole? Being with a guy who's a stranger when I've been honest with him. I trusted you."

She set her glass on the table. Oscar put a paw on her leg, as if to comfort her. She rubbed behind one of his ears.

She glared at Cole. "I don't think you deserve this dog. He's a lot nicer than you are."

"He shits in your shoes when he's mad at you."

Brie patted the dog's head. "I certainly understand the urge."

"I told you the truth about being part of a successful gaming company. But I wasn't an employee; I was one of the founders of Yeti Entertainment. We created a game while we were in college, and it turned out to be a hit. We made more games, and we also made a lot of money."

"A lot. I can see how that's open to interpretation. I follow the news. That company sold for several billion dollars, Cole."

He nodded. "And we dispersed funds to many of our long-time employees. We set up trusts for our families and split it four ways."

"So not rocket-man billions, but what did you call it—*a lot*?" She wanted to be angry, but the ache squeezing her heart didn't allow the emotion to slip in underneath the pain.

"So, you pretended to be Cole Moore, bar manager and cute scruffy dude. Was the offer to donate to the library real or just a pretense to fuck me?"

He winced at her choice of words. Then she remembered how her dirty talk aroused him. Certainly not the result she wanted to achieve tonight.

"Everything about the donation is real. Dylan and Wyatt and I still want to do that."

She stood slowly and crossed the room to glare down at him. "Are you telling me those two are your partners? Surfer Guy and Sad Man Bun are your former business partners?"

"What? Who calls them that?"

"It's not important." She glanced around the room, which reminded her this was an amazing house, and then also reminded her it belonged to the man formerly known as Cole Moore.

"What I need to know is the reason you lied to me. Why would you pretend to be a regular working man? Who are you really?"

She stood and considered him for a minute. "Is your name even Cole? Is that why I couldn't discover anything about you on the web?"

His eyes fired with a defiant blaze. "You were checking me out on the web? Why?"

Fury hit her like a quarterback racing to make the winning touchdown. "Because I'm a librarian and finding things out is what I do." She threw her hands up. "I thought it was strange that no one with your face appeared when I searched. You didn't show up on any of the social media sites or search engines. It's like you don't even exist."

She stared at him, then shrugged her shoulders. "Which you don't. You're the invisible man, Cole. How the hell did you even do that?"

He didn't answer, but took another drink of his wine and made a face. "I can't drink this. I'm grabbing a red. Do you want me to grab another bottle of this for you?"

"No, I'll be leaving soon. Don't bother." She could taste the acid in her voice.

He stopped at the door to the wine cellar. "I need to explain this to you. Please don't leave."

She wanted to stomp out of there. It would just show him, whoever he was, that she was seriously angry with him.

Then again, maybe there was a reasonable explanation for his deception. She might as well give him a chance to explain.

When he returned to the kitchen, he opened the bottle of wine and poured it into a fresh glass. He didn't bother to do the swirl and sip thing. He just gulped down the wine and refilled his glass before returning to stand in front of the fireplace.

"My actual name is Michael Cole Morrison. I changed it to Cole Moore after, when..." He took another long drink of wine. His face was shaded red, and she had a sliver of pity for him. But only a teeny-tiny, itty-bitty sliver.

Whatever he was going to tell her, it appeared to be really embarrassing.

"I had to do that because I was being blackmailed."

"Did you get involved with a crime syndicate, or was it a cartel?" She moved to the edge of the couch. "Was it the mafia? Are you *actually* in the Witness Protection Program?"

He stared at her. "You might want to cut down on the amount of Netflix you're currently consuming."

"I haven't been watching as much lately because I've been too busy, um." Her cheeks warmed with a blush. "Never mind."

"It didn't involve drugs or the mafia. It was a crazy ex-girlfriend."

She pointed at him. "Also available on Netflix, just in case you're interested."

He didn't smile, but his forehead wrinkled as if he was concerned about her mental state. He should be. She was vacillating between using humor to manage her anger and controlling the anger to avoid hitting him.

Brie should have asked for more wine. She wondered if it was too late. Also, she needed to stop interrupting and wait for his explanation. So, she kept quiet.

"When I was in college, I had a girlfriend. To be honest, she was my first."

She stared at him, waiting for the punchline. Then she realized that was the punchline.

"Your first girlfriend?"

He watched her reaction, and she finally nodded. "Got it. *First* girlfriend."

For someone who prided herself on her conversational skills, she was stammering tonight as if she'd forgotten what words were used for. Not that he was doing much better.

This man had put his lips on her most delicate parts, and yet he could barely tell her that once upon a time he'd been an innocent virgin. Stupid male pride.

"We were having, um, well, you know." She pictured it in her head and then tried to lose that picture immediately. She didn't like the image of him with another woman.

"Intercourse? Are we going to be using all the clinical names tonight, because that's really going to drag this shit out?"

"Fine. Yes. We were fucking, and she filmed it, and I didn't know that she filmed it, and it's embarrassing as hell to admit it happened."

Brie stared at him, and then she couldn't contain her reaction. She laughed. She knew it was a mistake when his expression transformed from contrite to furious.

"It's not a laughing matter."

She tried to stop. She really tried. Well, honestly, she didn't try that hard.

"A sex tape has created careers for some people. It's made nobodies into celebrities. It's transformed B-list actors into A-list actors."

His face turned as red as her lipstick. "You don't understand." He seemed to talk to the floor.

"I was a terrible lover. I couldn't last...sometimes at all. There were a few times I didn't get, didn't manage to..."

Brie stared at him. "So, your ex-girlfriend made a tape of the two of you having bad sex, and then—"

"She held on to it until our company sold. She found out about that and realized she could get rich by selling the tape."

It would be a cheap shot. Brie shouldn't say anything. He was already embarrassed.

"Ha! Exposing you." She wasn't proud of the remark, but he'd left himself wide open.

He glared at her. "This isn't funny, Brie. I had to pay her off, and then I had to wipe my identity in case she ever came back to demand more money from me."

Brie shook her head. "Rich people can afford good lawyers. I'm sure you forced her to sign away rights to her first-born if she, um, exposed you."

He put a hand to his forehead. She wondered if he had a headache.

"I get it. You were embarrassed. What I don't understand is why you lied to me. I trusted you." She stared at him, looking deep into his forest-green eyes. "I trusted you to meet my family, to get to know my friends, and I trusted you enough to be with you. We shared our bodies in some of the most intimate ways possible."

"When we were on the boat together, I wanted to tell you. It was the perfect time. I just didn't want you to look at me... like I wasn't skilled at—you know."

"Cole, er, Michael. Shit, what do I call you?" She shook her head. "It doesn't matter."

She'd been holding on to a thin edge of anger and now she let it flow. "Damn it, I slept with you. No, let's be honest. I fucked you—multiple times. Even if you'd told me about this, I'd never have believed you were a lousy lover. I had proof that wasn't true."

He blinked at her. "I couldn't tell you."

"You *chose* not to tell me. Maybe you were embarrassed. I can accept that. Except I think you wanted to be Cole instead of Michael. Cole is the cool guy who can sail into town on his super-duper boat or drive his macho truck around. He can hang out at the library ogling the staff and making them feel uncomfortable."

"I'm sorry if I did that. I didn't mean to."

She paced across the room behind the couch she'd been sitting on. "You were playing a part, and even when you could have told me the truth, you decided it would be too embarrassing for *you*."

He started to say something, and she shut him down. "Did you ever consider how embarrassing it would be for me when people discovered I was dating a ghost? What happens when my family and friends discover you're not who you told me you were? How do I explain that?"

"I'm sorry." A crease slashed above his eyes, signaling his regret. "I care about you." He took a deep breath, then released a jagged groan. "I don't want to hurt you."

"And that damn consent form!" She stomped closer to confront him. "You thought I might do what that other woman did to you." She turned to glare at him, her hands fisted at her sides.

"You wanted me to sign a form because you didn't trust me? Who are you really?"

"I'm the man who wants us to be together."

She stared at him. "I wish I could believe that. Unfortunately, I don't even know who you really are, much less what you're feeling."

"I can give you anything you want."

She took a deep breath and stared at him for a few moments.

"Can you give me honesty?"

Her question echoed in the silence.

"So, not that, right? I'm going to call Luna and ask her to pick me up at Three Geeks. I need some fresh air and some space, and I need to have some time to think things over. Please stay away from me. And don't call or text me."

"You don't need to do that. I'll drive you home or to the bar. Wherever you want."

She glanced at him over her shoulder as she stood at the door. "I need to clear my head and to stay away from you. I can't think clearly when you're around."

"Brie. Please don't go. I'm sorry. Let's talk about this."

She ignored his words as she slammed the door. She didn't glance back because she knew once she realized she'd stormed away from a gorgeous guy who made her laugh, who kissed her as if she was a delicate work of art, and who owned the most magnificent house she'd ever been inside of—and who gave her the best sex she'd ever had... she'd probably throw herself into Puget Sound.

Damn her parents for raising her with a moral compass that dictated she refused to be lied to. If she'd just budge a little, accept Cole's apology, and forgive him, things could go back to the way they were before he told her the truth.

She could be in that stunning house, engaging in some naughty behavior with a man who could make her toes curl when they fucked.

She stalked down the driveway, aware the sky signaled it would drop a deluge on her momentarily. Wouldn't that be poetic justice? The weather reminding her that sobbing her heart out could easily be drowned by a collection of clouds that didn't care if her heart was breaking?

TRUE CONFESSION: When people describe a broken heart, it sounds like it would shatter apart with a loud roar, like an earthquake ripping through the earth. For me, it's more of a wave of discomfort that starts in my throat and gets lodged in my chest, making it hard to breathe. Then it continues down the path to my stomach, where anything I've ingested recently reminds me it's there and could reappear at my feet at any time. It's painful, and achy, and causes acid reflux, wet eyes, and a runny nose. It's not at all attractive, but when you're experiencing it, you don't give a shit what you look like.

Chapter Twenty

COLE (MICHAEL)

COLE STOOD outside the Ancient Ways Apothecary trying to figure out why the hell he'd shown up there. This should be the last place he'd go to ask for advice about Brie. He wouldn't be surprised if Luna forced him to turn around and leave before he could say a word.

Or cast a spell on him that would make him regret ever hurting Brie. The information he'd gleaned about Luna was iffy, from Wyatt's description of her terrorizing him, to Brie's assertion she had a magical quality and read tarot cards, created amazing perfumes and elixirs, and sold unique art created by indigenous people from all over the world.

He straightened his shoulders, aware he'd probably receive a chilly reception from Brie's best friend.

A chime sounded above the door when he entered.

"I'll be right there. I'm bringing the tea out." A voice echoed from behind a multicolored curtain hung at a doorway in the back of the shop. He recognized Luna's voice.

"No need to rush," he said.

Luna appeared in the doorway. "No fucking way are you here to talk to me about Brie."

"Please," he begged her. "She won't talk to me."

Luna stepped toward him, her hostile dark eyes never wavering. "Why should I help you?"

Cole rested one hand against the counter. "I care about her, and I want her to know that. I need to, for her to know..." He ran one hand through his hair and looked down, then dragged the sleeve of his flannel shirt across his face to wipe the perspiration beading up on his skin.

Despite taking a deep breath, he couldn't seem to fill his lungs with enough air. Cole was supposed to be the calm guy who kept his cool. His heart beat so fast, he felt like he might pass out.

"Shit. Are you having a heart attack?" Luna said, a tinge of alarm in her voice.

He shook his head. "Panic attack. Haven't had..." He took another deep breath. "One in years."

"Shit! You better sit down!"

Cole didn't need the direction as he crumbled to his knees. He put his hand on his chest, feeling the racing of his heart. It beat too fast, and he swore it was so loud, Luna had to hear it.

Luna appeared with a pillow and held his head as he lay back on the floor. Once he was prone on his back, he closed his eyes.

"What the fuck should I do?" Luna's voice now held a note of genuine panic. "I'll call 911."

"No," he whispered. "Not an emergency. I'll be okay in a few minutes. An hour at most." He opened his eyes to see her hovering above him.

"So, you're planning to lie in the middle of my shop until you recover?"

"Give me a few minutes, and I'll be able to sit up."

Luna's lips pinched together. "Should I get you a blanket? Something to drink?"

Cole hated feeling helpless. He'd controlled these attacks

for years, and he didn't want to think about why he was suddenly experiencing them again. "I need to relax, get my breathing under control, and let my heartbeat settle down."

"I'm getting you a blanket anyway, just to make me feel better."

She returned with a throw, tossed it over him, and pulled it up to cover his knees.

"Whoa, this is soft," he said. "What's it made from, angel wings?"

"Yeah, we pluck them in the back room." She shot him a disgusted look. "It's knit from wool I get from Brie's farm. It's one of our projects."

She disappeared again, and Cole stared after her. Projects? Brie had other projects besides the library. How come he didn't know this?

Likely because, while he enjoyed talking with Brie, he enjoyed doing so many other things with her more. In fact, he'd focused a little too much on having sex with her over the past few weeks and not enough on getting to know her better. After they were on the boat together, when he realized he wanted to keep seeing her, his brain fogged with lust whenever he was with her.

"Here. If you can sit, drink this," Luna said, putting a stoneware mug on the floor next to him.

Cole craned his neck and glanced at the brown liquid. He picked up the mug, sniffed it, and lifted his gaze to meet hers.

A knowing smile turned her lips into an almost sinister grin. "It's chamomile tea with a lavender elixir and a touch of lemon balm."

He sniffed it again and cautiously sat up. She tipped her head to stare down at him.

"Think of it this way. If I wanted to kill you, you'd already be dead."

He held the mug to his lips, blowing on it while

considering her statement. "I don't find that very reassuring." He finally took a drink, then nodded.

"Actually, it's tasty. Thank you."

"Can you stand? I have a table in the corner where I do my tarot readings. I can draw the curtains to make it more private."

He nodded and handed her the mug to put on the table, taking her offer of an arm to pull him to a stand. An arm ridged with muscle. She helped him up with little effort.

"Damn, woman, you take working out seriously."

She shrugged as he dropped into a chair. "I enjoy lifting weights. I like the challenge." She put the mug in front of him. "Drink all of this. It'll make you feel better."

He crossed his arms on the tabletop and lay his head down on them. "I fucked up. I totally fucked up."

"Not gonna disagree with you, dude. Lying to her like that was a dick move. You hurt my friend, and to be honest, I wouldn't mind punching you in the face right now. Except I don't condone violence."

He lifted his head. "I'd deserve it, Luna."

"Maybe I'll punch you in the gut instead, with a reading." She stared at him before sitting across the table. "Let's see what the cards have to say."

Cole sat up straighter. "Sorry. I don't believe in any of that shi…" His gaze flickered to her. "Stuff."

Luna shrugged as she took something wrapped in a piece of fabric from a small box. She slowly revealed a stack of thick cards, a little larger than playing cards. "Not believing doesn't mean it isn't true."

His gaze settled on the cards sitting in front of them. "Is this the witchy thing Brie told me about?"

She shuffled the cards, then slapped them down on the table. "Cut the cards," she demanded.

He complied with her request but lifted an eyebrow to signal his skepticism.

"It's the Stregheria tradition. Part of my heritage is Italian."

"Witchy stuff, though?"

"Am I scaring you?" She pointed to the cards spread across the center of the table. "Choose four. Past, present, future, and advice."

"I feel better. I should probably get going."

Cole started to stand, and she slapped her hands on the table. "Don't fuck with the spirits, dude."

He slowly slid back down onto his chair. He swallowed as a shudder curled up his spine. A cloud slid over the sun, dampening the light inside the room.

"Ask your question," Luna directed. He pondered his choices. "Will I..."

"Shh. Not out loud," Luna hissed. "Silently. The spirits can hear you."

He closed his eyes, even though she hadn't told him to. It seemed appropriate. He figured you gotta respect the spirits. Just in case.

Is there any chance Brie and I will ever get back together?

He wished his question didn't sound like a Taylor Swift song. No, wait, maybe he should ask if she genuinely cared about him. Was it too soon to ask about love? Did he love her?

Now he'd asked four questions, and he couldn't be sure which one the spirits were going to answer. Not that he believed in any of this.

Luna directed him to flip a card over. "Past." Her mouth twisted as she studied the image. "Lovers. They face a choice. What will it be?"

Cole stared at her, then glanced down at the card. "Does it say?"

Luna shook her head. "The tarot doesn't make choices for you. It presents options. Offers guidance."

She pointed to the next card. "Flip it over."

He did, and she made a humming noise in the back of her throat that sounded judgmental.

"A card for the present. It tells us a fool needs to be more spontaneous. Someone needs to lighten up and go with the flow."

"Do you think that's me or my lover?"

His question hung in the air for a few moments. She closed her eyes, and he watched her and waited.

When she finally opened her eyes, it seemed like a darkness swirled through them. "Since I know you and Brie, I'm going to go with both of you. She works too hard, cares too much, and tries to manage everything without asking for help."

She flipped a thumb at him. "I don't know you as well, but she told me you're crazy rich, so I'm guessing you're ambitious and driven to achieve. And you work when apparently you don't need to?"

He nodded. "Another card? Which one is it?"

"The future," she responded. "The one everyone wants to see, but few will accept." Her voice held a warning tone. He figured she enjoyed teasing him, but her expression was somber when he glanced at her.

"Five of swords. Looks like someone made a mess and needs to clean it up." Her mouth twitched into a smile. "I'm going to guess that's you."

"How is it useful to be told what you already know when there's no suggestion for how to fix it?" His head felt clearer, so he stood to leave. "It's all abracadabra, hocus-pocus shit anyway. I hope you've enjoyed yourself at my expense."

He tossed money on the table and turned to leave.

"Your last card," Luna said. "You just need to turn it over

and see what it says. It's the advice card, so you might regret not looking at it."

He walked back to the table and turned the card over.

"Two of cups." She raised an eyebrow at him. "Not an unexpected card."

He stared down at the image of the two lovers on the card. "Does this mean we'll get back together?"

"It signifies you're in a passionate relationship. The fire is a symbol of desire." She settled back in her chair and tapped the card. "Sex. Really, really great sex."

His head snapped up. "Is that what she told you?"

Luna picked up the cards he'd chosen and laid them back on top of the deck. "She gave you a five-star review on Yelp. The woman is in lust, that's for sure. I just don't think it's enough for her."

Cole nodded. "I know she's a settle down, picket fence, make it real kind of woman. I think I could want that too, but I'm just not sure."

As Luna wrapped the tarot deck back in the silk, she remained quiet. Finally, she put the cards in the box and crossed the room to grab several small fabric bags. She took a few more steps to remove the lid from a glass container and filled one bag. After scooping a mixture from another container into the other bag, she added a small glass bottle to the collection in her hand.

"Here's some more tea, to help calm you down. I'm adding this mixture to help relieve stress." She handed the items to him. "And this, to give you more energy."

He glanced down at the items in his hand. "Um, thank you?"

"Don't thank me yet. Just drink the tea at least twice a day. Don't operate machinery or drive after taking it. Late afternoon and evening are perfect times." She waved toward the window. "Drink it outside if possible. It adds to the effect."

"I'll create an account for you and send you the bill." She was all serious businessperson now. "As for your problems with Brie, the only advice I can give you is to consider what's most important to her. You already know what I'm talking about. If you understand what her dream is, you can help her achieve it."

He nodded. "And what if she doesn't want my help?"

"That would be typical for Brie, so you'll have to be creative and apply yourself to finding a solution. Don't make it about you being her hero and rescuing her. Make it about giving her a moment in the sun and letting her shine."

He stared at the dark-haired woman. Clouds moved, revealing her beauty in the morning light. She looked like a statue of an ancient goddess. A tall, regal, and statuesque huntress who could throw a bow and arrow over her shoulder and race through the forest.

"Thank you, Luna. I appreciate your help, even if I'm not exactly someone who'd be your usual customer."

"You will be, dude. Just wait and see." She shot him a devious grin.

He turned to leave, then remembered something he wanted to ask her.

"Can I ask a favor?"

"More than you've asked for this morning. I'm going to need to charge you more next time."

"It's not a big request, but I'm hoping you'll pass it on to Raina and Shelby."

Now she looked interested. "Getting the entire gang involved, huh?"

"It's not about Brie. It's just something she said about Wyatt."

"The shaggy guy who kept drawing us at the photo

shoot?" She watched as two women paused to look at some plants displayed in the covered entryway leading into the shop.

He needed to make his request before they came in.

"Please don't call Wyatt Sad Man Bun. If he heard it, he'd be..." Cole swallowed. "It would hurt his feelings. Deeply."

The door chime indicated the women had entered the store.

"Hello, ladies," Luna greeted them with a cheerful smile. "Welcome to the Apothecary. Look around and I'll be with you in a minute."

She turned back to Cole. "You have my word. Wyatt seems like a nice guy, and I just learned about his wife."

Cole frowned at her. "You know about...?"

"Yeah. It's a sad story, and none of us want to make him feel any worse than he already does." A shadow of sadness crossed her face.

He crossed the room and grabbed the doorknob, then something occurred to him.

"Are you calling me 'dude' because you don't know what name to use?"

She glanced over her shoulder at the women chirping happily over a shelf filled with handcrafted baskets.

"Who do you want to be?"

Her question hung in the air.

"Cole," he finally said. "I want to be Cole. Michael wasn't a very nice person, and despite appearances—Cole is the better man."

Luna bowed her head. "Nice to meet you, Cole. And I believe someone who cares that much about a friend must be a good person."

He finally grinned as he headed out the door. When he climbed into the driver's seat of his truck, he stopped to consider the strange time he'd spent in Luna's shop.

He didn't believe in spirits, or Ouija boards, or cards that predicted the future. Well, actually—Luna had informed him the cards wouldn't be a prophecy.

He thought about the things she'd told him.

The lust-blinded lovers certainly fit. He and Brie had discovered so much mutual pleasure, and had been so compatible, they'd hardly moved their relationship beyond the hooking-up sex bubble phase. Carnal satisfaction was a great goal, but it shouldn't be the only thing they shared.

And there was more. He loved talking to her and listening to her ideas about the library renovation. Her face lit up when she described the things in a makerspace her kids would love.

Her kids. The ones sitting in the circle at story time, the ones who struggled with math, or science, or reading and showed up after school for tutoring. The creative kids who made art, music, and crafts. And the teens who played video games. All of them making too much noise, causing a commotion, creating a disruption in a place that traditionally valued silence.

Except she'd told him the purpose of the library was to be a place of knowledge and a gathering space for the people in the community. An institution that trusted you to carry away expensive materials and bring them back, because you said you would. A library operated on the honor system. It was a place where the door didn't open for an entry fee other than a card issued to you at no cost.

A place where the people who worked there would defend your right to access information, even if it were controversial. In fact, they'd protect it even more if others wanted to prevent you from reading it, seeing it, or talking about it.

Cole yanked out his phone and started a text message to Violet. He didn't know the time in London, where she'd settled into an apartment for a month, but he'd wait for an answer.

In the meantime, he'd recruit Wyatt and Dylan to his

cause. They'd both sat on the sidelines long enough. Time for them to step up and help him.

He couldn't know if Brie would forgive him, or demand he stay out of her life forever. Even the spirits hadn't managed to answer that question. Cole couldn't give up without fighting for her, though.

Now to recruit for the battle.

TRUE CONFESSION: If only there was a sure way to get the right answers to life's questions. Everyone develops their own practice when needing guidance. There's talking to a friend or relative, reading, meditating, and even using a Ouija board or tarot cards to get an answer, or at least to be pointed in the right direction. Yet every method forces you to think deeply, ponder, and weigh the alternatives. When multiple pathways lead in different directions, there's often no correct answer, only the answer that makes the most sense at the time. And time isn't static; what works today might be a total failure in the future. All you can cling to is hope.

Chapter Twenty-One

BRIENNE

"I THINK these are the best photos you've taken of the posse so far, Taffy."

Brie continued to watch her friend shuffle through the images on her laptop. "I agree," she said, tossing her hot-pink-hued hair.

"The light that day was perfect, and you bitches outdid yourself with costuming."

Brie blushed, remembering how the members of the Mermaid Posse had gossiped about having a male audience for the photo shoot. She hated to admit it, but there had been a frisson of sexual tension running through the day.

Especially for her and Cole. A thought she dismissed immediately.

"It's going to be challenging to choose the four images to complete the calendar. Should we try to balance the shots between posing in and out of the water?"

Taffy kept clicking through the photos. "I haven't edited these much, so you and the other mermaids should look at the file and choose your favorites. Then I'll work on them for the ultimate choices."

Brie sat back in her chair and stretched. They'd been looking at images from the photo shoot for over an hour, and she'd developed a crick in her neck.

Taffy lounged on the sofa and closed her eyes. "So, what's up with your red-hot lover? Are you guys a couple, or is it just a sex thing?"

Brie settled her legs on the arm of her velvet upholstered chair and gave a sigh composed of sadness, frustration, and a trace of anger.

"He's not the guy I thought he was," Brie admitted. "He lied about something important, and I'm not sure I can forgive him."

She tried every day. Remembering how thoughtful, sweet, and sexy Cole had been when they were together. He'd begged for a chance to explain more about the reasons for his deception, but she'd refused to talk to him.

Not exactly a grown-up response.

"Is he married?" Taffy sat up to stare at Brie. "I'll kick his ass myself if he's that kind of lying, cheating bastard."

"Not that, so I guess I should be grateful. It's more about who he..." She stopped and wondered if she should talk about this. She'd already shared the entire story with Luna, but Luna was her best friend. Taffy was a friend, but she also dated Brie's brother sometimes. It was a sticky situation.

"He had a terrible experience a few years ago, with an old girlfriend who did something really shitty to him, and he doesn't trust easily. It's...complicated."

"Trust issues are tough to deal with, but you shouldn't stop seeing him if the two of you can talk and work it out."

"We haven't been able to do that, and I'm the one who refuses to speak to him. I've been so angry, and just can't seem to..." She stared out the window and remained silent for a few moments, aware she'd been the stubborn one. "It's tough to think clearly when I'm around him, so I just shut down and refuse to answer his calls or texts."

"You guys haven't been together long enough to break up." Taffy stared at her.

Brie stared back. "You'd be the authority on that, Taf. How many times have you and Ryder broken up? I've lost count."

Taffy flopped back on the couch and shut her eyes. "The important thing is we're done. No more on-and-off booty calls. I won't play second best anymore."

Brie caught the sadness beneath the comment. "I don't think Ryder ever thought of you that way."

But there was a morsel of truth in Taffy's comment. Taffy and Brie's brother had been together since Taffy transferred to their high school when she was a sophomore. Ryder had been a junior. They dated, and when he was a senior, they'd been the "It" couple at school. He'd been class president, captain of the baseball team, and a leader in the popular crowd.

Taffy was beautiful, with soft blue eyes, blond hair, and developing curves that invited approving glances from the boys. And she had a vivid imagination that captured everyone with her fun, lighthearted personality.

Then Ryder left for college, and they broke up. That was the first time. Brie remembered the tears, the depression, the heartbreak that had overwhelmed Taffy. It took months for her to recover.

When Ryder came home for the summer, the couple picked up where they'd left off. After graduation, Taffy moved to Philadelphia to study fashion design and merchandising. They broke up again. That time it took two years before they reunited.

Their relationship was like that for years. Brie would assume they were finished, then they'd show up together for dinner. Her parents were as confused as she was, and everyone wondered if they'd ever be able to work things out permanently.

"I don't know why you put yourself through this, Taf. He's my brother, but he's kind of an asshole. I love him, but he's a self-centered shit."

Taffy nodded. "I know, but we have something magical when it works. The problem is all the time in between the magic when he ignores me." She dropped her gaze and Brie noticed her eyes glowed with unshed tears.

"Stop it, Taf. Ryder doesn't deserve your sadness. The next time I see him, I'll punch him in the stomach for you."

Taffy wiped her eyes and turned to study Brie. "Maybe you should focus on your own love life instead. You and Cole could talk and work out this thing you're fighting about."

"It's a big thing, Taf. A thing that hurt me deeply because I trusted him, and he lied to me."

"Did he have a good reason to lie? Was he protecting someone else, or was it something he kept private for a friend? Sometimes, people hide the truth to protect others."

"He protected himself to prevent being embarrassed." Brie stood to pace across the room. "And it wasn't one thing, the lies stacked up. It was like a Jenga pile of lies when he finally confessed."

"Ouch," Taffy said. "That's too bad, because it sure looks like the guy has it bad for you."

Brie snorted. "Yeah, I think he wanted to find someone for fun and games. Which is pretty much what he got. No expectations, no commitment, and no real relationship."

Taffy stared at her, then clicked a key on her laptop. "I don't think that's true. I took a lot of photos of everyone at the pool the day of the shoot. Look at these."

An image appeared on the screen of Brie posing on the rock near the waterfall. Luna fussed with her hair, and they were laughing. Taffy moved the mouse and enlarged the image.

Cole stood to the side, watching them. Taffy focused in even more. "That expression is adoration, girl. He's looking at you like it's his birthday and you're the cake."

Brie studied the image. "Sexual attraction looks like that, too."

"A man doesn't have to like you to fuck you. Believe me, I know." Taffy changed the image to one with Cole holding Brie in his arms. She'd been pestering him to set her on a lounge chair, and he was threatening to toss her into the pool. They were laughing, his dimple carved deeply into his face and his eyes bright with good humor.

And she snuggled against him, her arms around his neck, her body leaning into his and knowing, trusting—that he only teased her. She wasn't afraid because she knew he wouldn't hurt her.

How had that trust dissolved in a few minutes at his house the other night? Was she refusing to listen to him and accept his apology because of her pride? Had she used Cole's confession to avoid dealing with their relationship? Was she so humiliated and embarrassed that she couldn't consider his feelings or talk to him?

Cole told her he wanted more, but she'd never let him tell her what more meant to him. She'd shut the door and ignored his pleas to try to work things out. And she knew, deep down in her bones, it was because she was terrified.

Brie was comfortable with a superficial arrangement that didn't involve investing in a genuine connection. She'd walked off the night he'd been honest with her to avoid any kind of serious commitment and grabbed at the excuse that he'd lied to her because she needed to protect her own feelings.

She'd never considered how difficult it must have been for him to admit the truth. He'd been embarrassed, that was true, but he'd also been vulnerable. Cole needed to protect himself, and yet he'd wanted to be with Brie enough to expose himself to her ridicule and more shame.

He needed to hide something from her, but when he was honest, she punished him by getting angry and running away. She'd acted exactly the way he expected her to, which was the reason he didn't tell her the truth about who he was in the first place.

She should punch herself in the stomach, or at the very least slap herself to prove how ridiculous she'd been.

Taffy started to pack her things. "I need to catch the ferry. I'm doing costumes for a show tonight."

"Fun," Brie responded automatically.

Taffy let her gaze drop to the large bag on the floor. "It's the reason Ryder and I broke up. He told me he's looking for a life partner, and I'm not a serious candidate for the position. He said too many people know I was part of the burlesque scene in the city." She slipped her computer into her tote bag.

"His actual words were, 'No politician can be saddled with a wife who's been a stripper and taken her clothes off on stage.'"

"You're an artist, not a stripper!" Brie took offense on Taffy's behalf. Once again, her brother had proven to be an asshole, and she wished he were here so she could punch him.

"I'm sorry, Taf. He's so strung out on becoming a politician, he can't see how much he hurts other people. When he decided to attend law school, he told my parents to sell the farm and retire because he never planned to run it. He didn't even acknowledge how much they love this place. Everything is about his life and ambition."

"Yeah, I know that Brie. So, can you explain why I've been his midnight lover for so long? Why did I put up with it?"

"If I could explain desire, passion, and lust, I'd be rich. I don't know how we can still be attracted to people who hurt us. How can our minds warn us to stay away, and our bodies betray us with a need to be with them?"

"Girl, you're getting too deep for me." Taffy opened the door. "Just think about talking to Cole. We can be wrong about guys because they have such a hard time telling us what they feel and need. Maybe you should give him another chance."

Brie hugged her. "Thanks for the advice, and if my brother shows up for Sunday dinner, I'll run him over with the tractor."

Taffy smiled before ducking out the door. "I appreciate that."

After she closed the door, Brie leaned against it to consider the advice Taffy offered. Should she call Cole and let him explain? Did she want to hear his voice, or would that weaken her defenses? Did she even know what she wanted him to say to make her feel better?

Before she could settle her thoughts, her phone chimed. It was Luna.

"Girlfriend, we gotta talk," Luna said when she answered. "Cole was here today."

༄༅ ༄

A Week Later

Brie watched the meeting room at the library slowly fill with familiar faces. She waved at the members of the teen advisory group, pleased to see them willing to show up on a school night to support the library.

Several parents and their preschoolers took seats near the back, probably in case the meeting to review the plans for the library renovation ran late or if their little ones got bored, they could make a quick escape.

More local citizens shuffled in, chatting as they recognized each other before finding a seat in one of the folding chairs. She waved at Luna and Raina, who had promised to attend to provide support.

Watching the entrance to the room, she wondered if Cole would show up. She'd sent him a text to invite him to speak at the meeting.

He didn't respond. Which probably meant he didn't plan to attend. Which was fine since he'd sent her all the images she'd requested for the presentation, and she certainly didn't need him there to explain the makerspace project or talk about the donation.

It would have been nice to introduce him to the board members. She probably could handle the presentation fine. Probably. Maybe?

She licked her lips and glanced at Marion Rush-Talbot, who sat in the middle of the table in front of the room and shuffled some papers. Her mouth tightly pursed. When she looked up at the audience, her expression showed her displeasure at the turnout.

When the building committee met, Marion dictated the public meeting should be held in the morning, and surprisingly, most of the board members objected. She'd argued with them about the need to schedule the meeting at the regular time of their meetings on the third Wednesday of the month at nine in the morning.

Argus McLain had been the first to disagree, suggesting since the renovation of the library was important to the Horseshoe Island community, the meeting should be held in the evening when more people could attend. Rosalie Ortega agreed, which wasn't a surprise. Rosalie was one of the most outspoken board members and she didn't seem to follow Marion's direction as much as several of the other members.

Then Olivia Eriksson, one of Marion's most dedicated

followers, also spoke up to object to the daytime meeting. Everyone had to strain to hear what soft-spoken Olivia said when she'd suggested working people on the island should learn about the plans. The only person who voted with Marion was Dr. Williams, and he'd contended that if the meeting were held after dark, it might limit the number of older people who would attend.

Ultimately, they scheduled the meeting for seven in the evening, and those committee members who had objected to the daytime schedule were rewarded with a large attendance tonight.

Several of the teachers from the elementary school entered together, and a group of senior citizens she recognized from her book group strolled in to take seats in the front row. Brie had suggested they carpool, and they'd agreed that hearing about the plan for the library was important for their age group. Which also proved Dr. Williams wrong.

The room continued to fill, and Brie felt a flicker of nervous energy. Public speaking made her anxious, and as she fussed with the laptop and projector set up in the middle of the room, she wished Cole were there.

Brie couldn't even articulate her reasons for that wish. She'd practiced the presentation many times and knew exactly what she planned to talk about. The flutter in her belly signaled stage fright and it would disappear as soon as she started to speak.

At least she hoped it would, because becoming tongue-tied and losing the thread of the discussion in the middle of the presentation could doom her dreams for the renovation.

And it would disappoint so many of the patrons. From the preschool story time kids to the teen after-school crowd to the senior members of the community, she cared about them all. She wanted a library with programs and services that spanned the ages of the residents of the island.

The mayor, Ted Griffin, who also owned one of the local real estate firms, hurried in as the chairs continued to fill. He whispered something to Marion, who frowned in response and somehow, impossibly, squeezed her lips even tighter. She nodded while looking like she'd sucked on something bitter.

Brie twisted the string of pearls around her neck and glanced at the crowd again. She smiled at Shelby and Ryan, Shelby's fiancé, as they settled into seats. All the chairs were filled and now it was standing room only.

An impressive turnout for the middle of the week, and it inspired Brie's confidence to realize so many of her friends were in the audience.

Mayor Griffin, a prematurely balding middle-aged man wearing a rumpled gray suit, stood up and waited for the audience to quiet down.

"Good evening, ladies and gentlemen, friends and neighbors. I'm delighted to see such a magnificent turnout for our meeting tonight. It shows strong support for our library. We're going to listen to a presentation about the upcoming renovations for this building."

He paused as his words were followed by a rousing round of applause.

"We'll hear some exciting ideas tonight, but nothing is settled until the City Council votes their final approval."

There was less applause at this pronouncement, and he frowned, looking like a dog who'd been scolded by his master.

"I'm sure we'll all be delighted once we see the plans." He bestowed his most beatific politician's smile on the audience.

Brie didn't expect Marion Rush-Talbot to be delighted. In fact, Brie wouldn't be surprised if the woman voiced her objections loudly and forcefully. Marion had barely adjusted to the idea that the renovation plans would move forward.

Maybe that was the reason Brie wished Cole were here. He could stand with her against the venom she anticipated

Marion to spew at her. Although even his height and the breadth of his shoulders might not serve as much of a defense against Marion's meanness.

"I'll now turn the meeting over to the president of the library board, and one of our most distinguished residents, Marion Rush-Talbot."

Marion stood, pausing for a smattering of applause from the audience. Her icy glare slid across the people attending and settled on a face that made her eyes snap wide open and her jaw drop in surprise. Then it squeezed into an expression of even greater disapproval.

Brie followed her gaze and nearly laughed out loud as Taffy waved. Resplendent in a short denim skirt and pink satin jacket over a white lace top, with a dark black bra visible underneath, she'd obviously dressed to irritate her grandmother. Pink and white striped knee socks and black platform shoes completed the outfit. She hugged a unicorn backpack and wiggled in her seat.

"Hey, Granny!" she shouted.

Taffy's greeting made Marion's face turn beet-red, and she'd clearly swallowed the imaginary lemon she'd been sucking on.

Taffy Zodiac, or Elizabeth Marion Talbot, the name on her birth certificate, was a constant thorn in her stuffy, proper grandmother's side. A role Taffy cherished, as her grandmother despaired of ever controlling the young woman who shared her name and possessed none of the characteristics Marion thought of as ladylike.

Just watching the two women silently interact made Brie smile. No matter what else happened tonight, this clash of forces was worth the price of admission.

Marion sniffed and looked away, then gave a discreet cough before proceeding.

"The library board takes the responsibility of creating a

plan for the renovation of this building seriously. We've consulted with several architects about the direction of the planned design, and we'll offer those this evening as a preliminary review. While we will listen to your suggestions, you need to understand the final decision is for our board members to make."

Mayor Griffin lifted partly from his seat. "And the City Council, of course." He sat again.

Marion gave a frigid smile as she glared at the mayor. "Of course."

"Brienne Henderson will show us several plans, and we'll have a public discussion afterward," Marion announced.

Brie nodded and stood. "Could someone please lower the lights?" She glanced at Shelby, who sat next to the light switch to assist with the presentation.

After Shelby dimmed the lights, Brie began with several slides of the current building, with outside shots of the entrance, the sign on the front of the building, and the entryway.

"It's been suggested that we add a coffee bar in the area with the shelves for the Friends of Horseshoe Island book sales." That had been Marion's suggestion, and the one she seemed to be most focused on. She'd insisted the sale of coffee would serve as a fundraiser and pay for an extra employee.

That suggestion met with a murmur of disagreement from the audience, but Marion extinguished it with a reminder that there would be time for discussion at the end of the meeting.

The next images were of the current interior of the library, with the computer stations crowded together, the teen corner looking battered as usual, and the shabby carpet samples in the children's area that were used as designated seating during story time. The spaces were bland and colorless, with worn furniture and overloaded shelves forming the stacks.

"Brienne, move on to the first set of plans," Marion commanded.

The image flipped to a design rendering of the interior of the library. There were some new shelves, several more computer stations, but no additional lights or seating to divide the teen area. Brie worried the space would be even darker. There were two small tables with matching chairs that could seat younger children. A painted mural above a set of corner shelves designated the story time section of the library, merging the spaces for teens and younger children.

As Marion described the various re-designed spaces in glowing terms, emphasizing how inexpensive these renovations would be for the library, Brie closed her eyes. Marion tried to turn the proverbial sow's ear into a silk purse, focusing on how profitable a coffee bar could be, but the silence in the room showed little enthusiasm for this design.

Apparently, Marion could read the room. "Let's move on to the next design," she demanded.

The next layout for the main room changed the alignment of the computers, putting them around the perimeter of the room. A computer table pictured with laptops on it and two tall tables with chairs in one corner designated the teen area. Colorful shelving made the spaces more inviting than the previous design. A glass wall separated the main library from a story time room, and child-size furniture was scattered around the enclosed room.

The main room had more high shelving, and Brie winced at the towers of books that divided the space. The stacks were necessary, but this design didn't organize the materials to make them any more accessible, and the overall look seemed dark and crowded.

"Turn on the lights and I'll open this meeting for public discussion," Marion commanded.

"I'd like to share one more design," Brie said, her voice trembling.

Marion stood. "Brienne, the committee has only discussed two designs. Please don't waste our time with any of your ridiculous notions about creating a makerspace in the library. Libraries are for books!"

Brie's mouth turned dry as a desert wind. She'd planned every word of her presentation, but for some reason she couldn't muster even a squeak. As she stared at Marion, just as she feared, her brain fogged.

"Oh, Granny, stop being such a drag. Tell us about your ideas for the library, Brie." Taffy's voice cut through the brain clouds and Brie discovered her voice.

Taking a deep breath, Brie clicked on the first of the slides she'd created with Cole's help. "For this plan, we'd add nearly two thousand square feet of space to the rear of the library. We'd move the back room and offices and create a multi-purpose space that can be arranged for different kinds of programming, workshops, and events."

An illustration with long tables, chairs, and shelving was next. "We'll be able to use laptops and tablets to offer programs on coding, video game design, composing music, and more. With several 3D printers, we can teach patrons of all ages how to use CAD software." She paused before adding, "CAD stands for 'computer-aided design.'"

There was a sigh from the crowd at her explanation.

"In addition to technology, like a recording studio, there will be sewing machines, arts and craft materials, scanners, a turntable to convert records to digital files and more."

The room filled with a hum of anticipation. Brie went on. "The room could also be configured for large community meetings, training for local businesses…"

"Brienne!" Marion's sharp voice stunned Brie into silence. "This is ridiculous. You know we don't have the budget for this. Nor is it necessary for the library to provide these kinds of things. People spend enough time staring at their phones and computers. We don't need to encourage them to waste more time. The library is about actual books and reading quietly."

Brie shrank back, her voice drying up again.

"Nonsense," a voice erupted from the audience. "I'm eighty-two years old and Brie taught me how to download books to my tablet."

A woman from one of Brie's book clubs came to her defense. "Now I can adjust the type and it's made reading a lot easier on my eyes. Those are books too."

"My students would love to learn more about coding, and some of them don't have access to computers at home," one of the middle school teachers said.

"I've always wanted to learn to sew. If classes were offered here, I wouldn't have to spend a lot of money before I learned," a preschool parent added.

Several other voices joined in, suggesting ways they'd access the equipment in the suggested makerspace.

Marion wielded her gavel to quiet the room. "The library doesn't have the money for this sort of thing. We need to be responsible stewards of public funding." She lifted her chin and flung a triumphant glare at Brie.

"I've secured a promise of funding for this project from several community members." Brie took a deep breath. "I've been assured we can count on a million-dollar donation to support this design."

The room became silent as her announcement swirled around the space. Finally, Marion's dry, choked laughter echoed around them. Brie was shocked, because she'd never actually seen Marion Rush-Talbot smile, much less laugh.

The sound reminded her of a certain purple fairytale villain with tentacles. Or maybe the woman who wanted a dalmatian coat.

"This is nonsense, and I don't know why you're talking about this absurd idea. A million-dollar donation to our tiny library?" There was a snicker in her voice. "It's ridiculous."

"Because I assured her of the donation if that design was approved."

Cole's deep voice stunned Marion as her gaze jerked to the back of the room. The lights flickered on, and there he stood. His dark blue suit framed his impressive physique and emphasized his broad shoulders and long legs. He was clean-shaven, and Brie nearly swallowed her tongue as she noticed how his previous scruff had managed to hide the sharp cheekbones and angular chin. Cole was even more handsome than she remembered.

She bit her lip, trying to ignore the flash of heat whipping through her body.

"And just who are you?" Marion screeched.

Cole walked up the aisle separating the sets of folded chairs and stood in front of Mayor Griffin, extending his hand. The mayor shook it heartily. "Mr. Moore, so nice to see you again."

It hardly seemed possible Marion's face could pinch any tighter, but by some miracle of physics, it did.

The mayor turned to her. "Mr. Moore is a local businessman. He's new to our community, but his consortium has made several large real estate purchases in the past few years."

Brie stared at Cole, and he winked at her. She worked to regain her equilibrium when he moved closer to her. She inhaled the familiar cedar scent that trailed him, and it made her want to bite her knuckle.

Fuck, he smelled good. She wanted to dissolve into him and ignore everything else.

Unfortunately, that "everything else" was a room full of library patrons and board members. If her legs weakened and she fell to her knees, would they notice?

"Ms. Henderson has been assisting me with the details of the donation. I requested she not share any information about our agreement until tonight. She respected the privacy of the donors, who wish to remain anonymous."

Marion crossed her arms. "So, we're to believe you arranged this donation in secret, and Brienne kept it to herself despite a requirement she inform the board of any outside funding the library might receive." She glared at Brie.

"You have broken the terms of your contract, and I'll call a special meeting tomorrow to insist on your dismissal."

Brie stared at the older woman, trying to process her words. *Had she just been fired? In public?* She turned to stare at Cole, who seemed as shocked at Marion's pronouncement as she was.

"I doubt that will be necessary," a voice interjected. It was Rosalie Ortega, who slowly stood and walked across the room to confront Marion. "Arranging a huge donation for the library is a reason for a promotion, not for dismissing someone."

The crowd joined in with a whoop and laughter as Marion suddenly sat. "I won't stand for..."

Rosalie stared into Marion's face. "I'll be elected president of the board if you don't behave, Marion. As chairperson of the building committee, I have the support to replace you."

Brie's heart leaped at the words and her spirit soared at the possibility she might be named as the permanent manager for the library.

The meeting ended abruptly.

She noticed the expression on Marion's face as the older woman gathered her coat and purse and scuttled out the door, her complexion a frightening shade of puce.

Bless Taffy for being a good person and following her grandmother. She endured Marion's endless criticism to maintain their relationship.

Cole stepped away to talk to the mayor and several members of the library board. Brie's friends quickly surrounded her.

Shelby jumped up and down in excitement. "You did it, Brie. You beat that old witch and the new design is going to be amazing."

Brie accepted the congratulations of her friends and members of the public. There were more steps ahead in planning the renovation, but a major hurdle had been surmounted. They'd secured the funds for creating the modern library she'd dreamed about for so long.

And Cole was the reason she'd been successful. He'd let her prove she could handle the responsibility, but showed up when she needed him. Cole could have taken over the presentation, but he knew she could handle the pressure.

In fact, he'd recognized her abilities before she did, and placed a great deal of trust in her.

Could she trust him and give him another chance?

TRUE CONFESSION: It's amazing how fate can throw you a lifeline just when you think you've lost the things you genuinely care about. It's the moment when "your people" show up for you. When those you've supported and cared about during their own hard times know you need them.

Chapter Twenty-Two

COLE

COLE LEANED against Brie's Bronco, waiting for her to close the library after the meeting. He should have been inside, helping her and Shelby fold the tables and chairs to put them away.

Instead, he stood outside because he wanted to talk to her in private, even though she might ignore him, get into her vehicle, and drive away.

They still needed to sort things out between them.

Brie's refusal to answer any of his texts or calls convinced him he had to face her and break through the wall she'd built between them. He'd encouraged her friends to collect a supportive crowd for the presentation tonight, but he'd kept his distance from Brie. He'd known she could handle the explanation of the design for the makerspace, because she'd demonstrated time after time her commitment to her patrons and the community.

She taught him when you have the resources to give back to your community, you should be responsible and do whatever you can to help. And he'd used that logic to convince Dylan and Wyatt to help organize part of their foundation to fund local projects. Time for them to stop shutting out the world to escape their problems.

Telling Brie the truth about who he was might have destroyed any hope they could build a relationship together. At the time he'd confessed to the lies he'd told, it seemed the best choice to protect himself.

That assumption turned out to be false. The pain of losing her respect and trust hit him like a thunderbolt. He couldn't focus on work and spent too many sleepless nights tossing and turning in his bed. Her refusal to talk to him made him realize how much he missed her.

He missed her laughter, her joy at simple things, her sense of fun and her willingness to tease him as much as his best buddies did. Not to mention her hot, sweet mouth, the delicious curves of her body, and her eager response to his touch.

He couldn't imagine sex with any other woman after being with Brie. She was unique, a delightful surprise that kept him wondering what erotic pleasures they'd share if they could work things out.

Finally, Brie and Shelby exited the front door. Shelby glanced in his direction and pointed. She said something to Brie, who shook her head and watched as the other woman climbed into her car to leave.

As Brie crossed the parking lot, he rehearsed what he needed to say to her before she escaped into her own vehicle. He was as nervous as a gamer in his first tournament. Aware he probably would only have one opportunity to convince her to give him another chance.

She opened the rear door of the Bronco, and a surge of fear washed over him. He didn't have a Plan B for things not working out tonight. He'd hoped his appearance and support at the meeting would ease some of the tension between them.

Brie tossed several bags into her car, then rounded the back to meet him on the passenger side.

"I'm so sorry—" he began before she stepped forward and put a hand on his chest.

"Thank you." She stepped even closer, and he inhaled her unique scent. He needed to ask Luna to create a bottle of that for his personal use. Not that he'd confess how he planned to use it.

"I, um…" He couldn't remember what he wanted to tell her because her touch reminded a lower body part how much it missed this woman.

She gazed up at him. "I didn't think you'd show up tonight, but I hoped you would."

Now her other hand smoothed the lapel of his suit, and he swallowed a moan. How could he tell her how lonely he'd been and how much he wanted her if his mouth went dry and his heart pounded so hard, he hoped she couldn't hear it beating?

And he hoped he wasn't going to have a panic attack in front of her. He wished he had some of the magic potion Luna had given him. He still wasn't sure about the ingredients, but it worked so well that it had saved him several times this past week when any attempt at mindfulness had resulted in dwelling on the argument with Brie.

Her words finally struck him. "You hoped, but you weren't sure?"

"I've been a bit unfair to you." She stared into his eyes.

He raised an eyebrow as he tipped his head. "A bit? You wouldn't talk to me or even answer my texts."

"I know, but I had to sort some things out." Her hands continued traveling to smooth the fabric covering his shoulders.

"And I can't think straight when I'm with you." She licked her lips, and that resulted in another jolt to his already too-stiff erection. Maybe she planned to kill him with unbridled lust tonight.

He couldn't fight the temptation as he bent forward to kiss her. She pulled back from him as she dropped her hands that had been touching him.

His frustration escalated as he tried to control his reaction to her.

"Luna told me you visited her last week." Frown lines appeared between her stormy gray eyes.

"She did a hocus-pocus thing on me, and told me I made a mess of things, but tonight, I tried to fix some of it." He folded his arms in an effort to control his desire to wrap them around her.

"We need to talk." She glanced around the parking lot. "And this isn't the best place to have a serious conversation.

"A storm is coming." She glanced up at the dark sky. "We need to find a place to sort this out."

He nodded. "How about my boat?"

"Too many memories."

"Good ones, I hope." He pressed his advantage.

"A bit cramped, though." Her seductive smile told him what he needed to know.

"I never got the full tour of your amazing house."

"So, you think my house is amazing?"

"You have a tower and a wine cellar. I'm intrigued. Do you have a dungeon in the basement?" There was a flicker of teasing in her eyes and her mouth lifted slightly at the corners. He took it as a good sign.

He finally gave in to the temptation to touch her and put several fingers on the side of her cheek to trace a pattern to her full lips. Her skin was as soft and warm as he remembered.

"I don't have one now, but I can make it happen. All you need to do is ask."

"I'll settle for a tour. Should I meet you there?" she

whispered before turning to circle the Bronco. She slid into the driver's seat and waved at him as she started the engine.

He was too dazed at her suggestion to move. As she backed up, he finally realized he needed to get into his truck, or she'd get there before he did.

Her agreement to meet him privately added another jolt to his dick. If they talked things over, they might resolve things tonight.

Which meant they could end up in bed together.

He resisted the temptation to speed back to his house while working to maintain control of his overactive imagination and libido. There was no guarantee she wouldn't seize this opportunity to tell him off again before walking out of his life forever.

But the signals she'd been giving off didn't match that scenario. She'd admitted to avoiding physical contact between them to think more clearly about their relationship.

It was a point in his favor, and he'd take any scrap of encouragement he could get.

When he finally pulled into his driveway, she stood on the porch waiting for him. It cheered him up that she'd followed through and shown up.

Brie met him at his door and waited as he entered the code to unlock it. She glanced up and noticed the security camera.

"For a rich guy, you don't have much security," she commented.

"You don't see the security. I have a team in the boathouse. If they're doing their job right, you shouldn't notice them."

She paused in the entryway. "I'm not sure if I'm more impressed that you have a security team or a boathouse."

"The boathouse is amazing. I have a canoe, wakeboards, several kayaks, and a..." he paused, not sure if he'd sound like he was bragging if he told her about the yacht.

She stopped at the edge of the living room to blink at him.

"And?"

"Another boat?" he suggested.

Brie narrowed her eyes. "How big is it?"

"Under fifty feet. It has two staterooms, about the same size as the sailboat."

"Impressive," she responded. "Exactly how rich are you?" Her cheeks turned bright red, and she held up a hand. "Sorry. That's a nosy question and you don't have to answer it."

"Let's just say I won't make the top of the *Forbes* list. And remember, when all your wealth is reported, it's based on assets too, not just cash in the bank."

He grinned and glanced down at his feet. "Can we change the subject? Would you like a drink? I have more of that bubble gum wine you like so much."

"Fine. Change of subject and yes to the wine." She looked around. "Where's that precious doggie of yours?"

He headed into the kitchen and opened the wine cooler.

"My dog is in the boathouse. They spoil him over there."

He unscrewed the top of the rosé and held up the twist top to examine it. "Nothing says quality like an easy-to-open bottle of wine."

She squinched her face at him. "Try not to be a snob, Cole. Since I don't know enough about wine to be discerning, I'll just go with the one I like."

After he poured the pink bubbly stuff into a wine glass, he filled a tumbler with his favorite whiskey and carried both to the couch, handing the wine to her.

Leaving more distance between them than he preferred, he joined her on the couch. How could he figure out his status between them? Friend? One with benefits or frenemy? It remained to be seen.

"Well?" she finally asked.

He understood what it meant when someone referred to being a deer caught in the headlights of an oncoming car. He swallowed and didn't know what she expected him to say. Should he apologize again?

"I'm honestly sorry about…"

She stood and gazed down at him like he was unbelievably dense. Which, to be honest, was probably true.

She headed toward the huge staircase, glancing over her shoulder. "You promised me a tour of the house, or did you have something else in mind when you invited me here?"

The tone of her voice lit up all the cells in his already aroused body. He wondered if steam rose from his head because it seemed possible.

"That's where the bedrooms are," he replied as he stood.

"Hm." She started up the stairs. "How many are up there?"

He stumbled as he hurried into the kitchen to grab the wine bottle. "Five, and three have ensuite bathrooms."

Shit, now he sounded like they were on a *Hearth and Home* show, as he highlighted the exceptional quality of the real estate he showed her. Sometimes he really lived up to the "geek" identity. He'd worked so hard to overcome his quirkiness, but a home gym, some therapy, and money couldn't cure everything when you grew up an awkward kid.

BRIENNE

"Take a right," he suggested as she reached the top of the stairs ahead of him. She wondered if he was directing her to his bedroom. Or a sex room? She shivered at the idea of a room with an apparatus for tying her to the bed. Would she be disappointed he didn't have one? Could he be a Christian Grey type?

Cole dashed up the last steps to join her as she meandered

down the hallway to open the first door on the right. She stood gazing into the room, then turned to give him a playful grin.

"Is this your room, Cole? I love the pink roses on the wallpaper, and the chandelier over the bed is precious."

The soft pink and gray décor served as an unfluffy opposite to the design of her cottage. It had a feminine touch, but the furniture was mid-century modern and sophisticated.

"Hilarious. It's my sister Kate's room. She likes to come and stay here when she gets a break, which isn't often now that she's a resident at Seattle Children's Hospital and works crazy hours."

"That's nice of you, Cole, to let her have her own room here. You're a considerate big brother." She turned to gaze at him. He surprised her sometimes with his demonstrations of caring.

"We have a great relationship." He nodded. "I'm sure you love your brother, too."

"I'm actually contemplating running over him with the tractor the next time he comes home." She narrowed her eyes and thinned her lips.

"No!" Cole shook his head vigorously." You'll get blood all over the tractor, and then it'll get impounded as a murder weapon."

"Should I be worried your first concern is for the tractor? I just confessed to wanting to commit fratricide, and you're more concerned about the murder weapon than the victim?"

"I haven't met your brother yet." Cole shrugged. "But I love that tractor."

After rolling her eyes at him, she took another sip of wine and continued down the hallway. She opened a door and her jaw dropped as her eyes focused on the glass-enclosed shower room.

"I don't know what all of those knobs are for, but I'd love

to discover what they do." She continued to stare at the hardware and made a sound that might be confused with the noises she uttered when they had sex. She stared at the rain showerhead in the middle of the tiled room.

"We could strip down and try it out," he suggested.

Her head snapped around to stare at him. She actually considered his offer and turned back for one last lingering look at the showerhead before squeezing around him.

"Maybe later," she said as she exited the room and continued down the hallway.

She peeked into the two other rooms, which were basic guest rooms. He admitted he'd put little thought into the design since members of his family were the only guests he entertained regularly.

"They enjoy my boats, water sports, and island life. They don't pay attention to anything inside except the large-screen television sets and consider bedrooms a place to sleep so they can get up and get back to the water."

She grinned at him. "So basically, you offer them a pretty lavish B&B."

"Apparently, getting rich enough to build them a resort redeemed the skinny techie kid who couldn't live up to his dad's expectations growing up," he replied, his voice tinged with regret.

He'd never talked about his family much, but they would talk about that another time. She finished her glass of wine.

"Where's your room, Cole?"

Cole pointed in the opposite direction.

"My bedroom is a series of spaces. There's a lounge area, a massive bathroom, and an office."

She slid by him, and he followed her. She paused at the closed door. "Finally, the inner sanctum. I think our bedrooms can tell us a great deal about someone's needs and desires."

"I believe this can tell you more than my bedroom." He pointed toward his crotch.

"A little crass, Cole, but I get the message." She laughed, the sound echoing in the hallway.

Grabbing the doorknob, he turned it and gestured as if she were entering a throne room. "I doubt it can compare to your fluffy boudoir, my lady, but enter."

She laughed again, stepped into the room, then halted. Her mouth dropped open in surprise. Brie didn't hide her response because the room was impressive.

"It's the one room in the house I insisted on designing. My plan was for casual comfort with a touch of machismo. I also made sure it would never be called fluffy."

She wandered to the sitting area with a couch, chairs, and a coffee table, then turned to him. "Your bedroom is bigger than my entire cottage. I'm embarrassed. I was so proud of my tiny space."

"Your cottage is adorable, it's so...you."

Waving to encompass the room they were standing in, she shook her head. "I can't compete with this. It's so..."

"Impressive? Prodigious or possibly too big?"

She blinked at him, remembering she'd uttered similar words when describing a part of his anatomy.

"Impressive," she finally responded. Then she quirked a smile at him before crossing the room to open the door to the bathroom. One glance and she slammed it shut again.

"You are clearly a purveyor of house porn. We wouldn't need to go down the hall to use that amazing shower. You have one of your own."

She pointed at the closed door across the room. "Is that your dungeon?"

"Sometimes it feels like it. I'm afraid I'm not fifty shades of anything except possibly geek." He blushed. "There's a serious Lego collection in that room. My penchant for the Star

Wars sets might convince you I've never grown out of my ten-year-old boy phase."

"Now I'm truly intrigued." She crossed the room to open the door and gasped. "You have a Millennium Falcon hanging from the ceiling." She stepped into the room and squealed with delight.

"And you have the Ewok village! That's fucking awesome!" She slapped her hand over her mouth. "Sorry, that just slipped out."

Her gaze traveled around the room, taking in the various completed sets in his collection.

She fought the temptation to tease him about actually being a ten-year-old in a man's body. A man deserved hobbies, didn't he? Childhood obsessions turned into adult collections. Just ask eBay shoppers who tried to purchase the toys they played with as kids.

"Shall we talk?" he finally suggested.

She reluctantly closed the door to his office. "I plan to go back in there and discover all your secret obsessions. Did you bring the wine?"

He held up the bottle. He gestured toward the couch, but she crossed to his enormous bed and sat, then glanced around her. "I'm reserving judgment on this, except to wonder why you have a bed that could hold at least half a dozen people. Are there some kinks I need to know about?"

"Nothing you don't already know, but I'm open to suggestions," he replied before offering her more wine.

When he'd refilled her glass, she pointed at the fireplace. "Can you light the fire? I think the storm is moving in and it will cozy things up in here."

He hit the button to light the gas fireplace. When he turned back to her, she'd slipped off her shoes and was settling against a pile of pillows she'd arranged against the padded headboard.

He stared at her, then removed his suit jacket and flung it on a chair. She remained quiet and studied him. He slid his shoes off, apparently still waiting for her to say something.

When he started to unbutton his shirt, she held up a hand to stop him. "We have some important things to discuss before you get too excited."

"Too late." He stared down at the bulge in his pants and shrugged. "There are some things I have no control over."

She stifled a laugh and patted the space on the bed next to her. "Get over here."

He was quick to jump on the bed, and the wine in her glass swirled dangerously. When he finally settled next to her, she inhaled his familiar primal scent. It was so arousing; she felt the tips of her nipples harden and the heat at her core flare.

He took a sip of his whiskey, then leaned back, waiting silently for her to begin the conversation.

"Let's start with some important details," she said. "Which Star Wars film is the best? I'm talking about the original six in the franchise, not the later ones created to extend the market."

"That's the most important question you have to ask me?"

"I'm establishing a foundation for communication and understanding. If we can't agree on the important things, how can we possibly work out the finer details of our relationship?"

He held up his fist and raised one finger. "*Star Wars: A New Hope*, because it established the world and introduced our main characters. *Return of the Jedi* is second best because Luke returned to fulfill his mission to become a true Jedi." He grinned. "And it has ewoks."

"Acceptable choices." She sipped her wine before setting the glass on the table next to the bed. "Now we need to talk about us."

"I wanted to explain how I ended up here under a different name. It wasn't just to protect *my* reputation." He finished the whiskey and set the empty glass on the table next to him.

"Go ahead. I've been waiting for this." She slid down the bed to turn on her side so she could see him better.

"I told you who my business partners are." He stared at her. "But I didn't tell you the entire story." He took a deep breath, letting it out slowly.

"Dylan lives at Windswept, the house we were at for the photo shoot, with the incredible pool. When we were in college, we'd come out here during breaks. His mother designed it, and since his father divorced her to marry a woman younger than Dylan, the family doesn't use it anymore."

"And Wyatt? What's his story? He's not just an artist, right?"

"Much more," Cole admitted. "When we built our gaming business together, I became the CFO because of my degree was business management. I had a minor in computer science. Dylan oversaw the story narrative, writing the script and the music. He had double majors in music and creative writing, plus he has a knack for coding."

"I didn't know your friends were so smart and talented. I thought they were slackers."

"You don't know how pleased they'd be to hear that." He laughed. "Wyatt's the artist; he designed the skins, um, characters and he's a coding genius. We moved into an apartment after we graduated and worked ridiculous hours on creating the game that launched Yeti Entertainment."

"So that's how you got so rich? I can understand why *you* went into hiding. At least it makes sense. Why did they join you in going underground?"

"There was a fourth member of our team. Wyatt's girlfriend, who became his wife. Amy."

"I remember you mentioning her. She died a couple of years ago."

"She was the best coder on our team. More important, she was our cheerleader." He swallowed, and his eyes reflected a deep sadness. "When we'd get discouraged and wanted to quit, it was Amy who forced us to turn off our computers and take a break. She'd organize a special dinner and get us all involved in cooking and cheer us up as only she could. Amy wasn't just one of us. To be honest, she was the best of us."

His voice trembled with emotion as he gazed into the flames of the fireplace.

"What happened?"

"Ovarian cancer. She and Wyatt were trying to have a baby when they learned she was sick."

She placed a hand on his thigh. "I'm so sorry, Cole. That must have been hard on all of you."

"Wyatt was destroyed." He turned to gaze at her. "We all were. Then Dylan went through a very public separation from a Hollywood starlet, and I had to deal with my shit. We moved out here to Dylan's place, just to get away, and we never left. We could disappear on Horseshoe Island, so we did."

Now that she'd heard the complete story, she understood what made the three friends decide to disappear into obscurity.

"I'm sorry. I have no right to…"

Cole held up a hand to stop her. "I wanted to explain that some decisions weren't just mine to make. I created a foundation with Dylan and Wyatt, and the library project is the first thing we've funded. We're going to focus on donating to agencies and groups that help people here on the islands."

"You and your buddies are pretty cool geeks." She slid her hand along his clean-shaven cheek. "And I have to admit, this new look is really working for me."

"You don't miss the cute, scruffy dude?"

"I wouldn't go that far. I think I'm proof you can have more than one persona."

His gaze fell on the top button of her white blouse. "Isn't that the outfit you wore to our first meeting at Three Geeks?"

"Maybe." She fluttered her eyelashes and licked her lips. "I didn't realize you noticed what I wore that day."

"As if I'd ever forget. I couldn't get up to walk you out because, after you hugged me, I had a raging boner." He pointed at her breasts. "There's some familiar white lace peeking out."

"Library board meetings require conservative attire. I don't think it would be appropriate to show up in my corset." She formed her lips into a little pout.

"In my dreams." He grinned. "Can I take a little peek? Please?"

The heat that had been stranded between her legs flashed through her body. Excitement and anticipation created butterflies beneath her stomach. She nibbled at her bottom lip before casting a suggestive look in his direction.

"Sure, but turnaround is fair play. You unbutton me, and I'll unbutton you."

She lowered her gaze and could see his obvious reaction to her suggestion. She enjoyed teasing him.

"I want you, Brie. More than I've ever wanted any woman. I've missed you so much." He unfastened the top button of her blouse. "This isn't casual for me. I want..." he paused. "I *need* to be with you."

His fingers worked at the second button, exposing an expanse of skin and the delicate lace of her bra. He slid his tongue along the edge of the lace, and she realized she'd spilled a bit of wine on her breasts.

Someday she'd deliberately dribble wine there and invite him to lick it off. Just the thought of it made more heat pulse through her body.

A low growl showed he was as aroused as she was. He finished opening her blouse, then stared at the lace bra supporting her breasts. She could tell he enjoyed the view.

She set her wine on a side-table. As she reached for him, he moved closer to make it easier for her to unfasten the buttons of his shirt. After spreading the two pieces of fabric, she slid her palms across his chest, enjoying the firm muscles that rippled beneath her hands.

Cole leaned forward, grasping her chin lightly with one hand and capturing her mouth with a hot, possessive kiss that telegraphed all the yearning he'd experienced since they'd argued.

It was a sensual hunger she shared, as she opened her mouth and responded to him with tiny gasps and moans. She surrendered to her lust-crazed emotions.

Working to unbuckle his belt, she slid his zipper down, finally reaching into the opening to grasp his thick erection.

A deep, guttural sound rewarded her efforts as he responded to her touch. He covered her mouth with his again as his tongue slid between her lips to tangle with hers. The kiss was deep and demanding. She understood how much he wanted her because she trembled with pent-up desire.

He pulled back, sliding his tongue down her neck to nestle against the dip at the top of her shoulder. She closed her eyes to enjoy the path of pleasure he elicited as he explored further, pulling at the lace of her bra to expose her breasts and the hard nipples on the tip of her areolas. His tongue made a path around one nipple, licking the tender skin before he took it into his mouth to suck.

"We should get naked," she said as her eyes fluttered open, and he nodded. He rolled off the bed, and before she could stand, he flipped her over and slowly unzipped the back of her skirt.

It was the same skirt she'd worn weeks ago at the first visit to his office. The one with a flirty ruffle along the edge. He tugged at that ruffle to slip the skirt off.

He stared at her for a few moments before squeezing his palms around each ass cheek. She recalled the pure ecstasy of him taking her from behind when she appeared in his office wearing the steampunk outfit and fought the temptation to suggest they repeat the experience tonight. She wanted his lips on hers as he thrust into her, and she wouldn't make any attempt to control the sounds of pleasure she made as he fucked her. Most of all, she wanted to see his face when he climaxed.

After he turned her on her back, she watched him finish removing his clothing. He took his time, enjoying the way her gaze remained focused on him.

When he was finally naked, he joined her on the bed.

"Are you warm enough?" he asked, returning to tease her with his mouth and tongue.

"Yes," she answered, closing her eyes again and tossing her head against the pillow. "Hot. So hot."

She wasn't sure if she was talking about the ambient warmth of the room or how much she wanted him. It didn't matter.

She spread across the bed, whispering encouragement as he continued to arouse her. He rubbed his erection against her thigh so she could feel how engorged he was before he moved to lick the other breast.

Her breath was coming in small pants now. His tongue slowly made a path down her midriff, gliding across her stomach, and he paused for a moment, apparently to enjoy the view of her pussy.

The thong covering her didn't offer much resistance as he slid the small piece of white lace down her legs, finally tossing it aside. He slid his hands behind her, unfastened her bra and paused to enjoy the view of her lying naked on his bed.

"It nearly broke me the night you left after our argument. You walked away from me. I fought every urge to follow you, but you'd asked me to let you go. I regret I ever did that, and I'm never going to let it happen again."

He placed two fingers on each side of her mons, then opened her to expose the delightful pearl of pleasure seated at the top of the opening.

She wiggled as he licked her, then put his hands beneath her, lifting and spreading her as if he were preparing to enjoy a succulent feast. They were wild, wanton, and the scent of her arousal seemed to fuel his hunger.

When she gasped, he seemed to realize she was on the edge of a climax. He lifted his head and sat up, leaving a finger rubbing against the opening.

"Not yet, Brie. I need to be inside of you when you come." He moved between her legs, spreading them wider, and placing the tip of his thick erection at her opening. He eased into her slowly, measuring the slickness and being careful not to hurt her. Her dew made a wet path for him.

Finally, he thrust deep into her, and she responded with a moan. She watched him settle on his elbows above her. He nearly withdrew, then plunged into her again and again as she lifted her hips to meet each movement, their bodies engaging in a primal rhythm.

When he lifted one of her legs to settle it on his shoulder, it allowed him to slide even deeper inside of her. Brie made tiny sounds of pleasure as they moved together, their bodies shifting. She eagerly welcomed him to plunge deeper, harder, faster.

She climaxed first, as ripples of delight coursed through her body, and she screamed his name. Wave after wave of pleasure overwhelmed her senses, as she floated effortlessly on a cloud of intense carnal satisfaction.

Cole followed soon after, pulsing into her depths. His

own sounds of completion were as rough and wild as hers had been, and he took deep, shuddering breaths as he fought to recover some control. She listened to him struggle to breathe, and it took several minutes before he lifted off her, moving slowly to withdraw and then flop on the bed next to her.

Her own breathing was ragged, as if she'd run a relay. She put one hand on his chest, and she knew he was working to calm his heartbeat.

They studied each other.

"I don't know what you want, Brie, but I want you. On *your* terms. You can move in here with me. I'll even give you your own room and you can fluff it up as much as you want. Or you can stay in your cottage, and I'll sneak out there to visit you and hope your father doesn't get his shotgun fixed.

"I'm falling in love with you. I'm sure of that. Or I've already fallen. I've never felt the way I feel about you before. So, this feeling, it's probably love, right?"

She stared at him. "I think you're conjugating your emotions," she finally said. "We have feel, feeling, and felt." Then she grinned at him, and he let out a deep breath as the tension in his shoulders relaxed.

She needed to reassure him she cared as deeply as he did. Was she falling in love with him, or had she already fallen? She didn't know what they shared, but she wanted to be with Cole. That much she understood.

"We can work it out. There's no rush. We need to take some time and discover more about each other. That's the fun of a new relationship. We'll get to know each other better, then let's see what happens."

He nodded.

"And Cole," she added, "I am yours, and you are mine."

He blinked at her. "To infinity and bey…"

She put one finger on his lips. "We don't have to make any forever promises. Let's just go with happy for now."

"I can do that, for now, but just so you know, I'm going to do my best to not fuck this up."

"I agree to try that, too." She kissed him, her mouth just lightly sweeping across his lips.

"Now, let's get into that amazing shower together." She pushed him over the edge of the bed to the floor as she started to stand.

He reached toward the nightstand next to him and opened a drawer. "I have something to show you." He held out a card, and she squealed with delight.

"Cole, you have a library card!"

Grabbing one of her hands, he pulled her down on top of him. She sat up and realized she was posed in a very provocative position, with a leg on each side of his hips.

He grinned up at her. "This is going to be interesting, isn't it?"

She rubbed the firm muscles of his chest before standing and heading toward the bathroom.

"Let the adventures begin!" She teased over her shoulder.

She didn't know what the future held for them, but she knew in good times or bad, Cole was the man she wanted by her side.

TRUE CONFESSION: Mae West was supposed to have said, "Too much of a good thing is wonderful," and I believe she was right. Shutting down your ambitions, letting go of your goals, and giving up are sure ways to make sure you're never going to get what you want. If you give up, you're the one ensuring you'll never fulfill your dreams. A wish you don't make is guaranteed to never come true.

Epilogue

BRIENNE

December

"I CAN'T BELIEVE we finally managed to get Shelby and Ryan to the altar. Who knew one couple could create so much drama? I'd almost given up. I wasn't sure they'd work things out in time for the wedding." Brie moved her hand lower on Cole's arm, enjoying the bulge of muscle beneath his suit jacket.

He glanced at the happy couple dancing together in the center of the floor. "It proves love can overcome a lot when you truly care about someone."

"You've become quite a philosopher lately."

"I have the influence of a certain mermaid librarian to thank for that. She's teaching me to be grateful for all the gifts I've been given and to appreciate what she brings to my life every day."

"That's quite a testimonial," she said, smiling up at the man she loved with all her heart.

"Have you talked to Luna lately?" Cole wrapped his arm tighter around her waist, pulling her closer.

"I sent her texts while we were in Paris, but we haven't been able to meet and talk since I've been back. You and I packed a lot into those weeks in France." She gave him a flirty smile as a suggestive reminder of the *get better acquainted* part of the trip. They'd taken full advantage of the opportunity to spend uninterrupted time alone.

"I swear there's something going on between her and Wyatt. I went to see him the other day and there were paintings of her in his art room. Before we left, they could barely talk to each other without arguing. I have a sneaking suspicion things have changed."

She wiggled her eyebrows. "Are you talking about sexy time?"

Cole shrugged, and she moved her hands back up to his shoulders to give them a squeeze.

"I'm suspicious, that's all I'm saying. One painting was of Luna, naked."

Brie slapped at his shoulder. "You shouldn't be looking at my best friend when she isn't wearing any clothes."

He stared down at her. The edges of his mouth lifted into a sly grin. "Maybe your friend shouldn't be getting naked in front of my friend."

She peeked around his broad shoulders to see Luna dancing with Shelby's Uncle Mack, who was nearly seventy years old but could still strut his stuff on the dance floor. They were slow dancing and appeared to be having fun.

"Should I be worried Wyatt is painting naked portraits of her?" Brie bit her lip and frowned. "Do you think I should warn her?"

Cole stared over her head. "He's giving Luna and Uncle Mack a death-ray look. Something's up with those two, I'm telling you."

They moved across the dance floor, and she noticed Raina

sitting with Matt O'Donnell. Nodding at them, she turned her attention back to Cole.

"Should I tell Raina about him? I think she has a right to know he's more than a bartender at Three Geeks."

Cole turned her so he could see the couple sitting at one of the long tables set up for the reception at the Blue Moon Lodge.

"Let me talk to Matt before you say anything. He might just be her plus one for the wedding. I know women hate coming to an event like this alone."

"It's one of the worst things about being single."

"Something you don't need to worry about anymore." He grinned down at her.

She sighed. "Did you talk to my father yet?"

She glanced across the room, where her parents were seated with several other couples their age. They were all laughing, making toasts, and clearly having a wonderful time.

"Do you think we'll be like them in twenty years? Will we still look at each other with that special glint in our eyes?" she said.

"Even tarot cards can't predict the future." He leaned down to kiss her forehead. "But if I were betting on anyone, it'd be us."

"Can a librarian and a geek live happily ever after?" She blinked at him.

"Since we're talking about a mermaid librarian and one very lucky geek, I'll bet on every fairy tale I've ever read and say, yes, they can!"

She traced the deep dimple on the side of his face. "And don't let my father take advantage of you with his bride price nonsense. I'm sure he'll tell you it's an old Norse tradition that goes back generations in his family."

Cole's forehead creased into a look of astonishment. "What? It isn't?"

"What has my father done now? Did he already pull that on you?"

Cole swallowed. "I promised not to say anything unless I was tortured."

Brie stopped dancing to stare up at him. "What did he make you do? I only told you to ask for his approval before we announce our engagement because he's such a pain in the ass when he doesn't get his own way. He'd never let it rest that you married me without his consent. Which is crazy because I'm a grown-ass woman and I don't need him to give me permission to marry the man I love."

He gave her a look that made her toes curl and her panties damp.

"People are staring at us. We should either keep dancing or go back and sit," he suggested.

She noticed the funny looks from dancers surrounding them. She moved her feet. "Just keep dancing, and tell me what he said. I know how much he likes you, so I don't imagine he asked for much."

"I give him credit. He drives a hard bargain." Cole held up a hand. "Not that I wasn't willing to pay any price for you. I respect family traditions, and baby, you're worth it."

She was tempted to smack him on the shoulder, but there were too many witnesses.

"So, are you planning to share what he said, or should I march over there and force it out of him?"

"Is that the reason he mentioned torture? Your father negotiated a tough deal, but I'm the one who came out on the upside of the transaction."

She stopped dancing again to stare up at him. "Are you going to tell me or what?"

He laughed. "I got you, babe, and I'm now the proud owner of Diggin' Dirt Farm."

Her jaw dropped open in surprise. Then she burst into

laughter. He watched her for a few moments before joining her.

She couldn't contain herself, even when Shelby turned to glare at them, as if she were a stern teacher and they misbehaving first graders. The woman had pinched face perfected.

The music finally stopped, and she and Cole stood staring at each other. She had to wipe away the tears in her eyes.

"My father probably made you pay far more than it's worth because he knows you're a sucker."

"Probably," Cole agreed. "But not only did I acquire the prize, he agreed to bless our marriage."

This time, she didn't resist the urge to smack him hard on his bicep. "So, you finally got what you've wanted all along?"

The deep dimple at the corner of his mouth appeared again when he grinned. "Something unique and special doesn't come along every day. You gotta seize the opportunity when you can."

She grabbed his tie to pull his mouth down toward hers.

"I can't believe the lengths you've gone to in order to get that friggin' tractor," she whispered.

And then she made sure everyone attending the reception understood she was in love with this cute scruffy dude, who wasn't very scruffy anymore, and dragged his mouth to hers as they shared a deep, passionate kiss.

When he folded her over his arm in a dip, the room erupted in applause. He finally pulled her to stand in front of him again.

"What do you think they're saying about us?"

He laughed. "Probably what the hell took them so long?"

Acknowledgments

Edited by EMS Flynn, Flynn Books & Ideas
www.emsflynn.com

Cover and Promotional Art, Alexis Semeraro
www.nixkitcreative.com

Thank you, Anthony Semeraro, for the information about sailing. I look forward to our next time out on the water.

Thank you, Jade Cheung, an actual mermaid/librarian for the information about mermaid life.

Any errors about these topics are the author's mistake and do not reflect on their input.

Praise for Deborah Schneider

This story from Deborah Schneider (Confessions of a Domestic Goddess) has a delightful small-town feel, complete with a loveable cast of secondary characters begging for their own stories to be told.

LIBRARY JOURNAL

Five Stars

I'm a fellow naughty librarian, so I was really into this story. Either way, the characters are wonderful, and the romance it delightful. Cole is a thoughtful man who ticks off all the boxes for book boyfriend. I only wish there was more, but that's a good reason to read more in the series.

KRISTEANE B. GOODREADS
REVIEWER

So Many Emotions

Five Stars

I loved this book!! It really played with my emotions and the spicy scenes really were top tier as in sharing the connection between the main characters.

ALEXA – GOODREADS REVIEWER

About Award-Winning Author Deborah Schneider

The heroine of her first Western romance, _Beneath A Silver Moon_, won the Heart of Denver Molly award for "most unsinkable heroine" and was published as part of the Romantic Times New Historical Voice Contest. Her second Western, _Promise Me_ won the EPIC award for Best Western Romance.

She was employed by one of the largest library systems in the country and achieved a major career milestone when R.L. Stine called her "scary". She was recognized by Romance Writers of America as a Librarian of the Year.

Deborah lives in the Pacific Northwest, in the town that served as the location for the _Twin Peaks_ TV show and movies. She feels fortunate to wake up every day looking at a mountain and found her own happily ever after with an amazing, supportive husband.

She publishes romantic fantasy and gaslight romance as Sibelle Stone.

Social Media

For more information about Deborah's books, please visit her website at: _www.debschneider.com_

To see the inspiration for her books in the Bachelor Bay Series, _visit her Pinterest boards._

Follow Deborah on _Facebook_

Find her books on _Amazon Author Central_

Thank you for reading this book, and I invite you to write a review. An honest review is the way authors learn to be better writers.

Deborah

Also by Deborah Schneider

CONTEMPORARY ROMANTIC COMEDY

Confessions of a Domestic Goddess

Confessions of a Naughty Librarian

WESTERN ROMANCES

Beneath A Silver Moon

Promise Me

Say You Love Me

SIBELLE STONE BOOKS

Whistle Down the Wind

Prudence and the Professor